MARTYR FOR COWARDS

MARTYR FOR COWARDS

M. WARREN ASKINS

Martyr for Cowards
M. Warren Askins

Second Edition: 2025

ISBN: 978-1-7341200-8-0 (paperback 2nd edition)
ISBN: 979-8-3730485-5-2 (paperback 1st edition)
ISBN: 979-8-3748824-4-5 (hardcover)
ISBN: 978-1-7341200-0-4 (e-book)

Books by M. Warren Askins

Through the Thorns
Ian
The Dead Men are Dying Saga
Beyond the Spire of Navarene
Martyr for Cowards
Orphan's Rite
Ghosts of Halodwyth

Author's Note

This book occurs five hundred years before
the events described in *Beyond the Spire of Navarene.*

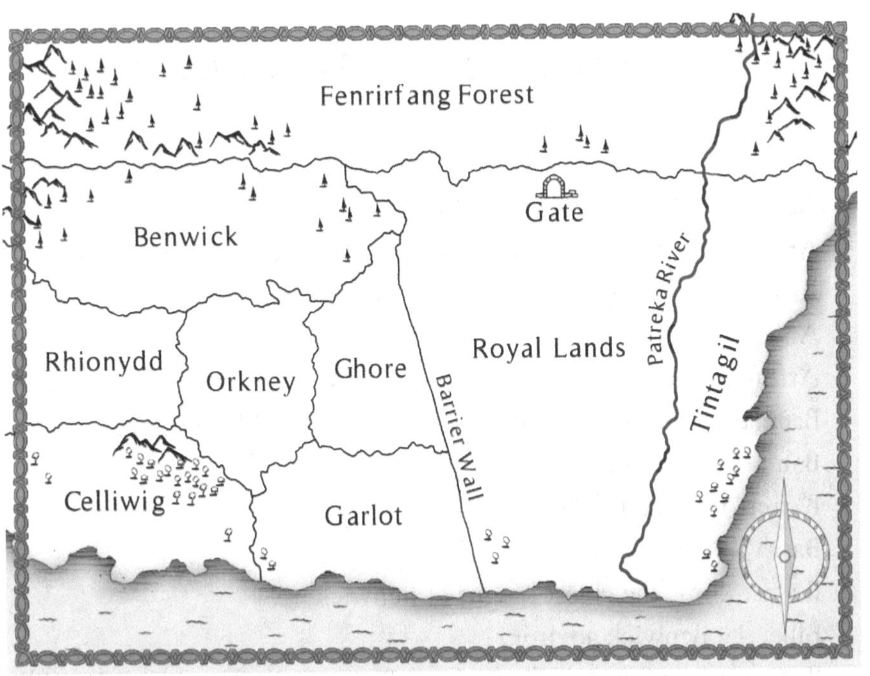

Fenrirfang Forest
Gate
Benwick
Royal Lands
Patreka River
Rhionydd
Orkney
Ghore
Barrier Wall
Tintagil
Celliwig
Garlot

Character Reference

Amyr – a First Laif, the first Arbiter
Ancel (Launcelot) – Lord Ban's eldest son and heir
Anders, Sir – knight of Benwick
Ankoreth, Sir – a wisp knight of Fenrirfang
Arthur – King of Camelot
Bactaal – a dragoon; a laif dragon hunter in golden armour
Ban – Lord of Benwick
Barrett Pentracil – Duke of Rhionydd
Basva – Kurrva's swain
Belfast, Sir – the eldest knight of Benwick
Bilka – a Benwick advisor
Bryndon – an unmarked man from Benwick, companion to Lanaelle
Byron – a Benwick advisor
Caestar – a Benwick laif ranger
Carlysle, Sir – an errant knight, sister of Lanaelle
Cass – a Benwick archer, employed by the bureau of taxation
Corbin – a mapmaker of Benwick, marked by the Architect
Craendir – a laif warrior stationed at Fort Navarene
Credence – a cleric of the Church, stationed near the capital
Daeban – protective forest spirit of destruction
Delevast, Sir – a wisp knight of Fenrirfang
Derathane, Sir – a royal knight of Camelot
Desdemona – a Benwick tariff officer, born Warrior
Deverin – a Benwick laif lampyr
Doncus, Sir – Seneschal of Lowthean
Earon – an apprentice spellcaster from Orkney

Ector – Lord Ban's youngest son

Elithiel – Royal Dancer (monster hunter)

Evaline, Sir – a royal knight of Camelot

Famyl – a First Laif, the first Healer

Flya – laif warrior of Fenrirfang

Gabriel – a son of Lord Ban

Geoffrey, Sir – a knight of Benwick

Gerald – a Celliwig cadet

Grandy – a Benwick werewolf, twin to Ren

Harold Pemberton – The Duke of Celliwig

Henrick – late brother of Kenna

Jekar – a Benwick physician turned werewolf

Jukaliska – an archenlaif

Kasyan – a sentry of Benwick, marked by the Observer

Kay, Sir – brother of King Arthur, and seneschal of Camelot

Kenet – the blacksmith of Fort Navarene

Kenna – a Benwick farmer, the father of Linette

Kravit – the royal mage of Camelot

Kurrva Pentracil – a lady of Rhionydd, betrothed to Ancel

Laevephen – a laif lampyr of Benwick

Laiernaten – a dragoon; a laif dragon hunter in golden armour

Lanaelle – an unmarked woman from Benwick, sister of Sir Carlysle.

Lavenche, Sir – a knight of the Isle of Lowthean

Lavernia – a queen fae of Fenrirfang

Lhaewyn – the first lampyr, son of Famyl

Liesel – daughter of Kenna

Linette – youngest daughter of Kenna

Natalia – daughter of Kenna

Nedok – a laif warrior stationed at Fort Navarene

Nolan – a son of Lord Ban

Pelant – a laif guide

Perla – daughter of Kenna

Price, Sir – knight of Benwick

Priraeda – a drevnigost (ancient guest) of Joyous Garde

Raymond – a red knight stationed at Fort Navarene

Ren – a Benwick werewolf, twin to Grandy

Rowan – a Church vicar

Saeva – a laif lampyr of Fenrirfang

Sandrin, Sir – a knight of Benwick

Seyfried, Sir – a knight of Garlot

Stacey – Sir Carlysle's squire

Subin, Sir – a knight of Orkney

Tamarah, Sir – a knight of Benwick

Tawny – a woman from Benwick with shimmering hair

Traskal – a laif warrior stationed at Fort Navarene

Uljae – a laif of the Hold

Vashal, Sir – a knight of Benwick

Vuko – an outcast werewolf harbored on the outskirts of Benwick

This one's for you, Dad

Where the weak belong;
below the strong

With better days grinding to a halt;
hold the vigil, please,
for those who have gone before.

Avalon seems so far;
Avalon is so far away.

-an excerpt taken from a laborer's song

PROLOGUE

Five hundred years before the Slaughter at Knotwithstadt...

Mistakes had been made.

Walking the battlements of Fort Navarene, Raymond contemplated the decisions that had led him to this particular position. His past was abundant with bad ideas and poor calculations that could fill the Valley of Lichmere to overflowing, the scar adorning his throat a reminder of his most recent error in judgment.

If only that git would have sliced a bit deeper, he thought, tugging the cold steel of his breastplate, *then I would be drinking wine in Avalon, instead of stuck with this miserable assignment.* Who was he kidding? When death came for him, he very much doubted that he would be welcomed on the shores of Avalon. As terrible as the predicament was that he found himself in, joining the red knights on the frontlines and facing a rumored Archenlaif threat, deep down he preferred this to the lonely death that he had avoided on the gallows.

"How are we holding up?" a regal voice cut through the ebon night behind him. Raymond turned to see Elithiel, the Royal Dancer, place a leg up on a nearby crenellation.

Raymond could not deny it was comforting having such a skilled warrior with them, fighting alongside the ranks of nobodies and upstarts that comprised the red knights. He hid his admiration as best he could. "Not quite dead," he replied, turning to survey the area in front of the north gate.

"Getting there, eh?" Elithiel did not turn his head. "I must congratulate you..." he trailed off, obviously unaware of Raymond's name.

"Raymond," the red knight completed.

"Raymond. Yes, yes, of course." The laif gazed deep into the vast darkness before them as if he could see beyond. "You are the only scout still awake. Well done. You won't be as startled when the hailstorm begins."

Raymond nodded as if he understood, wanting to come across as knowledgeable about war and battles. *Does he mean an actual hailstorm, or is this some sort of obscure laif reference?*

"The weather is about to change," Elithiel explained, noting the confusion in Raymond's eyes. He peered above to the night sky. "And we're about to get..." he paused, meeting Raymond's eyes before continuing, "Handled roughly. In more ways than one." The laif cleared his throat and patted the red knight on his shoulder before walking away.

"Wait!" Raymond shouted. The laif stopped and turned his ear toward the red knight's voice. "Have they seen something from the spire?" he asked anxiously.

The King's monster hunter responded with a single nod and vanished into the darkness.

"What about the forward scouts..." Raymond petered off, his question posed to no one. Turning back to face the gloom, he rapped his knuckles against the stone parapet.

Perhaps the length of two breaths passed before a battering from the skies descended upon the fort. *Oh, so he did mean actual hail,* Raymond chuckled as he struggled to pull his cowl over his helmeted head. The clinking of tiny ice crystals buffeting steel plate and stone filled the atmosphere, and Raymond's vision was heavily obscured by the falling wall of ice shards.

The feeble rays of moonlight penetrating the overcast sky offered limited visibility beyond the torch lit walls of the fort. Raymond blinked hard, wondering if the sleet was forming strange spectral shapes in the distance.

Nope, he thought, fumbling for the horn on his chest.

Dark armoured silhouettes were funneling down the hillside in a co-ordinated pattern that left little room for speculation as to who was calling at such a late hour.

Raymond lifted the horn without thinking, and the instrument was immediately filled with chunks of ice. Bending down in urgent frustration to unclog it proved to be quite fortuitous, for as he did so, the sound of shaft and fletching coursing through the air whistled above his head in the exact location his head had been a mere moment ago. Strength and smarts were two examples of qualities that Raymond was lacking, but speed, speed was something he *did* possess. Instantly the new recruit dropped to all fours and bolted to the protected side of a crenellation, pressing his back to it and tucking his chin to create the smallest of targets.

He rotated the horn to the side and attempted to blow it once again, to rouse the regiment, to save the regiment, but his nerves failed him. There was no wind in his lungs, fear clogged his arteries and he shuddered trying to dispel the intense panic that had overtaken him. His armour felt suffocating and the walls were beginning to tighten around him. Closing his eyes, he shored up as much strength as he could, not realizing that he had been holding his breath. When he released the pent up air, somehow his hands found sure purchase on the horn. The trembling ceased for the moment, and Raymond took full advantage of the reprieve

With a heave, he sucked in the cold night air and held it, leaning forward as far as his breastplate allowed, he put his lips to the mouthpiece and blew with all the strength he had remaining, infusing the instrument with his very soul. In a moment of triumphant confusion, Raymond believed that his horn was resounding from the heavens and not from the lowly crenellation he had wedged himself in. At that precise moment, the scouts at the top of the spire took notice of the approaching enemy and offered their horns to bolster his, stirring and waking every human and laif inside Navarene.

The stones he sat upon began to shudder from the force of their blast, infused as they were with ancient laif magics. Lowering his horn, the red knight felt a strange sense of accomplishment. *The archenlaives are now further into Fenrirfang than they have ever been,* Raymond contemplated his predicament, *and guess who is somehow at the vanguard of all this?*

"Rayford!" Elithiel shouted to his right.

Raymond, still huddled on the stone battlement, looked up to see the laif loosing arrows into the night, facing the enemy alone.

"To arms!" the laif cried. "They will be upon us in moments!"

1

"He has only a few hundred breaths left in him," the lampyr cautioned, fangs dripping as he placed a hand on the young lord's shoulder. "You must hurry if you wish to say your good-byes." Ancel nodded solemnly, watching his father's blood roll down the lampyr's chin.

"Thank you for this, Laevephen. It means the world to me," Ancel said, squeezing the lampyr's hand perched on his shoulder. Not wishing to waste any of the fleeting moments, Lord Ancel strode briskly through the hallway. It was lined with servants and vassals with grave expressions, their eyes shimmering with sorrow. Some clung to medallions, muttering prayers, pausing as their soon-to-be liege walked past.

Pressing through the heavy oak door inlaid with the shape of their family crest, Ancel entered his father's chambers.

The minstrel playing a stringed instrument in the corner ended his interlude mid-sweep and solemnly stood, taking a slight bow before exiting discreetly, leaving Ancel alone with his father.

The older man turned his head at his son's approach, revealing the fresh fang marks on his neck, the blood already dried from the lampyr's final treatment.

"Son." Lord Ban reached for him, his battle-scarred hands trembling, the very hands that had built the firmament of this estate. "My son, Launcelot," he said, almost inaudibly. The name was rarely used when addressing Ancel, though it was his true birth name, but it had been almost completely abandoned.

"Remind me," Ban continued, struggling to sit up, "which of your brothers was it that had difficulty pronouncing your name?"

"It was Ector, Father," Ancel replied, feeling there was so much left to talk about with his father.

"Yes, yes, it was wasn't it?" Lord Ban smiled, tears collecting in his eyes at the recollection. "Such a pity that 'Ancel' became so popular. I always favored 'Launcelot,'" he laughed. "It's much more *regal,* in my opinion," he said before a bout of coughs overtook him.

Ancel reached down and placed his hand atop his father's. The black and green blankets emphasized how pale the Lord of Benwick had become. The coughs began to subside, diminishing into growls of aggravation.

"Cyclones," began Ancel, tears forming along the rim of his eyelids. "How is it that they work?"

Ban's growling cough was drawn short by laughter. "I think this foolish old man has taught you everything you need to know."

"But still."

"You know the answer," Ban said gently, rotating his hand to squeeze his son's. "When hot and cold air collide in the right conditions—" he was interrupted by violent coughing. "Why waste this time on such things?" Ban queried once his chest settled. "I want to know what you plan to do with your wandering betrothed."

Ancel was taken by surprise, not prepared for the abrupt change in subject. "Kurrva and the man that she left me for shall make the Walk of Atonement."

"Of course they will... but..." Ban trailed off.

"But," Ancel paused, looking toward the window, the morning rays piercing through the mountainside, "they will be given a laif."

Ban's laugh was hampered by hacking coughs, blood evident on his hand when he withdrew it from his lips. "You are giving them a laif to guide them," he said, shaking his head in admiration. "Such mercy! You are a better man than me."

"Father, your hand."

Ban hardly took notice. "My time is short, son. I am off to Avalon to finally be with your mother again. This is not an early grave for me."

"It feels like it to me, Father," lamented Ancel.

"You will find love again." Ban's eyes shimmered and wavered, "and wisdom and glory... and glory... there will be challenges, much and greater than your old father ever faced..." The coughs were no longer full coughs, but rattles from deep in his core. He fought against them, prevailing for just a moment, his eyes clearing with lucidity. "You will see," he said, feebly lifting his hand to pat his son's crown for the final time.

Ancel aided his father's attempt, resting the old hand where it wanted to go.

A flicker of joy rushed behind Lord Ban's eyes before it was washed away with gray.

"Farewell, Father," whispered Ancel with surprising composure, still holding his father's hand as it rested atop his head. "I will never give up, I will never give—" His words were choked off, sorrow surging up, and Ancel broke down, clutching the blankets and weeping like an abandoned orphan.

The door creaked open behind him, but Ancel took no notice, wracked with grief as he was.

"The Lord of Benwick has passed," said Laevephen gently. "While this would ordinarily be a time for grieving..." he trailed off as the sound of heavy steel-shod boots entered the dimly lit chamber.

Ancel lifted his head from the bed.

"There will be time for that after..." Laevephen finished, walking to the foot of the bed.

One of the knights who had entered cleared his throat. "Lord Ancel," he began.

Ancel groaned, knowing that it would take some time to grow accustomed to that title. "What could be so important at a time like this?" he asked, not turning to face the unwanted guests.

"Lord Ancel, the king is summoning you," stated the knight.

"Oh, the king, eh? This should be rich." Ancel finally turned to see who had spoken. The two knights were unfamiliar to him, but their regalia identified them as Royal Knights: gray and black heraldry surrounding magnificent plate. The cowls on their mantles had been pulled back to expose their rain-soaked heads, and Ancel's eyes were drawn to the water dripping onto the floor from their fingertips and from the ends of their scabbards.

The other knight present stepped forward. "The king needs his finest knights and fighters," she said softly, seeming a bit more sensitive to their poor timing. "Arthur has requested you by name."

"Did he now?" Ancel sneered.

"The archenlaives have reached Navarene."

The room seemed to grow darker, the direness of the situation sinking through Ancel's fog of grief. He gently placed his father's hand back onto the bed, clasping it one last time, and rose to his feet.

"Lead on."

2

"It's nothing more than a hobby patch!" Kenna tossed his shovel on the ground and rounded on his daughter. "Just stop scribbling for a crack and listen!" he demanded, reaching for the small board of black slate clutched in his daughter's hands, but she pulled back quickly avoiding his grasp.

"I'm not going to fight ya, lass!" her father said, turning his back to her and flinging his hands up in frustration. He could hear Linette writing on her chalkboard as he bent down to retrieve the shovel. "Ban is gravely ill on his deathbed as we speak, so forgive me for thinking that the fate of some tiny garden would even register as a priority!"

Linette held up the chalkboard for her father to read, her tongue pressed to the inside of her cheek in irritation.

The man leaned forward, squinting, and walked toward her to read the words.

"I'm not embarrassed!" he insisted, poking the board with a forefinger and whirled around. "I need to get back to work! And you should do the same!"

Rushing to face her father, Linette held up the next phrase.

In frustration Kenna buried the blade of his shovel into the soil and scanned the letters. "Look, Linette," he said, wiping the grime from his hands before placing them on his daughter's shoulders. "I love you very much. You're the most precious thing growing on this farm to me. But unless you have the coin to hire an errant knight or some other champion for your cause, there is not much else to be done."

He felt his daughter's shoulders wilting under his hands. "Isn't most of the fun just growing those pretty flowers?" he asked brightly. "Can't you just be happy with that?"

She stepped free from his light grip, fervently scratching the plate with chalk before raising it yet again.

He didn't bother to read it, instead glaring into her eyes, "That is enough! I don't want to hear any more about this! Just be content for once! The keep's collectors are coming in a week, as you well know, and I must get these vegetables into the cart!"

Linette was not swayed by her father's argument and continued to tap the board, putting it in her father's face, but he refused to give it even the faintest glance.

Looking to the sky, Kenna blurted, "Of all the daughters that I have been blessed with, why is it that the mute is somehow the loudest?"

For a moment Linette's mouth gaped open, but she quickly snapped it shut, forming a scowl below a narrowed gaze that gave her burly father a bit of pause. Before he could offer an apology, she stormed away, leaving her father to his tasks.

It's not just a hobby to me! Linette thought, sitting on the grass a few paces from her humble cottage, proudly gazing at the three silver flowers springing from the ground.

Her four elder sisters had married and moved on, leaving all the farm responsibilities to her and her father. Generations of her family had served as vassals to the lords of Benwick, happily providing a portion of their yield, gratefully toiling in the fields to feed themselves as well as provide support for the demesne.

It wasn't all that bad for Linette. She loved growing plants. Her sisters, however, despised the labor of it all. They hated the sweat staining their garments, reducing the appeal to potential suitors. The dirt accumulating under fingernails could be humiliating, especially at fine dinner parties where one may find one's hand exposed when wrapped around a goblet of wine. And jewelry! Jewelry could not be worn at all while tilling soil or rooting around in the dirt beds for pesky weeds. Their eyes had been ever elsewhere. Not Linette's though. *My little tiller,* her father would call her. Or *my little cob* was sometimes a favorite, always spoken with a proud gleam in his eye. She was the one daughter who would rise before him, ahead of the sun, chasing the darkness of night an hour before the ground was scattered in daytime shadows.

Has it been ten years already? Linette wondered, plucking a blade of grass and snapping it in half. A full decade had passed since the day her father had returned from Market Days with his hands behind his back and a mischievous grin on his face. Taking her by the hand, he had led her outside the cottage, away from the prying eyes and curious ears of her sisters.

"Pick a hand," he said, lifting his chin, trying to conceal the losing battle he was waging with a smirk. She was eleven at the time, a year or so before she hit her teenage growth spurt, and when her father lifted his head like that, she found it impossible to read his face. She hopped in place with excitement, unable to contain herself, guessing what he held behind his back.

Since she had first read about silver shadesgill in a crusty old almanac, she had begged Kenna for just a few drops of aspis venom, or the even more spectacular faewort. Both of these elements, expensive and dangerous to procure, were used to ensorcell the soil to grow the intensely delicate flowers that had overtaken her imagination. A powerful mage could probably whip up an incantation, but the odds of that happening for her were as likely as her slaying an abowraith bent on revenge. Neither event was ever going to happen. Her best bet was the faewort, but she would settle for the venom.

She pointed an excited finger to his left.

Her father tilted his head down, frowning with bright eyes, and revealed an empty right hand. "Guess again," he urged, "the odds are in your favor now."

Linette chewed her bottom lip, her eyes narrowing to slits, then pointed at the same hand again. She was wise to his tricks.

"You outsmarted me again," he laughed, bringing a closed hand to his front.

She hopped up and down, clearly projecting, *What is it? What is it? What is it?!*

Rotating his wrist and creaking the cage of his fingers open, her father revealed a thumb-sized vial with a milky substance sloshing around its bottom containing maybe six or seven drops of aspis venom.

Far beyond elated, she had rushed her father, ignoring the gift for a moment. If she had been taller and longer of limb, she would have wrapped him up in the biggest hug ever in recorded history. At the time though, she was still quite small in comparison to the broad shouldered and sturdy frame of her father. Nevertheless, he groaned and laughed as she clutched the gritty fabric of his favorite old paltock at his waist, the furthest distance her embrace could reach.

Kenna held the vial above his head, protecting it from the onslaught of joy. "Alright! Alright, Linette!" She had begun weeping, unable to control her emotions. As she had no voice, her crying sounded closer to choking, which always made her father vastly uncomfortable.

"Alright, let's get it together, little one," he soothed, lowering himself to her level with the vial between his thumb and forefinger, he gave Linette the gift she had been wanting for most of her life.

Linette smiled at the memory, but the wistful moment of remembrance was soured in an instant.

"Are you deaf now too?" a harsh voice sniped.

Having no desire to turn around, Linette instead scratched at the slate in her lap, raising it over her shoulder to the women who had silently gathered behind her.

The interrupter read the words on display. "Go away!" She grinned at Linette and pivoted on her heel. "Oh, we will be going away, little snail." Moving faster than her frame seemed to allow, she brought her chin to hover an inch from Linette's shoulder. "We found ourselves nearby, monitoring the Lord's harvests, and I thought to myself, 'Self? What say you? Ought we check on the progress of our special little crop of gray gilly?'"

Linette began to scribble again as the woman rose to her full height and looked to her companions, all of whom were armed and adorned in Benwick's regalia. "I'd say the blossoms are *almost* ripe... nearly there. What do you think, ladies, maybe another week?" the woman guessed.

The slate was lifted again.

"Not your crop, Desdemona," one of the women read aloud in a mocking tone.

Desdemona wheeled to stand before Linette, glowering over the small patch of shadesgill. "You're right, snail, this is not *my* crop," she said, straightening up, hands on her hips. "It is Lord Ban's crop. And who are you to withhold the annual contribution demanded of his vassals? What makes you so special, snail?"

"Actually," the shortest of the retinue interjected, adjusting the longbow on her shoulder. "It's Lord Ancel's now," she corrected sadly.

"Eh," Desdemona waved dismissively at the marksman, "it matters not. Ban didn't give a tinker's rib about this snail and the caitiff she calls 'father.' What makes you think his whelp will be any different?

Lords have their lording to do... busy, busy, busy while the rest of us scurry around underfoot, picking up the scraps."

Though disagreeing most heartily with the statement, Linette did not have adequate space on her chalkboard to educate the sheer ignorance of this woman. Instead, she fixed her adversary with the most bewildered look that she could muster.

"Have something to say, shit snail?"

She shook her head.

"You want to go get your daddy to come out and scare us away?"

Linette rolled her eyes, settling them on the horizon where she noticed a murky cloud rising up on the road.

"Remember what happened the last time your daddy tried to have a chat with us?"

Another member chimed in, with obnoxious enthusiasm, hand to the pommel at her waist. "We slapped him good 'n proper-like, and sent him crawling back home."

The woman was so pleased with herself that Linette half expected the dunce to take a bow.

Desdemona saluted her friend with a nod. "That's right," she confirmed, baring her teeth. "And I'll bet that sordid tale has not left the confines of this pathetic little grange," she added, giving the back of Linette's head a shove. "We'll be back in a week for our gilly. See that you make sure they make it until then." Her last words came out in a rush, interrupted by the sound of mounted knights passing on the road.

"Already?" the marksman remarked. "The Benwick knights are already on the move? Wasn't it only yesterday that we got the missive?"

Desdemona's tone shifted to one of authority. "They have reached Navarene. The Killing Fields are finally coming to Camelot's doorstep."

Leading the spectacle of shining steel was a man rarely seen in public, his head barren of helm, his long hair trailing behind like a banner.

Can that be? Linette wondered, trying to guess the man's identity.

"They may actually be able to stem the tide," one of the women pronounced with admiration.

Desdemona shrugged, dispelling the moment, "Never thought I'd see the day when Lord Ancel would answer Arthur's call."

"Never thought I'd see the day when Arthur would actually *call* Ancel," the marksman scoffed.

Linette admired Ancel's features as he passed, believing he appeared to be a man of honor and reason. *Perhaps,* she thought, *the new Lord would be more sympathetic about my flowers?* Perhaps he would listen to her plight and deal with the parasites that preyed upon her... that had been harassing her for almost a decade. If he only knew the sheer amount of labor that silver shadesgill required and he listened to her, then maybe, she would be able to expand her tiny plot.

Linette was well aware of the reason why these tax collectors wore fine armour and sported more fashionable weaponry than their peers. It was due to her silver shadesgill. It was her toil, and it was a father's gift to his sad, silent daughter that had made it possible.

Desdemona seemed to read Linette's thoughts as she watched her follow Ancel's silhouette fading off into the distance, the warhorses' tails nipped by the swirling road dust in their wake. "You think the new lord will have any time for a cur's cur like you?" she asked, thumbing toward Fenrirfang. "Your time would be better spent in a choir."

* * *

Unseen eyes watched the scene unfold. Standing by, year after year, spectating, doing nothing while the farm girl was harassed by those meant to protect her. It was not that the eyes did not want to intervene. No, the spirit attached to these eyes wanted nothing more than to interrupt the annual display of cruelty. Eyes and spirit were alone in this, it seemed, for Famyl's hands were tied.

Life with the Creator in the Hold, residing and existing by His right hand truly had its many advantages... as well as its great disadvantages. One of the latter being the restriction regarding a return to the terrestrial sphere he had abandoned.

Fairness was a concept that he had scoffed at long ago, when he was flesh and blood, the immortal physical embodiment of the Healer. His mind flipped through the pages of his history, recalling the battles and heartache, the heroes and villains, with, of course, the villains always believing themselves to be the standard of morality.

"This is not what I wanted," Famyl growled, tucking his chin in shame and wiping the tears from his eyes. His mind settled on a memory that often plagued his dreams, when he actually had dreams. It was the battle that had claimed his son, his only son, Lhaewyn, the first of his kind that came to be known as the lampyr. The saviors of wounded and sick humans, in war and in peace, they eased the dead men's incremental descent toward death.

Famyl felt that his bones had been graying, decaying, while his body lived ever on, rising to face the drudgery of a new day. It clung and pressed heavy to his chest, no matter how hard he tried to shake it. No matter how much vomit he expelled, the ache in his stomach would never dissolve into peaceful, placid coolness.

Famyl's time of reflection was interrupted by footsteps. "You're watching that farmer girl again, eh?"

The laif swiveled his neck to match the intruder's voice to its body. "I am," he replied. "Do you need aid, Uljae?"

"No," Uljae commented. "Just curious."

"Be curious elsewhere," Famyl ordered, waving a dismissive hand at the other laif, returning his focus to Linette. The girl was alone now, lying next to her garden, her body curled around the flowers as a hound protecting her brood.

"Why kill yourself over her?" Uljae taunted, standing close to his elder.

Famyl arched an eyebrow. "Kill?"

"Apologies." The laif neatened a kink in his sleeve and looked up, "perhaps a more appropriate word would be *torture?*"

"Ah, you speak as if time still matters to me."

"Clearly time is not a source of stress for you, as if it ever has been for a born-immortal such as yourself?"

Famyl only nodded.

Uljae continued, placing his hands behind his back, "Do you not see the humans born unmarked now offering themselves up to become werewolves? Has that escaped your sweeping optics? Why not intervene in those endeavors, big brother? It's pretty obvious that it will only end poorly for all involved."

"Everything ends poorly," murmured Famyl.

"And you turn a blind eye to the archenlaives bearing down on the Creator's favorite ruler, Arthur, and his ever-dwindling army!" Uljae continued. "I hear the good king now calls for aid beyond the boundaries of Camelot. It's actually rather fascinating. A laif becoming the ruler of humans. Such an experiment! Such a tale, Famyl, for even a laif as boring as you, you must admit." This garnered no response, so the younger laif pressed on, counting on his fingers as he spoke, "We have wisps and fae embroiled in a heated confrontation with ogres over the marshlands of Talanth, dragoons journeying to Ruma where a red dragon has decided to make humans its primary source of sustenance... Oh! And how can I forget the random violence and sorties raised by kapreta, goblin, ghoul, gorgon, victus, danegust... need I go on?"

"I am sorry," Famyl blinked. "Were you still speaking?"

"Yet," Uljae went on, undaunted by Famyl's apparent disinterest, "I find you here, day after day, watching this... this child. This human. This *insignificant* mortal. The world could burn around you, and yet, you, the Healer, would keep his gaze fixed firmly upon..."

* * *

"Linette," Kenna called to her in the gathering gloom of evening. She had spent all day with her garden, but now the day was coming to a close. "Supper is on." Before he turned to head back inside, he saw her lift her slate. "You know I can't read that in the dark, sparrow," he said kindly. "Come inside."

3

"Is everyone else dead?!" Raymond asked Elithiel, finally reaching a moment free from bloodshed. The archenlaives had taken the fort with relative ease, but Elithiel and Raymond had somehow fought from the front line, fallen back with the retreat, and miraculously survived. Leaning back against a tree after following the Dancer into the forest, Raymond poked at himself, checking for any wounds on the fleshy places that were not covered by armour.

"Not everyone," Elithiel noted, nodding toward the spire. The smoke twirling up from the fires enhanced the sight of arrows raining down from the spire. Arrows, like the hail that had ceased moments before the battle, fell in torrents, the final death knell of a broken regiment. Many an archenlaif would be cut down, but it would not win the night.

Raymond watched the archers, still confused that he was somehow breathing. "How many are up there?" he asked, speculating that there had to be at least thirty or forty laives in the spire.

"Hm..." Elithiel's smirk drew a single crease around his mouth. "Four, I think?" He peered around the tree for a brief moment, then turned his gaze back to Raymond. "Wait, no," he corrected. "I saw Craendir make a run for the spire right before the call to retreat."

"So, five?" said Raymond, astounded.

"Yes," Elithiel glanced past the tree once again. "So I understand you red knights are supposed to fight to the last man, hold the line and whatnot," said the laif, seeming fairly composed, "but, I'm wondering if you would be alright with—"

A black arrow struck the tree, showering splinters in the precise spot where Elithiel's head had been moments prior. "That was close!" he exhaled.

"They spotted us!" Raymond hissed, tugging at the collar of his breastplate, making sure it was still in place.

An archenlaif seemed to materialize in the forest just beyond Elithiel's shoulder. Raymond meant to warn him, but the Dancer turned out to be much faster than Raymond's voice. The laif had little time, the space between foes was tight, and he quick-drew an arrow from his hip and punched it through the archenlaif's throat. The tip, dipped in basilisk venom, resisted Elithiel's attempt to pull it back through, as the archenlaif's neck was already stone, so the Dancer abandoned it. At first it seemed that the archenlaif was not concerned in the least, drawing her scythe back as if she would have the time to bring it down on Elithiel's head.

Elithiel turned away and spoke to Raymond as if they were friends enjoying a relaxing moonlit stroll in the forest, "We need to get across the road." Behind him, the archenlaif, a frenzied look on her face, slowly brought her weapon down toward the back of Elithiel's head.

"Uh, Elithiel..." Raymond interjected, nervously pointing at the threat. Before Elithiel even had time to lazily glance over his shoulder, the venom completed its cycle and the archenlaif grew rigid, turning to a harmless statue. "Nevermind!" said Raymond. "What were you saying about crossing the road?"

"Ah, yes," Elithiel responded, eyeing Raymond with something resembling pity. "We must make for the road. Beyond it is safety. But be wary, as I know your duty does not permit you to abandon the fray."

Raymond played with the visor on his helm. "You're going regardless?" he asked, knowing the answer. Escaping with the Dancer wouldn't be the first time he broke some sort of code of conduct.

The laif quickly surveyed the area and lifted a hand to call for silence. "Wait for it..." he murmured. Screams of humans and laives dying continued to rise from the confines of the fort. "One moment more..."

There were more sounds of steel smashing steel, arrows bouncing from rock and plate and bone to pierce exposed flesh and armour. The screams gradually diminished into articulated shouts, orders from archenlaif captains to their soldiers overtaking the racket. Arrows no longer rained down from the heavens, though Raymond was unsure when they had stopped.

"Make haste! Now!"

Without another glance, Raymond slammed his visor down and steeled himself as he bolted for the road. Branches battered his shoulders and bracken hinted that they might trip him up if the mood took them. He pumped his arms feverishly, gripping his arming sword tight, and steeled himself for death, acknowledging that this was not for the first time he had done so this evening.

Here we go again, you buffoon, he chided himself. Free from the shadows of the trees, the red knight found his feet upon solid ground. A flurry of movement to his left drew his eye, and from behind the eye slit he recognized the silhouette of several archenlaives. Their conical helms rose and fell rapidly as they rushed for him, but Raymond did not falter, remaining intent on his goal.

They're gonna catch you! The voice in his head was tugging at the reins. *You may as well stop and face them. Either way, you're done. Go down swinging!* This sort of valiant effort was new for him. With a shake of his head, Raymond found himself abruptly stopping on the paved ground, his boots sliding sideways to a halt.

"Let's get this over—" he shouted. Before he could complete his statement a hail of arrows sailed in from the right and overcame the three archenlaives. Their bodies were punctured, completely riddled with arrows, their ghosts abandoning them long before their bodies struck the cobbles. No need for further encouragement, Raymond turned and sprinted for the trees, adjusting his course toward the savior archers.

Fort Navarene's front gate was wide open, revealing the bodies scattered like refuse, and archenlaives teemed freely within. Never before had the archenlaives made such an effort in their battles, such a surge toward Camelot. The frontline defense had failed and was completely shattered by this unexpected clash.

Through broken beams of moonlight illuminating the shrouded forest floor, Raymond caught sight of silvery armour rushing away, putting as much distance between themselves and the fort as possible. Raymond knew the knights must be Navarene's final resistance and he felt an overwhelming need to join them.

"Wait!" he shouted, counting at least three retreating forms. *And where the hekk is the Dancer?!* Suddenly spotting the largest archenlaif he had ever seen stalk into the forest, Raymond hurriedly pressed himself against a tree. The brute did not exhibit the ordinarily slender build of your typical archenlaif, but instead appeared as if his ancestors had interbred with ogres somewhere down the bloodline. The red knight silently cursed himself for shouting, gingerly easing his visor open, desperately wanting to keep his location from the hulk.

He was alone now, save the enemy. *Elithiel, you son of a—*

An arrow ricocheted from his chest plate, a grazing shot, the terror causing Raymond to nearly soil himself. Dropping to a knee, he surveyed the surroundings for cover, which proved to be a mistake. At first, he falsely believed that the sharp pain springing from his shoulder was from the sudden weight he had distributed upon his arm when he had steadied himself with a hand. Betraying his instincts, he paused to glance down, and noticed a bewildering discontinuity. A dark wooden shaft adorned with fibrous fletching jutted out from his left shoulder, parallel to the earth.

"Creator's honed tusks!"

He now fully realized the end would be nigh, one way or another. Archenlaives regularly dressed their tips with an array of horrifying venoms and poison, bringing about a sure end even if the shot was not fatal upon impact. His mind reeled and his cognitive biases took over. *Is it becoming difficult to swallow?! Is my arm turning to stone? Now that you mention it, it is much harder to lift...* A myriad of outcomes pervaded his mind before abruptly screeching to a halt as a shadow lurched before him, blocking out the moonlight.

Blood and drool seeped out from under the massive archenlaif's helm as he tilted his head toward the dying man below, salivating at the slaughter.

Raymond lifted his hand from the moss and straightened up, still remaining on his knees. "Are you waiting for an invitation?" he asked, exhausted.

Suddenly the amount of blood dripping from under the archenlaif's helm began to overflow, overtaking the translucent liquids. Letting his halberd fall, the archenlaif mimicked Raymond's pose, dropping to his knees. A tremor passed from armoured knees to his shoulders, and the quake was just enough to upset his helmeted head, now teetering at an unseemly angle.

The severed head toppled, revealing Elithiel standing behind with his blade drawn. "Follow!" he beckoned to Raymond.

"I can't," Raymond replied softly, drawing the laif's eyes to the protruding arrow.

A pained expression passed across the immortal laif's face. Elithiel was suddenly by his side, surprising Raymond. Ahead of him, he could see the tide was rushing through the trees toward them. A volley of arrows obscured the tree limbs, passing into the atmosphere beyond the forest. More than a handful of archenlaives dropped to the ground, purchasing time for Elithiel.

"Get going, you twit," Raymond urged, groaning back sobs as the laif hauled him to his feet. "Save yourself."

"There'll be plenty of time for that later," Elithiel said to Raymond. Turning to the darkness he shouted, "Lampyr!"

Raymond hobbled alongside Elithiel, struggling to keep pace. "They're right behind us!" he urged through shudders. "Leave me." The poison or venom or whatever was about to take him, his words replaced with an enveloping surge of froth that slavered from his mouth. Vomiting was not at all painful and he hardly felt like he was even regurgitating anything at all.

Elithiel watched the red knight's deterioration with distress. "Lampyr!" he screamed, his voice cracking with emotion. "I need a fucking lampyr!"

Raymond wagered the odds that another soul was nearby with the will to help, much less a lampyr, was slim, the odds greatly diminishing the longer he pondered. As he stood, his vision faded, quickly beginning to tunnel, and soon Elithiel was shouldering his burden without aid.

"Give me space," said a new voice, rousing Raymond from his stupor.

Warmth suddenly washed over him as he lay flat on his back, his sole discomfort a needle prick to the side of his neck. He opened his eyes to see the skies were dotted with stars where the trees allowed passage to the heavens. It was still night, and he wondered how long he had been unconscious.

"It hasn't been long," Elithiel revealed, answering the question plainly visible on Raymond's face. The Dancer was kneeling to Raymond's left and an armoured laif was across from him, mirroring the pose. Beyond them a skirmish raged.

"I must rejoin the fight," said the unfamiliar laif to Elithiel. "I have done all that I can." Looking at Raymond, he smiled, two parallel blood trails dripping down his chin. "You'll be fine," he promised. "For a dead man."

"Why do you stay and fight?" Elithiel queried, wiping his face in frustration. "Why, Saeva? All is lost!"

As soon as the lampyr opened his mouth to reply, a steady sound became audible, drawing closer and closer, unwavering, until it was right behind them. It sounded as if the forest were being chewed up and spat back out in a churning, sweeping commotion.

"Randall!" Elithiel shouted at Raymond. "Get yourself flush to the tree! Now!"

He did not have the time to inquire the who and why, and followed the order immediately, uncoiling his body from the ground and pressing against the nearest tree. A moment later, Saeva launched himself at the tree, his clutch of arrows riding awkward as he pressed close to the red knight.

The lampyr glanced at Raymond, not even a flicker of fear in his eyes. "The forest is unhappy," he explained, which was not reassuring in the least.

"What is happening?" Raymond demanded, quite the opposite of the composed laif with whom he shared the shelter.

"The Daeban comes."

Very descriptive, Raymond thought. "What is that?!" he shouted, needing to raise his voice in order to be heard.

"You shall see," Saeva smiled, then seemed to settle into the bark. The lampyr closed his eyes, and the roiling and cracking of the forest overtook everything around them. Deer-like forms leapt around the trees, reaping pathways as the rumbling began building to its climax.

What followed behind the sea of stags branded Raymond with a new kind of fear, one that he had yet to experience in his short life.

Wraiths!

Raymond would have turned and plunged his body into the cork if he weren't utterly frozen with fear. And if such an act were possible.

The vanguard of the enraged spirits was all he saw, for as soon they entered his vision, he battened his eyelids as Saeva had wisely done moments before. The ground trembled through the soles of his boots, chattered his teeth, and knocked his visor down over his face. The wind felt both arctic and volcanic at the same time, scorching and freezing simultaneously. The late summer leaves stood no chance against the wind as they were shorn from their anchors. Debris, twig, stone, and soil were all whipped up in the frenzy, making Raymond grateful that his protective visor had dropped over his face.

After what felt an eternity, the rumbling began to wane, the particles of earth gradually lessening their clicking against his armour, and Raymond felt that perhaps it was safe to unfasten his eyelids. Looking around, he saw leaves tumbling to the earth in spiraling patterns, drawn by the wake of the wraiths. Realizing that Saeva was no longer beside him, he was seized with the fear that he was the lone survivor of the Daeban.

"Can you run?"

Raymond jumped, his heart pounding in his throat. He nodded at Saeva who had appeared in the thicket before him, having overlooked the laif upon his view of the aftermath.

"We must move now," Saeva stated, already making for the fort. Raymond hustled to catch up, noticing that the vast array of the vines along the forest floor were now gone. Saeva continued, "We must re-supply our arrows if we are to stem the tide."

"You—You're staying?" Raymond stammered.

"Arthur will be here soon, and we are all that stands between the kingdom of men and misery."

"Where's Elithiel?"

"It matters not."

Raymond found he had to jog in order to keep up with the laif's strides.

"When we meet with the others, our pace will quicken beyond your capabilities. Keep up as best you can..." Saeva's voice faded as they entered a clearing that spanned for a dozen yards.

Within several blinks, four laives appeared, barring their passage. Their typically impeccable vestments and armour appeared dappled and marred by the sheer amount of blood spattered upon them. Just above them, the spire jutted up into the starlit sky.

Bounties of information seemed to have been exchanged silently between the laives with a series of single nods. Raymond, as usual, found himself out of the loop.

"He will die," the slender female laif insisted, indicating Raymond.

"And deny his nature?" Saeva said, causing the other laives to laugh.

Raymond joined them, laughing hollowly, his eyes darting to their faces as the unease in his gut continued to rise. The red knight was unsure whether Saeva was referencing his station as a red knight, or the plight of being human. *Or perhaps it's both column A and column B,* he thought as the four laives facing them swiftly turned heel and dashed for the fort, Saeva and Raymond following closely behind.

Dismembered corpses littered the ground along their path to the fort. The bodies grew in number and frequency the closer they drew to the fort. To Raymond's immense relief, most of the dead appeared to be archenlaives, likely caught unaware when the Daeban tide had swept through. While Raymond was, in fact, much slower than the surefooted laives, the bodies piled around did not aid him in his mission. He felt like he was running an agility course, similar to the sort he had endured after joining the red knights in penance to avoid execution. To his limited credit, it actually was the only trial he was moderately good at. It really didn't matter though, for as deft as he was at skipping through the carcass pond, he was still a league behind the laives.

By the time he reached the base of the wall, the laives had already disappeared. A series of stones protruded from the stronghold, only visible when standing directly beneath them, each allowing the precise amount of a foothold needed for a skilled climber to ascend. Raymond found it to be ingenious, another example of how infinitely more clever laives were than any other race.

"Dead man!" an urgent voice above him barked.

Looking up, Raymond caught sight of the striking visage of the female laif. "Catch!" she commanded, dropping a man-sized satchel over the ledge.

He positioned himself under the falling parcel, gritting his teeth in anticipation of a painful collision. To his relief, nothing of the sort happened. The parcel struck as light as a bundle of feathers, and Raymond's confusion turned to awe when he felt the density of the contents.

Arrows, he realized in disbelief, *hundreds of them!*

Setting the satchel aside, the female laif appeared next to him, having descended without notice. "Can you shoot?" she asked, startling the red knight.

Though he considered himself to be a good liar, the gravity of the situation he found himself in encouraged him to be truthful. "Not at all," he admitted, knowing the disappointment such an admission would bring.

The laif shrugged. "It's probably for the best," she said. "You'll better serve as a distraction anyhow."

An awkward silence stretched between the human and laif, breaking only when the other laives appeared above them, successful in their mission. In no time at all, they were back on the ground and tearing off in the direction from whence they had come. Raymond followed behind as languidly as he dared, grateful for the brief respite.

Will the morning ever arrive? he wondered, trailing in the wake of his new companions. He had lost sight of the entourage almost immediately upon reentering the forest, but he resolved himself to simply plot the course before him, and to hekk with those inconsiderate laives. Maybe luck would take him elsewhere, leading him to better housemates that would refrain from constantly referring to him as "dead man." In addition, the notion of holding the post of "distraction" was extremely unappealing.

The wind whistled, rattling calcified branches, ushering the memory of the wraiths surging to the front of Raymond's mind. He shivered, not only from the lack of sunlight, but also from the instinctual fear that chilled his bones. Fenrirfang was certainly not a forest to trifle with.

His pace began to slow and soon he was briskly walking, bearing in the direction he had last seen the laives. Some forty paces ahead, he saw tree trunks aglow, lit by a roiling orb of light. Drawing close, he crouched down as he closed the gap. If he could have silenced the scraping of his armour, he would have, but tried to instead compensate by taking very small, almost creeping steps.

"Move as slowly as you want," said the female laif, nearly causing the red knight to collapse into himself.

Startled, he doubled over, clutching himself. "Fack!" he hooted.

"It's not your footfalls that attract attention," she continued, "it's your scent." She leaned over and took an exaggerated sniff, inhaling loudly and violating Raymond's comfort zone. "And you will make the perfect distraction," she said with a nod, smiling as if she were gazing at a simmering soup.

4

"You didn't waste any time getting here," said Ancel to the mounted laif waiting outside Fenrirfang's boundary.

"With a swift horse and a purpose," Caestar replied, a crooked smile on his face, "you'd be amazed at what you can accomplish."

Halted behind the Lord, the retinue from Benwick waited. Thus far their travel had been rather leisurely, the knights saving their horses for the harsher terrain of the forest. There had been no spectacle, no banners, no frills attached to their mounts. They were not heading to a tournament, this was not a friendly melee of any making. Some of the knights had been roused from pleasant naps, others interrupted during their daily tasks with the news of war. Sudden, jarring news, and for a few, absolutely thrilling.

Piling more shock onto their day was the revelation that they would be following their Lord into battle. Not Ban, the lord they had grown accustomed to serving, but the new lord, Ancel. Even the knights who had salivated at the notion of finally facing the archenlaif threat had simply smiled uneasily and noted, "Interesting..." The more reticent of the ranks had been entirely at ease with the development, especially when considering what was at stake.

The laif settled his gaze on the knights of Benwick. "Is this all?"

"It's all that Benwick has," replied Ancel. "It's all that Arthur will need."

"If you say so," said Caestar. "Well, if I have read the missive correctly, we will be the vanguard. From here, Navarene is a two day journey, though I imagine we will be meeting the enemy *much* sooner." The laif fidgeted nervously, expecting curious questions. Ancel simply squinted up into the trees, completely disinterested.

The laif sighed and continued, "Tintagil and Ghore will be joining us sometime soon, they are perhaps a day or so behind."

"And Arthur?"

Caestar blinked and adjusted himself. "The King is embroiled in another sort of battle. As we speak, he is—"

"Naturally," interjected Ancel.

"Our King will be there."

Pulling the reins, Ancel steered his horse broadside to his knights. Grim faces peered back at him under lifted visors, the shade underneath obscuring their features. The knights of Benwick had always answered their King's call and were always first into the fray. Be it manticore, ogre, laif, gorgon, or human, the knights of Benwick could be relied upon. Benwick's close proximity to Fenrirfang, the nearest threat to Camelot, often gave them the advantage and ability to strike first. Every time dire news reached the keep, rushed through the air on hurried wings, the response beacon was instantly lit, and the knights would ride forth. Each and every time. Through the years, however, their numbers had dwindled. Be it from death or cowardice, their ranks had been noticeably thinned. Furthermore, children born with a Warrior's mark had been few and far between within Benwick, making replenishing the ranks quite difficult. Where hundreds once rode out, Ancel surveyed the knights as his horse shied beneath him with unease, now rode thirty.

Ancel turned to face the forest. "Let's get this over with."

As they passed the boundary with no incident, the final knight in the cavalcade breathed an audible sigh of relief. The sun still had plenty of time before it was resigned to rest, but in the more cramped sections of the path, one could believe time had flown carelessly by, skipping dusk, pitching the riders straight into night. Throughout the forest birds shrieked warnings to their kin, heaving the thrum to near deafening volumes, and when the knights believed their ears might actually bleed from the clamor, the songs would crescendo downward to a manageable racket.

"Brother," Ector called, spurring his mount to catch up to Ancel at the front of the line where the pathway had generously widened to comfortably ride three abreast. "What say you? If these tweeters are the harshest beast we face until the enemy, I'd say we would be blessed," he said, a hopeful look in his eyes.

Ancel turned, chewing his unlit pipe. "Aye," he agreed. He was opposed to the youngest of his brothers joining them on this mission, but all Warrior-born had a responsibility to the realm, and affection must be brushed aside in such circumstances. Looking over Ector's plate and weaponry, Ancel noticed the strap on his brother's right vambrace was hanging untethered, swinging like a pendulum.

"Secure your bracer," he said sternly, returning his eyes forward.

Ector's horse slowed. "A thousand pardons, my Lord," the young knight muttered sarcastically, obeying the command, his glare unwavering from the back of his brother's head as he did so.

He briefly considered riding back up to Ancel, but thought better of it, and continued to slow his horse's pace, drifting back to his place in line. He knew that his brother greatly preferred silence, and the simple pleasures of a tome in his lap and a pipe in his mouth after a day of labor. Though he held renown as perhaps the most powerful knight in the realm, one would never know it by looking at him. There was no swagger, no posturing at the taverns, not ever. After victory at a tourney, Ancel would return to his chambers and close the door, shutting out the world with its applause and expectations. Its trumpets and finery completely ignored and rejected, all of it could burn as far as he was concerned. Tourneys and melees were simply part of his job, a burden that he silently shouldered without complaint as the eldest son of Ban.

In the past, Ector had idolized his brother, but struggled to find common ground. Where Ector fumbled and failed with the ladies, Ancel could stride into a room and cause a breeze to whip up from all the heads turning his way. Between match-ups in tourneys, Ector was sizzling with energy, chomping and salivating, awaiting his next opponent. Ancel, however, was more than likely to be found napping, needing to be roused by whichever unlucky lad or lass had drawn the shortest straw that morning. Ector longed for a loving family with its loud conversations surrounding and filling any voids of calm, but Ancel had always seemed as though he could take or leave company without sparing a second glance.

Father's body was not yet cooled when he gave the orders to ride, Ector thought bitterly. His father's death march had been long and arduous, his eventual demise no surprise, but the pain Ector felt when the news finally came was no less severe.

Up ahead, Caestar lifted his arm, calling for a halt, breaking Ector from his reverie.

At first glance the creatures that crossed the path appeared human, walking upright in a hurry. The leader swiveled his head, distinctly rodent-like, in their direction and took in the knights with a level gaze. No one moved, save the distracted bobbing of horsetails.

"Victus," someone whispered behind Ector, putting a name to this particular forest-dwelling race.

Caestar waved at the victus patriarch with two fingers and a thumb in a gesture of goodwill. Returning the laif's signal, the patriarch steepled his hands as if in prayer and bowed. From the forest, more victus quickly crossed the path knowing that no harm would befall them from the knights. The patriarch remained in place as his kin passed behind in a wave of controlled desperation. Mothers clutched their young to their chests with fathers leading others by the hand. Families linked together, grasping the tail in front of them as they crossed, all flanked by victus guardians carrying cudgels and other makeshift weapons. The sudden archenlaif occupation, so deeply entrenched and so close, had repercussions that Ector had not considered.

Watching the last of the rat creatures disappear under the forest's shroud, Ector turned to the knight beside him. "Most will run from a fire," he commented. "But fools like us will run straight into it."

The knight he addressed, Sir Sandrin, lowered his chin. "The world needs fools sometimes," he said to Ector, finishing the statement with a grim smile. The long, tight curls of Sandrin's hair billowed out from under his helm. The only times that his mane ever seemed tame was when it was locked under a helmet, and even then it managed to escape in wild increments.

"I suppose so," replied Ector, incredulous. He let the conversation die off, and Sandrin returned his attention forward, clicking his tongue gently and urging his mount onward as the retinue renewed their trek.

At the forefront, Caestar attempted to coax a conversation out of the Lord of Benwick. "You are aware that your knights are only a single dressing upon a gaping, weeping wound?" queried the ranger.

Ancel did not reply to the laif, and only closed his eyes in acknowledgment of the statement.

The ranger continued, "The army before you is an actual *army*," he rotated in his saddle and surveyed the knights behind him, nodding his head as if counting their numbers. "And it appears as though you are at least a few hundred shy."

"This is what we do."

Caestar leaned toward Ancel, as if suddenly activated by the rebuttal. "You know as well as I that this is an ill-conceived plan," he argued. "It's simply a knee-jerk reaction, an arrow into a swarm of wasps! It is entirely fruitless!" The laif seemed on the verge of panic, an unnatural state for someone in his station. The victus departure had a chilling effect on him, and he was clearly rattled.

"Are you frightened, laif? Do you feel your immortality in check?" Ancel swept his eyes up to the branches impeding his view of the heavens. "It is not as if you will even be joining us in the fray. What would you have me do?"

"Feign retreat! Run!" Caestar hissed, leaning further in his saddle. "Your numbers are small and Tintagil would not suspect a thing! In truth, they would be glad to add you to their ranks, despite their numbers being quite inadequate for pitched war, the odds of survival would greatly increase. At least, until the King's army sweeps over the enemy, securing a sure victory."

"We stay the course, Caestar," replied Ancel, yawning.

"This is insanity!"

Ancel shook his head.

"We must run! Join the ranks of Ghore and Tintagil, I tell you! You will hardly register as a hiccup to the enemy!"

Ancel did not bother to respond this time.

"You will die!" Caestar spat, speaking loud enough for all to hear.

Ancel paused, locking eyes onto Caestar. "If the need arises," he concluded, speaking with the surety of one already in the grave.

Caestar replied with a tenor growl and encouraged his slender horse to move ahead of this suicidal mortal, no longer interested in futilely attempting to reason with him. "I will take you past the ward before Ir-phen's Downfall," he announced. "No further will I go."

Overhearing the conversation, Ector abruptly found it difficult to swallow, his windpipe parched, the dryness below in contrast to his eyes. Tears began to pour down his face, foreign and unbidden.

Sir Sandrin peered at the grieving rider and offered a scarf. "When it passes," he said to Ector, "steel yourself. You are a knight of Benwick. You are already dead."

Ector accepted the offering. "It's not that," he sniffed. "I do not know what has come over me. I mean, I know that *this* is all hopeless," he said, waving a hand at the surrounding knights. "We will not be returning to the fields and streams of my youth. I know I will never see them again." The tears began to abate, and Ector sniffed, steeling himself as the knight beside him had recommended. "This foe... we have never faced a foe like this. But I do not mourn us, and I do not mourn me."

Sandrin nodded, pretending comprehension, retrieving the scarf as it was handed back to him. "I am sorry to hear of your father's passing. It came as—"

"It's not that either," Ector interjected. "Maybe it is? I have always found it difficult to reconcile my feelings."

"Ah," said Sandrin, perception beginning to bloom. He buried his hand in the satchel on his hip, stowing the scarf in one movement, and as if by magic, seemingly transforming the scarf into a flask as he withdrew his hand. "Take this, my friend. I have brought others." He smiled reassuringly as he passed the container of spirits to the younger knight and patted the satchel.

The remaining tear streaks had begun to dry in the meager breeze, but renewed as tears sprang forth once again from Ector's eyes. "My thanks, Sandrin," he said laughing, swiping at his cheeks. "Cheers, mate."

The pair lifted their flasks in salute and took a deep draught of the burning fluid.

Sandrin coughed for several rounds, pounding his chest plate. "Into the flames," he finally managed to say.

Ector artlessly replied by taking another painful slug, choking back the sting traversing his trachea. "Into the flames," he croaked.

* * *

"Do you think it will work?" Bryndon hustled to keep up. The woman ahead of him was in much better shape and her legs were considerably longer.

"It's all we can hope for," she replied, stopping at the peak of the grassy embankment, looking down as her companion struggled his way up the steep grade. "Keep up, will you?"

"Why are we—" he reached out for help and Lanaelle clasped his hand and heaved him up. The stocky man wiped his brow. "Why are we rushing so? It's not like the werewolf is going anywhere. He hardly ventures outside anymore." Admittedly, he too spent far too many nights at the tavern and not nearly enough in training, as Lanaelle was prone to do.

She took advantage of their pause to withdraw her canteen. "I don't know," she admitted, eyes clinging to the horizon. "I'm just excited, I guess. I have wanted this for so long."

Bryndon eyed her speculatively. "*This* being?" he asked, waiting for her to finish her sip.

"*This* being the answer to all our frailties." With one finger she swiped the trickle of water that had escaped from the side of her mouth and used the same finger to indicate the space on her neck bereft of any mark. A glossy spot appeared where her finger traced the line, drawing Bryndon's attention.

"A possible answer," he corrected, his mouth suddenly dry. "There is no guarantee that it will work... or that we'll even survive!" He unstopped the cap on his canteen and took a drink, his eyes remaining on Lanaelle.

Lanaelle affixed her fists to her hips. "It will work," she insisted. Without waiting for a reply, she wheeled around and took off. "Keep up!" she shouted behind her.

Surprised, Bryndon recklessly jerked the canteen away from his mouth, soaking the front of his jerkin in the process. With an enamored sigh, he fumbled the canteen back into its holster as his feet resumed a faster than comfortable pace.

"No, no, no," the unkempt and noticeably thin man repeated. "A hundred times, no!" His lips retained the circular shape as he shook his head in dissent.

"Come on," Lanaelle begged. "Just one bite!"

"Creator's crimson peaks, woman!" the thin man shouted, rising from his breakfast. The term *breakfast* was implied loosely, what sat upon his plate was merely a raw haunch of hastily skinned rabbit meat. "No!"

"Why not?" She rose in unison with the werewolf, spreading her arms belligerently. "What have you got to lose?"

He wagged a finger at her and turned his attention to Bryndon. "Talk some sense into your girlfriend, will ya?"

"She's not my—"

"Answer the question, Vuko!" Lanaelle cut in, refusing to be dissuaded. She called the man by name, pressing her luck with the beast in human form.

"For one," Vuko said, closing the distance between them, bristling. "You would not survive the transformation," he paused, glancing side eyed at Bryndon, his gaze falling on the man's paunchy gut, "and your boyfriend would *certainly* not make it out alive."

"I'm not her—"

Lanaelle's eyes glimmered, hungry for a fight. "Oh yeah?!" The tight space between woman and werewolf became nonexistent. Their chests pressed against each other, and if one were not any wiser the scene would appear to indicate a lover's quarrel. This, however, was assuredly not the case.

"Yes," Vuko growled from somewhere deep in his chest. It was an alarming sound that would send most sensible folks to flight. Bryndon, being fairly sensible, inched toward the door, ready to flee at the faintest glimpse of a sprouting fang.

"Lanaelle..." Bryndon spoke slowly, cautiously. "Maybe we should—"

She waved dismissively at her frightened friend, mustering more than enough courage for the both of them, her eyes intent on the beast. Vuko did not move an inch, and neither gave ground as the intensity in the room escalated, nearly popping the hairs from Bryndon's scalp as he trembled. The single room cabin hummed with an energy almost palpable enough for him to see if he squinted just right.

"Explain yourself," Vuko spat, verbally conceding. "How are you so sure you won't die?" The werewolf detected something in the woman's eyes that sparked his interest. He was not a people person and rarely sought company, choosing to live on the outskirts of Benwick. The fact that Lanaelle was willing to enter his abode, *and* request something so absurd, as well as stare back at him with such defiant intensity... this was beyond unique.

"Because," Lanaelle began, snapping her fingers and holding out her palm to Bryndon. The man was cowering a half dozen paces away. "Bryndon! The vial," she demanded, continuing to snap her fingers impatiently as if the man was an aloof servant.

The notion struck him like a blow to the head, causing him to reel and hold his forehead. "Oh, yes! Yes!" he exclaimed, fumbling in his pouch. "One moment... not this," he mumbled, tossing a mushroom aside, "Or this," he continued, discarding what appeared to be a stalk of broccoli. "Ah, here we go," he said in triumph, lifting a small glass bottle. He held it at arm's length and marched toward the pair who had reluctantly withdrawn from each other, easing a bit of the tension in the small space.

"And what is that exactly?" the werewolf queried, cocking an eyebrow. The sapphire liquid sloshed around the vial, coating the insides in its tiny wake.

"A concoction," Lanaelle replied, lifting her chin haughtily. "Procured from a mage, guaranteed to allow a blank like me to survive the werewolf transformation."

"Impossible."

"Doubt all you want, but it's true," Lanaelle unstoppered the cork and angled it toward Vuko's nose. "Care to take a sniff?"

Vuko instantly shot back, clamping his nose and cursing. "It's authentic!" he wailed, wheezing as if he had just completed a marathon. The slim frame of his shoulders rose and fell with each labored breath. "Alright! Alright!" he relented, taking a seat by his breakfast.

"Excellent!" Lanaelle bobbed up and down on her tiptoes and clapped her hands in elation, beaming at Bryndon. He tried his best to imitate her excitement, his body and limbs reflecting her movements, but his eyes told a different story, showing trepidation from the nostrils up.

Vuko snapped a bite from the meat. "Take a seat," he said, nodding at the chairs on the opposite side of the table. They were in pristine condition, in marked contrast to the rest of his furnishings.

Lanaelle and Bryndon took a seat, the male counterpart in clear discomfort. His eyes never ceased tumbling around the room and his hands wrung endlessly, liable to wear themselves raw if he continued for much longer. In distinct variance, Lanaelle was the picture of ease, a placid stone adjacent to a quivering lump of jam.

"Tell me," Vuko began, speaking through a chewy mouthful of tendon, "How did you manage to get such a potion? The cost must have been quite high." He was losing the battle in his mouth, and he removed the band of sinew with a scowl and tossed it over his shoulder.

"Uh..." Lanaelle flexed her lower lip and looked to the uneasy man next to her, who did not appear excited to divulge details. "Uh, we *helped* him with a portrait, er, painting?" she paused, biting her bottom lip, "Yeah, we helped him with his painting..."

Vuko sat quietly, one eyebrow raised in a request for more details.

"A painting that required a particular model..." Bryndon offered, wishing the conversation would shift.

Silence hung in the room as Vuko's canine eyes darted between the pair, awaiting a conclusion. Neither wished to venture further, which became grossly apparent as the beads of sweat on Bryndon's forehead became rapidly descending torrents. Not for the first time that day, the werewolf relented.

"Fair enough," Vuko said, sliding his chair back and folding his arms. The points of his elbows jutted out in dangerously sharp angles under his bristly arms.

Both visitors breathed a sigh of relief. Lanaelle closed her eyes and recalled the scene in question, wishing she could dispel it forever. As hard as she tried to forget, the image was seared behind her eyelids. *But why did the mage need Bryndon to take his shirt off?*

Vuko caught the woman's movement. "That bad, eh?"

She twitched again.

"Hey!" Bryndon interjected, offended. "It wasn't that bad." He looked Lanaelle up and down and huffed.

For the first time in many days, Vuko laughed. "Once I am done with my meal," he announced cheerfully to Lanaelle, as if they were discussing an impending gala, "I will bite you."

Lanaelle cleared her throat and flicked her eyes at Bryndon.

"Both of you?"

5

Linette's spoon swirled the stew in her bowl, aimlessly shoving the bits of meat and vegetables aside. Her mind meandered and wandered, much like the spoon carving its path in the gravy. The kitchen was the largest room in the cottage, and it held a massive dining table crafted by her father years ago when the realization struck that he would be spending meals with six women for the foreseeable future. Evening meals with all the sisters attending were loud and raucous, and at times, rather screechy. Kenna was forced to cover his ears on many such occasions when the din would reach ear-splitting pitches. The ghosts of happier days seemed to haunt the room, lingering on the fringes of sight. On quiet nights like this one, the memories almost seemed palpable, like one could almost reach out and pull them back. Where seven once sat, now only two remained.

"Are you not hungry?" her father asked softly, his brow furrowing with sincerity. "I added some new seasonings in with the broth. Maybe it's too spicy?" He rose abruptly and reached for her plate, "perhaps I can soften it up a bit—"

Linette gave him a look that made him stop, then shook her head and held a hand over the bowl.

"Ah, I see," Kenna said, settling back into his seat. "Do you like it?"

She returned a solemn affirmative nod, and graciously dispelled any suspicion by dredging a heaping spoonful and bringing it to her mouth.

As she struggled to chew, her cheeks bulged and her lips puckered, barely containing the tide behind them.

"Oh, good, good," Kenna dabbed his chin whiskers with a napkin. "Do you think Perla will like it? I think I recall her taking quite a liking to spicy foods and I was—" He broke off at the expression he was receiving from his youngest, the serious look made less impactful from the slight smears of soil adorning her forehead and cheeks. He had found her outside not a half hour ago, lying down, curled protectively around her small flower garden as twilight gathered around. He had heard the small commotion earlier in the day, and upon discovering the source, he had shamefully returned to his work. The last time he had tried to intervene on his daughter's behalf, in concern to those wicked agents of Benwick, he had befallen the most humiliating of experiences. Afterwards, he had assured himself that it was best that Linette learn to deal with adversity on her own. It's what a good parent did. At least, that's what he told himself.

"What's the matter?" he asked, attempting to abate the glare he was receiving. "Your sister has some news to share with us."

Linette held up her board.

Kenna read the words, his head following the letters. *"You did not tell me we would be having company tonight,"* he recited the lines evenly, snapping his mouth shut at the end and settling his hands into his lap. "The message arrived just this afternoon, Linette. I'm sorry that I did not inform you." He tugged his beard and smiled. "But won't you be happy to see your sister? I wonder what tidings she has, eh?" He bobbed his eyebrows playfully, bringing to mind a pair of graying caterpillars struggling to stay afloat.

Setting her spoon aside, Linette scribbled another message.

Her father laughed as his eyes danced over the letters. "Yes! Perhaps! And that would make you an aunt! How about that?" He shoveled another bite into his mouth and grinned. "Grandfather," he happily proclaimed, chewing the stew. "Do you like 'grandpa' or 'poppa' better?"

Linette replied by scratching another phrase.

"Deda?" Kenna squinted for a moment before laughing with recollection. "That was what you called your grandfather on your mother's side!" Memories swam behind the older man's eyes and he fixated on the wall above Linette's head, lost inside the past for a spell. "Well," he said at length, bringing himself back to the present, "it's something to think about. And who knows, maybe it's some other news?"

Raising the board, Linette smirked behind the single word she had scribbled.

Kenna took a moment to swallow, his eyes comprehending the word before he spoke it: *Doubtful,* he chuckled. "You're probably right."

Spoons scraped the wooden bowls as father and daughter ate, deciding not to wait for Perla to arrive before serving food. They were famished from the day's labor, and Perla had the habit of being consistently late for all engagements.

"Oh," Kenna broke the silence. He waited for Linette to look up before continuing. "What was it that you had written on your board when I found you earlier?" He pointed his spoon at the panel of slate resting next to her bowl, the tool never far from her reach.

Linette decided that now was not the time to bring up the subject of the silver shadesgill. Her father was practically radiating in the hopes of his first grandchild, and she did not want to sour his mood.

"It can wait," he read the plate with a full mouth and chuckled. "Alright sparrow, that sounds good." He happily resettled into his chair and continued to eat, his mind clearly elsewhere.

Moments later, a knock resounded from the front stoop. The door was open to allow the spring breeze free access, and before Kenna could rise from his seat, a pair of slippered feet scuffed through the entryway and a sweet voice spoke.

"Hello?" there was an ironic tremolo in the vowels. Kenna and Linette shared an excited look and stood, nearly rocking their chairs to the ground. A wide-eyed face poked around the dining room threshold, feigning confusion. "Hello?" she repeated in a higher pitch, eyes roaming the kitchen ceiling.

"Perla!" Kenna received his daughter with his arms opened as wide as he could manage. Perla's eyes snapped to her father and she did not waste another moment playacting, but instead hurried into his embrace.

Clapping her hands and rising onto the balls of her feet, Linette stood beside her father, awaiting her sister's greeting. How long had it been since they had last seen each other? Two years? Three years?

Stepping free from her father's welcoming arms, Perla appraised Linette from sole to crown. "You look *sturdier,* little sister," she said, eyes gleaming with mischief. Linette replied by flexing her biceps and baring her teeth, a very unladylike display for sure, but one that caused the elder sister to roar with laughter, as was intended.

After the sisters shared an embrace, a full bowl of stew was placed before Perla and the meal resumed.

"In truth," Perla began as she took up her spoon, "I already had supper, but for some reason I feel like I can eat again." Her eyes roamed over Kenna and Linette, the mischief from moments before still visible.

This time, Kenna's chair flew across the room from the force of his movement. "You don't mean?!"

Patting her stomach and smiling, Perla confirmed their suspicions.

Kenna hopped in place with his hands on the tabletop, looking much like a boy in a toy shop. He did not wait for his daughter to rise before flinging his arms around her, teetering the chair onto its back feet. Only a second behind her father, Linette fastened herself to the pair, and if she could laugh and shout, she would have. In their stead, tears of joy poured down her cheeks.

"Alright, alright," Perla playfully batted them away. "Allow me some space to eat!" She squinted and wrinkled her nose in mock outrage. "Knaves!"

Linette returned to her seat, but Kenna's feet would not let him leave his daughter's side. He stood over her with his hands clasped, smiling down upon her with shining eyes.

"Father," Perla said curtly.

His smile branched to his earlobes. "Yes?"

"Your shadow is making it difficult to see what I am eating."

"Oh!" Kenna rebounded bashfully and moved to take his seat, forgetting that it was still prostrate against the wall. When his hand found nothing but air where he believed the chair to be, he awkwardly danced sideways. In his attempt to remain standing, he ended up tumbling onto the floor, skidding to a halt on his chin.

"Father!" Perla cried, hastily rising.

Linette was at his side within a blink.

His chin bounced from the floor as he howled with laughter, his arse in the air. "Honestly," he began, interrupting himself with another bout of laughter. Every attempt to help was waved away. He rolled onto his back with a groan and stared at the ceiling as if it were a vast tapestry of stars. "Honestly, I'm okay right here," he murmured contentedly.

Feeling her initial alarm was a bit misplaced, Linette returned to her seat. After all, Kenna was a sturdy man and it would take more than a small tumble in a dining room to remove the wind from his sail.

Turning her attention back to the table, Linette wrote, "What else is new?" on her slate, though she knew full well it was a lazy question. She lifted it to her sister.

A mouthful did not deter Perla from responding. "Where to begin?" she mused. Although the words came out garbled, Linette could easily decipher them.

With a furrowed brow, Linette scribed a more specific query.

"*How is life with the Cartographer?*" Perla read. "Ha, ha." She rolled her eyes. "Corbin is..." she trailed off, fishing her spoon aimlessly in her bowl. Her tone abruptly shifted. "That's actually something that I need to talk with Father about."

A small commotion began on the floor as Kenna worked to find his chair and right it. "What are you going on about?" he asked, face pink around his beard as the blood rushed back to his head.

"Daddy," began Perla, her lip trembling.

"What is it?" Kenna urged her in a soft voice.

She flipped a lock of hair over her shoulder and composed herself, abandoning her spoon and straightening up. "Corbin is not leaving me," she stated, her lips becoming a solid line. "But... I feel like I will be losing him." Her chin drooped. "Soon."

Before Linette could scribble down a question, her father posed it. "What is happening, dear one? Start from the beginning."

Perla's eyes chased across the ceiling as if it were littered with scudding clouds. "We were happy. Very happy, actually, at first. The first years were total and complete bliss. He would go off to his work every morning, but not before giving me a kiss and an apology for his absence." She seemed to withdraw into herself. "But, as of late..." The ceiling above no longer held her interest, her gaze now favoring the knurls and lines on the table. "Perhaps it was a few months ago it started?" She scratched her chin. "That was when the discontentment began to settle, and a month or so after that, the spite really began to dig its claws into him."

Startled, Linette and Kenna looked to one another in confusion.

"I knew the problem had grown more severe than I first guessed when the news—" she paused, gesturing at her belly, *"Our* news... that we would be expecting a child," she hesitated. "His face hardly moved when he smiled. The news seemed to cause him more pain than pleasure."

Kenna leaned forward, inclining an ear. "Well, were you both trying..."

"Yes!" she interrupted, her voice more severe than she had intended. She stopped and smoothed her dress to calm herself, working out her misplaced emotions, before clearing her throat and speaking again. "I mean, it was a desire we held jointly. Yes."

"Ah."

"Map making was not something that Corbin ever dreamt of making an occupation. He has always held the desire of being... well, of being a knight."

Linette gagged, attempting to squelch a laugh.

Her sister did not favor the response, and simply peered at Linette sidelong. "Absurd, I know," she said, glossing over the slight. "He was born in more fortunate circumstances than others, having been marked with the sigil of the Architect at birth. A blessing from the Creator, to be sure! And in conspiracy with his ridiculous handsomeness, he was destined for success. Any fool could spot it from miles away." There would be no argument concerning that notion. It was a cruel yet accepted fact: prettier people tended to be more approachable, therefore more opportunities would be granted to them over those less fortunate in the looks arena.

"It was a smart match. The two of you," Kenna agreed, scratching the stubble on his chin. "Your children will have—"

"Exquisite bone structure? I know." Perla huffed in agitation. "Corbin's mother has already relayed such information ad nauseam."

She waved the recollection away, "Have you heard any rumblings about the archenlaif invasion?"

Kenna leaned back in his chair and folded his arms. "Our little farm might be far from the common pulse, but yes, such news has reached our doorstep."

Perla nodded. "And have you heard the rumors about men looking to change their station? Men and women looking to fight alongside the warriors?"

"Common folk are looking to join the war ranks?" Kenna asked, blinking in confusion. Warriors were warriors for a reason, and the only commoners sent to battle were those unlucky enough to be conscripted by the red knights. But those people were, by and large, brigands. "Whatever for?" he queried, remaining perplexed.

"Well, apparently some fur trader, some woman," Perla clarified, clearing her throat. "Has found a means to change the stars of those born bereft a mark. Or for those who are unhappy with their current mark."

"It is never good," Kenna stated, his chest heaved as he inhaled, "When people attempt such things."

"Well," Perla interjected. "That's not the whole of it. Allow me to finish, please."

"By all means!" said Kenna.

"I'm sorry, it's just—"

"No, it's alright, Perla. Please continue."

With a growl and a shake of her fist, she spoke. "It's just *that* stupid woman and my stupid husband!"

"Oh, Perla..." her father deflated.

She shook her head. "No, no, no. It's not like that. He's not having an affair. Well, not in the carnal sense."

This puzzled both Kenna and Linette, and in concert, their brows furrowed. Perla looked from one to the other and calmed the tension with a laugh. "Let me start again. I believe I am being too cryptic about this. This pregnancy has brought with it many blessings, but it has also ushered in new and more emotions than I have ever encountered. It can be overwhelming at times."

Without a request, Linette rose and fetched a cup of water for her sister.

"Thank you," she said, accepting the offering, but not partaking. Acting as if she were about to receive a lashing, she placed both palms on the table. "They want to turn themselves into werewolves," she revealed, the color draining from her features upon the admission.

Doing his best to take it in stride, Kenna opened his mouth and pointed, but made no statement. Linette remained silent as usual, but behind her eyes it was evident that she was formulating a response.

Perla looked to the upraised slate in her sister's hand. "*Why?*" she read, and briefly looked back up. "Because—" she stopped, needing a moment to regain her composure. "Because it will give him exceptional strength and agility and all the other qualities that he believes that he lacks," she explained with a pained smile.

"Will he survive?" Kenna had found his tongue at last. "Not too many make it through such an ordeal."

"He has a mark," Perla snapped. "He is more likely to survive."

Linette quickly scribbled something down then held up the slate. "*Says who?*"

"Says the woman," responded Perla. "What was her name? Landel, was it?" She chewed her lip trying to conjure the name. After a few seconds of pained thought, she smacked the table, "Lanaelle!" she blurted in triumph. The abrupt noise made Linette flinch.

Her father nodded with narrowed eyes. "Well, she sounds dreadful."

"She is," Perla nodded along, scrunching her face. "Her death would benefit this world greatly," she said before quickly slapping a hand over her mouth in horror. "Creator forgive me," she whispered through the cracks in her fingers.

Scratching at his beard as if it were infested, Kenna suddenly appeared markedly uncomfortable. It was apparent that he was about to share something that he was not comfortable making known, especially not to his daughters.

"When I was young," he began, "probably around Linette's age, maybe younger? Maybe a little older? Bah! Makes no difference!" Rising to his feet, he strode to the cabinet where he kept his smoking pipe. He paused, pulling smoke into his mouth while extinguishing the match in his hand, the cherry flashing and growing red in the pipe bowl.

"Where was I?" he said, his furrowed eyebrows almost connecting at the bridge of his nose. "Oh, yes. When I was maybe your sister's age," he repeated, pointing the pipe stem at Linette, "I knew a group of boys, almost men, mind you. Local boys that I grew up with. And like me, they were blank, absent of the Creator's gift." He tapped the side of his neck in emphasis with the pipe stem and clenched his jaw. "We grew up with tales of knights and valor and all that nonsense, so it was only normal to want that. To be a brave knight. To be a warrior. But such notions tend to flee when reality sets in, along with the settling of your life's station. Some, like me, picked up a hoe and shovel, while others reached for the hammer and anvil, or pen and parchment..." His words diminished as his thoughts left the table.

Perla reached out and touched his hand, snapping him back to the present.

"Yes," he blinked and shook his head. "We blanks do the best we can with what we've got. Anyhow, these particular boys got it into their heads that they would become knights. One of them had a sister that was an artist, blessed like your Corbin, she had the Architect's gift. And they decided to have her tattoo the Warrior's insignia on the flesh of their necks. Right where it was supposed to be. Now at that time, as it is now, there was a Warrior shortage. Always in demand. And so they believed that they would get accepted as squires, no questions asked."

Kenna paused his tale to take another draw from his pipe. The smoke twirled up from the bowl, and he sent a round of smoke rings into the air. Darkness had fallen outside, and the candles flickering gave the smoke a lingering life as they gradually distilled into mist.

The daughters waited for their father to continue, though a glimmer of impatience was held within the elder's eyes.

"The tattoos looked real," Kenna smiled without mirth. "Too real. Desiree was so talented with her drawings..." he began to drift away, but something caught the current and he brought himself back. "She made their necks look like they had the gift. I was so jealous." A hollow chuckle surfaced before he continued, "and the boys trained and trained, trying to bulk up to better play their part. To fool the world. To fool themselves." He sighed and placed the pipe stem at the corner of his mouth. "But in the end, they were simply *fools*."

A palpable silence fell, the sisters not accustomed to their father speaking so seriously, and they were hesitant to press him further. But Perla took it upon herself to push the subject.

"What happened to them?" she said. When he did not reply, she tried again. "Daddy?"

The cherry in his pipe had been extinguished, snuffed from the lack of wind.

"They all died," he replied, staring off at the ghosts. "Horribly and embarrassingly."

Perla gave Linette's slate a double take, reading the etching that her sister held aloft for their father.

A lump formed in Kenna's throat as his lips silently read the statement. He shuddered back a sob but did not give in to weeping. "Yes," he admitted, holding his head in his hands. "That is what befell your uncle."

The truth of their Uncle Henrick's demise had never been revealed to his girls. It was something that he had held close to his chest all these years, revealing only the good while omitting the bad.

"Oh, Father!" Perla shrouded her mouth with her napkin. "We never knew..."

"You were never supposed to know," he said. "Mark my words, dear daughters. This world has a nasty habit of punishing good intentions, no matter how noble," he said firmly, his finger emphatically stabbing the table, "with blood and death and misery."

6

"You want me to do what?" Raymond asked in disbelief.

The female laif, Flya, gently cupped his chin in her leather-clad hands. "Run over to that glade and pretend that you're intoxicated or mad or something," she said with a crooked smile. "Improvise."

Their first order of business had been to root out the archenlaives that had spilled into the surrounding forest. Which was where Raymond's part came into play. The bait.

"Yes," Saeva nodded in agreement with his kin. Though they shared similar physical qualities, their personalities contrasted rather sharply. "Make noise and rouse their attention. That is all."

Raymond got to his feet and reached for the sword he had propped against a tree, blade down. "Oh, is that all?" he spat incredulously, gripping the sword's hilt and waving his weapon around, testing his wrists.

"You won't be needing that," Flya said, concluding the statement with a crack of laughter.

Raymond looked to Saeva, and the laif nodded. "She's correct," he sighed. "You'll likely only hurt yourself, or worse, one of us."

"You're going to have to trust us," Flya said as she passed behind him, leering at him. In the brief period of time he had known her, he had been unsure as to whether she wished to bed him or to drown him.

They had allowed him a dirk only to be used as a last resort. He had been advised that he should only draw if all else failed, though, in all honesty, there was not much that could be done with such a weapon.

"You'll look a right twat waving such a darling weapon around anyway," Flya said before shoving him out into the glade. "Now get out there and do what you do best!" After regaining his footing, Raymond turned around and found that the five laives had already disappeared, leaving him feeling remarkably lonely.

"Oh," he said, beginning to limp. "Oh, man! I'm feeling very discouraged and hurt!" he exclaimed loudly to the vacant trees encircling the glade. "And drunk!" he added. He swore he could hear a tinkle of laughter somewhere off in the distance. He was no mummer, that was certain, but he did know how to feign an injury. "Ah, it hurts!" He allowed the limp to become utterly hampering, and dramatically collapsed onto his knees while issuing the whiniest moan he could conjure. A rustling in the bracken drew his attention. He whirled around, his knees carving a divot in the soil, to see a solitary archenlaif knight stalking toward him. The pale light of the moon gave the knight's armour a speckled eggshell luster, which Raymond found himself rather curiously focused on in the moment. He wanted to reach out and touch it to see if it was as textured as it appeared. The knight took less than two steps into the clearing before each gap in his armour was filled with arrows, penetrating nearly to their fletching. The invader made no sound, save the scraping of steel as he collapsed, dead long before his toes pointed to the sky.

"Whoa, whoa," Raymond clambered to his feet, adjusting the visor on his helm. That was way more startling than he had expected. Another sound issued from behind him, and he jumped, spinning to see what approached. His temples pounded as he scanned the area. Nothing. No one. He spun back to the dead knight and immediately reeled at what he saw. Or rather, what he did not see. Nothing, the dead knight was gone.

"What in the Holy Handsome Death Caverns..." he muttered, frantically scouring the glade for the body. "What in the—" he uttered again before the breath froze in his lungs. A dozen or more archenlaives burst through the trees, perhaps thirty paces from the dumbstruck red knight. Any admiration Raymond had once held for the archenlaif armour was completely forgotten, abandoned, and replaced with bowel draining terror.

Arrows sang past his head, their whistling heard clearly from under his helmet. The volley was chaotic and concentrated, precise and swift; not one arrow bounced or missed its target. The archenlaives fell in heaps, their rushing steps cut short.

"Damn it!" Raymond screamed at no one in particular as he shuffled away, creating as much distance as possible between himself and the mess of bodies. Arrow shafts grimly projected from every angle of the tangled corpses. He kept his eyes glued to them, waiting for them to disappear as their comrade had, but his hopes proved fruitless. A bone chilling hiss emanated from over his shoulder, and Raymond closed his eyes, having little desire to investigate such a terrifying sound.

Stillness blossomed in the atmosphere, and the temperature tumbled at least ten degrees. With his eyes fused shut, Raymond creaked his visor down over his face, shutting out the surrounding horrors. *Trust them, trust them...* he whispered, the fog of his breath swirling out from under his helm. The dirk he had securely fastened to his ankle felt incredibly far away. It may as well have been locked in a chest and buried in a marsh for all the aid that it would bring. The shivers began as mere twitches, originating at the nape of his neck and cascading down his spine, but soon increased in frequency and grew into teeth rattling spasms. Whatever approached was something that placed the insignificant red knight far, far out of his depth.

The noise continued to grow closer. If feet could slither, then slither they did.

Raymond was certain that he was about to die.

"Hurry!" Flya said, slapping his back as she careened past him. He opened his eyes and saw the friendly archers sprinting through the glade, obscuring the bodies littering the ground and disappearing into the trees. "Come on!" she commanded, halting and turned back fiercely, "these pricks won't cull themselves!"

Whatever frigid evil had attempted to creep into Raymond's soul seemed to dissipate at the laives' presence. He shook his head and began to trot forward. His limbs felt as if he had fallen into an icy well, causing his movement to be rather sluggish. By the time he reached the edge of the glade, the laives had fanned out behind cover, hidden from his sight, save for Flya. She stood waiting, impatiently tapping her foot.

"Come along, come along." She hurried him over to her, waving her hand and placing a finger to her lips. As he drew closer, she lowered herself onto one knee, and Raymond did the same. In hurried whispers, she spoke, "That was a good start, but we still have more work ahead of us, my little dead boy."

"Okay, but where—" Raymond began.

"That way," she bit him off, pointing an arrow in the direction of the spire. "We saw some more of them walking the perimeter of the battlements. Probably only six or seven of them..."

"Alright, but what—"

"Best of luck, mate," she offered the words of inspiration with a gentle push. "Now off you go!"

He set off and when he turned back, the laif was gone. Any more objections that he wished to raise would have to wait. *Alone again.* He pressed on, his thoughts spinning. *Six or seven? That's laif math for you. It's probably more like thirty or fifty.* The torchlight ahead quieted his thoughts. It was in motion, roving dozens of feet in the air, and Raymond guessed that he was approaching the crenelated walls of the fort. Bumping into a tree, he fastened his arms around the craggy bark, digging his fingernails between the crevices that ran down its trunk like rivulets. Leaning his head out to survey, he quickly realized that he was only a stone's throw from the fort. The torchbearer stalking the parapet did not notice him, but his light revealed a handful of archenlaives working away at something on the ground below. Their movements appeared frantic in the flickering torchlight, but the shadows on the wall revealed little to Raymond as to what they were doing.

"No matter," Raymond said under his breath with an assurance that felt peculiar. "They shan't be finishing!" He cringed at his own words before striding out from cover.

The jingling of loose buckles in conjunction with the sound of Raymond clearing his throat drew the archenlaives attention. The sentinel above, however, did not react and continued to pace without breaking stride. None of the archenlaives before him wore helmets, revealing faces exuding pure hatred accompanied with an undercurrent of contempt. It was the first time he had glimpsed an archenlaif's face, and Raymond was disappointed to find they simply looked like laives, albeit really pissed off laives. Before he had time to admire their features any further, five arrows flew over Raymond's shoulder, almost inaudible on their course to five separate throats.

Their deaths were silent, not one uttered a sound. Raymond capitalized on this good fortune by shrinking back from the torchlight, backpedaling until his haunches connected with a tree in the safety of the shadows. The sentinel was none the wiser as he continued to traipse the walkway, completely oblivious.

Where to next? Raymond wondered. *To hekk with it. Let's improvise!* It wasn't every day that one found themselves shadowed by guardians who whispered death at the faintest provocation. Confidence surged in his core, though his toes still felt traces of frostbite at their tips, from whatever... from whatever that *thing* was back in the glade. He tried to rationalize it as a figment of his imagination as he ran between the trees, skirting the fringe of the forest.

It's from all the ale, he reasoned. *You didn't think you could go on bender after bender without some sort of repercussions? Your mind and soul are always at odds, but I think that they agree on this one thing, you're tarnished goods.* He shook his head, wishing that his mind would ease up on its harsh truths.

Just keep on running, jackass, he thought, renewing his speed.

Suddenly another voice invaded his thoughts. *Yes, just keep running, Raymond. Just keep running until you finally meet the death that you know that you deserve.*

The entire world abruptly fell silent, every sound absorbed into oblivion, leaving Raymond's ears with a dull momentary hum. The unexpected change was disorienting, and he stumbled a step, but managed to find purchase on a waist high rock wall from a long-abandoned foundation.

"What manner—" he uttered before being cut off.

An eye-searing flash emitted from the top of the spire, immediately followed by a cataclysmic explosion. Radiating waves sliced through the moonlit smoke, parting the clouds, offering a rare glimpse at the peak of the spire.

An urgent tug on the back of his collar caused him to nearly crumple in fright.

"Back to camp," said a voice from behind him, a brief glance showing it to be one of the male archers. "We will see what we can do on the way back. But for now, the hunt is over."

Saeva returned, and with him came the daylight. The night had proven to be the most frantic game of tag that Raymond had ever played.

"Our enemy believes that we are many," the lampyr reported, smiling as he refilled his quiver. "Simple minds," he added, shaking his head. The laives had spent the night successfully preventing the archenlaives from leaving the gates of the fort.

Wrapped in blankets, Raymond lay on the ground watching the laives prepare their armour and weapons for another campaign of confusion. There was nothing for him to do, except keep the fire alive, and that was perfectly fine with him. At the moment, the laives believed him to be fast asleep.

Saeva had remained in the forest, doing whatever it was that lampyrs did in the dark. Something that was probably far from the practice of the healing arts, Raymond speculated.

On Raymond's trek back, the archers had dropped another half dozen of their skulking enemies and, judging by the retreating horns and shouts, the archenlaives had decided to hole themselves up behind the walls of the fort for the time being.

For Raymond, the night offered a sleep that was harder and deeper than any he had ever known, in spite of the armour he was still wearing. When his bladder roused him from his warm blankets, he drowsily wandered to the nearest tree, out of sight, but able to catch fragments of the laives' late-night conversations. During one of Raymond's semiconscious piss walks, he overheard a male speaking, and the word *karbaled* stuck out to him like a red berry growing in the dead of winter. He mouthed the word to himself, for ease of remembrance, hoping it would cling to the back of his throat.

Karbaled, karbaled, he had repeated as the tension in his groin gradually depleted, steadying himself with one hand on the tree. *Do not forget to ask Saeva about the karbaled.*

"I believe that we have bought ourselves at least a half day," said Saeva. "Or more, perhaps. Their numbers are still many, but if we are prudent, we may yet walk away from this."

"Do you have any idea when the armies of Arthur will arrive?" a male laif inquired. Raymond recognized him as the laif who had clasped his collar right after the explosion the night before, almost startling him into oblivion.

"Of that, I do not know, Craendir."

Flya spat into the flames. "So the games will continue, eh?" She arched one eyebrow. "Fine by me. I just hope our decoy holds up," she commented, probing the outskirts of Raymond's blankets with her foot.

Raymond, who had been eavesdropping, while still swaddled below them, finally stirred. "Saeva," he began. Flya started, clearly believing her touch had been delicate. He wrested himself free of the bedding and continued, "What is..." his voice cracked. Clearing his throat, he made a second attempt. "What is a karbaled?"

Flya's expression of mild shock suddenly jolted into immense amusement. "And what do you know of karbaleds?" she asked.

"Nothing, actually," Raymond replied. He was distracted by the heel of his boot getting caught by one of the thinner quilts, and he kicked at it like it was on fire. Finally, his boot was clear, and he stood up and yawned. "It was a phrase I overheard in my sleep, and it gave me chilly dreams." Though he spoke false, he felt compelled to steer the conversation toward the icy apparition he had encountered in the glade.

Saeva fixed Raymond with a stern glare and spoke to his companions. "I see no reason for any further deception." The laives all nodded their heads in agreement.

"A karbaled is a practitioner of hoarfrost," he explained, the tips of his fangs protruding just below his upper lip as he spoke. When all he received in return was a look of confusion, he tried to clarify but was interrupted by Flya.

"It's an ice wizard," she said bluntly. "And with where we currently find ourselves," she paused, sweeping a hand around them, indicating their present location, "Facing such a foe is practically suicide," she concluded dryly.

"Why is that?"

"Because, in brief, to slay an elemental conjurer, you must first stem the source of its power. When that's all well and done, you go for the wizard's throat."

Raymond looked from Flya, then back to Saeva. "And the source of this wizard's power is?"

"Underground," replied Flya. "Out of our reach. She is drawing from underground springs, which, as even you should be able to comprehend, are nigh impossible to stop."

A dawning realization bloomed on Raymond's face and Saeva sensed something deeper beneath the red knight's reaction.

"You were touched by the karbaled," the lampyr stated, thoughtfully tracing a finger across the sharp angle of his jaw. "Last night at some point."

Raymond nodded.

"When exactly?" Saeva pressed, stepping toward the human.

"In the glade."

"Before the spire detonated?"

"Yes. Right after your second volley."

"What did you feel?"

He closed his eyes and peered back into his memories. "I felt very cold and very frightened, like I would be overtaken by some great beast. And I kept telling myself to trust that you would kill whatever was behind me..."

Flya narrowed her eyes at him. "And?"

"You didn't." Raymond shook his head and stared at the ground. But when you entered the clearing and urged me on, urged me to leave, the terror and the icy cold lifted all at once."

Saeva, typically calm and unflappable, turned a heel and cursed loudly toward the heavens. This sudden and unusual outburst was unsettling, not only for Raymond, but for all those in the group.

"What does this mean?" the lampyr growled at the sky, scratching his head.

"Uh," Raymond's eyes darted from laif to laif. "Maybe it—"

"You should be dead," Saeva cut him off, speaking without turning. "By all rights, Raymond, you should no longer be among the living."

7

"You woke me up to tell me *what?*" Sir Carlysle whined, flopping over to face the wall. "And which inn is this?" Basic bedchambers all looked the same through a drunken haze, and distinguishing them often proved impossible.

"The Sly Spectacle," her squire replied through gritted teeth, heaving the blankets away from the knight's tightly wound grip. "Why can you never remember anything?" she asked, knowing full well that it was because her knight was rarely sober.

"Didn't I fire you yesterday?" The knight now lay supine upon the bed, still in her gambeson and boots, and squinted at the ceiling.

"Indeed," the squire replied, folding the coverlets and scrunching her nose as the stink of cheap liquor wafted up from the fabric. "And the day before that and the day before that," she mumbled.

"You don't need to shout, Stacey."

"I'm not shouting, my liege." She headed for the curtains to drench the scene in morning light.

"Hey! Don't!" Carlysle protested, shielding her eyes. "My head!" She cursed as the brilliance passed over her, catapulting her dull headache from a four to an eleven. "Well, consider yourself fired for the hundredth time!"

"Yeah, yeah," Stacey muttered indifferently, collecting more of the errant knight's belongings. "Shall I draw a bath before we shove off?"

From under a pillow, Carlysle croaked, "Yes, please."

"Has this sky never heard of clouds?" Carlysle grumbled, wincing, as the pair left the Sly Spectacle and re-entered the world.

Stacey enjoyed the brief sober moments with her knight a bit more than the drunken ones, though the former were rather rare. It was only a matter of time before they entered another pub or tavern or inn and Carlysle ordered round after round until her feelings and memories were swept away on the foaming, bubbling river of abstraction. Whatever had befallen her in her past that caused such intemperate behavior was soundly locked away, and even the overindulgence of alcohol never loosened the hinges. It was why—at least it's what Stacey told herself—the squire remained loyal for longer than any of her predecessors. Life with a drunk was not easy, but Stacey believed that one day it would pay off. And every so often, the squire thought she saw a glimpse of *something* underneath the slovenly veneer. One time while sitting in a tavern, Carlysle had made a statement, while intoxicated, that Stacey would think of often in the time to come. *It's hard to see death coming when time passes in flickers...*

"So anyway," Carlysle continued, peering at Stacey blearily. "What manner of trouble is my sister in?"

"You're aware of the archenlaif incursion?"

"Yes, yes, of course I am," drawled Carlysle, "what of it *now?*"

"Well, apparently your sister has decided to take it upon herself to organize an army to aid the king and Camelot."

Carlysle snorted and swiped at her nose with the back of her wrist. "Lanaelle?!" she guffawed and cursed as her headache suddenly thrummed anew. "Lanaelle is a cobbler! What is she going to do? You can't *shoe* away an archenlaif!"

Stacey's mouth became a firm line. "I'm being serious, Carlysle. Your sister is a werewolf."

"I'm sorry, what did you just say?"

"Your sister. Lanaelle." Stacey spoke slowly, carefully articulating each word, "is a werewolf."

"How did this come about?" the knight demanded.

Her squire shrugged and dipped her chin. "I heard it was some sort of potion or something. After she drank of it... it kept her alive," she concluded, averting her eyes from the knight's unexpectedly focused gaze.

An alley offered Carlysle an escape, and she grabbed Stacey by the elbow and forced her into it. Pressing her against the wall, the knight's lip curled as she seethed with hot anger, an emotion that eclipsed the usual listlessness that pervaded the knight's bearing. Inwardly, the squire was actually rather impressed that the drunkard had it in her.

"Where are they and how many are there?"

"Uh," Stacey choked out, finding it difficult to think with her air restricted. She glanced frantically at her clavicle, hoping Carlysle would catch her meaning.

"Oh! Sorry..." the knight removed her forearm from Stacey's neck and took a step back.

With a shaky hand, Stacey smoothed her collar and rubbed her neck, refilling her lungs. "Last I understood, your sister and *her pack* are currently staying near a farm somewhere in the northeast of Benwick."

"Good!" Carlysle released a sigh. "Then she's not far."

* * *

"How long do you think they'll be staying?" Kenna's frown deepened as he peered at Linette, momentarily turning his attention from the activity on his lawn.

Their reunion with Perla had been cut short when her husband had unexpectedly turned up on the front stoop, trailed by over a score of freshly changed werewolves in various states.

Now, the sounds of stakes being driven into the ground, plus the general din of camp being set up filtered through the front kitchen window.

Linette held up her slate. *You're the one who agreed to this.*

"Yeah, yeah, I know." Kenna ran a hand over his tired eyes and down his face. "Well, I hope that they don't expect us to feed them!"

Linette half-heartedly reassured her father with a curt nod devoid of confidence.

"Oh, here she comes," said Kenna. His eyes followed Perla as she stormed toward his front door. The frills along the hem of her dress swirled as they tried to keep up, grasping at her rushing heels.

"He's going to do it," Perla stated, ice infusing her voice. She swept into the room where her father and sister were still gaping out the window at the spectacle.

Kenna's shoulders sank as he watched his daughter cradling her head in her hands, despair branching across her frame. "There's no changing his mind?" he asked, trying to be delicate. "Did you remind him that he is to have a family soon?"

Linette shifted her focus from the window and offered a sincere nod, agreeing with her father's line of questioning.

"Oh, he's fully aware," Perla snipped, shuddering as her anger finally gave way to sadness. "He believes that he'll be a paragon..." Her eyes flitted around the room, searching for the proper translation. She still loved her husband and did not want to paint him as a buffoon. After another sigh, she continued, "He wants to set an example for our child. He thinks that becoming *this, this, this* monster—this new shape—will make him exactly the sort of father and husband that our family deserves. He's utterly convinced of it."

With a gentle hand, Kenna interrupted Linette from showing the word *delusional* she had scribbled onto her slate. The look in his eye conveyed that while he agreed with her assessment, perhaps in this circumstance, it was best to just listen.

"They only lost two, he said!" Perla cried, joining her family at the window. "Two people have died from the bite!" She placed a protective hand over her slightly distended belly and faced the window. Whatever she was going to say next got caught in her throat. Beyond the pane, Corbin could be seen removing his boots, preparing himself for his gifted curse.

* * *

"There will be no going back after this," Lanaelle warned, watching the man tug himself free from his tunic. Oddly, her voice remained unchanged, though her body was that of a beast.

Corbin scratched the long hairs that clung to his cheek and tucked them behind his ear. "I am ready," he confirmed. The mapmaker's bare chest inflated as he trapped a breath, steeling himself against the ensuing agony. There was laif magic that allowed one's clothes and armour to expand upon transformation, and Corbin wished he had been able to obtain such garments as he stood completely nude in the broad afternoon's sunlight. He was the only remaining human among the group. "Lord Ancel departed yesterday," he said, peering toward the forest. "And I wish to join him, and, at the very least, beat Tintagil to the battle."

A resounding growl of assent rose from behind him. The pack was ready to meet the archenlaif invasion.

"Oh, we shall," Lanaelle said, drawing her tongue across her fangs.

Bryndon stood beside her—his previously pudgy features had tightened into firm muscle, but his stature had remained at its low sum. After surviving the transformation, he had been glued to Lanaelle's side, acting as an informal and unnecessary sentry. Though the pack had yet to establish an alpha, it was obvious where Bryndon would cast his ballot. Impatiently, he shifted from one clawed foot to the other, drawing Lanaelle and Corbin's collective attention.

"Where would you like the bite?" Bryndon blurted, hastily hovered a step backward as Lanaelle's curious gaze flashed into a glare.

Cocking his right elbow at an angle, Corbin indicated where he would like to receive the puncture wounds. He had actually given it a good amount of thought, and he wagered that it would be the simplest place. The crook of his arm, at the bend, offered a good amount of meat, and the bone directly underneath would limit how deep Lanaelle's fangs would penetrate. Most of the others had requested a bite at the neck, the place where a lampyr would suck out the evil from the sick, while several had offered a wrist. The two incumbent werewolves who had died, screaming and foaming and writhing uncontrollably in the dirt, had both requested their bites on the wrist, and after that, no one else had dared anything but the neck.

"I am giving you one last chance to back out of this, Corbin."

"Do it," he commanded, planting his feet and raising his elbow, thrusting it closer to Lanaelle.

* * *

Perla latched herself to the window. "No, no, no," she whispered, watching her husband try to remain on his feet. Convulsions had overtaken the man, and his entire body began to tremble.

"I can't look," Perla whirled away from the viewing, frantically scratching her scalp and bundling her hair into her fists. "That stupid, stupid!" she spat.

"He's, he's..." Kenna could not remove his eyes from the scene.

Corbin's knees had eventually buckled beneath him, and unlike the other transformations they had witnessed, this one was eerily silent. He rent the soil with his fingers, flinging earth onto the bystanders nearby, but there was not one sound of anguish from the man, though his jaw was locked open as if he meant to scream.

The werewolves who had been erecting tents and shelters had abandoned their work and approached the scene. Everyone, both on the lawn and in the kitchen, was utterly enthralled and horrified all at once.

"The fur should be springing by now," Kenna muttered behind a cage of fingers. His eyes met Linette's and they exchanged a troubled look.

Perla sucked in an anxious gasp, but she resolutely kept her back to the window in staunch opposition.

A familiar scratching to his right caused Kenna to avert his eyes for a moment. Linette was scribbling a message, and her shoulders moved to allow him to read a rather peculiar question.

When is the next full moon?

Kenna pondered the question, the horrifying display abandoned for a time. the flesh around his eyes wrinkled as he performed a series of mathematical equations, trying his hardest to recall what phase of harvest they were currently in. He returned his attention to the lawn where several werewolves had begun to revert back to their human form. A few retained their wolf heads, while some became completely human save for their extremities. When the collective was in their full werewolf regalia, there was a swath of colors to behold. Mostly unremarkable shades of brown and tan, but when they all stood together, bristling and preening, the patchwork was, without a doubt, quite impressive.

Kenna noticed that the only werewolf that stood out from the others was the female, Lanaelle, the woman that his daughter did not trust. She now stood towering over the form of his son-in-law, retaining her predatory shape, not a fractional change to be seen on her coat. She was, by far, the tallest and most intimidating of the pack. Her limbs were inches longer on her steady frame, and her movements were more bestial, more feral than the others, and yet more controlled. All of this aside, her fur was a striking obsidian, setting her apart from the others at the first glance, especially when compared to the runty werewolf that clung to her side like a shadow. Lanaelle was the clear alpha, even to Kenna's untrained eyes.

It had been the span of several breaths since Corbin had last displayed any sign of life. From where Kenna stood, he could not make out any rise and fall of his chest, nor expansion of his rib cage.

"Two or three more nights, I believe," he distractedly replied to Linette. His eyes followed a pair of werewolves, who had retained their wolf form, striding toward Corbin at the behest of Lanaelle. With their muzzles downcast, one shrugged at the other before lowering down and retrieving the fallen, dead man.

"Where is Deverin?" Kenna shouted, his voice solid, devoid of anger, but wholly urgent.

Perla quailed at the name, and if the wall had not been nearby to slow the descent, she would have crumpled to the floor. Linette rushed to her side, angling a shoulder beneath her sister's armpit, effectively becoming a crutch.

"Where is the lampyr?!" Kenna demanded, looking Linette in the face. The girl was helpless to reply and tried to convey confusion to her father, as best she could, while bearing the weight of his crestfallen daughter. She did not know where the lampyr was. Kenna recognized the expression, and he knew that Deverin was likely far away, too far to help, more than likely off with the knights of Benwick where he was most needed.

Turning back to the window, Kenna closed his eyes. "Aw, hekk."

* * *

"He still breathes," the gray werewolf murmured, lifting his chin as Lanaelle approached. When she ducked under the tent flap, her ears scraped awkwardly against the fabric.

"That is a relief." Lanaelle could tell before she even drew close that Corbin yet lived. From beyond the tent poles she could sense the blood still flowing in his veins. "What can be done, Jekar?"

"His future is uncertain," replied Jekar, still hunkered down beside the dying man. He was a physician, though born unmarked, he was intelligent enough to practice the healing arts, but not trusted enough to work on humans. In this rejection, he had turned his skills and knowledge toward the healing of animals. "The others had expired by now..." The physician leveled his gaze and swiped a claw at his eyebrow, a movement that shared equal realms betwixt human and lycan. "Perhaps the fact that Corbin is marked plays into his prolonged survival?"

A flurry of movement from the entrance drew their attention. "Is he dead?" Bryndon bellowed, blustering in awkwardly, his eyes alight with curiosity. Like the others, he still required more time before he would be comfortable in his new skin.

Jekar held the interrupting werewolf with a measured stare. "No," he said, moving a hand to adjust the spectacles that he no longer needed to wear, spectacles that no longer sat upon the bridge of his nose. It was an old habit that his soul clung to, having suffered from piss poor vision for his entire life up until now. "He may survive, and he may not. Only time will tell."

"We can pray that he survives," intoned Bryndon. The expression that crinkled his muzzle did not exude benevolence.

"I suppose," Jekar said, waving a dismissive hand. "Now, please, he needs rest."

"I see." And with that, Bryndon brought himself to his full height.

After giving Lanaelle a look that bled desperation from its seams, he departed from the coolness of the tent and reentered the daylight.

After a few moments of shared stillness, Jekar looked to Lanaelle.

"Keep your eyes on that one," he advised. "I am not convinced that everyone is meant for this life."

8

"Draw anything but a breath," a deep voice hissed from behind them. "And we'll pull your tongues out through your bum-holes."

Carlysle and Stacey lifted their arms in surrender as they turned around, slowly, taking tentative baby steps. The feat proved more difficult for Carlysle, the pounding in her head had been an endless thrum all morning. And Stacey had not allowed her to cut the pain with a bit of alcohol, a tried and true method she had discovered over the years, to dull the ache by just a few wheel cranks. Her squire was correct, after all, they did have actual work to do and the hazy, blissful mist of drink would not be helpful for the day's activities. Most every circumstance could be complemented very well with a few cups of ale on the side, especially when family is involved... but perhaps not when you couple family with *werewolves*.

"That seems a bit of work, don't it?" Carlysle had been facing the rising sun all morning, and this direction offered a welcome reprieve. "I mean, are your arms even long enough to—"

"Shut it!" a rough-looking woman snapped, twitching a dirk back and forth between knight and squire. She was young, but the severity of her visage made her seem decades beyond. Three other brigands, each donning dry and cracking leather armour, flanked her sides with weapons in hand. They had set this ambush on a path that bisected a field of sheep, nearly barren, and the perfect location. It was far enough from any sort of aid, but likely to be tread by those transporting some manner of goods. A set of rocky crags that overlooked the pasture provided excellent optics, and that is where they had sprung from, undetected.

The man who had first spoken was handling a menacing poleaxe, and his eyes darted all about as he rotated the handle, facing the hammer side to the dirt.

Carlysle continued, ignoring the order to keep quiet. "This is rather bold, I must say. Robbing a knight and her squire, both warrior born I might add, in broad daylight? Bold. Very bold!" She nodded appreciatively, squinting at the light reflected by the steel buckles on the bandits' armour.

"As they say," the man replied, "when the cat is away..." he trailed off, glancing toward Benwick castle.

"Ah, yes." Stacey quirked a smile. "Lest we forget the *actual* threat at our doorstep, now we must contend with idiots like you. A mugging? Really? If it's violence you seek, why not join up with the red knights? Or just do us all a favor and walk right into Fenrirfang and join the fight?"

The man coughed and spat. "It's not violence we seek! It's coin," his voice came out in a rasp, and he cleared his throat and spat again. "Though the fighting is a bit of icing, I gotta admit."

"Couldn't agree more," Carlysle said, grinning then flinching quickly as if she were drawing a weapon.

The bandits all started, their eyes like saucers.

Carlysle barked a laugh at their reaction. "Would have caught you flat-footed on that one!"

Her demeanor was very unsettling, not only for the brigands, but also for her squire. "Let's just take it easy," Stacey cautioned. She was worried that her knight had failed to notice that these were not your basic highwaymen, easily dispatched, for each bore warrior marks.

"Drop your swords," the man said, breathing heavily. His upper lip was dominated by a nautilus of a moustache that would make eating soup rather strenuous. "Today." He worked his jaw, replanted his feet.

Knight and squire complied, quietly, both submissively dangling their weapons before letting them fall to the soil. Each was careful not to allow their blades to land in the copious piles of sheep dung.

"Perfect," the severe woman chimed in. "Now the boots."

"Oh, come on!" Carlysle whined. "There's shit everywhere."

"Can't have ya chasing after us."

Without protest, Stacey began unlacing her boots.

Looking to the clear skies, Carlysle groaned. She bent down and staggered, stumbling toward the male bandit, leveled as if she were to grovel right before him.

The bandits took a collective step back, save the man with the poleaxe and moustache.

In a sweeping step, Carlysle found solid ground and planted her hands into the field deftly, as if she were about to perform a cartwheel. Whirling around in a flourish, her tabard flagging behind, the knight launched a back kick, looking much like a crazed horse, yet much more precise. The force of the impact splintered the man's knee, the loud crack carrying clear to the trees and startling a flock of resting grouse. His hip buckled, unable to bear the burden, and he dropped to his left, his weapon hanging by the thread of a few fingers.

Blacking out from pain, his consciousness waning, he did not see the knight's knee rise to lay waste to his nasal cavity. He saw no more after that, dropping to the ground as if dead.

Carlysle looked to her left as she stepped over the twitching and gurgling shape of the bandit. One of the brigands was covering her eye, blood flowing through her fingers as she ran in mincing steps, appearing as one who had just soiled themselves. Perhaps she had? It was tough to tell, and Carlysle had deeper concerns for the moment.

Looking around, Carlysle found Stacey facing off with a bandit.

Where did she find a farmer's hand scythe?

Her opponent wielded an arming sword in his left hand, complemented by a buckler on his opposite wrist. One of Stacey's bootlaces was snaking free as she sidestepped, mirroring her opponents' movement, estimating his center of mass as she had been taught.

Carlysle tore toward the remaining bandits. The severe woman was locked on her and was swinging a chain grapple hook, appraising the knight with a heavy scowl. In truth, this was unusual, Carlysle admitted to herself, she had yet to face a foe with such an unconventional weapon.

"Come on," the bandit said, "doff the boots!"

"What's with you and boots?" Carlysle questioned, closing one eye against the sun.

"Nothing in particular, really."

"I suppose everyone has their thing." She shrugged.

The bandit recoiled, scrunching her chin into her neck. "It's not my *thing!*"

"If you say so."

"Get on with it, and don't try any of that stumble business. I'm wise to that." The heavy steel grapple threateningly increased its speed in its centrifugal sphere. The bandit's eyes continually flicked from Carlysle to her companion who was locked in combat with the squire. Stacey was still holding her own, maintaining a healthy distance from the arming sword's limited reach.

Bending down, Carlysle fought the urge to lay down and sleep, and tugged the top lace of each boot then sat to wrench the footwear free.

"Where is your horse?" the bandit asked, her eyes lingering on Carlysle.

The knight tossed one boot aside and began to work at the other. "Equine care is not my strong suit."

"Isn't that what squires are for?"

"Not her strong suit either." Carlysle sighed and flung the second boot toward its mate. Sitting cross-legged on the ground, she leaned back on her hands and gazed up at the bandit.

"On your feet," the woman demanded, her spinning weapon slowing a bit. "And just what is your strong suit?"

A pained grunt issued from the male bandit and the woman turned for a moment, but immediately regretted it.

In the length of a breath, Carlysle was beside the bandit. Thrusting her wrist between the weapon's rotation, the knight coiled the chain around her vambrace, effectively defusing it. As the weapon ended its final lap, the razor-sharp grapple latched onto the knight's wrist like an enraged wasp. Two of the barbs lanced through her steel armour, punching into the bone below her thumb, and the knight, having gripped the bandit around the throat, spoke. "Numbness, you poor sod." Carlysle eased back, opening the space between them just enough to pass her injured wrist through, and she violently, although a bit clumsily, backhanded the bandit. The claws that had not penetrated Carlysle's flesh found a new home, puncturing the bandit's cheekbone and mandible. The woman attempted a scream, but the vice-like grip on her trachea did not permit such passage of air.

The knight began to press her wrist into the bandit's face, twining it deeper, encouraging retreat. The bandit hastily backpedaled, trying to get away.

Seeing that her knight had gained the upper hand, Stacey doubled her effort, feinting to the left, leaving a trace of her spirit near the ground for her opponent to focus on. He did not see the scythe slide itself between his temple and ear, discarding all the light from his eyes long before he collapsed.

The remaining bandit inevitably stumbled and fell as the knight pressed her. Carlysle remained on her feet and allowed her opponent to topple, arching back to not share in the fall, intending to dislodge the grapple with the movement. She did not, however, anticipate the sharp whipping motion that ensued. The bandit's neck was snapped sideways, cocked in an unnatural pose, remaining as such even as her body struck the earth.

Stacey appeared beside Carlysle. "Where were we?" she asked, kneeling to lace her boot, but a peculiarity on the side of the dead brigand's neck drew her focus. "Before we were interrupted..." she trailed off. The squire's bootlace remained dangling as she approached, on all fours, and swiped her thumb with her tongue and ran it across the dead woman's mark.

"Hold the reins," Stacey inhaled sharply, gazing at the dark smudge that remained on her thumb. The warrior's mark on the crooked neck was now smeared, a clear forgery. She looked up at her distracted knight. "How did you know they were faking it?"

Carlysle shook her head, confusion in her eyes. "I thought they were legitimate—" She broke off, a look of revulsion suddenly flashing across her face. She craned her woolen-socked foot over the opposite knee to inspect the bottom. "Fack!" Appearing a ruddy bronze in the daylight, a gooey clump of sheep excrement could be seen clinging, encompassing the arch of the knight's foot.

The knight dropped the tainted appendage, dangling it inches above the ground as if she had suffered a sprain, and stood upright on the other foot with a pained grimace. "Do you think we'll have time to stop for lunch soon?"

Stacey worked her jaw, still swirling in awe of her knight's bravery, *or was it sheer stupidity?* "If we are to make it by tomorrow's noontide, we need to take minimal stops."

Appearing wounded by the proclamation, Carlysle looked to the ground dejectedly, and her squire rolled her eyes and continued, "If we had horses..."

"You know better. Come along, let us press onward."

Stacey laced her boot as quickly as she could, and raced to get over to her limping knight.

"Let me get this straight," Stacey said, pulling Carlysle's left arm over her own shoulder, burdening a portion of the knight's weight. The steel on the knight's vambrace, normally smooth and well maintained, oiled by Stacey's own hands, was strangely tacky. "Wait." Stacey halted their movement. "You're bleeding."

"I'm aware."

"And there's a hook embedded in your wrist."

"It's keeping the rest of my blood at bay."

"Maybe stopping for lunch is not such a bad idea."

* * *

Nothing irked Famyl more than watching Linette suffer any sort of discomfort and unnecessary hardship. Hardships could be good for so-lidifying character, and they built the cornerstones for a decent per-sonality, but when the young woman was brushed aside, her potential completely overlooked, it was almost enough to make him shout.

The werewolves had arrived the day before, disturbing the sem-blance of peace that Linette and her father enjoyed. An interesting turn of events, to be sure, but the idea of harm befalling Linette, from these beasts, was more than Famyl could bear. Any guilt he may have felt for focusing all of his attention on this little farm had been abandoned as soon as the werewolves appeared. The First Laif sensed that this was the epicenter of something larger and much more significant, and that his time spent gazing here would not prove to be a waste. News of dragons in the eastern crags, or troll communities disbanding and breaking apart, setting their sights on the fae kingdoms... Famyl responded to those missives with a shake of his head. Humans were becoming beasts in order to move up in the caste, circumventing the natural order, selecting a destiny and donning a mantle with unknown consequences.

Most of the humans, now a pack of werewolves, were blank, born without the Creator's blessing. Really, there was only one among them born marked. Ordinarily, this assured a safe transformation, but this man, Corbin, was still abed. His body had trembled throughout the night, stricken with fever, and now the daylight had arrived and the man was still not seeing any relief.

Very odd.

Famyl shifted his attention from the suffering man, across the lawn, to Linette, seated cross-legged, engrossed by her small patch of shadesgill. The muddy morning skies were beginning to give way to another radiant, warm afternoon.

Famyl smiled mirthlessly. *If any of those devils harm a solitary*—a movement down the lane drew the First Laif up short. A group of Benwick officials on horseback was working its way toward the farm. *She is surrounded,* Famyl thought, *and she doesn't even know it!* The rather peaceful existence of Linette, which he had enjoyed watching for so long, was beginning to roil and rattle like a kettle on the verge of boiling.

* * *

The werewolf in charge had told Linette's father that the pack would be departing in a few days, no more than a week at the most. She had also assured him that he would be paid for his troubles. At first he had vehemently declined any payment, but after much insistence he relented and agreed to a reasonable sum. Kenna later admitted to Linette that he found it quite difficult to argue with a creature baring claws and fangs in such close proximity, even if the conversation was far from violence.

A darkling beetle began its trek upward from the soil, stuttering a few steps on the trichomes protruding from the shadesgill's mature stalk. Lowering her belly onto the grass, Linette watched the little creature's journey with amusement, nestling her chin in her hands. *Here comes the sun, my friend,* she thought, *you're just in time.*

A voice displaced Linette from her moment. "Is *that* gray gilly?" The question was posed with reverent astonishment. The girl swerved onto an elbow to regard the speaker.

She found, to her surprise, Lanaelle in human form standing several yards away gnawing a bovine thighbone. "That is quite impressive," Lanaelle said after seeing the slight nod from the girl. "Why the hekk are you living in a hovel like this when you have a smuggler's treasure springing up before you?"

Instinctively, Linette reached for her slate to render a response. It was not where her fingers probed, and she swept her hand along the grass hoping to find it, but came up empty. Furtively she looked around, and realized that she had left it inside, probably on the dining table.

With eyes still alit with amusement, Lanaelle smiled. "Ah! Your sister told me that you had been gifted with silence."

A gift? Linette did not regard her condition as such.

The werewolf tilted her head back and swallowed. "And apparently, you have other gifts, though they may seem to be lying dormant."

The statement was awarded with Linette's full attention.

"I come from a family of artisans," she explained. "Craftsmen of raiment, if you will, and we deal with many different fabrics and elements. In these dealings, we consistently rub elbows with other tradesmen who are on the lookout for magicked goods. I could, with great ease, find you a buyer of this small harvest, if that is something that interests you?"

Feeling mildly desperate, Linette wished she could speak and ask the woman just how much she believed the patch was worth. She had never had the value assessed, though she assumed it was a decent sum, but nothing that would rearrange the stars for her and her father. But by the way this woman was speaking, Linette was beginning to believe that perhaps she had been grossly underestimating just what she possessed that was summarily grifted by the "state of Benwick."

As if by clairvoyance, Lanaelle offered an estimate, "I'd say you're sitting on twenty gold farthings, maybe?" she squeezed her eyes tight, "or twenty-five?"

Linette recoiled as if a handful of ice had struck her full in the face.

"You had no idea, did you?"

That's five years of father's wages! Linette quickly crunched the numbers. She sprung to her feet and nodded her head emphatically, transmitting her approval.

"Fair enough." Lanaelle shucked another strip of meat from the bone and spoke through a full mouth. "As soon as I return home, I will put out some feelers and see—"

She was cut off by steel shod hooves drawing to a halt some distance away on the roadway. A mist of dust continued to meander past the riders who were sitting upright and staring aggressively in Linette's direction. Each of the riders wore the regalia of the office of Benwick, a total of near a dozen tax collectors. The leader, riding a magnificent palfrey with a plaited mane, was noticeably taller than the other women in the retinue. She, in particular, was wearing a most distasteful scowl upon her countenance, her gaze remaining uncomfortably locked on the mute farmgirl.

"Friends of yours?" Lanaelle disrupted the tension, chewing loudly.

Without looking away from the harsh-looking leader, Linette returned a single shake of her head.

With a rattling of maille, the officers dismounted in near unison. Their well-disciplined horses remained in place, not venturing an inch from the roadway.

Linette's posture was rigid, her arms locked at her sides, and Lanaelle could smell the acrid scent of fear emanating from the girl. For reasons unbeknownst to her, the werewolf began to salivate.

"I know, I know," Desdemona said, using placating words, though all else was hostility. "We told you that we'd be back in a week for your *little* contribution." She spread her arms wide as the retinue formed a crescent around Linette and Lanaelle, hedging them in from retreat. "But, what can I say for myself?" A smile tugged the corner of her lips. "I lied."

The scent wafting from Linette shifted, tainted with something new. Lanaelle wasn't certain exactly what the girl was feeling, as it was a bit more complicated than the other emotions she had been able to sense since her transformation.

Desdemona hooded an ear with her hand. "What's that?" she laughed, "you'll need to speak up."

Without a means of communication, Linette fiercely shook and punched her palm with a finger, indicating a point in time.

The Warrior-born tax collector understood the gesture. "Nuh, uh, uh," she said, wagging a finger. "You see this is tax season, little snail, and we can come to collect any time we wish, regardless of past promises." Desdemona nodded toward a pair of officials who stepped forward, one armed with pruning shears and the other a wicker basket. "So, please step aside."

Lanaelle lazily punched the top of the basket as the woman passed, using the bone she had been gnawing on, effectively popping it loose and sending it directly into the grass.

"Eh!" Desdemona narrowed her eyes, acknowledging Lanaelle for the first time. "None of that, please."

The flustered official near Lanaelle bent down and retrieved the basket, hissing under her breath, "Bitch." As she straightened up with her arms encompassing the basket as she had done before, Lanaelle repeated the gesture, and the basket struck the earth a second time.

"Bitch!" This time she shouted it loud enough for all to hear.

"You don't realize just how accurate you are," Lanaelle said lightly, crouching down to remove her boots.

Desdemona jolted forward two steps, cutting the distance between them in an instant. "Do that again," she warned, blotting the sun as she stood over Lanaelle. "And you will regret it most deeply."

"Talk some sense into your friend, snail," the shear wielding official goaded. Instantly the group erupted into derisive snickers, their shoulders quaking, delight highlighting their eyes as a few covered their mouths.

"Whoa. That's..." Lanaelle said before rising to her full height. "Hilarious," she growled, eye to eye with Desdemona.

"Why did you take off your boots?" Desdemona said, working her jaw. "Make it easier to fly?"

Not shying from the conflict, Lanaelle did not falter with her reply. "They're made from Cantotlian fleece—" As she spoke, her front teeth gradually transformed into fangs. "Ridiculously expensive."

Desdemona blinked in disbelief, reeling backwards. For the first time in her remembrance, the warrior gave ground, entirely confused.

"What are you?" she shrieked, placing a hand to the pommel of her arming blade. The surrounding officials followed suit with their captain. An archer among them deftly drew and bent, aiming the fletching at Lanaelle's throat.

Lanaelle sniffed the atmosphere. *Despair.* The recognition took her by surprise. Linette's scent that she had not been able to quite place a finger on—*it's despair*—and it cut through the hymnal of aggressive aromas billowing from the Benwick officials. *Hate, fear, envy, spite, rage...* Lanaelle placed them all, but the despair was the most distinct. It smelled as a decadent truffle in a plain chocolate cake.

Attempting to obtain a bit of safety, Linette withdrew as the officials pressed forward. She managed to ease between and underneath their shoulders, coming out on the other side, placing bodies between herself and the conflict.

Claws sprang from Lanaelle's hands.

Swords rasped from sheathes, gilded crossguards glimmering above shaking hands.

"I see what you have been squandering a bit of your gold on," Lanaelle said, admiring the ornamental swords, still mostly human. "But what else have you been doing with the wealth proffered from this girl?"

"How does that concern you?" Desdemona wiped her mouth in irritation, pacing. "How does *any of this* concern you?"

"Sausage and tarts?" the werewolf guessed.

Desdemona drew up short and shook her head incredulously.

Lanaelle leveled her gaze on the plumper of the officials and fluttered her fingers under her chin, then nodded approvingly. "Yeah, definitely tarts and sausage."

"I will give you the courtesy of a single warning," Desdemona said sternly, dispelling the werewolf's nonsense. "Leave. Now. Or I will have a new fur rug to adorn my study."

"And I will extend the same courtesy," Lanaelle responded, her raven fur beginning to glisten as it bristled from her flesh. "Excluding that whole furry rug thing, of course."

The horses on the road began to whinny and shy, as if a storm approached.

Their attention shifted for a note, and in that moment, Lanaelle became a monster.

The lesser officials danced back as if the ground had caught fire. The archer retreated along with them, slackening her draw.

Lanaelle bore down on Desdemona, wielding the femur bone as a cudgel, leaping and bringing it down in a vicious stroke. The warrior was more prepared than she appeared, and caught the bone midway through the lycan's leap. Lanaelle's momentum carried her forward while her one hand was held in suspended animation, locked in her opponent's titanic grip. She stumbled clumsily on her clawed feet, disbelief flashing in her eyes as she released her grip. She instinctually knew that holding on would have been her end. Upon her dismount, she wheeled around to face Desdemona, and saw that her instincts had not led her astray. In the warrior's opposite hand was a dirk, and if Lanaelle had held on to her makeshift weapon, the warrior would have drawn her in and punched it through her snout.

"Perhaps a bit of advice is in order?" Desdemona said, ceremoniously flinging her dirk into the waiting hands of a nearby official, and freeing her longsword from its scabbard. "No matter what form a lesser being, such as yourself, decides to take, you will always fall short of those born marked. It's a simple fact."

Lanaelle found the warrior's composure unsettling, unable to sense any fear from her. And perhaps she was correct, Lanaelle thought, cocking her head, and sizing up her opponent. This was indeed both a trial and an experiment, all at once, for the newly minted alpha.

With an emphatic wave of Desdemona's sword hand, the circle widened, affording more ground for the duel. Linette remained frozen in place, awaiting the outcome with one eye to the tents beyond.

"This is shaping up to be a banner day, girls!" Desdemona announced, squaring her shoulders. "We'll obtain our crop of gray gilly *and* procure a mighty fine werewolf pelt on the side," she paused, "a prized *ebony* werewolf pelt, at that."

anaelle had mucked up. She had mucked up pretty badly. She had
wrongly believed that becoming a werewolf would give her the upper hand, no matter the foe. Every notion she had held as truth was
now rattled loose from certainty, blooming into question.

Her first attempt had been a colossal failure and her second attempt
proved just as fruitless. When she finally managed to get under the warrior's weapons, belly to belly, she was able to make her foe release the
bone cudgel. A victory, yes, but also very *small*. And then the warrior
dropped a hip, securing the werewolf's center of gravity, and heaved her
into the air. Moments before her snout carved a nice little path in the
turf, Lanaelle experienced the blissful sensation of flight. Getting to her
feet was easy, but bearing the jeers and mockery of the spectating officials was another matter.

In her mind, all she needed was to get within claw-length, at which
point, all disputes would be considered settled. She had never studied
combat techniques. Her only experience was watching her sister spar
when they were younger.

This must be why wolves hunt in packs, she thought, swiping the muck
and grass from her mandible. She feinted a step at the nearest Benwick
officer, causing the woman's eyes to widen in terror, kicking up the fra-
grance of fear.

"Hey!" Desdemona shouted, clearly not impressed. "I'm over here."
The warrior held the longsword with a balancing hand upon the blade,

a few inches shy of the tip. She wisely maneuvered the weapon as a staff, a simple change of tactic that proved additionally irksome for the werewolf, and compounded the sense that she was out of her depth.

Lanaelle charged again, this time feeling a bit less clunky as she grew more comfortable in her new skin. With a simple step to her left, Desdemona avoided the lunge, and gave the wolf a randy swat on the rump. The warrior once again completely avoided tooth and claw. Yet another harmless attempt. This was beginning to appear as no more than sport for the tax collector.

Hope began to wane, but Lanaelle was not yet flagging with exhaustion, so she pressed on. Experience she lacked, but not ardor. This time she leapt feet first, zeroing in on the warrior's abdomen, estimating that the maille would not survive a swift downward claw stroke. Unfortunately, her hypothesis would need to be tested at another time. Desdemona whirled a pace away, once again just out of the werewolf's reach. This time she thrust her longsword out, still holding on with her left hand near the tip, and Lanaelle latched her hands to the blade at the end of descent, trying to strip the warrior of her weapon. Momentarily feeling that she had secured the upper hand, Lanaelle's sense of victory plummeted almost immediately. Desdemona rocked back as Lanaelle wrenched forward, and the warrior rolled onto her back with a boot stuck into the werewolf's midsection, the force and sensation akin to a catapult. Lanaelle was once again airborne, grasping and clinging to nothing as she careened helplessly over the earth, some fifteen feet from the fight.

Rising to her feet, her snarling roar was loud enough to drown out the rapturous laughter that had erupted after her second midday flying lesson. Her guttural frustrations echoed throughout the surrounding landscape, but the only response she garnered was the shivering of the trees as a few perched larks took flight. Even the horses no longer deemed the beast to be any sort of threat and nonchalantly chomped at the grass rimming the road.

Lanaelle's hands felt damp and sticky, and they puckered when she flexed them. She glanced down and noticed the sheen of blood pouring from her elongated palms. The blade had sunk in deep when she gripped the steel, and it was fortunate that she had not shorn her fingers completely off.

"I grow bored," Desdemona complained, unscathed, "and you don't seem weary."

At the same time, Lanaelle flicked her clawed hands and Desdemona snapped the wrist holding her blade, each dispelling excess blood.

Desdemona smirked and looked toward the archer. "A warrior, I suppose. But *not* a knight," she said and gestured at the werewolf. "Honor is not required here."

The archer gave a solemn nod, bringing the bow to full draw before releasing, aiming at the werewolf's lower limbs. The arrow sang, then the werewolf howled.

"Try to leap again." Desdemona held the longsword with her hands stacked on the pommel, no longer on the defensive. "Please."

Lanaelle plucked the broad-headed arrow from her shin, where it was embedded a few inches above her left foot, narrowly missing the tendon that connected to her heel. The archer had intended to sever that crucial tendon, but the werewolf had managed to flinch, driven by pure instinct, into the safer direction.

Desdemona appeared disappointed. "Another, Cass," she said to the archer. "This time, aim a bit higher."

Lanaelle attempted to charge the archer, but the deep laceration in her leg caused her to stumble, opening enough time for Cass to release a follow-up. This one struck Lanaelle between the clavicle and shoulder, rendering her left shoulder useless.

"Fack!" Lanaelle spat, recoiling from the blow and the ensuing arc of pain. She draped a hand over the fletching, which was buried much deeper than she hoped, and tested it with a meager tug. She immediately felt an obstinate pull on her back as she applied pressure. The arrow had passed clean through. Before she had the time to release the curses behind her lips, another arrow struck the opposite clavicle, and mirroring its predecessor, it punched out into daylight, showering the earth in crimson.

This is it. Lanaelle wilted onto her knees. *This is how it ends.*

She felt the arrows jostle as she dropped to the ground, the wounds excruciating.

Cass had nocked another arrow and was drawing back once again. "Just say the word, Des," she said coolly.

From the ground, Lanaelle lifted her hands in supplication. Murky drool dripped from between her fangs as she heaved her muzzle to look into the archer's eyes. Desdemona cut through the space separating them to stand between the arrow and its target, inclining her head at the werewolf. A cold smirk pulled the corner of her mouth as she lifted her sword arm, placing the blade against the froth-encrusted fur of Lanaelle's throat.

"This can't be the end!" Lanaelle wheezed in disbelief. The warrior cocked her head, but before she could speak, her attention was drawn elsewhere.

From somewhere beyond Lanaelle, a howl erupted. It began as one distinct roar, dominating the others that followed suit, as the other werewolves lifted their voices in unison. It ended as abruptly as it had begun, followed by a heavy, tangible silence.

Lanaelle, having more keen senses than the humans surrounding her, heard the heated breaths of a host of avenging angels approaching. *Her* avenging angels.

As the growls grew in volume, Desdemona wavered. She shifted her focus, hurriedly sheathing her sword. "To the horses!" she shrieked, though more than half of the officials had already started running in terror, not needing the order.

The archer remained, the only one to hold her ground. Lowering her weapon, she stared, frozen in abject horror at the flanking tide sweeping toward them.

"Impossible..." Lanaelle heard the archer mutter. "How could they..." she withdrew the cowl from her head and narrowed her eyes, following the approach.

The horses stamped and whinnied, though terror bulged their eyes, not one broke rank and fled. Brave souls they were, watching their masters tear in their direction, waiting for them to mount. As completely as a shadow swallows, the werewolves overtook the horses without breaking stride. The faster officials halted as if they had reached a precipice, flinging their arms out to brace the others behind them, afraid of being swept away.

It was an intelligent and concentrated strike, and Lanaelle stared in bewilderment as the werewolves decimated the horses but left the humans standing rooted and helpless only a few feet from the carnage. Mere inches divided them from their mortality, but not one was struck down.

"I have instructed them to harvest the bones," a voice from behind Lanaelle said, sending a chill down her spine. "We don't have time for this nonsense."

Swiveling her head around to identify the speaker, she spied Linette huddled on the grass, gaping upward.

A huge silver werewolf stood above her, a look of controlled madness glowing around his crescent pupils. He towered larger and broader than the king's prized battle destriers, and though his voice was free of warmth, it kindled a welcoming growl within her. Lanaelle probed her mind, scrabbling to identify this titan.

"The full moon is nigh, Lanaelle," he said, offering her a hand. "We leave before nightfall."

* * *

"Remarkable!" Famyl gazed down upon the scene. The werewolves had stripped the horses clean of their flesh within the span of several breaths, but had completely ignored the officials. Treading past the humans, who eagerly gave way, the werewolves carried the horse bones with ironclad purpose, stopping before the great silvery-white wolf.

The laif willed his optics closer to hear the dialogue. The setting filled his view.

* * *

"Corbin?" Lanaelle said, recognition finally taking hold as she was shakily brought to her feet by the silver wolf.

A slender, gray wolf stepped out from the crowd. "We need to get her to the tent now," he advised. "She should heal rather quickly, once we remove the arrows."

"Very well, Jekar," Corbin replied, turning his attention to the shorter wolf who had latched himself to Lanaelle's side. "Bryndon, escort her there now."

Ardently bobbing his head in acknowledgment, Bryndon looped Lanaelle's left arm over his shoulder, causing the wounded werewolf to wince in pain.

Sweeping his gaze around the clearing, Corbin settled on a pair of werewolves with markedly similar appearances. "Ren and Grandy," he addressed the brothers. "Go with Lanaelle and give aid as best you can. If she is not ready by twilight, I want you to be her guide. Between the two of you, I trust you can manage the course to Navarene."

"Aye," Ren agreed, driving an elbow into his brother's ribcage, who responded with a snarl and a shove back. A bit of laughter rippled out from the surrounding wolves as they parted, allowing the brothers to catch up with Lanaelle. Without needing any urging, Jekar broke rank and followed.

As if noticing her for the first time, Corbin peered over at Linette. The girl was still seated on the ground, hugging herself and trembling. "You need not fear us, sister," he called out to her, keeping his distance. "Those ones, however..." he began, swiveling his gaze to the diminishing shapes of the officials fleeing on foot.

He did not need to finish his statement. The wide grin spreading on his face adequately conveyed his meaning.

* * *

"How much further?" Carlysle whined. It was probably the third or fourth time she had raised this exact query while they traversed this particularly desolate stretch of road. The knight and the squire both walked in the canals worn by wagon wheels from decades of use, some five or six feet apart.

Initially, Stacey had ignored her knight, opting to rip into a hunk of bread and chew loudly with an open mouth, ejecting crumbs with each chomp.

Carlysle looked her up and down. "Well?" she demanded.

"How should I know?" Stacey shrugged and took another bite. After a round of labored chews, she continued, "I only know the general vicinity. I imagine it will be rather obvious when we see it."

"Ah! Of course" Carlysle was not accustomed to being this sober after noontide. She nodded, reassuring her squire that she was not *that* slow on the uptake. "The werewolves will be a dead giveaway!"

Nodding, Stacey acknowledged her knight's moment of catharsis. "Precisely." She reached into her satchel and she squinted. "Would you like some more of my bread?"

"No thank you," Carlysle cupped a hand to her stomach. "I am fine on bread for the moment, possibly for the next year. I fear if I eat any more bread, I will have to—"

"What in the..."

The distinct sound of steel violently rattling on maille abruptly shifted their attention. It grew closer, and human voices shouting and cursing could be heard within the din. The road ahead curved around the base of a hillock, obscuring clarity of what was approaching.

Carlysle leapt from her tread and cut across to Stacey. "That sounds like a small army," she whispered, needlessly.

"Aye," Stacey said, pointing toward the toe of the hillside. "Step clear then." The pair quickly surrendered the road, giving more than enough space for the incoming squad to pass. As soon as Stacey's boot settled in the grass behind Carlysle, she spied what appeared to be a Benwick tax collector rounding the bend. Her curly locks battered the breeze as she frantically pumped her arms, surging lengths ahead of the rest of her retinue. Fear mingled with exhaustion emblazoned each of their faces as they passed. Though Stacey attempted to flag one for information, she was met with only a terrified glance which offered zero explanations.

"Nine, ten..." Carlysle calmly counted the armoured women.

Stacey gave up trying to obtain any rational news after the third woman she attempted to accost drove a vambrace into the squire's chest, toppling her backwards onto the spongy soil. "Coward!" she shouted as she rose from the remarkably comfortable ground. The woman who had knocked her down did not look back at the accusation, but merely continued her dash.

"Well, that's not something you see every day," Carlysle remarked, stepping onto the road, regarding the diminishing retreat. "Are you alright? That was quite a tumble you took."

"I'm fine," Stacey spat, retrieving a satchel that had fallen on the grass. "If I wasn't so heavily laden like a pack mule, perhaps I would not *tumble* so easily!"

"I swear, Stacey," Carlysle said, rounding on her. "If you go on about horses one more time..."

"Then what?"

"Then I will..." the knight fumbled for a proper threat. She recognized that she had very little leverage in this situation. Stacey was the longest running squire that she had ever taken under her tutelage, and, the knight had to admit, she had proved very handy to have around. Which was a surprise for Carlysle every day. Each morning, she expected to rise, blinking back a splitting headache, to find that she had once again been abandoned. Just as she had been on the many mornings before, though she had never blamed any of them for their desertion. And she certainly would not blame Stacey when she finally decided to bolt. The knight's shoulders slumped. "Nothing," she sighed, extending a hand.

Her outstretched arm was met with a smirk. "What are you doing?" asked Stacey.

"I'll take the cargo."

"Are you sure?"

Carlysle nodded.

The squire could not free herself of the burden fast enough.

"This isn't even heavy at all..." Carlysle muttered as they selected their wagon treads and set off once again. "Annoying, yes, but not heavy..."

Afternoon shadows loomed ahead as the sun, now past its peak, dipped behind them. Sparsely populated farmland stretched onward, and the travelers carefully surveyed every homestead, hoping to see some sign of werewolf activity. They merely found peaceful country settings, trickling brooks, and examples of those who had opted for simpler lives. Those born warriors were not often given such options. Their lives were filled with responsibility, drifting on the flowing tides of other's expectations. Power came with it, yes, and prestige, and a life riddled with envious looks in equal measure to those of admiration. Though when one stopped to think, they would almost suffocate under the weight of it all.

Up ahead, Stacey was the first to notice a figure navigating the distance between them.

"Eh," the squire grunted.

Carlysle turned her head from a gown that she had been momentarily coveting that was fluttering upon a nearby clothesline. "What is it?" she asked before spying the road's occupant ahead. "Oh."

As they drew within shouting distance, Stacey lifted one hand in a friendly gesture and called out.

The woman's outfit seemed to match those of the contingent that had torn past earlier. Her expression, however, was leagues more composed, not a hint of panic tinged her features. She languidly returned the greeting, an unstrung bow in her other hand.

"I believe your companions passed us a little while ago," Stacey said, thumbing behind her. "Their bearing was not very..." the squire gritted her teeth as she trailed off, not wishing to offend.

"Calm?" the archer offered.

Nodding in agreement, Stacey replied, "Yes, calm, yes."

The archer raised an eyebrow, glancing back and forth between knight and squire. "I would recommend turning back," she advised, adjusting the quiver strap on her chest. Though she was courteous, it was clear that she wished to be on her way.

"What makes you say that?" asked Stacey.

"Well..." The archer offered a fleeting glance at her feet. "I am walking back to our barracks because a pack of werewolves ate my horse," she said, articulating the phrase with the candor of a statesman.

"How far?!" Carlysle demanded with sudden urgency.

Stacey was taken aback by her knight's sudden outburst.

"Only a bit further down the lane," the archer said, holding her ground as the knight strode closer. "You can't miss it."

"How's that?"

"When you stumble over the bones of my mare, look to your left. It's the only farm with a teeming mass of werewolves running all over it."

10

Aday passed. Or maybe it was two or three? Time was running together and intertwining, and Raymond struggled to keep track. He slept whenever he caught the chance, whether the sun was in the sky or the ever-brightening moon glared down through the masking leaves.

One of the laives had died sometime in the night. Nedok was his name. When four had returned to the camp and the fifth never showed, they all knew something was dreadfully wrong. The last few excursions had thankfully not included Raymond, and he admitted that he was grateful for the reprieve. Spending the last string of hours resting and oiling his armour, he thought, if there had been a spare bow lying around, he would have used it for some target practice. But now that there was a spare bow, Raymond would rather cut off his own hand than dare pick it up.

The plan, as far as he understood, had been that four of the laives would position themselves near a corner of the fort, effectively giving them a clean view over the majority of the structure. The fifth would act as a go-between of sorts, stalking around the boundary and giving aid if the need arose. Saeva had assigned himself to that post.

It had all been unfolding quite favorably. Each laif controlled their corner well, and not one archenlaif had poked a single foot outside the walls in more than a day. But truthfully, it had only been a matter of time before a fracture started in the foundation of their design.

Flya was the first to happen upon Nedok's body. The laif was well beyond the aid of a lampyr when he was found. While Saeva could not regret holding his post, as the leader, he felt responsible for the loss. As all good leaders should.

"His neck was severed clean, like a snapped icicle," Flya recounted to the others. "And I could not find his head anywhere. Sprinkled around his torso and on the grass and leaves were these peculiar damp spots. A few shards of ice and an archenlaif arrow buried in the soil told me the rest of the tale." She went on to describe her theory, which to everyone seemed to be the most plausible explanation. The karbaled had cast a freeze spell that had encapsulated Nedok's head in a shell of ice, leaving an archer to pierce an arrow directly through his brittle head, crudely shattering it into a thousand fragments.

Now, another night was falling, and Saeva would take up the now empty position. "Here," the lampyr said, handing Raymond a bone horn. "I want you to run the forest tonight, as I have been doing."

The red knight accepted the instrument and held it far from his body as if it were covered in thorns. "Uh, what do you want me to do exactly?"

Flya was the first to respond, slapping Raymond on the back as she passed. "If you see something, just blow the horn."

Saeva nodded his head in agreement.

Raymond tried to speak, but the sudden jarring to his back had brought on a bout of coughing. "Simple, right?" he finally managed to eke out, with tears welling in his eyes before the coughs returned.

"Just think," Flya said cheerfully, regarding the red knight as he doubled over for a second time, "of the number of scars you'll have if you survive all of this." She whistled and bit into an apple that she had seemingly conjured from the darkness. "That's one of the few things that humans receive that we do not." Turning to Saeva, she gestured toward Raymond with her dagger. "Imagine how marred our flesh would be if *every* cut we sustained left a blemish of some sort? We'd be stippled like a trout!"

"I don't know," Saeva mused. "It might be nice to have a physical chronicle of battles past."

Flya's lips crested into a thoughtful smirk. "Just when I think we're on the same page, blood sucker, you somehow manage to flank me."

"You'll catch up one of these days."

The skies were clear and the endless stars sparkled, aiding the moon as it boldly illuminated the empty parapets. Raymond felt that nights like this one could be almost pleasant. Actually, they would be pleasant, if he exchanged his current setting for a lakeside dock, a stiff drink in one hand and his pipe in the other. In that case, yes, most assuredly, it would be a most magnificent night.

He was much fleeter of foot after Flya had convinced him to doff his armour. Feeling as light as a wood fae, the red knight darted from tree to tree, keeping one eye fastened to the fort.

"After all," she had said, "a helm and chest plate will freeze just as quickly as your skull."

Good advice. He spun around a rather jagged looking sapling just in time to prevent his groin from getting speared. He breathed a sigh of relief with his back against a tree. *Perhaps I should slow down a bit, eh?*

A swampy scent caught his attention. He sniffed the air again, and the smell lingered. Cutting to the next large tree, he tested the air once more, and it was there as well. He briefly wondered if there was marshland nearby. While there were many dead bodies strewn about, this was not the scent of decay. The smell of death was one he would recognize instantly.

He wiped the sweat from his forehead with his sleeve and was struck with another, more intense wave of stench.

"Well, damn it!" he whispered, lifting his collar over his nose to confirm his suspicion. "It's me," he shook his head. "I need a bath!" A voice inside his head added to his thoughts, *You need more than a bath.* "Like what else?" he asked the voice.

You need to take this opportunity.

His eyes darted about looking for the source of the voice. "What do you mean?"

Run, you idiot! Drop that dumb horn and book it. Get as far from this occupied fort as you can. The laives won't notice for hours. And even when they do, what are they going to do? Chase you? They are the ones honor bound to this place. You are not.

"Come on, now. I can't do that."

Why not? You owe them nothing.

"That's not true. Saeva gave me my life back. Remember?

Fair point. But still...

"No."

You're a red knight. A nothing. A nobody. Fodder. Just look at Elithiel and Saeva's armour, for example.

The voice stilled for a moment, as if it were drawing an extended breath.

"Go on," Raymond encouraged, wondering what their armour had to do with anything.

Oh, yes. Think about it. Why are you even called a red knight? Is it not a term of derision?

"I suppose."

They call you that, although the station is officially named otherwise, because of the state the armour is in when you receive it. Covered in dried blood. The blood of the poor fuckwit who went before you and died in battle. Who knows how many predecessors your particular set of arms has had? Twenty? Fifty? Three hundred? Sure, they halfheartedly try to scrub the armour clean, but you can see firsthand just how tainted the steel has become.

This was a better argument than Raymond believed that he was capable of conjuring on his own.

Just run.

"No."

Now, you fool!

"No."

The forest is vast. You will be able to survive this.

He shook his head, wishing the voice would grow still.

You only need to run.

"I will not!" he shouted, immediately regretting the outburst. If only he could reach out and catch those words before—

He heard a stirring on the walls, the rustling of an archenlaif rising to his feet. Phrases were shouted, directions given, and somewhere in between the garbled phrases he swore that he heard the word *karbaled.*

Just look at what you did!

He felt his spine bristling against the trunk of the tree as he straightened upward. "Oh, would you just get bent."

And with that, he became the only minstrel in Fenrirfang.

The horn blast ruptured much louder than he had anticipated, or perhaps it only seemed so loud in contrast to the quiet of his surroundings. Either way, his shout had drawn the attention from only a handful of the enemy, but his latest action arrested *everyone's* attention, both friend and foe. Although right now he was much more concerned with the foe in this equation.

"Well," he said, his posture slackening. "I guess that's that."

He waited, watching the torch bugs flit about, expecting to feel a frigid hardening at any moment. Silence stretched overtop the trees and over the fort, creating a canopy of frenetic stillness. The potential for disaster crept between every heartbeat that thrummed in his chest.

The torch bugs had fled.

There was a fathomless darkness, despite the opposing moonlight, that began to loom.

In disbelief, Raymond tried to blink away the vision to no avail. Against his better judgment, he craned his head around the tree in another attempt to dissipate the fringe of the dark clouds, slowly realizing he was not imagining things. It did not seem possible, but yet, here he was, a witness to an unbelievable phenomenon.

Raymond withdrew his head and bounced it against the bark. "Why does it grow so dark?" he cried.

"I have no clue," said a voice to his left.

Nearly wetting his pants, he shuddered in a breath. "For all that's sacred!" he breathed, belatedly recognizing Flya's voice.

"Why did you blow the horn?" Flya asked, remaining still as stone behind a tree.

"Did they make to breach?" a voice to his right asked, yanking at Raymond's remaining nerves. With a start, he snapped his neck toward the speaker, sighing in relief to find it was only Craendir.

Saeva appeared a moment later. He was hunkered down at a safe distance, opting to hide within a patch of fronds, his eyes piercing the dark like a cat. "The karbaled is near," he warned, managing to whisper loud enough for all to hear.

"But where is Traskal?" asked Flya, looking for the unaccounted-for member of their party.

The only reply was an unnerving quiet.

Craendir broke the silence. "There is no breach. We should away back to our posts," he urged. "The human signaled in vain," he added contemptuously.

"I fear that we are now three," Saeva answered grimly. "Returning to our corners would be an error at this juncture."

"Then what do you propose?" Craendir challenged.

Flya spoke up, cutting off the lampyr's response. "We focus on the ice wizard. We kill her at all costs."

"She is a powerful asset," Saeva agreed. "Eliminate her and we would cripple their advance."

An aggravated grunt issued from Craendir's throat. "As you say," he said, slumping, displaying the first measure of defeat that Raymond had yet to note.

"An ice wizard needs to see her target, right?" Raymond piped up, against his better judgment.

Through the dark, Saeva's eyes bobbed in agreement. "Yes, and?"

"So, we're safe as long as we stay behind cover?"

"Not necessarily..." said Saeva.

Flya gripped the tree and glared at Raymond. "What are you getting at?"

"Perhaps we should," Raymond began, then licked his lips nervously, "return to camp."

"And after that, what then?" Flya scoffed.

"I don't know, stay close to the fire?" Raymond suggested. For an instant he thought that Saeva had departed, but the lampyr had simply closed his eyes.

Flya covered her mouth to conceal her laughter, but her eyes did not share in the mirth. "Perhaps you wish us to make hot cider and toasted bread while we're at it?" The laif shook her head, dismissing the idea. "I say we make a stand, *right here*. If we rush the wall, she can't freeze all of us at the same time."

"Well—" Saeva tried to voice his concern.

"We only need one good shot, Saeva!" Flya said, prodding the air with a finger. "One good shot. One of us stays behind, and the rest of us make for the wall. We *know* she's right over there. You can feel her."

A few tense moments hung in the air, weighing heavy. The thought of an immortal giving up their life was not a decision made lightly.

Craendir was the first to speak. "I'm with the human."

Flya clicked her tongue. "Really?" she said in disbelief.

"We regroup and formulate some sort of plan. I feel a bit caught with my pants down at the moment."

"Well, hike them up then," her voice was rising, making Raymond quite uneasy. "Would you prefer to be the one to fire the shot?"

"That's not what—"

"We are going back," Saeva said, biting off the argument.

"Oh, come on!"

The lampyr was already rising to his feet. "I would be more comfortable carrying out this discussion at a safer distance," his voice diminished, retreating back, favoring the shadows. "With me. Now."

As soon as they returned to camp, Saeva made for his parcel of supplies. He went to his knees and began to pull the items out, placing them on the ground and stacking them in a particular order.

"Raymond." Craendir tugged his sleeve. This was the first instance that the laif had actually used his name. "Help me build up the fire." Urgency was reflected in his tone.

"No!" Saeva commanded, then rhythmically pounded his forehead with a fist. "I mean, yes. Yes, build the fire, but Craendir I need you to find a pine tree, a white pine if you can, and scrape it for resin."

Craendir nodded his assent and set off.

"Raymond," Saeva beckoned.

The red knight swept past Flya, making his way to the lampyr's side.

"Build the fire tall," Saeva advised, rotating to face the fire, and lifted a thumb-sized vial to better ascertain the contents. With a grunt of disappointment, he turned back and placed the bottle back into its slot.

"How tall?"

"Pretend that you're building a pyre... no..." he trailed off, straightening his spine and placing his hands on his upper thighs. His eyes darted about as he searched for the proper description. "Like you're building a beacon."

"I like where this is going," Flya said with admiration engulfing her eyes.

The happier Flya became, the more it distressed Raymond. "Alright," Raymond agreed, backing away. "I'll get to work."

"Flya," Saeva called out unnecessarily, "fell a few trees for Raymond, if you please?"

Before he finished his sentence, the female laif had already begun toppling a cedar and the red knight was hocking logs onto the blaze, blasting cinder and embers into the skies.

It was remarkable how much work one could accomplish when the threat of an icy death floated above your head, thirsty as the executioner's axe. Such senses of looming dread were not alien to Raymond, but still, that did not decrease the discomfort by any means.

The blaze had reached beacon status, and Raymond and Flya stood a healthy distance away to admire it. Saeva, after making a noise that sounded mildly joyful, was laying out dozens of rags onto a flat rock while Craendir was melting down his resin mixed with charcoal over a smaller fire.

"Careful not to allow the pitch to boil, Craendir," Saeva said, not looking up from the rags he was carefully dabbing with a yellow powder.

"I will be careful."

"If you see one bubble—"

"Saeva."

The lampyr paused his chore.

"I know what I am doing," Craendir assured him.

Flya rolled her eyes at Raymond. Between the three laives, she was the only one that did not seem apprehensive. "That scar," she began, tracing a finger across her throat, "where did you acquire it?"

Involuntarily, Raymond touched his throat. "I was sentenced to death," he answered, coughing to clear his throat. The wind had shifted, billowing smoke into his face. He tried to face it without cringing, attempting to outlast it until the wind changed again. But no, his eyes began to water, and he retreated for fresher air. "I was meant for the gallows."

Turning her back to the flames, remaining in the smoke, Flya appeared troubled. "What crime did you commit?"

"Uh." Raymond itched his scar. "More like multiple crimes, actually. But the latest one..." he pursed his lips, then continued, "I am a very fast runner... and you see, well, that can have its advantages. But there's always someone faster."

Flya scowled in mild irritation. "That doesn't answer my question."

"I'm a thief," admitted Raymond.

"But what did you steal?"

He took a deep breath, which proved to be an error. A lungful of smoke invaded his throat and nostrils, gagging the red knight, relieving him of speech.

"What was it?" Flya demanded, stepping out from the smoke. "Out with it."

Raymond pounded his chest. "A child," he coughed. "I stole a child."

"So, you're a filthy kidnapper?" Flya sneered.

"Well, no, not really. I wouldn't go that far." Raymond squinted into the flames. "It's a bit more complicated than that."

The snap of a bow interrupted their discussion. Particles of bark ignited and sprayed from where the arrow struck, showering the area around the tree in red-hot tendrils.

Flya whirled to the origin. "What was that?!" she demanded, pointing at Craendir.

The laif was lowering his bow. An expression of hope began to take root. "Have you never encountered a flaming arrow before?" he asked, his smile widening as the hope took hold of him.

Saeva strode next to Craendir, the shadows cast by the rolling flames battered their faces and armour. "Tonight, we are going to ignite the skies."

Not five or six breaths after the lampyr made his declaration, the very skies that they planned to be filled with flame instead began to pour rain.

<h1 style="text-align:center">11</h1>

"We must get dry!" Saeva screamed. Everyone understood what an exceeding amount of water upon your skin could mean when facing a karbaled. Squinting against the pelting deluge, Raymond followed behind Saeva and the others. They passed the fire as it continued to rage, hissing in protest, but it would be only a matter of time before it succumbed to the overwhelming damp.

As usual, Raymond, fast as he was, trailed behind.

Craendir turned back to offer encouragement. "Try to keep up! I will maintain—" His voice broke off. A stalagmite of ice sprung up from the ground puncturing the laif's chin, bringing him to an abrupt halt. A series of others followed suit, piercing his upper chest and lifting him from the earth. His eyes were crazed as he stared down at Raymond, attempting to speak, but it all came out as a gurgle. With a violent jolt, the ice shifted, and the laif hitched downward. Before Raymond's eyes, all life fled from Craendir.

The red knight felt a tug at his wrists, and was suddenly launched onward, his feet struggling to maintain the clip. Saeva and Flya each held one of his hands in theirs, rushing him along like a child through a crowded market. The rain striking his cheeks made it impossible for him to determine if he was crying or not.

He thought perhaps his sense of direction was impaired, what with all the trauma and whatnot, but he was fairly certain that they were heading *toward* the fort, not away from it. And when a patch of clarity opened between the branches, sure enough, piercing the skies ahead of them was the Spire of Navarene.

"We're going the wrong way!" Raymond shouted, pulling back, his rain slick wrists dispelling their hands.

The laives latched on again. "It's the only shelter!" Saeva urgently explained.

"If we run, they will only give chase!" Flya shouted. Her face was soaked and a fan of water sprayed out from her words. "If we run, all will be for naught!"

Nedok, Traskal, and Craendir flashed through Raymond's mind. Immortals who had given up everything to keep this evil contained within Navarene. "Fack!" he cursed, and bolted between the laives, continuing on before he lost his nerve.

They reached the west wall without any more stalagmites erupting. There was not an arrow, nor a shout of recognition. None of them held the belief that they had somehow traversed the forest without detection. With their backs pressed against the wall, Raymond pushed up onto his tiptoes to tighten his profile as much as possible. Saeva and Flya had their fingers pressed to the stone, as if they were searching for something beyond the wall.

"Raymond!" Saeva rasped. "Are you still bearing that dirk?"

It was only then that Raymond realized that they had crossed the enemy's boundary void of any armour or proper weaponry. He nodded and fumbled at his belt before retrieving the implement. He quickly passed it to Flya, who handed it over to the lampyr.

Nodding his thanks, Saeva swiped the drenched locks of hair out of his face. "I'll go up first. Flya, you boost up Raymond, then I'll toss down the dirk, and you can make your way up."

This particular segment of wall, much like the rest, was very tall.

Raymond eased his head out to survey the wall. "I don't think you'll be able to boost me up that high," he commented. "Unless you believe that you can fling me..." he trailed off at the incredulous stares he was receiving from his companions. "Well, never mind," Raymond concluded and leaned back against the wall.

Not wasting another breath, Saeva plunged the dirk into the wet stone several feet above his head. Water blasted around the steel, but the driving rain dampened the sound. With a dagger between his teeth, he pulled himself upward. Once his chin reached the dirk's hilt, he removed the dagger from his mouth and drove it higher. He continued upward, driving the weapons into the stone, using them as makeshift handholds. When he reached the top, he folded over at his waist, and with tremendous force, planted both blades back into the wall.

I was told that laif-forged weaponry held no peer, thought Raymond with admiration. *Seems the boys had been right.*

"Prepare yourself," Flya intoned with a wink.

Unsure of what that implied, Raymond simply smiled.

The laif dropped to one knee and slapped her thigh. "Place a boot here," she instructed. He obliged, and Flya latched onto his foot and surged upward with an unthinkable amount of speed and strength. Her back arched and her arms acted as a ballista, launching the red knight from the ground. He was propelled upward, sliding against the rain-slick surface. His chin and knees bounced along the stone as the pair of protruding handholds rushed to meet him.

"Take hold of them!" Saeva shouted, indicating the dirk and dagger.

In the exact instant that Raymond's head breached between the weapons, his momentum petered out.

"Grab them!"

The dirk was the first that he clasped, and for whatever reason, his other hand decided to ignore the fact that there was an alternative option. He dangled, incongruously, with both hands wrapped around only one of the handholds. His left hand scrabbled to stay put, but the knuckles on his right hand did not offer any sort of helpful resistance. And his right hand was not faring much better. The leather hilt felt like a sponge, pleasant and comfortable, but not very grippy.

Just when he thought he would slip, Saeva lurched down and snatched his left wrist. With a great heave, he pulled the red knight up to safety.

"Get down!" Saeva said, immediately pushing Raymond down against the parapet.

Crouching against the stone, Raymond stared straight ahead and took in the familiar, yet surreal surroundings. Over his shoulder, he could make out the lampyr retrieving the handholds with a grunt. The walkway was empty, Raymond could see no sign of the enemy. Saeva handed him the dirk.

"Wait," Raymond protested. "Aren't you supposed to—"

The expression that Saeva returned was adequate explanation; Flya would no longer be joining them. Her path lay elsewhere. "The barracks are underground," he began, and flinched as an arrow ricocheted from a crenellation. Forcing Raymond to his belly, the lampyr, maintaining a tight grip on the red knight's mantle, lowered himself down in kind. A few more arrows skittered on the stone, kicking up water along their course. When an arrow cracked directly above their heads, Saeva leapt to his feet and wrenched Raymond along with him.

An archenlaif archer's helmeted crown appeared ahead, rounding the stairs, and another could be seen on a ladder a few feet beyond the staircase summit. Saeva reached the juncture first and whirled down the stairs. He placed a boot into the startled archenlaif's chest, sending her down. Her body came to an abrupt stop on the landing, her lifeless form briefly halting the ascension of yet another archenlaif.

"The other way!" Saeva shouted, wheeling back toward Raymond.

The archenlaif on the ladder tried to slide back down when he noticed the lampyr's approach, attempting to avoid a head-on confrontation. Saeva grabbed the enemy about the collar and heaved him onto the walkway without breaking stride, quickly ending him with a dagger to the temple. With a brisk slide of his right hand, he unsheathed the dead foe's sword, and tossed his dagger back to Raymond.

"It will prove more favorable than that dirk," he called.

The confidence in his voice lifted Raymond's spirits a fraction.

They continued to sprint over the parapet, avoiding the archenlaives surfacing from the stairs. Arrows continued to pepper the path. The steel heads clicked harmlessly onto the ground with each miss, their trajectory hampered by the continuous rainfall.

Suddenly Raymond recognized where they were headed. In moments they would be passing the very parapet he had stood upon when first spotting the archenlaif invasion. His eyes lifted to the forest beyond, swatting away the water to clear his vision. In unison, both the lampyr and the red knight's tempo slowed.

"No, no, no..."Raymond whispered, overwhelmed with despair,

A vast swath of shimmering armour was approaching under the flickering torchlight. Yet another force of archenlaives had arrived at the fort, this one the size of a grand army.

Once again, Raymond found himself the unwilling vanguard in a war he did not want to wage.

"What do we do now, Saeva?"

The lampyr shook his head, anguish clear on his features, and suddenly darted sideways. A spear of ice shot up from the stone floor, bisecting the space between the human and lampyr. Vaulting the parapet, Saeva disappeared over the wall toward the forest, and into the dark. Raymond moved to follow, but another spear violently emerged by his feet, almost catching his right ear. He bounded to his left and rolled, hoping that unpredictable movements would make the karbaled's work more difficult. Raymond had heard that you should zig and zag if you're ever chased by a kapreta, and though it was more than likely fool's drivel, Raymond had very few tactics to draw from.

The darkness and poor visibility somehow made it easier for Raymond to select a path. If he could not see the danger upon the stairs, maybe it did not exist? He broke for the nearest ladder leading to the ground, gripped the rails with hands and feet, and slid down. In anticipation of the approaching army, the north gate was opening, and Raymond wanted to be as far from that as possible. He bounded for the nearest building, any hesitation abandoned when he had been nearly skewered by the last barrage of frozen pikes. Expecting to be met by dark armour and drawn blades, he pressed through the door of the smithy shop with Saeva's dagger in his fist.

"Oi!" A heavily bearded face recoiled behind a mist of embers. The forge was in operation, billowing wonderful heat throughout.

With an overwhelming sense of relief, Raymond recognized the man. He was the fort's blacksmith, a real jack when it came to repairing damaged steel.

The archenlaives must be keeping him alive until their own smith arrives, Raymond thought. Which would not be long, judging by the size of the force descending upon the fortress.

"Kenet!" Raymond said, calling the man by name.

"How do you know my name?" the man asked, stepping closer, clearly not recognizing the red knight. His face crinkled around patches of soot, screwing his eyes, appraising the young man as if he were a damaged sabaton. "I don't know you," he admitted dismissively.

"I know you don't," Raymond said, cutting across the room to glance out a window. His mantle and tunic were drying quickly, and he wanted to spend as much time as he could within this heat box. "Look," he began, watching the archenlaives rush all around, their feet kicking up water. "I know we are not well acquainted, or anything but I'm—"

"A red knight," Kenet finished, reaching for his tongs. "You may hide here as long as you want," he said, rotating what appeared to be a hatchet, the steel head flaring white hot above the blaze. Raymond glanced around the shop, unable to keep the longing off his face as noticed the array of weapons and armour adorning the walls.

Kenet easily interpreted the red knight's expression. "Take whatever you want," he said with a shrug. "It's not like I'll be around for much longer."

"Why don't you fight with me?"

The smith coughed a laugh into his fist. "You're a funny one!" he said, wagging a gnarled finger at Raymond's chest. "Fit yourself with a decent blade if you'd like, but I would recommend that little strelsam over yonder."

Raymond blinked. "What the hekk is a strelsam?" he asked, approaching the gadget the smith indicated.

"I don't know where it came from," Kenet's bushy eyebrows rose as his smile spread, watching the red knight handle the dainty weapon. "But I do know how it works." The smith reached for the strelsam. "No, no," he chided, "you hold it like so." He pointed the device and chuckled. "And it needs bolts..." The smith began to tug out drawers, rushing between tables and machinations. "Ah!" he announced in triumph. "Here they be!"

Catching up to the smith, Raymond gazed down at the tight bundle of miniature arrows that were displayed inside the drawer. Retrieving one, Kenet placed a bolt in the strelsam and flicked a switch above the handle.

"And like so..." the bolt seated with a click. "Easy enough, right?" he asked.

"What is the point of—"

Kenet answered preemptively. With a flick of his finger, the strelsam activated with a vicious snap, loosing the bolt with such velocity that it punched a hole clean through the wall.

Raymond's jaw dropped.

"I've always wanted to do that," confessed Kenet.

"Do you have any pitch?" Raymond inquired, and snapped his fingers, trying to remember the name of Saeva's smelly yellow powder. "And any..."

"Sulphur?" Kenet offered, admiration coaxing a grin.

"Yes! Sulphur! That's it!" said Raymond excitedly.

Kenet placed his hands in his pockets and shrugged. "Fresh out. But I do like where your mind went."

Raymond bit his bottom lip and growled a curse. "I thank you, Kenet," he said, composing himself. He thrust his hand out and the smith accepted it with a bone shattering grip. "Perhaps I will be seeing you at the crossroads."

"Aye," the forge light glimmered in the old man's eyes. "Take care of yourself, friend."

"You as well," Raymond said, attempting to wrench his hand free from the smith's vice-like hold on his sword hand. "And I fear that I must take my leave."

Pausing at the threshold as the smith shuffled away, Raymond pursed his lips and thought of saying more, but decided against it. The smith and red knight shared a parting glance, and with a final nod, Raymond stepped back out into the night.

The rain continued to pour, and the dryness that Raymond had enjoyed was instantly swallowed by the deluge. The moon accented the flagstone walkways, painting the puddles in its light and torchlight flashed as archenlaives rushed past the sconces embedded in the walls.

Raymond worked his way toward the south gate, keeping the strelsam cocked and loaded.

As he posted up against a projection along the inside of a wall, the irritating voice in his head began to prattle once again. *You should have run when I told you to.*

"Oh, come on," Raymond said loudly, instantly covering his mouth.

Just what do you think that you will accomplish?

"Now is not the time," he whispered.

You want to see her, don't you?

"Who?" he countered.

The karbaled, of course! The voice shifted and became suddenly serious. *Hold still! They are about to pass!*

Obeying the command, Raymond stood still as stone. Not three seconds later, pounding feet rushed past him.

Well done, the voice cooed, *perhaps you may last the night.*

"Alright, what should I do next?"

Run.

"That is very helpful."

You are not equipped for time travel, so the only option you have is escape. Or death, I suppose. Which is a bit more realistic.

"I'm going to kill that ice wizard."

Oh ho! Where did this sense of duty come from?

"Can you help me?"

Maybe...

"That's all I needed to hear!" The red knight broke from cover. "Where is she?" he shouted as the rain poured down his face.

A nearby sentinel heard the proclamation, and rounded the corner of a building. Rushing to meet the foe, Raymond decked the sentinel's peering face before he had time to react. Acting quickly, the red knight raised the strelsam and punched a bolt into the archenlaif's throat. Well, actually, it went completely *through* his throat. And without another thought, Raymond reloaded the weapon and continued on.

Where did you learn that trick?

"Shut up."

Glancing through the drops of rain, which was rather painful, Raymond scanned the parapets. "Where could she be?" He knew that the karbaled needed to see him in order to conjure attack spells. He spun in a semicircle, and a grim dawning struck him. "The bloody spire," he breathed, the knowledge making him want to drop to his knees.

Archenlaives began rushing toward him, funneling between the buildings and staircases. It would be only a matter of time now. He backpedaled toward the south gate, his mouth agape in horror, facing his impending mortality. Lifting the strelsam, he fired a useless bolt into the rushing sea of blackened steel. Stemming the tide was akin to beseeching the impossible. Rotating on his slick heels, Raymond took off on a hopeless, desperate run for the south gate. Though he knew he would not have time to crack open the great doors and escape, he could not see any other options.

The gates loomed ahead.

Yes. Run.

Steel shod feet pounded and sloshed on the wet cobble behind him. Shouts of aggression lifted into the air, filling the atmosphere with the exhilaration of a hunter finally bringing down a prized stag.

Raymond ran and ran, even as his body began to betray him. An arrow hissed over his shoulder, and the muscles above his knees flagged, causing him to stagger. More arrows careened over him, and he knew that soon one would strike its target.

When the blow finally struck, he almost welcomed it. The arrow punched into the back of his left shoulder, the force nearly taking him off his feet. A dazzling pain rattled his jaw, but he was determined to stay upright, and did not succumb to a fall.

He wanted to pluck the shaft from his body.

He wanted better traction for his feet.

He wanted to live longer.

Suddenly more pain tore through him, arresting his movements. Another arrow had struck, this one several inches above his right buttock. His momentum was beleaguered with pain, and his right leg constricted immobile.

"The gates..." he whimpered, collapsing to his knees, giving in.

Are open.

The darkness carved between the gates filled with green and black, rushing like glorious spectres. As he slumped into the mud, Raymond believed he was seeing visions in his delirium. The wind whipping up around him proved that he was wrong. Hooves battered the stone, shaking the earth that Raymond's ear was pressed against.

Enraged screams pierced the night. "Into the flames!"

Raymond began to laugh, sputtering blood into the puddle as he recognized the war cry of Benwick. His vision began to tunnel, suffocating his elation. "The fools opened the gates..." he whispered, and then the red knight knew no more.

12

Ector couched his lance and his destrier plunged in through the gates of Navarene, spurred on by pure hatred. He could feel it in her flanks. Tessa only got this angry at goblins… and apparently archenlaives. Even though his dropped visor obscured his periphery, he could sense that he had lunged ahead of the rest of the knights. Ancel had positioned him in the second row of the assault line, but old Tessa was pissed and now he was going to be the first to strike.

They had been waiting just over the bridge in Irphen's Downfall for their forward scout to return. When he did, informing Ancel that the south gates were wide open, the Lord of Benwick nodded solemnly and wheeled his horse to face his knights.

But there was something else that the scout wanted to add.

"There's a monsoon in the fort, Ancel," he revealed. "But nowhere else."

This admission furrowed the Lord of Benwick's brow.

Magic. They all knew it. They weren't stupid.

Ancel's mount danced in place, feeling his master's ire through the saddle. He addressed his knights, allowing the horse to stamp out his nerves.

"Elithiel's report claims that there are three hundred archenlaives within the fort," he said, finally bringing his horse to heel. "This means we each are tasked with felling ten." His eyes swept over his meager host, examining them for frailty. "No less."

"Into the flames!" a knight cried. The others took up her shout, and the knights of Benwick charged headlong into battle, funneling down the stone path into Navarene's mouth.

Raindrops pounded Ector's helm as he entered the fort. Water fell in sheets, but it did not deter Tessa in the least. Actually, it seemed as if she was even angrier now. "Into the flames!" he screamed through his helm, securing his lance in its stop and balancing it on the saddle's rest.

A host of the enemy was charging the gate on foot, and Ector's mouth creased into a dark smile. *Ten apiece, eh?* he thought. *I'll push for twenty.*

He noticed that a few of the black armoured archenlaives were armed with pikes, but none matched the length of a Benwick lance. An arrow glanced off his right pauldron, making him laugh in response. A flurry of motion to his right drew his attention. Even through his sliver of an eye slit, he could recognize the rider. Only one knight rode with that manner of abandon, helmetless, his long hair twirling behind.

Brother.

Exhaling, Ector watched his brother crouch, level his lance into a frontline archenlaif, and carve a path through flesh and steel. Shards of armour burst into the air. Following a breath behind, Ector did the same, striking the second blow. Scraping and sheering, swords bounced cleanly from his leg armour, and Tessa was hardly slowing. He could feel the horse crushing fallen foes beneath her hooves, the soft flesh between armour bursting. Foam sprayed from the sides of Tessa's mouth, meeting the rain, flowing in a white-clear liquid down her neck. Ector's lance had already plastered three foes to the ground, and he aimed for a fourth, when suddenly he realized that he was on the other side, free and clear of bodies. Tessa reared, wanting desperately to go in for another run.

Ector eased open his visor, finding Ancel already there, his lance up-raised, calmly watching his knights lay waste to the invaders. Pelting raindrops struck his armour, causing more discomfort than their enemy had. Turning toward his younger brother, he inclined his head at the battle, inviting him for another round.

With no words needed, the brothers took off, Ancel hooking for the left flank and Ector wheeling for the right. Ector found this charge proved even easier than the first. He felt as if he were riding downhill. The enemy did not see him coming, and the ones that turned in the confusion were trampled before they had a chance to counter.

Several knights had shivered their lances upon the premier jolt, and now wielded maces or longswords in the midst of the melee. They swung ardently, cleaving foes left and right.

Ector drew up on the other side of the battle without suffering any injury to self or mount. He regarded the landscape, and saw Sir Price overtaken, pulled from his horse, and lost in the teeming mass. Sir Anders was favoring his left arm, but still drove forward, despite the fact that his left hand had been completely severed.

"We must get free of this place before a spell is conjured!" Ancel shouted into his ear.

Ector watched helplessly, wishing to offer aid to his falling comrades. The knights fighting on foot were heavily outnumbered, despite Benwick dwindling the archenlaif force down to a fraction of its former number. It appeared that the original three hundred was now far below one hundred. The young knight turned to see Ancel, along with over a dozen still-mounted knights, beckoning him to follow in retreat.

He fervently shook his head. "No!" he screamed. The proclamation rang his ears. He raised a finger and shouted through the air holes, "Just one more run!"

"Don't be a fool!" Sir Sandrin shouted, appearing next to him and reaching out.

Ector lifted his visor to argue further when a shrill cry cut him off. Rounding onto the pitch, he saw clear-blue pikes issuing from the ground, impaling the knights, heaving them from their feet. The horses were not exempt, they were also hoisted into the air just as their masters, kicking and howling as wounded animals do.

"Away!" roared Ancel.

Ector hesitated before making his retreat, and in that second, he spied the prostrate form of a knight far from the fray with several arrows protruding from his back. He did not recognize the man, but felt drawn to the lifeless form.

A twitch.

The man lives! Ector thought. *I can't save my fellows, but I can save this poor sod.* He leapt free of Tessa, urging her to continue on, and landed a few feet from the dying man. He rose and bundled the man's mantle in his gauntlet, finding him to be quite light. Tessa whinnied impatiently just beyond the gates. "I'm coming!" he insisted, collecting the survivor in his arms, and shrugging him up onto his shoulder.

The knight swiftly cut the distance, sliding his first steps on the slick flagstone, but he quickly found his footing and made it to the exit. As his heels cleared the threshold, a shimmering wall of spears burst upward, sealing the gate. In truth, if Ector had been a touch slower, he would have been collected up into the magic, becoming quite the morbid gate ornament.

Slinging the body up onto Tessa's saddle, Ector gave the horse a pat on her flank. "Thanks for waiting, old girl."

"Any wounded?" Ancel asked, pacing around his dismounted knights. He had called them to a halt within the ancient, damaged fortifications of Irphen's Downfall. The stone husks of glory past provided little service these days, aside from a bit of cover from archers. The fall of Irphen was a bloody bit of history, and like their current predicament, magic had been heavily involved. At first glance, one might believe that siege engines had been employed, or dragons had been responsible for turning the carved stone to glass. But they would be wrong. Spellcasters, on both sides, held equal blame. Surrounded by such stark examples of the destructive capabilities of spellcasters, the knights could not help but be apprehensive in the face of their current predicament.

"Cuts and bruises." Sir Tamarah stepped toward Ancel, bridle in hand, leading her destrier. "Nothing too severe."

Ancel nodded, counting their numbers. They had struck a severe blow, but the toll it had taken on Benwick was even greater, he feared.

"We are less than half, my Lord," Sir Sandrin added as he approached, standing beside Tamarah. "Fourteen strong."

"Including me?" inquired Ancel.

"Including you."

"And my brother?"

Sandrin worked his jaw and snapped his chin at something over his Lord's shoulder.

Strutting up the road, far behind the others, Ector rocked with his mount's careful footfalls. To Ancel's relief, the young knight appeared whole and relatively unscathed. But a second rider behind Ector's saddle replaced the joy Ancel felt, shifting him toward concern.

Ector was close enough to see the emotions change on his brother's face. "I could not leave him behind," he explained, still mounted.

Ancel rushed to lift the wounded man's hood, inspecting his face with worried eyes. "Who is this man?" he asked, stepping back to regard his brother. "He is not from Benwick."

"I know," Ector sighed, leaping down from Tessa. "He was a mere stone toss from the gate, Ancel. I only had to stop for a second to—"

Ancel gripped his brother tightly. "It is alright to lose," he said, his eyes boring into Ector's. "I want you to remember that." His hold on Ector slackened, and gradually released.

"What do you wish me to do with him?" Ector called to Ancel's retreating back.

"We are without laif or lampyr," Ancel said without pausing. "Dress his wounds as best you can. We can't fall back much further, so if he is able, give him a sword." He motioned to Sandrin and the knight stepped forward. "Aid my brother, please?"

Sandrin, his hands clasped behind his back, nodded and strode to Ector's horse. Helping carry the man toward the fire, Sandrin recognized the tunic beneath the mud and grit. "This bloke is a red knight," he remarked. "He could have been laying there for days." The knights carefully lowered the man to the earth, propping him up on his side, trying to prevent the protruding arrows from causing a painful jostling.

"I don't think so," Ector disagreed, easing a bundled blanket under the man's head. "His fingers don't seem pruned enough, do they?"

"Ah," Sandrin scratched his beard, "you may be right about that."

"Should we try to remove the arrows?"

"I don't know these things, mate."

"Maybe we should just try and keep him comfortable?"

"I'll boil some water and see if I can retrieve a spot of salve," the older knight said. "You see about undressing him so we can treat the wounds."

Ector sneered at Sandrin as he departed. *We're both suddenly hand-maids, but I'm the one who must deal with naked parts,* he thought. *Prick.*

Withdrawing a knife from his satchel, Ector went to work slicing apart the red knight's tunic. As he scored a line from the shoulder fletching, his elbow bumped the man's side. The red knight suddenly surged forward, clutching his throat, wheezing and gagging, crimson misting from his mouth.

Ector sprang back, but kept a steadying arm on the man's back to keep him from pressing the arrows deeper as he convulsed.

"The spire!" the red knight choked out. "The spire!"

Ector drew close. "The spire?"

The red knight bobbed his head and covered his mouth, sputtering through another fit of coughs.

"Yes? What of it?"

"Can you see it?" Raymond blurted out.

Ector lifted his head, noticing that, yes indeed, he could see the nee-dle-like spire from his place by the fire. "I can," he replied. It was dif-ficult not to see that gratuitously tall blade of a building. The thing nearly pierced the heavens, prodding the Creator's bum.

It began to drizzle.

"We must!" Raymond suppressed the coughs battering his throat. "We must get out of its sight!" he shook with urgency, clutching Ector's newly slick vambrace.

Finally understanding, Ector shot to his feet, loosing himself from the red knight's grip. "To the glade!" he yelled, receiving bewildered looks. "The caster is in the spire! We must free ourselves from its eyes!"

Most of the knights had already removed their arms and were enjoy-ing a bit of peace by their fires. Some were about to enjoy the first bite of a venison stew, but immediately dropped their spoons upon Ector's announcement. It was a flurry of motion as the knights broke for the corner glade, the trees creating a barricade from Navarene's view.

Raymond screamed as Ector dragged him across the ground on his belly. Each rock, mound, and knoll sent shockwaves of agony into his skull.

He was not alone in his screaming.

As lances from the heavens, shafts of ice began to rain down, piercing and slaughtering those who had been slower to react. Once again, Ector found himself a helpless spectator. Despite his burden, he outran the magic curtain and was one of the first to reach safety. Instinctively, he reached for his longsword.

"This is not something we can fight using physical means," Ancel said from beside him. "How did you know the caster is within the spire?"

"He told me," Ector gestured at the red knight. "I fear he is on the brink of death."

"Those are archenlaif arrows," Ancel said, kneeling. "Who knows what manner of venom the tips have been imbued with?" He sniffed, and fluttered his eyes for a moment, then gave another sniff. "Is that onion?" he asked, beckoning his brother to join.

Ector obliged and concurred, wrinkling his nose. "I think you're right."

"Now why would they dip their arrows in onion sauce?" Ancel asked, his tone betraying his knowledge.

"To enhance the seasoning of their game?" Sandrin offered, revealing that he had been eavesdropping on the brother's conversation. He extended a flask, wagging it between them. "Not a bad idea, now that I think of it. You're basically injecting your meat with flavors right at the moment of kill," he smiled, "rather brilliant, if you ask me."

Accepting the flask, Ector slugged a hit and passed it back. He winced as the liquid burned a fiery course down his windpipe. "I've never known the archenlaives to have such an affection for adding zest to their meals. But I guess it's possible?" he looked to his brother for approval.

Ancel's expression was often difficult to ascertain. The knights could not determine in that moment whether he was delighted or disappointed. Perhaps it was somewhere in the lands in between. "What manner of creature is repulsed, to the point of death by onion, garlic, leek..." He questioned the knights, hoping they might supply the solution on their own.

The answer arrived, but not in the way Ancel expected.

From the bracken nearby, a stirring could be heard, and though the rainstorm barred any sound ahead, the forest behind had been still and silent. The remaining knights rushed the flurry of movement, swords at the ready.

A pair of laives staggered into the moonlit clearing. The female, gravely wounded, leaned heavily upon the male.

"I believe the answer you are seeking," the male laif said, opening his mouth and revealing a striking set of fangs, "is a lampyr."

13

When they had finally reached the farm after walking all across the Creator's green hills, Carlysle had been directed to a tent by a surprisingly courteous and proper sounding werewolf. Unfortunately, since blood and bits of horseflesh still clung to the area where a bib would have been appropriate, she could not help but stare during his explanation.

Carlysle wanted, *really* wanted, to knock on the farmer's door and ask for an ale or wine, or any sort of sauce, but her damn squire prevented such activity, practically pulling her into her sister's tent. A human-shaped Lanaelle was asleep beneath the doting gaze of a short, plump man, with another man seated an arm's length away reading a scroll in a chair.

"It smells like a dozen wet dogs crumpled up and died in here," Carlysle complained.

Stacey gave her a withering look. "My apologies for my knight. She oft speaks afore thought."

"You grow accustomed to it," the man in the chair replied, dismissing the apology. He set the scroll aside and rose to his feet, extending a hand to the knight. "I am Jekar, and this is Bryndon and—"

"Lanaelle," Carlysle faltered. Her sister's lips were so pale. "What happened to her?" she asked. She strode past Jekar to stand beside her sister. "Did one of you monsters do this?" Fury filled her as she looked between the men.

Bryndon appeared offended. *"Monsters?"* he spluttered, his face puckering. "As a matter of fact, it was *humans* who did this," the man swung an accusatory finger between Stacey and Lanaelle.

Following the man's finger, Carlysle's eyes took on a murderous gleam.

Noticing the look on her face, the squire quickly stepped forward. "Which humans?" she asked, remembering the tax collectors they had encountered.

Bryndon sniffed haughtily. "Doesn't matter. We set them to flight."

"And ate their horses," Jekar added.

"Aye," Bryndon agreed, finally lowering his finger. "So what does Lanaelle mean to you lot?"

"She is my sister," Carlysle replied, seeming to wilt upon the admission. "Will she be alright?"

"Most certainly," Jekar said good-naturedly. "I administered a sleeping draught only an hour ago. The arrow wounds should be completely well before sunrise." He adjusted his spectacles. "While we still have much to learn about werewolves, our swift healing is well-known."

Kneeling, Bryndon clasped Lanaelle's hand fervently. "We'll be running behind the pack, but we'll catch up in no time." He leaned closer and spoke directly to the sleeping woman. "Won't we, Lanny? Won't we?"

Carlysle turned away. "Wait, they're leaving?" she asked Jekar.

"Oh, yes," Jekar explained, "the pack is making for Fenrirfang aiming to aid the crown against the archenlaif threat."

"When?"

The physician peered through a rift in the tent. "They may have already departed," he replied.

"They have," a voice growled somewhere to Stacey's left, nearly lifting the squire from the ground.

Stacey reeled. "Fack!" she cursed, then retained her wits. "Where did you come from?"

A pair of matching auburn werewolves, seated in chairs, cocked their heads, examining her as a peculiarity. "We have been here the entire time," the one on the left replied, arching a fuzzy eyebrow.

"Oh, my mistake," Jekar assuaged. "This is Ren and Grandy. The twins here have been tasked with leading us to the fort of Navarene at sunrise."

"We aren't *twins*," Grandy grumbled. "I was born a year before this chode," he claimed, slapping his brother's bicep. Aside from a white circle around Grandy's left eye, the pair looked identical.

"My mistake," Jekar apologized, and whispered to Stacey, "even when they're human, they look like twins."

Stacey half-heartedly suppressed a giggle.

"I do not know your plans," Jekar said to Carlysle and Stacey, "but we can offer you a tent for the night, and thereafter it is up to you." He paused to clear his throat, "I fear we have upset the peace for the landowner, so I do not believe it would be prudent to knock on their door under any circumstance. After today's business, they will be happy to be rid of us."

As per usual, Stacey spoke for her knight. "I thank you, Jekar," she began, but swallowed her next words as Carlysle lifted a hand for silence.

"I will not be leaving my sister's side," she insisted, leveling hard eyes upon Bryndon. "*You* will find shelter elsewhere. Go ahead and shapeshift, mutt. I'll cut you down no matter what you are."

Shooting up to his full height, Bryndon faced the knight. "You, you, you!" he sputtered. "You don't, you don't—"

"Don't what?!" Carlysle challenged, not bothering to stand.

"You don't, you don't tell me what I can—"

"You're spitting all over my sister, you daft hound!"

Jekar and Stacey instantly transformed into diplomats, stepping between the heat radiating from the werewolf and the knight.

"Alright!" Jekar placed a hand on Bryndon's shoulder, causing the man to flinch.

"We are staying here," Stacey asserted, brushing up beside Carlysle. "I think it best that you leave," she said to Bryndon, indicating the exit with a firm nod.

"No!" Bryndon yelled, flinging Jekar's hand away. "You lot leave!"

Jekar made an earnest attempt to soothe the angry man. "Let's be sensible," he calmly placated. Whatever else he was about to say remained unspoken.

"Will you *all* please shut up," Lanaelle said from her place on the floor, her eyes snapping open. "My sister stays," she commanded. "Everyone else leave."

Bryndon's shoulders heaved in protest, but abruptly stilled when Lanaelle's lip curled aggressively, challenging the man to utter just one more word.

Stacey lingered after the others had left, before being dismissed by her knight. "Stay near Jekar," Carlysle advised. "He seems a good sort."

Lanaelle rubbed the arrow hole on her shoulder. "What are you doing, sister? Do I look like I need rescuing?" she asked.

"What are *you* doing?" Carlysle said, suppressing fury.

"Mother and Father—"

"Mother and Father would be appalled!"

"Since when did you start caring about our family?!"

Carlysle jolted back as if she had been punched in the chin.

"Exactly!" Lanaelle angrily ran her fingers through her hair. "You spend more time staring at the bottom of a bottle than you do being a proper knight."

"Lanaelle, I—"

"Can you even remember how much Father sacrificed for you? How much we all sacrificed so you could earn your belt? And how do you repay us?"

The knight shook her head, wanting to be better. "That's why I'm aiming to make things right," she said softly.

"Oh, yeah and how's that going to work?" Lanaelle asked angrily.

"I will come with you," said Carlysle. "I haven't had a drink in..." she trailed off, trying to count the days, before realizing it had only been a few hours since her last foray with alcohol.

"I don't need you," the younger woman asserted. "I can fight on my own now, sister. I do not need you."

Admiring the bandages covering the woman, Carlysle nodded. "Clearly."

Lanaelle laughed. "*This?* This was practically an ambush," she worked her jaw defiantly. "And I survived. And we won."

Sighing loudly, Carlysle knew her sister was correct, but she still needed to make things right. For herself certainly, but even more so for her family. Liquor had taken hold of her for far too long, and now was as good a time as any to put aside the bottle. Was it the drink that had hampered her so? Or was her true nature simply craven? She figured there was only one good way to determine that.

"I am coming with you tomorrow, sister," she said.

Lanaelle sneered at her. "Good luck keeping up," she said, her sneer morphing into a wicked grin. "And good luck getting past the wards."

The knight rushed from the tent, finding her squire entrenched in a discussion regarding the destructive properties of an ogre's hammer in comparison to one created in a laif forge.

"We need horses!" Carlysle said, frantically.

"Some free horses are tethered by the bigger barn," one of the not-twins said.

"Help yourself," the other added, resuming the debate.

Carlysle's head trembled as if she were seizing. "Stacey! Let's go!"

"I never thought I'd see the day," Stacey exclaimed, bounding to her feet. "Where are we off to?"

"We need to find a laif."

Reluctantly they had abandoned their horses on the outskirts of the forest, as their laif guide had advised. Apparently the route they would take to Fort Navarene was far too dense for them. And Carlysle soon discovered that finding a willing laif guide had proven much easier than sticking with the werewolves' forest velocity.

Good luck keeping up.

Her sister's words needled Carlysle's mind as she navigated the dense thickets of Fenrirfang, feverishly trying to match step with the werewolves. They had not slackened since taking off, and she knew that Stacey was being gracious by staying within eyeshot. Her squire and laif guide seemed to enjoy this. Perhaps, a bit too much.

"Come on!" Stacey urged, lifting a thorny branch with her vambrace. "They aren't running *that* fast."

Catching a moment's respite, Carlyle wiped her brow. "Why are they expending themselves so? The war will still be there when they arrive."

Stacey shrugged. "Not sure, but their pack has a healthy head start, so I wager they're just anxious to catch up." The younger woman tugged at the knight's mantle. "Come on!" she said, and darted away, swift as a stag. Pelant, their laif guide, nodded reassuringly before bounding after the squire.

"Keep up!" the squire and laif shouted in unison from inside a ravine.

"Oh, I'll keep up," Carlysle muttered, simmering with anger. "I'll keep up with a greatsword to your scrawny necks…" And she set off again, jogging at first, then charged into a sprint. *Not too bad*, she thought, settling into a comfortable gait. *The trick is maintenance.* She equated the run with a night at the tavern. Too much drink, too fast, led to oblivion, and the same idea went with her current situation. *It's all about balance*, she nodded. *Finding that sweet, sweet pocket.*

Though knight, squire, and laif all possessed the stamina to keep up, they were not as physically equipped as a claw-footed werewolf. It was barely noon before their companions were out of sight. Only Jekar, acting against his new nature, lingered back, stating that he felt obligated to guide them.

After completing the blood ritual required for passing the first ward, Pelant waved farewell as he wrapped his freshly sliced hand. The first layer of the cloth bandage bloomed crimson, and he continued wrapping it to block the scent, not wanting to be pursued by one of the many predators lurking in the forest.

"Take care," Stacey called from across the ward.

"Thanks for the coin," Pelant returned.

"Thanks for the blood!" Stacey said, turning away slowly. When she looked back a moment later, the laif had disappeared.

"He was a good fellow," she said to Carlysle and Jekar after she caught up.

Carlysle shoved a bramble with the side of her arm. "Aye," she nodded. "He got us past the wards like he said he would."

"I thought he was also a bit easy on the eyes, eh?" Stacey bounced her eyebrows at the knight and nudged. "Eh?"

"Not my type," Carlysle responded distractedly, her attention on the werewolf a few steps ahead. Since they had shed their laif, he had been sniffing the air and calling halts regularly. Forest travel was much more dangerous without a laif. "How long do you wager it will be before we meet your kin?" she asked to his back. Jekar's left ear flicked back in response, but the rest of him ignored her question.

She repeated herself, louder this time. "How much longer until—"

"Heh!" the sound issued from the depths of his chest. Rapidly turning on the women, the werewolf motioned for them to find cover.

They darted for a thick circle of vegetation, albeit Carlysle a bit less gracefully than her squire. Her left greave caught on a root, sending her on a sideways spiral that concluded with her staring straight up at the boughs, flat on her back. An unfavorable position that left her feeling like a terrapin flipped onto its top shell.

"Quiet," Stacey hissed.

Carlysle glared at her squire.

After a gratuitously long pause, at least Carlysle thought it was gratuitous, the knight began to roll onto her stomach. The armour rattled and Stacey laid a hand to her knight, stilling her. "Shush!"

"Don't you shush me, you little—"

Carlysle never completed her insult, as clever and biting as it had promised to be. A ferocious snarl exploded several feet before their hidden post, interrupting her words.

The women froze, waiting anxiously for the inevitable violence to erupt.

But there was no return growls or gnashing. No tumult ensued from the initial racket. And after the span of several bated breaths, Jekar hurried to the patch of undergrowth, and made a surprised double take at the knight gazing back up at him.

"We are clear," he said, offering a hand to Carlysle. "For the time being, at least."

"What was that?" the knight asked, sitting up and accepting the werewolf's paw.

"Merely a small colony of troll," he said, sounding almost disappointed. "The sudden archenlaif presence ushers an imbalance that upsets every denizen of the forest. The trolls are fleeing the potential upheaval, no doubt."

"How sad," Stacey intoned, adjusting her arming belt.

Jekar shrugged. "It is often how events occur."

The three set off again at a reserved jog.

"So," Carlysle began. "How long will this journey to Navarene take?"

The werewolf's eyes bounded from tree to tree. "The pack should be there just after nightfall," he replied. "We, however, at our current rate, will join them in two days."

Carlysle whistled. "You werewolves can cover a lot of ground."

"I only hope that we will still be able to offer assistance when we arrive," said Jekar.

"I can tell you one thing for certain," the knight remarked, pausing to leap a boulder and duck a spiky vine, "we will make it to the battle long before the king."

Without breaking stride, the werewolf bounded a hillock and passed underneath a tree whose roots rose from the ground like a pair of splayed legs. He waited on the other side, craning his neck between the gap. "Somehow, I do not find comfort in that statement," he said, and stepped aside, freeing space for the women to pass.

14

"Above all else," Saeva noted. "He has a remarkable proclivity for survival." The lampyr glanced at Raymond, peacefully curled beside a fire, with admiration.

The ice shards had ceased falling as abruptly as they had begun. Thanks to the laives, the knights learned that the karbaled would need time to regain her strength, and they should get some sleep in the meantime. The next day would surely bring more blood and frost.

Three hunched forms sat around the fire, the still night allowing the crackling embers to spiral unhindered into the heavens.

Ancel was the only man of Benwick still awake. "What can men do against such power?" he inquired, looking between Flya and Saeva. "In the annals and tales, opposing sides each employed a spellcaster."

"Didn't you mention earlier that Orkney has an apprentice?" Flya asked, needling a log with a tree branch.

"I did," Ancel replied, his voice filled with hesitation. "But I do not believe him capable to combat what we face."

"Youth?" said Saeva.

"Aye," Ancel confirmed. "Along with many other..." he thought for moment, "*qualities*," he concluded. His eyes settled on the flames. "I would not place my faith in him. Our time is better spent on strategy."

The female laif giggled. "Unless you know of a way to choke the underwater streams, or shield the clouds, then our time would be better spent digging graves."

"Flya," Saeva chided, lifted a hand toward her before turning to Ancel. "Forgive my companion. She is very valiant, but her tongue often proves—"

"Annoying?" Flya finished. She brushed at the fang marks on her neck. "Or maybe you mean realistic?"

Saeva lowered his chin. "I was about to say, 'quicker than her good sense'." He lifted his eyes to Ancel. "But I suppose in this case 'realistic' would be appropriate."

The Lord of Benwick would not be persuaded to change his course. He rose to his feet and turned to face the spire as the first whispers of sunrise began to pervade the leaves. The hours seemed to slide through his fingers like oil.

"We cannot prevent the enemy from leaving the fort, and continuing on," he said softly, "but we can at least put a hitch in their step."

"How?" Flya asked with a loud sniff. "She will quench any blaze you light."

"Tintagil and Ghore should arrive soon," Ancel said, speaking mostly to himself.

"I recommend retreat," Saeva stated. "Wait and combine with Tintagil and Ghore. That would create a more formidable force, would you not agree?"

"Nay," Ancel spat. "The only retreat I will be making will be to my tent for the night." The knight began to walk away, the dancing shadows nipping at the green of his tunic.

"Let me get this straight," Sir Belfast, the eldest veteran in what remained of Benwick's army, called out. "Are you asking us to abandon all codes of chivalry?" The old knight mustered a terrible scowl beneath a nose that was bent in over half a dozen places.

Ancel's silhouette carved a hard line from the ground. "In short, yes," he replied.

"Have you lost all sense?!" Belfast broke rank and seemed ready to charge. The vein on his forehead pulsed. "Your father would throttle you!"

The knights of Benwick had quietly gathered on the crimson stained grass of Irphen's Downfall to receive their daily instructions. Most appeared unexpectedly fresh, showing little signs of fatigue. Sir Belfast, however, appeared hot under the collar. "Let us die as befitting our stations!" he shouted, whirling his back on Ancel to beseech his fellow knights. "Let us die in glory! Die as knights of Benwick! Let the chanters sing of our sacrifice to our grandchildren's children!"

A few faces nodded dourly. The rest ignored him and focused on their Lord.

Belfast did not receive the response that he desired, and not to be cowed, he circled back to Ancel and marched toward him. "Your orders are craven! For cowards!" he raged, an inch from Ancel. "Cast your gaze over what remains of your knights, Ancel! I don't see any cowards among them!"

A long pause followed. Ancel did not falter during the silence. Neither did Belfast; he only seemed to swell as he gathered more ire.

"We will not die among the trees as children at play!" the old knight continued. "We will die mounted on the field of battle, as our brethren did, not one day hence!"

This garnered a response that Belfast deemed appropriate. Seven of the twelve knights heaved a passionate arm in salute.

Ancel deftly stepped past Belfast. "Keep those arms up," he commanded. "Please."

The seven were suddenly unsure, wavering under their Lord's measured gaze. One knight nearly dropped her hand, but Ancel gestured for her to keep it up.

"Let's see," he began, counting. "That gives us seven." He paused, nodding at the indignant knight before him, "eight, if you are inclined, Sir Belfast?"

"Inclined for what?"

"Why, to remain mounted, my old friend!" Ancel clasped a hand to Belfast's pauldron and squared his shoulders. "I need to divide the force and was just about to request volunteers." The Lord of Benwick removed his hand and gestured for the knight to return to his place among the ranks. "You have my deepest gratitude for performing that portion of the work for me."

Shifting his weight to one foot, Belfast prepared to return to his position, but hesitated. "Are you saying that there is going to be a charge?" he asked, furrowing his brow.

"Light that fire within you, Belfast. Perhaps it will be enough to melt the ice witch in her tower," said Ancel sincerely. "Lead the charge."

Belfast straightened his spine and drew a fist across his chest. "Into the flames," he said. And somehow, he returned to formation with even more ardor than he had begun with.

Behind Ancel, the knights of Benwick had begun preparations for the day, and if the Creator kept them, for the following day as well.

"You are not wasting time," Saeva said to Ancel, matching his stride.

"I try not to," replied Ancel. His tone was perfectly balanced between dismissive and polite. "How long does it take a karbaled to regain her full prowess?"

"I do not know with any full certainty, but if I could wager a guess..." the lampyr's steps slowed, and Ancel slowed with him. "Perhaps a day of rest to regain full strength?"

"We will run with that belief then," replied Ancel. "Best of luck to you today," he added, turning a heel and leaving the lampyr to his business.

Walking through the camp, Ancel scanned the knights, seeking his brother. He was not among the knights counting arrows and divvying them out. He was not among the knights preparing their mounts as if a grand tourney were about to commence. Nor was he among the knights kneeling under a shady copse, pleading for the Creator's mercy, for his favor, and for their families' survival if the worst should occur.

A tall knight with long hair plaited to match his destrier's was oiling his dagger, and the meager amount of armour that he would be sporting on the day's mission. Approaching the man, Ancel was hesitant to disturb him, but if anyone knew Ector's location, it would be Sandrin.

"Apologies for disturbing you," Ancel said, drawing up beside the knight.

Sandrin did not pause in his work. "No need, no need," he said, sliding his gaze from the blade to the Lord. "How may I be of service?"

"My brother?"

"Ah."

Placing the glistening dagger on a nearby stump, Sandrin retrieved his helm and admired it for a moment. Easing the visor open and closed, he worked the simple mechanism. "Look to those blokes holding their own personal vigils," he recommended, gesturing to the knights in prayer, "and follow the trees to the right."

"Yes..."

"See that remarkable banyan tree just beyond those maples..."

"Aye..."

"It's quite a ways in."

"I see it, Sandrin."

Dabbing the oily cloth on the hinge of his visor, Sandrin smirked. "Well, I saw him traipsing toward that tree with that scary but pretty laif. You know the one."

"I thank you," said Ancel, hurrying toward the aforementioned tree.

"Mind you, she's scarier than she is pretty," Sandrin called to Ancel's retreating back, as if it mattered in the least. "You wouldn't catch me mucking about with the likes of her," he muttered to his helmet, making the helmet nod in agreement.

Entering the forest, the cooling shadows fell upon the knight as he scoured the space for his brother. Before his eyes could properly adjust to the dimness, he heard the snap of a bow, and instinctively dropped to a knee.

Fifteen paces hence, light filtered down upon a man in the greens and blacks of Benwick holding a bow beside a slender framed laif. The man's quiver, filled with arrows, was bobbing nearby on one of the branches undulating from within the banyan's obscured trunk.

"Not bad, not bad," Flya said, gently clapping her hands in feeble praise. "I'd like to see if you're that accurate with a target in motion."

Ector beamed. "Soon enough you will," he said, reaching for his quiver to nock another draw. He started, noticing his brother leaning against a tree just beyond the quiver. "Ancel," he called out, resting the limb of his bow on the soil. "What brings you to my woods?"

"I am checking to make sure that you have all your affairs in order," Ancel replied, not moving from the tree.

"How thoughtful of you," Ector said dryly, smiling at the laif. "My brother is always very helpful."

"You understand that I would not place you in this battle, but I cannot spare a single knight."

"Yes, yes," Ector replied, wishing whole-heartedly that his brother would disappear. "You need as many as you can get. Is there anything else I can help you with?" He spoke through gritted teeth, transmitting to Ancel that he wished to be alone with Flya. For obvious reasons.

If Ancel picked up what Ector was dropping, he showed very little signs. "Remember brother, if all seems for naught, I need you to speed away to the nearest ward and wait for Ghore or Tintagil. Do not get caught up in the battle and forget your—"

"Yes, yes," Ector snapped, snatching an arrow. "I will stay as far back as possible during the advance. One eye to the gate and one to the exit." He drew the bow and stared down the shaft. "I heard you the first time," the knight said, exhaling. The arrow buried itself in its target with a resounding thud. Ector lowered the weapon and turned. "So, if that's all..."

But Ancel was no longer there.

Ancel wandered, allowing his mind to do the same. Knowing full well that they would not be coming out of this alive, he offered apologies to the ghosts and spirits of bygone days.

There is no magic in Benwick.

The phrase reverberated in his mind. It had been Sir Vashal who had spoken the words earlier in the day. She had been speaking to Sir Geoffrey as they discussed the fall of Irphen, and the reason the grass grew red in the valley. Both knights had been assigned to Saeva's contingent.

It was all very simple, really. Three knights would accompany each laif, dividing the total archers evenly, four and four. Vashal, Geoffrey, and Tamarah would accompany the lampyr in the forest, along the west side of the roadway, and Flya would lead Ancel, Sandrin, and Ector along the east side.

"Keep the enemy inside the fort," Ancel had commanded, "that is all that I can ask of you."

Saeva and Flya, with only three others and a red knight, had been able to keep the archenlaives in the fort for several days. Though Benwick's knights were admittedly less skilled than the laives, perhaps with extra bodies, they would be able to hold out for at least one day.

The fact that another force of archenlaives, well over three hundred strong, had entered the fort from the north, consistently grounded the Lord of Benwick, reminding him that unknown variables *always* proved to be a crippling factor concerning strategy and tactics. Adding the karbaled into it only worked to compound measures. And he had only eight... *eight* mounted knights to act as a failsafe if the archers failed or were overrun. Six of the knights would be employing salvaged lances from the first battle. The weapons had been re-honed and sharpened but were now at only half their original length. In their haste, Benwick had packed light for this campaign.

If only we had a spellcaster of our own, thought Ancel.

After all, *there is no magic in Benwick.*

15

Raymond rolled over, sweating and unready for consciousness. Particles of light streamed through the pinprick holes in the canvas, finding his eyelids no matter which way he turned. He must have been enthralled in quite the fever dream the night before. He swore that he had heard the haughty timbre of Saeva during the night, which clearly was not possible. He ran a finger over the fang marks on his neck, remembering his first meeting with the lampyr. The holes had only just begun to itch with healing.

With another flop, the red knight realized that the arrows that had been jutting from his back had been removed. When he made to reach for the wounds, a stabbing pain infiltrated the nerves running the entire length of his arm, so he decided it best to simply imagine that a skilled physician had treated and dressed the damaged parts.

"Aye!" the fresh-faced knight who had rescued him poked his head through the tent flap. "We're off to our deaths, so try your best to keep things together here, eh?"

Raymond tried to sit up, but beacons of pain flared up all over his body. "Wait!" he shouted.

The outside breeze returned along with the knight. "Yes?" he asked.

"Did I..." The red knight's tongue felt like paste. "Can you bring some water?"

"Over there," Ector said, helpfully gesturing to Raymond's left hip.

"Ah, yes." Raymond, still remaining on his back, carefully drizzled some water onto his mouth. After his throat felt adequately dampened, he began again, "Did I, by any chance, hear a lampyr last night, or was I imagining things?"

Lowering his head, Ector entered the tent and crouched down. "Yes," he admitted cautiously. "They didn't want me to tell you, but I fail to see the harm."

Raymond's body shot up with exhilaration. "Saeva?!" he exclaimed, and immediately wished he had not moved. Lowering back down with a groan, he received an affirmative nod from Ector.

"And he brought with him another laif," Ector said, running a thumb across his stubbled chin. "She was in pretty bad shape when she arrived but—"

"Flya?!"

"Indeed."

The red knight ignored his pain and struggled to his feet, fighting back the jaw clenching anguish. He had almost planted both feet when Ector moved between him and the exit, placing a hand to the red knight's chest.

"You'll reopen your wounds!"

"Where are my friends?" Raymond demanded, his words beginning to slur. His knees buckled and his head felt light as a feather.

Ector caught him and lowered him down to the ground. "Easy now, man," he said, bringing him to rest and adjusting the pillow, "this is probably why Saeva didn't want me to tell you..."

A knot formed in Raymond's throat. "Why hasn't he healed me?" he asked, tears cresting his eyelids.

"He said it would take a few days for the onion to work its way out of your system."

"Ah, yes. The onion," Raymond brushed his wrist across his nose. "Clever archenlaives."

"Fortunate for Flya, they had tipped her arrows in some type of venom, so the lampyr was able to make short work of her recovery."

Raymond looked the knight in the eye. "You mentioned that you are all going to your deaths?" He did not wait for a response. "What are you planning?" Raymond asked with trepidation.

"We plan on picking up where you left off, my friend."

"But the karbaled..."

"Concern yourself with healing," Ector said, eyeing the scarlet stains that were beginning to advance under Raymond's armpit. "Roll onto your stomach. I fear that I must re-dress your wounds."

Obliging with a grunt, Raymond shimmied onto his belly and inched his arms out in front of his face. Everything hurt. Before, everything hurt, but now, *everything* hurt.

Ector peeled off the damp, sticky cloth. "Do not worry though," he said, bundling the first mess and tossing it aside. "I have been tasked with fleeing if everything seems lost. I'm the special messenger boy. And if that happens, I will make sure to shout an exclusive warning as I sprint past."

"How very thoughtful."

"It's the least I can do."

The sun was at its peak.

The eight archers set off, leaving the other knights behind, crossing their fingers and hoping that the karbaled was still in recovery. Each hour they bought for Arthur's realm, for Camelot, was one more hour for Tintagil and Ghore to arrive. And after them, Rhionydd, Orkney,

Celliwig, Garlot, and Lowthean were expected to follow. But Ancel doubted that half of those domains had even begun to oil their armour.

Such is the way of things, he reflected, offering one final glance at his knights before pressing into the dim coppice.

"Soft!" Flya's whisper was harsh as she gestured for the knights to slow. She had spotted a sentinel leaning out on the fort's balustrade, intently keeping watch.

Ector wiped his brow. It was hot and humid, but there had been a favorable calm in the winds. "How many can you see?" the knight inquired with a tentative step toward the laif.

She lifted a single finger to her lips, calling for silence, then flashed three fingers. The knights digested the information for a moment, but a concerned look suddenly graced the laif's face, and she amended the number, brandishing her whole hand: five archenlaives.

Flya was no dope. Before they had ventured into the forest, she had made a plan for their attack. Upon her signal, Saeva and Ector would remain and Ancel and Sandrin would flank.

A question lingered in Ector's mind, but he knew better than to voice it. As he pantomimed what he was searching for, Flya made the agreed upon signal, firmly crossing her arms and locking eyes with each knight, effectively freezing Ector's gesticulation. He raised a hand, wanting desperately to voice what he believed was of grave import. The laif waved a dismissive hand at him, misreading the troubled look on the knight's face as youthful doubt.

Five archenlaives, adorned in their obsidian-black armour, stood upon the southeast corner of the fort, just as the laif had conveyed. If an army of over three hundred souls remained within those walls, Ector could not tell. The atmosphere was hauntingly quiet and still.

The second bit of Flya's instruction dictated the *when*. Once she released her first arrow, the rest of the company should loose until the enemy was down. She had emphatically urged, *"do not fire before me,"* and added, *"do not miss."* The knights found the latter command more difficult to agree to follow than the former.

Treading delicately near the wall, Ector withdrew an arrow and nocked, watching Flya from the corners of his eyes. His question needled at him still, and he cursed himself for not imagining such a circumstance before they had set off.

The laif drew and raised her bow, leveling the arrow toward the enemy furthest to the left.

If there are only four of us, Ector thought, matching Flya's movement, stretching his weapon to its fullest draw. *And there are five of—*

Flya's bow snapped, and Ector saw her target drop instantly. The knight unwittingly flinched, sending him off-mark, but before he could correct himself, his target tumbled back, a fletching sprouting from just under his chin. With a fluid bump, Ector angled his arrow toward the next archenlaif, releasing a breath, the arrow following suit. Within the span of a single arrow's release, the five archenlaives had dropped, their heels kicking up and tunics whirling upon their descent to the stone.

Flya nudged Ector. "No matter the number, I'll always handle the overflow," she whispered. "Perhaps I should have covered that before, eh?"

The dark look Ector returned was an adequate response.

The laif's lips were suddenly inches from his ear. "Well, now you know." She slunk back, giving ground to the fort. Ector followed, twirling a finger in his ear and shaking his head.

Cries erupted from inside the fort, the first real, notable din. It was a response not dissimilar to that of a stick puncturing a hornet hive. At first, Ector believed the tumult had been drawn from the discovery of the dead sentinels, but the roiling voices seemed to be congregating toward the opposite bank.

Sandrin and Ancel reappeared from the brush, lowering their cowls, recognizing the undeniable sounds of battle in its infancy.

This was far too soon, and they all knew it.

"Oh, Saeva," the laif murmured toward the west walls. "What have you kicked up?"

This was not what I had in mind! Saeva thought, wheeling back and surging toward cover. A mossy hillock proved the perfect shelter from the hail-fire of bolts and arrows that flew in his direction. The knights were close behind the laif, and the last, Geoffrey, barely tucked a heel before the steel shafts began to burgeon from all over the forefront of the knoll. Missiles whistled over their heads, terminating in the beyond, snapping hundreds of leaves from their stems.

The lampyr turned back and eyed the green flags as they swirled downward. "They are pinning us down!" he shouted, drawing his blade.

Geoffrey's lips were pale. "I'm sorry!" he claimed. "I didn't know that their eyes were so sharp!"

"Now ya know," Tamarah snapped, easing cautiously over the grade to spy any approach.

Saeva placed a hand to Tamarah's back. "It was my fault," he admitted. "I should have been leading." He rose by fractions to speak to Tamarah. "Does the enemy approach?"

"I can't—" she flinched as tiny fronds of mossy debris spewed onto her forehead. She pressed her back to the berm. "I can't get a good look," the knight confessed with bitter frustration.

"We need eyes..." Saeva muttered.

An idea struck, and the laif dropped to his hands and knees, crawling to where the hillock gradually leveled itself flush to the plane of the ground. On his back, the laif extended his sword, incrementally, praying for a miracle. He grit his teeth, expecting a bolt to smash into his steel, but his progress went undetected.

"Tamarah!" Saeva said urgently. He caught her attention and flicked his eyes toward the upraised weapon. "Can you see them in the reflection?"

The knight's mouth and eyes formed solid lines, focusing as hard as she could. "Tilt it down just a baby's hair..." she signaled with her hand. "Ah! Yes! Perfect! Hold fast, right there!" Her expression of victory slipped into shock.

"Vashal!" She rocked back, violently punching the air over the startled knight's head. "Draw and loose!"

The knight swiveled onto his side and hastily drew his bow, siphoning as much strength as he could in such an awkward pose. At the same time, a poleaxe crested the mossy bank, hammer side down, followed by the wielder's helm. The unmistakable black of the archenlaif's armour almost appeared surreal in that dreadful moment.

If not for his hesitation, young Vashal would have come out of the exchange unscathed. Unfortunately, he shuddered a breath and his shoulders arrested him for only a second, but so much can happen within the length of a second. The looming poleaxe dropped, and then Vashal released his shot. The arrow struck true, finding a breach under the enemy's armpit, forcing a spasm, but it was not enough to stop the heavy weapon. The archenlaif was huge, a head or more taller than the others they had seen. His momentum was not broken, nor was his grip, and the hammerhead fell, striking a tremendous blow to Vashal's leading leg. Boldly, Geoffrey rose with dagger in hand, and pressed the giant. He drove the blade upward into the enemy's chinstrap, buckling the enemy's knees, and toppling him rearwards.

Vashal screamed in anguish. The enormous weapon had been wrested free from the giant's grasp as he fell, but it remained anchored atop his shattered leg, locking him in place. He screamed again, this time in fear, as he watched his fellow knight fall in a tangled heap, caught up in the archenlaif's embrace, over the side of the berm, leaving him fully exposed to the enemy. "Geoffrey!" the injured knight shrieked. But as much as he wished to stay the execution, there was nothing he could do.

The arrows suddenly shifted their focus, funneling a concentrated torrent directly into the brave Benwick knight, still struggling to free himself from the fallen enemy. Though he could not see it, Vashal knew that Geoffrey was no longer among the living. No one could survive such a rain of steel.

Tamarah rushed to Vashal's side. "Heal him!" she begged the lampyr. While keeping her head down, she strained, attempting to pry the poleaxe off the knight's leg.

"We don't have the time for that!" Saeva explained, placing a firm hand to Vashal's thigh.

Gathering her strength, Tamarah heaved the weapon upward, revealing shattered devastation in its wake. Vashal wailed and nearly passed out, wavering for a few moments after spying the splintered bones marbling the mossy earth.

Arrows continued to thud against the earthy barrier, pelting their heads with dirt and soil. The lampyr and Tamarah scoured the bank, waiting, expecting another wave. Shock had taken hold of Vashal, and one might believe the knight was dead for the way he stared listlessly upward toward the heavy limbs of the ancient tree boughs. With a flash of clarity, Vashal latched a hand to Saeva's wrist.

"Why?" he asked, his eyes darting over the lampyr's face.

Saeva freed himself of the man's grip. "We simply do not have time for the healing to—"

"No!" Vashal corrected. "Why do the archenlaives *hate* so much?"

Reacting as if he had taken a bite from a bitter fruit, Saeva took a moment to gather his wits. It was common knowledge that archenlaives despised mortals, but the *why* was a convoluted and archaic tale, not the sort of story that one could wrap up into a single, clever phrase.

"We're nothing more than chattel to them!" Tamarah answered hurriedly, proving that there was, indeed, a nutshell-sized explanation. "Now reach for your sword, you dense prat!"

Focusing on one point ahead of him, Vashal acted as though he had been struck blind, fumbling for the dagger at his hip. He had neglected to bring his arming sword, opting for a lighter load in favor of quickness and a tighter profile.

Clutching the leather pommel in trembling fingers, time began to slow as Vashal waved the dagger before him, fending off the ghosts assailing him.

"We've lost him!" Tamarah's voice suddenly seemed far away to Vashal. "Look to the center!" The arrows that had been striking all over their position, evenly fanned, had suddenly opened up an empty cone at the median, which could mean only one thing.

Tamarah and Saeva seized their bows and latched their chests to the berm as they surveyed the dark armour rushing to meet them. Not requiring words, the knight and lampyr loosed arrows in unison, desperately trying to remain steady while their hands trembled, betraying their masters.

Within a breath, Saeva cleared four arrows, felling four foes. As he drew back the fifth, a black shaft struck his left pauldron, burying into the flesh beneath. The force of the impact hardly garnered a reaction from the laif, who merely grunted, steeling himself to drop his fifth adversary. As soon as his hip locked into place, another arrow slapped into the same pauldron, and this time, he could not shrug it off.

The laif dropped to a knee before Vashal, nearly falling onto the shattered remnants of the knight's outstretched leg. "Why?" Vashal begged the laif. "Why?" he asked again, peering intently into Saeva's eyes.

A pain-drenched groan issued from Tamarah. The knight reeled back, an arrow jutting from beneath her collarbone. Terror infusing her eyes, she searched desperately to see where it had struck, but the shaft obstructed her chin. In disbelief, she dropped her weapon and placed a hand to the arrow, locking eyes with Saeva.

"Get down!" the lampyr screamed, reaching for the mortal knight.

She merely shook her head in response, and as she did, an arrow grazed her scalp, billowing her hair and cocking her head violently to one side.

Saeva rushed to catch the knight with his right arm. "Creator, no!" He fought back his instincts to bite her neck and subsume the damage. Time was not an ally today.

Her eyes fluttered open. "Fight, you idiot," she gurgled.

A stillness gripped the trees, wrenching his attention from the dying knight. The feeling built to a jarring sensation that enveloped the lampyr's sternum. His breath was hindered by whatever stirred beyond, traveling swiftly, and near.

What is that sound? Saeva wanted to stand.

He looked to Tamarah. "Is that..."

...a growl?

The knight offered no response, for she was no longer conscious. Saeva spun from Tamarah and stared at the forest to the right, his left arm dangling useless, his right arm pressed to the knot growing beneath his chest.

That was not a growl.

That was a roar.

Riders! Glorious riders! Their mounts were swift as stags, navigating the forest as if it were open road. With heads bowed, the laif-bred horses rent the soil, plunging toward the fort, destroying all forces of resistance. The riders, armoured in brilliant gold, got to their feet as the forest flew past them, standing atop their mounts in stark defiance of reality.

Vashal stirred behind him. "Angels..." the knight murmured.

Not angels, Saeva corrected in his thoughts. "Dragoons," he said aloud.

The moment the lampyr spoke the word, the red-eyed destriers cleared the forest boundary, immediately halting their motion, gouging the soil, carving deep trenches in the earth. In a display of sheer brilliance, the laif-horses reared at the last moment, launching the warriors onto the wall.

There were only two dragoons, but to Saeva there may as well have been two thousand.

The golden knights clung to the wall a mere arm's length beneath the balustrade. An unseen signal passed between the pair, and as one, they rushed upward, overtaking the summit. Retrieving the cruel spears adorning their backs, the dragoons sprinted off eagerly, bringing to mind reapers before harvest.

The sloping hillock prevented Saeva from viewing the dragoons' attack, but he heard the repercussions. It felt like a coffin slamming shut, a tremor of silence ensuing behind. Not one more arrow was flung from that crenelated wall to strike nearby.

Saeva peered over the berm, surveying the aftermath. The walls, where once a tide of black armour had amassed, were now barren. Several armoured bodies were strewn on the ground, tracing a path to the knoll he was sheltered behind. The lampyr started when his gaze fell upon an archenlaif mere inches from their position. She had almost reached them, but Saeva could not tell what manner of death had befallen her.

A voice from behind spoke, disrupting his reverie. "We should not tarry, brother."

Saeva swung around to see the dragoons, their spear hafts planted in the soil, standing above him, their armour slick with scarlet. Both were slender, but one was smaller than the other and appeared more feminine. With their visors still dropped, it was difficult to ascertain which warrior had spoken.

"There is a restless magic that watches from above," the dragoon continued, offering a hand.

Saeva looked to his gravely injured companions. "But, these brave knights..." he protested.

Shadowy presences arrived behind the dragoons, huffing and snorting impatiently. "Our mares will spirit them from this locale," the smaller dragoon said. "And thereby, you may ply your healing trade."

16

"We are divided enough as it is!" Ancel was adamant. "We will not split this force."

Flya balked at the knight's audacity. "You seem confused, Lord of Benwick," the laif argued. Ordinarily a very close talker, she held her ground. "I don't answer to you."

"Fair enough," Ancel conceded, wearily. "Sandrin and I will hold here as long as we can." He turned his back to the laif. "Best of luck."

Scoffing, Flya made for the road, bounding through the brush, hardly making a sound. Ector, unlike his companion, hesitated.

"Ancel," he called to his brother's retreating back.

The Lord of Benwick paused and turned his head.

Ector wanted to say something profound, something memorable, something remarkable, something akin to what Ancel himself would say. After all, this could be the final moment he would share with his older brother.

Instead, he just froze.

Ancel lowered his chin into his cowl. "Remember, when you hear the horn," he reminded, "make for the ward as fast as you can." And without a glance, he disappeared into the daylight shadows.

Treading closely behind Ancel, Sandrin paused. "Keep your head down, Ector," said the knight with a wan smile. "And give my love to my family, will you?"

The knights exchanged somber nods and passed from one another's sight.

It did not take long for Ector to catch up with Flya. She had not gone nearly as far as he had expected. The laif was easily detected, standing beneath an elm, her back to his approach, the smooth contours of her armour standing out against the tree's mottled bark.

"...and somehow this... this..." Flya paused, pointing fiercely toward the spire. "This does not concern you?"

A small voice twittered back, but the knight could not distinguish the words.

"Ogres?!" Flya was becoming a tad belligerent, cutting a wrathful step away from the tree. "Ogres in the outskirts take precedence over a wizard in the fucking spire?"

Now that the laif had moved from the tree, it allowed Ector to see with whom she was holding such a debate. It was a fae. A rather elegant fae, actually. Her tiny translucent armour glowed, radiating brilliance from within. "I do see your point, Lady Flya," the fae said calmly. Her moth wings languidly batted the air as she hovered, respectfully, at eye level. "But our armies have already been pledged, and there is no turning back now."

"There is nothing you can do?" Flya implored. "Nothing at all?"

The fae shook her head. "Well over half of our forces are in Talanth as we speak."

"Then give me the rest!"

"Flya, I do not—"

The laif stormed toward the fae. "Send them up to the bloody spire and knock that witch from her roost!" she demanded, shaking with fury. "Are you blind to what is before you, Lavernia?!"

"It is not so simple," said Lavernia, her essence darkening a shade. "You know what such a pledge entails for those of us bound to the forest. I do not have the power to bestow any blades to your cause."

"Give me fifty," Flya requested desperately.

"I cannot."

The commotion from the walls was not waning.

"We don't have time for this!" Flya gestured toward Ector, who had drawn closer. "This knight's lands have given all they have! Even his brother, the Lord, is fighting at the front! Less than a third of their forces remain, and yet," the laif's voice tightened, "and yet, they abide!"

Lavernia would not be dissuaded. "I simply cannot—"

"Thirty!"

The fae stared at the ground and pressed her fingers to her lips in grave uncertainty. More shouts rippled from the fort, more snapping bows and loosed bolts, more steel pounding upon stone parapets. "Ten," she finally said, gazing back up at the laif. "I can afford ten."

Rushing relief filled the laif's voice. "Thank you, Lavernia!" Flya seemed prepared to embrace the fae.

"Save your gratitude," Lavernia raised a halting palm. "It will take some time, and you will need to remain here."

Flya cast an urgent look toward the east tower. "But, Saeva..."

"You are the one who made such a brazen request of the fae, and now you quail at the response? I will not fling my knights out into uncertain skies without a commander." Lavernia's tone brooked no argument. "I am entrusting them to you, Flya." Her radiance vacillated as flames. "Do not waste them."

Lavernia shot upward into the endless symphony of leaves overhead, disappearing from view.

The ways of fae and laif were entirely foreign to Ector, and while he was hesitant to approach, he did anyway. "How long do you wager this will take?" he asked the agitated laif.

Luckily, no rain had begun to fall thus far, but the fighting on the ramparts was not lifting. Flya wished for nothing else but to run to Saeva's aid, but an invisible chain of obligation tethered her in place.

"I do not know," she said. "But I pray that it is soon." The relief that the fae's promise had brought was swiftly replaced with trepidation. She sought aid, but she had no desire to be the one to lead. She was the striking arrow, not the one who guides. She had always briskly shrugged off the yoke of responsibility, and now, now she feared that she had struck a bargain that she could not see to fruition.

Flya hugged herself and paced, but suddenly drew up short. "Do me a favor, Ector," she said, her voice unnaturally soft. "There is no need for the both of us to wait here. Move swiftly and silently to the roadway, and see what you can, please?" Her arms fell to her sides. "Find out what has befallen our friends."

"I want you to pull the arrow as soon as my fangs pierce her neck," Saeva instructed the dragoon. The lampyr was behind Tamarah, propping her up with his knee pressed to her spine. The knight was dangerously close to being somewhere between Fenrirfang and Avalon and would soon be beyond his reach.

"Are you prepared?" Saeva asked, readying his mouth.

The dragoon, now helmetless, nodded curtly.

As the lampyr fastened his mouth onto the dying knight, the dragoon withdrew the arrow with a quick, decisive wrench. Tamarah's eyes sprang open and she croaked out a horrible wheeze. Removing his knee, Saeva gave the confused knight some space.

"Who are you?" she demanded, her eyes were wild, darting from dragoon to dragoon. She placed her hand to the fresh bite wound on her neck and gasped at the scarlet stains upon her fingers. Kicking frantically, her feet scrabbled on the soil, propelling her backward into Saeva.

She peered up at the familiar face. "What has—" Before she finished her query, she stopped, her memory returning in a rush.

"We have received some unexpected aid," Saeva explained, almost beaming. "These dragoons, Bactaal and Laiernaten rescued us and led us to this motte and tower. We owe them quite a debt."

"Banish such inclinations," the more feminine of the warriors spoke, waving a hand. "Aside from dragons, archenlaives are the most repulsive creatures walking among us. We gladly partake in any opportunity to strike them down." If not for the deep voice and the thick muttonchops that filtered into hearty stubble, Tamarah would have believed Bactaal to be a very pretty female laif.

"Well, if it means anything, you have my deepest gratitude," Saeva said, cupping his hands over his heart. The dragoons returned the gesture.

"Yes, yes, thank you very much," Vashal interjected, his words slurred. He was propped against the base of the tower, looking much like a worn and weathered puppet with his legs together, and extended before him. The left leg was oddly several inches longer than the right. The grotesque disconnect between shin and knee socket was clearly to blame for the obvious incongruence. How the knight was not writhing in anguish was perhaps a testament to his iron-like resolve. "Saeva, would you be a dear and heal me up, please?" he asked, tapping the side of his neck with a hiccup. An empty bottle of wine kicked out from beside him and began to roll down the motte's semi-steep grade.

"As you wish, my friend," said the lampyr to the knight.

"Blessings upon thee, friend," Vashal replied with unmistakable relief in his voice. He abruptly straightened up and cocked his head at Saeva. "But what of your wounds? Who will heal you?"

Saeva was pulling the long strands of Vashal's hair aside and bundling them in his hand. "In healing, so we heal," he intoned the old adage. "Now hold still, you are about to feel a bit of pressure..."

The strength was returning to Tamarah's limbs, and with a trembling hand, she reached out to Bactaal. The dragoon received her hand and hoisted her to her feet.

"How far is the fort?" she asked the warriors in gold.

Laiernaten responded first. "This long-abandoned tower was built as a watch for the knights of Navarene," he said with upraised eyes.

"I like this one," Bactaal remarked, scraping his chin with admiration. "Prepared to rejoin already?"

Tamarah, who had been plucked from death's warm embrace only moments prior, was indeed prepared for another go. She nodded her agreement and repeated her question, "how far?"

Grinning at Bactaal, Laiernaten spoke, "I like this one as well." Turning to Tamarah, he answered her question, "not far, not far at all."

A raised root hooked Ector's toe after he hurdled a fallen log, causing the knight to stumble, though he managed not to fall. He was returning to Flya after reaching the road, as requested. While en route, however, the sounds of the battle were abruptly swallowed, giving way to a disturbing silence.

The enemy must have claimed their quarry! A tremor of despair issued up from his toes, vibrating his bones, and eventually took hold of his chest. He found it difficult to breathe.

The knight continued running back to the laif, drawing in ragged breaths, rapidly losing himself to hopelessness. Through the leaves, he spied the laif waiting against the same mottled elm.

"It was quiet," he said, bending over, both hands gripped to his thighs as he sucked air. "The ramparts were silent."

Startled from her lean, the laif rocked forward and met the knight. "What do you mean by *silent?*" she demanded.

"The bows stopped!" Ector's face was undone by distress, "I fear..."

Flya began rubbing the knight's back in a comforting circular pattern.

"I fear that they are all dead," Ector admitted after a moment.

"How can you be certain?"

The knight shook his head. His words had run dry.

"So you don't know for sure?" She bolted upright and looked at the elm. "Hurry up, will you?" she yelled, "my friends are dying down here!"

The echo of her shout reverberated into the distance, and in its wake an uncomfortable silence hung. The laif immediately regretted her outburst, feeling a whining whelp.

"If I told you," a small voice began, somewhere behind her. "That my pain is greater than yours—"

Flya whirled around to locate the speaker. The voice continued, "it does not make your pain any less relevant."

A retinue of armoured faeries and wisps hovered amongst the boughs.

"I'm sorry, I did not mean any—"

Without a fractional drift in their formation, the ten small knights fluttered down to the laif.

A faery among the host shook her head. "Lead us..." she said.

"And we will follow," a wisp concluded.

Flya and Ector crossed the roadway seemingly without detection. No shouts or flares went up, and not one pointy icicle rained down upon their heads.

Dusk was upon them, and the small company kept their distance from the fort walls, which appeared empty upon each careful glimpse. Favorable indeed, but also highly suspicious. Ector had been concerned that the sentinels would easily spot the glowing fae but the fae knights easily reduced their radiance to that of a lowly torch bug. The knight admired the tactic, but with the gathering darkness, part of him wished for their full glow. His human eyes did not have the sharp night vision that Flya and the fluttering knights possessed.

One of the wisps that had been sent to scout returned.

"Lady Flya," the knight said gravely, hovering with a hand to the pommel of his sword. This solemn wisp had the head of a nightjar, which was a rather stern-looking bird to begin with, and only added to his somberness. "I believe we have discovered the site of the skirmish…" he trailed off, tightening his hooked beak.

"Yes?" Flya encouraged the wisp to continue, waving an impatient hand. "Go on."

"My lady," the wisp's eyes were buttoned to the ground. "One of your knights was claimed in the conflict."

The laif's mouth wrinkled at the sides. "First of all, they are not my knights, Sir…?"

"Sir Ankoreth," the wisp volunteered.

"Yes, Ankoreth," the laif repeated, drawing a breath. "Man or laif?"

"That we could not determine," the wisp replied. "The body is…" he was reluctant in the recounting.

"Lead us there."

Ankoreth bowed brusquely and set off. Flya eagerly followed the wisp, and Ector hurried behind.

When the fae that swirled around the laif and knight paused to indicate the trail of dead, they slowed, drawing closer together. Drifting at the peak of a hillock ahead was another wisp, the other scout, bobbing in place over a particular patch.

Ankoreth appeared suddenly before Flya. "The knight fell upon the knoll," he said, gesturing toward the other scout, "Sir Delevast is marking the place."

Ector and Flya approached the tangle of bodies. Ector instantly recognizing the fallen knight. "Geoffrey!" he gasped, careful not to shout.

"I'm sorry for your loss, Ector," Flya said gently, secretly relieved the dead ally was not Saeva. "But we should not linger here." She turned to Delevast. "Are you sure that this is the only body that is not archenlaif among this mess?"

The wisp, whose head was that of a sooty owl, peered upward. "No, my lady," he replied dourly. "But this is, as you adequately voiced, quite the mess."

Ector sadly stepped around the body of his fellow knight and overtook the hillock. "It looks like they used this mound as cover," he noted. "There's a lot of scrapes and evidence of battle." His fingers traced the gouges.

"That's also a bit of blood," Ankoreth said, admiring a dark patch impossible for Ector to distinguish. The wisp landed on Ector's shoulder, uninvited, but the knight did not mind. "Beyond us there are horse tracks," Ankoreth revealed, pointing behind them. "A pair of them. Laif-bred judging by how they manage the terrain."

Flya bounded past the hillock. "Should we follow?" she asked, inspecting the hoof marks. As if in answer, a swelling clamor suddenly emanated from the interior of the fort.

A pattering of rain began to slap the leaves above their heads.

The gates! Flya's mind reeled. She drew the bodkin at her hip and sliced her hand, lifting the wound to allow the blood to collect in her palm. Returning the bodkin to its sheath, she shrugged her bow into her hand, and worked the grip into the tacky blood, giving herself a sure handhold.

"Ector!" she shouted, striding in the direction of the road.

The knight heaved himself over the berm and hurried to catch up.

"Take up your bow," the laif commanded as the knight drew to her side.

The fae swirled and dipped around her, awaiting her instruction. "My fae knights," she said, turning. She punched a finger toward the spire. "Take that tower!"

The radiant knights bolted for the heights.

Ankoreth still clung to Ector's shoulder, the last fae to take flight, and he turned to the knight. "I pray the Creator see you through this, Sir Ector."

"I pray he do the same for you," replied Ector. A moment of understanding passed between the knights, and the wisp bent at the knees and surged upward, joining the rest of the fae.

The fae hurtled toward the witch in her spire. Miles below, Ector and Flya tore through the forest, striving to reach the west side of the roadway.

Flya slowed and frantically waved at a nearby tree, urging Ector take cover behind it. "If we can halt them just a little bit," she said, pressing her chest against the tree, and angling her head out to survey the road, "maybe we can bring their numbers down enough for your knights to deliver a healthy blow?"

The archenlaif vanguard had been distracted by something from the opposite side of the road, but the rest of the army continued to march forward. From Flya's vantage point, she saw two archenlaives fall backward, the surrounding company moving to brace their fall. Another caught an arrow below the jaw, and fell to his knees, never rising again.

Taking full advantage of the occasion, the laif loosed arrows into the backs of the enemy. One by one they toppled onto each other, creating panic within the ranks. Ector joined, snapping off several shots, though he admittedly brought more distraction than death. The front archenlaives whirled around in panic, halting their progress. The archenlaives near the gates gathered themselves, preparing to mount a focused charge into the forest. But suddenly, bulwarks of ice burst up from the road's border, effectively shielding the army's flanks.

The drizzle seemed to be growing irritable. The drops grew in size, dragging leaves from branches, smacking waves into puddles. In moments, monsoons scoured the forests, but left the marching army completely dry.

"She's going to turn the forest to ice!" Flya screamed. Water poured down her face and glazed across her teeth.

Ector could only stare back in shock. Before another thought passed behind his eyes, a familiar baritone sliced through the dense air.

Ancel's horn!

He turned and ran, glancing back briefly. The disbelieving expression painted on Flya's face was something that he would never forget.

17

❦

His tunic clung to him like a second skin. He doubted that it would ever be dry again. His sodden boots felt weighted, and his socks slid and burped with each footfall. Blisters were something that he could look forward to in the future. *If there was a future.* For the first time in his life, Ector welcomed the thought of dealing with blisters.

He shifted the trajectory of his course when he felt that he had gained enough ground from the enemy. Banking left, he exited the forest, choosing the dry terrain of the roadway. He did not look back.

The gradual upward slope of the road would eventually lead to a bridge, and after that the road would open up to a meadow. Within the meadowland the remainder of Benwick's forces waited. He had been instructed to signal their charge if they had not caught it on the winds.

As his first soggy steps overtook the stone bridge, he leapt onto the parapet. The knights of Benwick had indeed heard their Lord's call and were eagerly plunging across the bridge. Ector's breath caught in his throat as he watched the warriors whip past him. It was merely eight knights storming down toward an army of well over two hundred. One might believe that they had victory in hand by the way they charged forward. But Ector knew better.

"See you in Avalon, sisters and brothers," he said, the striking of hooves upon stone drowning his voice. Soon they were well past him, over the bridge, and fanning out to form a single wave. "Into the flames..." he murmured. After a brief pause, the young knight sprinted across the parapet, tearing off to complete his mission.

Cutting a course through the tents, Ector delivered on his promise to warn the wounded red knight. Rushing past, he lifted his voice, "We're fallen, Raymond!" he called, swiping the canvas as he passed. Not waiting for a response, he continued to race onward. The ward was still a ways off, and every hiccup of time that Benwick bought was precious.

Sir Belfast spurred his charger, leaning forward in his saddle to pat her neck with his free hand, knowing that she was aware to their impending fate. Animals did not need to understand arithmetic when facing such odds.

The archenlaif army was a dark ribbon against the falling night, spreading toward them, permeating the entire span of the roadway. As they pressed on, the bordering forest was buffeted from the heavens. Tree boughs bucked and chopped at the tremendous rainstorm, and the trees, engaged in their dance, reminded the old knight of the joyful crowds from tourneys past. Under his dropped faceplate, Belfast grinned as tears began to roll down his face.

Abruptly, the rains ceased. The trees began to recover, straightening their posture, returning to form. To Belfast, it appeared that they were now offering a farewell salute.

Raising a palm in disbelief, Flya barked a laugh borne of pure incredulity. Her little flock of knights had somehow done it! In exhilaration, she rained arrows upon the archenlaives no longer guarded by the rapidly dissolving ice shields. Soon her quiver was empty, but she had retrieved Ector's quiver. There were only a dozen shafts remaining, but she would savor each one.

From the east side of the road, Ancel and Sandrin had taken up their bows, renewing their effort. The archenlaif numbers were decreasing with each bow twang. In truth, it registered as merely a small dent, considering their numbers. But each time an arrow smote down another foe, Flya could not deny the grim satisfaction that she experienced.

She reached to draw another arrow from Ector's quiver, but her hand registered only blank space. "It was fun while it lasted, I suppose," she said, drawing her bodkin. The self-inflicted wound on her hand had just begun the healing process, but the laif halted that, slowly carving the blade, renewing the flow once again. She worked the scarlet trail into her palm as if it was pine tar.

Looking toward the spire, she drew her sword, the bitter steel flashing in the moonlight. "It has come to this," she laughed, breaking for the enemy's flank.

"Swear to me," said Ancel, gripping Sandrin's mantle, "that you will cleave at least ten skulls before you pass from this existence."

Sandrin laughed and seized his Lord's hand. "Sure thing," he agreed. "As long as you cleave twenty."

"Twenty? Not a problem," Ancel smirked. "I plan on culling the entire host."

Raymond had been enjoying the most luxurious of dreams. He was inside an open-air temple, surrounded by the most exquisite laives. The cleanest, bluest skies stretched above him, and the most temperate of breezes drifted through the windows. Exotic fruits and perfectly spiced meats aplenty were offered to him upon silver trays. And the raiment worn by the serving laives, well, that was not very plenty. It was all so pleasant, and his belly never seemed to fill uncomfortably no matter how much food he shoveled down his gullet. Endless, impeccable joy abounded, with nary a hitching step or a bolt through the back.

Then—"We're fallen, Raymond!" upended everything. Scandalously dressed laives and fancy sauces went flying into the fathomless atmosphere, lost forever.

He shot up from his bedroll. "Ector, you prat!" he cursed, waking with rancor. He felt as if during his sleep some jerk had swapped the bones of his back with sharpened fragments of glass. He wanted nothing more than to return to that dream, and he swore that he could still taste the faintest notes of wine upon his tongue.

A whittled lance proved to be an adequate walking crutch, and the red knight staggered toward the bridge to observe the battle.

"Not many people get to enjoy the luxury of watching their death rush to meet them," he joked to himself, moving faster than his body desired.

He stood upon the apex of the bridge, finding it to be the perfect vantage point. And, honestly, he had no desire to venture any further. He watched the knights, far below, tunneling down the path, seemingly uncaring that it would lead to their end.

His eyes flicked to the forest with the realization that he would be able to hide when the knights of Benwick fell. It was always good to have an escape plan. Though his wings had been clipped, metaphorically speaking, he would actually survive this. *However...* his mind wandered back to the forest daemons, or wraiths, or whatever those enraged spirits were, that had nearly snuffed him out. If Saeva had not been there to warn him...

His attention snapped back to the road. The knights were now only forty paces from the army, barreling forward fast as ever. Several forms cleared the forest from the east and west banks, and charged the enemy flanks. He recognized Flya's gait immediately, rushing from the west, but wasn't sure who the two knights opposite were.

Eleven, Raymond counted, scratching his eyebrow. *Eleven against a garrison of archenlaif knights.* He had never been much of a numbers sort of man, but he did favor odds. And these odds were beyond hopeless.

Biting down and settling his trembling chin, the red knight began to cross the bridge.

Twelve! he thought, hobbling down the road to join the war for Camelot.

Sandrin fell almost immediately. Amidst the bewildering confusion of battle, Ancel struck at knees, bringing archenlaives down. The ones who were responsible for taking Sandrin no longer enjoyed the privilege of drawing breath. He scoured the ground where his companion had collapsed but could not find him.

Gripping his longsword with both hands, the Lord of Benwick pressed forward. In his periphery, he saw his charging knights now seconds from impact.

Feeling his right arm tugged, he pivoted, smiting the foe with the pommel of his sword. Blood burst from the air holes on the caved-in visor, and the archenlaif stumbled back. Ancel pressed forward again, swinging a circular overhead arc, managing to create space before the inevitable. It would not be long before the archenlaives would overtake him. He could feel them enveloping him, subsuming him like a river coming from thaw.

Without warning or direction, the Benwick horses suddenly reared and broke. Their hooves scrabbled at the stone as they shrieked in panic. From the west, remnants of archenlaif armour could be seen peppering the night sky. A pair of golden warriors appeared, mounted upon daemon-laif mares, and dispatched the archenlaif vanguard. They flashed past Ancel, their heavy spears passing a hair's breadth from his scalp. Regrouping and turning upon the east bank, one of the warriors flashed a salute at Ancel, then spurred his horse for another tilt.

Breaking free from the melee, Ancel ran across the road to his knights who were striving to bring their horses to heel. "Strike!" he shouted, waving his sword as a banner. "Gather yourselves and strike after their next row!"

Several knights heard the order and hurried to obey. "Assemble!" one shouted, leading the knights back onto the road.

Ancel turned back to the clashing of steel. He squinted for a moment, finding Sir Tamarah fighting side-by-side with Flya. And somehow, Sandrin, with blood dampened hair, had returned to his feet and was embroiled along with them. It was all he needed to see. Bloody purpose flooded his veins. He waited for the proper moment. The golden warriors carved another swathe through the army, and, in their wake, Ancel surged forward, stepping into the gap that had formed. Almost as if he wielded magic of his own, Ancel whirled from his feet, spiraling downward to his knees, a savage pirouette that cleaved through steel and flesh. Stepping to his left with expert timing, he moved to avoid Benwick's charge. The center ranks of the enemy army burst apart like a freshly opened wound.

Ancel was fairly certain he had not been seriously injured. Scraped and bruised, yes, but his suddenly clammy tunic gave him pause. Amidst the screams of wounded, between the ringing and scraping of steel, a gentle plinking caused Ancel to blink.

The sky was weeping once again. Ancel cursed and flung himself deeper into the scrum, aiming to reach Sandrin. If he was to die upon this field impaled by ice, then he wanted to at least share his final moments with a friend.

"That coward karbaled," Raymond muttered, raising a palm to the sky. "Every fucking time."

He was still far from harm, slowly hobbling his way to war. From the angle of the road's gentle decline, he caught the unmistakable sight of what he believed must be the karbaled. A bluish feminine creature within a protectorate of black armoured knights strode beneath the fort's gated threshold. She now had an expansive view of the battlefield, which, as far as Raymond was concerned, was not at all a good thing.

The golden knights had wisely returned to the forest from whence they had come. Their surgically precise strikes had taken a decent toll on the archenlaif advance.

Now the remaining brave eight were gradually being swallowed by the archenlaif force. One by one they fell, unseated by halberds or pulled down by grasping armoured fists. Two remained seated, fighting frantically, and Raymond heaved a ragged sigh. The army abruptly parted for the knights, opening a sinister path that led directly to the feet of the karbaled. Believing that they could turn the tide, the brave duo drove their mounts forward.

The karbaled's retinue did not even pause. She snapped a gesture, a simple flip of her wrist, and two pillars of ice shot up from the wet stone. The horses suffered first, pierced at their bellies. The ice penetrated through the animals' flesh and bone, and skewered the riders. The tips of the pillars continued up to puncture through their chins, lifting their helms free.

Raymond gasped in horror.

Flicking her wrist back the other direction, the knights were instantly encased in solid crystalline ice. As she passed them, she lifted her chin, as if in boast, and the fresh statues crumbled to powder. An improper and vulgar burial for knights so bold, but this was war, not the classroom.

The path sealed shut, and the karbaled became a singular fleck of pale blue against a sea of glassy moonlit armour. Ignoring a minor skirmish to their right, the karbaled ordered the force to renew their march. She did not seem remotely concerned that Benwick had not been completely vanquished.

The distinct flashing of steel caught Raymond's attention, and he focused on it, wondering who might still be fighting. *Any moment now,* Raymond speculated. *She's going to put up a barricade, or worse, punch a wall of icy lances through their chests. Any moment now...*

"Any moment now!" Ancel shouted. He had hewn a path to the others. Sandrin appeared delusional from his wounds, yet still bore his weapon. Tamarah miraculously was in fighting form, and Flya was a tapestry in motion.

"My Lord," Sandrin wheezed, drawing behind Ancel and Flya. "I need a breather."

"How are you still alive?" Ancel asked, deflecting blows.

"I'm still alive?" Sandrin gasped, doubling over in an attempt to gulp as much air into his lungs as possible. From the right, Tamarah reappeared, lugging herself back from the fight. She joined Sandrin, seeking the last shred of refuge.

Steadily, Flya and Ancel were driven back.

The karbaled seemed to be floating past them, carried upon the shoulders of the knights beneath her.

"Any moment now!" Ancel repeated, waiting for the frozen attack.

She was not too far from his reach. If he surged toward her, however, he would leave Sandrin and Tamarah vulnerable. Yet if he succeeded and ended the icy terror, Benwick's sacrifice would not have been in vain. The battlefield would be leveled. Tintagil and Ghore would present a fair showing, Ancel prayed, and this conflict would perish along with the spellcaster.

Flya could sense the knight balking beside her. "Do it!" she encouraged, nodding toward the karbaled.

He parried an archenlaif's downward strike, navigating the blade down and away, and whirled to the foe's rear. Ancel met Flya's eyes, and placed a kick directly into the archenlaif's back, sending him into the laif's waiting blade.

No longer wavering, Ancel sprung toward the karbaled, cleaving and sundering each foe that stood in his path. He had yet to encounter an enemy that was his equal on this battlefield. And still, the karbaled did not seem to notice his approach.

An unseen dagger licked out from a dying knight, bringing Ancel to one knee. He rebounded, but his steps became hampered.

The karbaled was merely two sword strokes away. He staggered but carried himself forward. Pivoting on his damaged calf, the exquisite pain collapsed half his body. The sliver of a shimmering blade coursed toward his face, and Ancel gracelessly rolled, avoiding the assault by fractions. He rose and planted his trailing foot but found his heel frozen in place.

The army was backing away, opening ground for the stage.

Ancel gazed upward, meeting the eyes of the karbaled.

She posed with an upraised hand, signifying armistice.

"I want you to understand," she began, her voice chilling the night air. She lowered her hand and pressed it to her sternum, her exposed flesh a striking pallid blue, nearly that of the sky. This was not a creature native to the planes of man. "This army surrounding you is only the faintest of waves. Behind this, a rolling ocean awaits. You are receiving merely a paltry taste of what is to come."

Ancel had to give her credit, she knew how to stick with a theme.

He cleared his throat. Every minute he could stall, was a minute saved for Camelot. "Well, behind me is a..." *What's that word? Not canyon, no, not gorge... oh, yes!* "A dry gulch. Parched paths. Scorched soil."

The bridge of the karbaled's nose crinkled.

"Burnt bracken," he continued, beginning to run out of alliteration. "Crispy... curtains?"

Seeming to savor the moment, the karbaled's lips curled upward. "Do you see now," she shouted, addressing the dark host, "with your own eyes, that humans were designed for labor? That they were created for service. Created to be under thumbs."

Keep her talking as long as you can! Ancel reminded himself. *Prevent them from gaining more ground.* "Under whose edict?" he demanded insolently, jerking his leg in an effort to free his foot from its icy prison.

The karbaled peered at Ancel with a flat stare. "This freedom you enjoy is blasphemy."

"I'm not convinced that there's any truth to that."

"Dissenters," she spat. "Are destined. To drown."

Rain striking the flagstones emphasized the hush that fell. In the distance a wolf howled, filling the void.

The karbaled's countenance shifted, and she unexpectedly appeared oddly rattled.

Standing in his soaked clothes, Ancel glanced to his companions by the wayside. They were each disarmed and on their knees. Damaged and pitiful. "What are you waiting for?" the knight asked, steeling himself for the end.

Seemingly without provocation, barriers suddenly flung up around the blue spellcaster. Flinging himself backwards, Ancel miraculously avoided getting caught inside the barrier despite his foot remaining tethered to the stone. He swallowed a scream, falling and grasping the twisted bones above his ankle.

The archenlaif knights rushed past him, ignoring him, forming a barrier around the clearly frightened karbaled.

Another wolf lifted his voice to the heavens, the sound emitted from the other side of the road. And now leagues closer.

Ector finally reached the ward. His tattered mantle had begun to dry, but the night breezes icily branded every wet patch on his tunic.

It was the most tormented waiting of his life. His landsmen, brother, and Flya were dead or dying as he stood idly by. He restlessly snapped branches between his fists, discarding the splintery remnants. As he plucked another branch from a nearby poplar, he heard a snapping, not of his making, and it jolted him to attention.

A laif stood on the opposite side of the ward, a torch battered his armour with light.

"Elithiel?!" Ector cried in disbelief, dropping the branch in his hand.

The laif nodded at the knight, and unsheathed his dagger to begin the ward's blood offering.

"W-wait," Ector stammered. "What are you doing all the way..."

That could only mean.

The most magnificent of laif-bred chargers stepped into the meager torchlight.

All breath escaped Ector, and the knight's knees buckled.

Before the notion had fully formed, he exhaled. "The King?"

18

A rushing sound from the forest behind made Flya believe that the karbaled had summoned an ice river to come and claim her. But the manner in which the archenlaif knights backed away, led the laif to believe otherwise.

It was most certainly a wave, but not the sort of wave that a karbaled could summon.

Flya dropped instinctively to her stomach, her companions following suit. Sandrin in particular appeared in rough shape, and the laif was unsure if the knight would rise again. His shoulders and neck had been torn open, and with his cheek pressed to the dirt, his lips puckered like a fish struggling to breathe.

The laif believed that it must be the glorious gold knights approaching, coming back for another sweep. Or perhaps they had merely been the scouts for an imposing golden army, sent to weigh and measure the enemy force. Lying on the ground, she could make out distinct footfalls and snapping underbrush.

That doesn't sound like hooves, she thought, rolling her head to raise a different ear to the sky.

The karbaled was blocked from sight, concealed behind a barrier of ice. The archenlaif force, completely halted, was braced for an assault, raising their weapons and shields in defensive postures.

Flya could smell them before she saw them. *Wet dog?* her nostrils flared.

Moments later, the underside of a great silvery wolf leapt over her head. Flya buried her face to avoid the muddy debris and pebbles that scoured the air behind him.

At first, Raymond believed that the avalanche issuing from the forest was those ethereal wraith-daemons, *the Daeban*, as Saeva had called them. But he was mistaken. The forms pouring from the east and west, converging at the center of the road were not nearly as endless as the Daeban.

"Fuck me," Raymond hovered a fist before his mouth. "Those are werewolves..."

A tremendous silver werewolf led the pack from the west. In a flash, he smashed his shoulders against the karbaled's ice blockade. The distinct sound of cracking glass could be heard for miles. With a seething renewal of rage, the werewolf reached into the gap and sundered the ice. The karbaled pressed herself against the opposite wall, utterly terror stricken.

Her panicked scream was violently ripped short, and the rain immediately dispersed. All of her frozen constructs crumbled, wafting into mist.

The archenlaives response was anything but cowardly. Notoriously silent, the dark laives rarely shattered the air, even when facing imminent peril. But screams of indignation rent the air that night. The archenlaives set upon the incursion in a vengeful frenzy, which the werewolves were more than happy to meet.

Feeling out of place, Raymond set aside his broken lance and lowered himself to the stone. It was a painful slide, and sitting up was halfway to anguish, but he refused to lay down. He locked his knees to his chest and resumed his vigil.

Ancel tried to stand, but both of his legs were useless. One was twisted at the ankle and the other was streaming blood. He could feel the loss with each pulsation from his chest.

The great werewolf, after relieving the karbaled of her head, looked at the Lord of Benwick with faint recognition in his eyes. In the moment before the beast turned and spewed karbaled gore over his shoulder, Ancel felt sure there was a connection between them.

The archenlaives parted the air with fury and filled it with blades, bearing down upon the werewolves. A channel formed between the archenlaif forces, and Ancel found himself at the epicenter. To his left and right were archenlaif backs, engaged in battle, and surging forward and backward, much like the waves of the sea. The knight rolled onto his knees and searched for the last place he had seen his allies. His eyes combed through the flurry of legs and falling bodies, hoping desperately for a sign of Sandrin.

Two sets of hooves brushed up along the roadside and golden sabatons hurriedly splashed through the mud. Reaching down, the golden knights retrieved two sodden bodies and eased them up and out of Ancel's view. He thought one of those rescued appeared to struggle against it, but Ancel was not sure. Between the flickering movements of battle, he was unable to distinguish whom the knights had saved. And as swift as their arrival, the horse's legs disappeared from sight. Taking in a battered breath, Ancel realized exactly who had not been rescued.

Sandrin lifted himself onto his elbows, locking eyes with Ancel, an anguished grin painting his face. He shook his head slowly, knowing that Ancel would try to reach him. "Do not!" his lips formed. He repeated the phrase over and over in the hopes that it would be acknowledged.

Ancel understood the message, choosing to ignore it. He tried to stand, but collapsed.

Sandrin pounded the soft earth. "Do not!" he yelled, vehemently shaking his head. "Do not! Do not!"

With an effort that would make an angel weep, Ancel crawled through the battle. Following the man's trajectory with his eyes, Sandrin shuddered, draping his head in defeat.

Reaching the discarded bastard sword he had been edging toward, Ancel planted it into the ground, using it as a walking cane. He dragged himself toward Sandrin, his useless ankle scudding behind. Focusing all his strength into his fists, Ancel clenched the sword's pommel, slamming it into stone and drawing himself to it. He duplicated this action over and over, nearing the fallen knight. Sandrin, still on his belly, continued to plead to his Lord to stay away.

An archenlaif with a werewolf fused to his chest somersaulted backward, abruptly parting Ancel from his sword, dashing him onto the stone. The knight could feel his ribs cracking under the archenlaif's heavy fluted armour. A vicious tumult ensued on top of him, splintering Ancel's ribs to the point of agony. Suddenly the werewolf hefted the dying archenlaif upward, instantly relieving the sharpest of the pain.

Breathing had become very difficult, and Ancel batted away the tunnels that chased his vision. His left lung felt deflated and he could only sip air into his throat. Finding the sword once again, he returned to his feet with difficulty. He felt almost feverish and was beyond dizzy, the sky pressing down on him. The stars themselves seemed to squeeze like a vice.

Through the madness, Sandrin was miraculously standing. He teetered on his feet and waved a farewell.

Ancel wanted to call out to him, but he was unable to gasp in enough air for speech.

It was the last he saw of dear Sandrin.

Ancel released his sword and swooned, finally surrendering to mortality's curse of rest.

If it had been possible for Ector to call out to his brother through the void dividing them, he would have. "Fall back!" he would have told him. Or, "Flee to the forest! Relief is nigh!" But it was not possible. Instead he had stepped aside, allowing passage for the King and his knights.

After safely crossing the ward, the King had spurred his mount forward and tore off for Navarene. His knights, all astride laif-bred horses, streamed through the thick of the forest, following close behind their liege.

Elithiel approaching Ector, leaned a shoulder to a nearby tree. "I imagine that you were dispatched to deliver a message?" he asked, wrapping the fresh cut on his wrist.

"Yes," Ector agreed. He flinched, his answer interrupted by the sudden falling of branches over his head.

"Gargoyles," Elithiel explained sedately. "They like to skim the treetops, for whatever reason."

"Gargoyles have come as well?" Ector asked in awe, his eyes dazzled.

Elithiel shrugged. "The King's not playing nice," he said. "So what was the message?"

"Doesn't really matter anymore," replied Ector. "The archenlaives have probably reached Irphen's Downfall by now. Their force is down to less than two hundred."

The laif whistled and bounced his shoulder from the tree. "Early dispatches estimated six hundred," he said, straightening up. "I saw at least three hundred with my own eyes on that first night's assault."

"Plus, there was an ice summoner."

Elithiel appeared concerned, but not the least bit surprised. "Ah." Elithiel nodded. "I thought I sensed a bit of sorcery in the air."

"The King should—" Ector began.

"The King should have this well in hand," Elithiel interrupted, gesturing at the garrison of azure armoured laives marching past.

"Are those?" said Ector in awe.

"Those would be Amyr's personal sentinels," Elithiel confirmed, gazing down, admiring his own gauntlet. "On loan from the First Laif himself." He followed the passing army with his eyes. "If the King doesn't strike the enemy down on his first run, I would be shocked. But," the laif continued, slapping Ector's shoulder and pointing back beyond the ward, "following Amyr's force, we have Tintagil and Ghore," the laif paused for a moment, considering, " and then Rhionydd and Orkney, and behind them, I believe it's Celliwig? Don't hold that against me if it's not. And after that..."

Ector was no longer paying attention. *The entire realm came!* he thought in disbelief. *Ancel, for all his wisdom, didn't see this coming. If only he was still alive to see how foolish he had been.* Ector's smile turned grim, realizing that his brother had sacrificed all of Benwick for nothing. *If he survives, he should see the gallows for this!*

"The werewolves put up a good showing," Raymond said to himself with admiration.

Upon entering the fight, the beasts were already vastly outnumbered, and inevitably, their numbers dwindled.

The red knight watched another werewolf driven to ground. *If only they would work together,* he thought as archenlaif spears began to thrust down upon the fallen beast. Detached from the pack, a lone werewolf was slain easily.

The silver one, that huge monster, had claimed a great deal of skulls on his own, but even he was being driven back. He bellowed, attracting the remainder of the pack to him. Stragglers strove to join the pack, urgently extracting themselves, but more were cut down in the attempt.

A good showing indeed, Raymond reflected, finding his makeshift crutch and preparing to move. He had been sedentary for too long. As he got to his feet, his wounds began to tear open once again. The spark inside of him had been dampened, and he decided to opt for the safety of the forest. Glancing down the road to the battle, he saw the tail of the last werewolf retreating under the immense canopy. The few surviving werewolves had many wounds to lick.

Leaving behind a field of broken bodies, the archenlaives continued onward. Why they did not simply turn and regroup in the fort, Raymond could not fathom. Strategically, that would be a sound decision, but this enemy often did not seem to adhere to logic. Or perhaps, they simply knew something that Raymond did not.

The red knight hurried as best he could toward the nearest thicket, having no interest in meeting the same fate as his most recent companions. He thought it rather funny that he had never considered Fenrirfang to be a safe place, not by any stretch of the imagination. Yet, here he was, seeking its embrace. *From one treacherous path of vipers to a forest brimming with venom,* he thought, exiting the moonlight. The murky darkness within the forest, as unnerving and perilous as it was, felt almost welcoming.

Clattering armour sounded off parallel to Raymond's position. The army was now passing where he had watched the ruinous melee over the past hour or so. *Had it been merely an hour?* the red knight wondered, doubting his senses. The position of the moon assured him that it had not been nearly as long as he first presumed.

Acting against his better judgment, he decided to shadow the archenlaives. Shambling from tree to tree was far easier than containing the yelps of searing pain that threatened to burst out. Swallowing down one such jolt, he whimpered and sagged against a tree steps from the edge of the forest, giving him a clear view of Irphen's Downfall. A few archenlaives searched the tents, seeking any craven soldiers that may be sheltering from the war. They did not understand that this was a Benwick encampment and scouring for cowards was a complete waste of time.

Raymond watched as the archenlaives navigated through the meadow with measured trepidation. An abundance of stonework and abandoned bulwarks dappled the space, supplying ample opportunities for ambush. These knights, since first laying siege to the fort had not had an easy go of things. They had dealt with sporadic sniper strikes and bold knights who seemed to never quite die completely. There had also been the mysterious golden warriors and their ferocious horses, followed by the unexpected werewolves assailing their flanks, and ultimately stripping them of their magical upper hand.

These guys have really been tossed to the wolves, Raymond snickered.

The forefront of the army began to split, and Raymond wagered that they were exercising some sort of formation shift. But then seemingly without provocation, the vanguard began to flee, barreling straight into the knights caught unaware behind them. The rearward knights lifted their visored helms to the cliffs overlooking the meadow, realization spreading at a startling rate. A few remained rooted in fright, sustaining buffeting blows from their comrades furiously rushing past.

Raymond eased himself forward, needing to see what had sent these warriors to flight. Whatever had caused this army to collectively piss their pants was not something he had any interest in encountering.

A mist dragon, maybe? Raymond speculated anxiously, craning his head under the canopy. *It must be something pretty huge...* "Blast!" he spat. He could not manage a clear view of the clifftop, and there was no way he was going to move any closer. With all the speed he could muster, which admittedly was very little, he turned tail and hurried away.

"I hope that monster isn't attracted to the smell of blood," he muttered, feeling his damp clothing sticking to his wounds as he plodded along with the agility of an old crone.

From atop the cliff, a horn belted out a valorous note.

It was a familiar note.

Raymond froze along his pathetic retreat, combing his mind. As the tone began to evaporate into the distance, he keyed in on it with a jolt of recollection. "The gallows!" he breathed in disbelief, sinking painfully onto a knee. "The crown."

Ancel felt weightless, stirring awake as gloomy figments of a night forest flashed past his blurry vision. The journey to Avalon was much more jarring than he had imagined it would be. The sages had determined ages ago that it would be a pleasant transfer across planes, near instantaneous. All pain would be discarded along with the mortal coil. But Ancel felt only inescapable pain. He gasped as his shattered ankle caught the trunk of a sapling.

"My apologies," a tender voice spoke. The voice was soft, but not nearly angelic enough for a courier of Avalon. "You will be with the others soon."

Wait a moment now, Ancel thought. *Am I not dead?* He wanted to give voice to his query, but his current riding position, belly pressed to a saddle, prevented him from conjuring the proper air. Amidst his personal debate, a tremor filled the air above his head. It was a grounding note that permeated the endless fronds and needles, providing an answer to his pressing riddle.

I am alive, he concluded bitterly. *Arthur, in perfect fashion, has arrived just in time to bury my knights.* He cursed and clenched his jaw. *You're welcome, prick.*

ACT TWO

"The annals would proclaim that King Arthur struck the decisive blow that drove the archenlaif incursion back from whence it had derived. His arrival, and his alone, had been what rescued the kingdom from slavery and slaughter. Though the retellings around the campfires and within the schoolhouses would not be in error—they would not be wrong at all. But like most of history, the dead cannot lend their voice for clarity...

Certainly the footnotes would mention the employment of gargoyles, which signified Arthur's abandonment of all defense in lieu of attack. A controversial decision, but time and time again we see how victory makes fools out of dissenters...

The rousing of Lord Amyr and his holy sentinels would also bear mentioning. For without him, the expedience of the King's travel would not have been possible."

-Excerpts retrieved from *The Sunset on Camelot*, courtesy Rouse Flanagan

19

Irphen's Downfall, two days after the King's victory.

"Where is my sister?" Carlysle asked no one in particular. The knight and her squire were ambling around the tents allocated for "the dying and the recovering." The moniker had first been used by a stern-faced lieutenant from Celliwig, whose jaw looked like it had seen one hundred punches. She had pointed a blood-encrusted cleaver toward the section of camp and hastily turned back to butchering a hare.

In front of the tents, a row of knights in their undergarments were sunning themselves, enjoying a bit of holiday. Each had been gifted with two dots, courtesy of a lampyr, on the side of their necks. Carlysle surreptitiously eyed the bottles the knights were drinking from, wondering about their contents.

"You blokes must be considered *recovering,* I assume?" she said, awkwardly rising on her tiptoes and tapping her neck. "Saw some battle did ya?"

The glances she received in return ranged from baleful to aggravated.

Carlysle's upper lip began to twitch. "What ya drinking?"

The knights resumed their activities, drinking and carrying on blissful conversations as if Carlysle did not exist.

"What my knight is trying to say," Stacey interjected, stepping up and attempting to salvage Carlysle's unskilled effort to ingratiate herself. "We are looking for her sister and we..." she trailed off, also totally ignored. The only directed response she received was one knight waving farewell between casual sips of her drink.

Stacey appeared ready to draw daggers, but Carlysle unexpectedly encouraged temperance. "Come," she commanded. "I'm sure there's more *intelligence* elsewhere among this camp." The pair turned and strode away.

Overhearing the pointed conversation, one of the knights gagged on a spit-take. He bucked forward and coughed while receiving helpful blows upon his back by his neighbor. "I'm alright, I'm alright," he croaked, tears welling in his eyes. "Wait a moment, please," he called, bounding to his feet.

Carlysle and Stacey turned, both glaring down their noses at the man.

The knight was clutching his chest, still fighting coughs. "In the wake of battle—" he stopped. His pitch was a higher octave than he desired, and he pounded his chest until he felt confident that he would no longer sound like a shrill goblin. "Many knights hold those who did not fight in low regard, and it's very clear that neither of you has recently seen war," he said, beaming at them, relieved that his voice had returned to his natural tenor. "Please don't take it personally."

"I don't give a shit about any of that," Carlysle said quickly, concerned that Stacey would employ unnecessary vulgarity. "I'm just looking for my sister."

"What does she look like?" The knight's eyes seemed on the verge of glassy. "I've seen a few pretty knights around camp, but none that quite match you."

Creator's crooked tusks! Stacey thought, but tried to temper her words, "Well, in her current state you may not have placed her in the *pretty* category."

The knight responded with a confused expression.

"My sister is a werewolf," Carlysle explained.

"Oh," he replied placidly. "Oh!" he repeated, clarity dawning on him as he sucked air between his teeth.

"What is it?" Carlysle demanded. Both women stepped closer to the scowling knight.

He scratched the back of his head. "I didn't actually see any of the werewolves in the battle. It was well before our army took to the field," he said, wincing. "I can't really say anything for certain, but I heard that not many of them made it out alive." His eyes carved channels in the grass, appearing ready to say more, but did not.

"Perhaps Jekar has had more luck," Carlysle said to her squire. She turned and half-heartedly thanked the knight, and made to depart.

"There are a few in the camp," the knight offered brightly before they could leave. "Werewolves," he expounded. "There are a few werewolves in the camp. They'll be more help than I have been."

Pausing her gait, Carlysle lifted her hand and gave the knight another flimsy wave. When they were out of his hearing, Carlysle turned to Stacey again. "Let's see if Sir Squeak's story checks out. Keep your eyes peeled for werewolves."

"Or my nose," said Stacey. "It's often easier to smell a werewolf."

Pavilions had been erected all around the camp, meticulously arranged throughout the meadow. Banners clapped the air before them, signifying households and lands. Innumerable tents stretched across the boundary, kissing the treelines, resembling a massive tourney ground. The scent of meat on spits stung the air, causing a careless passerby to recall their hunger. Steel rang upon steel as knights trained in designated areas, employing blunted weapons, aiming to keep their muscles lithe and ready. Smiths belted out the sounds of repair, stoking their forges, signaling their locations with heaven bound embers.

Carlysle and Stacey climbed atop the husk of an ancient watchtower to survey the grounds. Glancing at each other, they each resigned themselves to the hours of work that lay ahead.

"Are you hungry at all?" Carlysle asked, shielding her eyes, seeming to be looking for something in particular.

"I could eat."

"If you spot the black and green banners of home, let me know," said Carlysle. "Maybe we'll be able to score a morsel or two."

Stacey nodded and began scouring the banners. It did not take her keen eyes very long to complete her search. "Found it," she said with a hint of triumph. A solitary pennant with frayed edges was strung to a lance. "Oh my," she whispered, the triumph in her voice fading when she saw all that remained of Benwick's force.

Leaning in, Carlysle strove to see what her squire was regarding. "What's the matter?" she asked with concern.

"Let's go," Stacey shook her head as if wresting herself from a trance.

Carlysle blindly followed behind, sliding downward and leaping from the decaying parapet. She rushed to catch up. "What's the matter?" the knight repeated.

"You'll see."

After thirty rushing steps, the squire led her knight to a small fire surrounded by three tents. There was no one to tend the fire and the tents seemed barren. The space was deathly silent.

Carlysle looked around in confusion. "Where are we?"

Stacey reached out and snagged the frail pennant that dangled from a lance. "This is Benwick's encampment," she stated, releasing the cloth.

"Where's the rest of it?" Carlysle spun. "This must be a joke."

A woman groggily poked her head out from a nearby tent. "This is Benwick," she groaned. "Or what remains of it."

"Sir Tamarah?" Stacey gasped.

With the confusion that lingers right after waking, Tamarah's face tightened around her mouth. "Yes?" she asked, wobbling to her feet. Two distinct lampyr marks adorned her neck, and she wore an elegant sleeping gown that curled about her bare ankles.

That gown had to be a gift, Stacey guessed. The quality was far above a simple knight's station. "Do you not remember me?" she asked, still a bit distracted by the woman's garment. "I'm Sir Belfast's niece, Stacey. We've only met on maybe two occasions, but..." She faltered at Tamarah's expression. "What is it?"

"Your uncle," Tamarah shook her head. "He did not make it out of this one," she said, smiling sorrowfully. "Tough old man. Died honorably though."

Momentarily, the world seemed to upheave around the squire. "Did he die in battle?" she managed to ask, unsure of the etiquette.

"He did," Tamarah confirmed. "He fell during Benwick's final charge."

"My father must get word..."

Carlysle placed a steadying hand on Stacey's shoulder. "We will send a bird," she said reassuringly.

"Birds went out at sunrise," Tamarah said, turning back to her tent. "Allow me a moment, ladies, I'm beginning to catch a chill." The knight disappeared between the folds of the canvas and could be heard rummaging about inside.

The fire was bothering Carlysle, the way it flickered feebly. It was unseemly for a Benwick fire to behave so poorly. She gave Stacey's shoulder a squeeze before setting off in search of logs. Walking to the left, she noticed the nearest banners were emblazoned with the buttery gold of Tintagil.

"Nope!" Carlysle muttered, backing away. She skirted across Benwick's site as if she had stirred up a hornet's nest.

Seated on a stump by the fire, Stacey stared into the powdery ruins. After donning a tunic and hose, Tamarah joined the squire. She cocked an eyebrow at Carlysle rushing past them.

"What's with your knight?" she asked, prodding the dying embers.

Stacey was still in a daze. "I'm sorry, what was that?"

"Your knight," Tamarah repeated, pointing her stick at Carlysle. "What is wrong with her?"

"Oh, her," Stacey said, one corner of her mouth slanting into a smile. "She was banished from Tintagil for 'reasons.'"

Tamarah leaned back with her hands locked behind her knees. "Ah," she said, narrowing her eyes. "I see."

"My knight," Stacey began, quickly correcting herself, "*Sir Carlysle* is rather... unique."

"*That's* Sir Carlysle?" Tamarah blurted. "I have never had the pleasure of meeting her! But I have definitely heard quite a few tales about her. What's it like serving under such a notorious character?" she asked, swiveling her head toward the younger woman. "Stacey, was it?"

Stacey responded with a nod.

"Well, Stacey, I apologize for not remembering you." Tamarah sat up and wiped her hands together. "Hungry?" she asked, getting to her feet to retrieve a covered bin.

From nowhere, the clatter of a thousand spoons filled the air. The women snapped their attention to the racket, and Carlysle reappeared, stumbling toward them with an armful of dry logs.

"Who put that armour stand there?" Carlysle demanded, unlocking her elbows and dropping the logs. "I really should..." she indicated the steel arms strewn across the path and darted over to amend her mistake.

"Believe it or not," Stacey commented to Tamarah as she plunked a few logs onto the smoldering ashes, "she's sober."

Tamarah snorted a laugh. She was on her knees blowing life back into the flames. "I'd love to see her drunk then."

"No, you don't," Stacey assured her. "So, what's on the menu?"

Between gusts of air, Tamarah wrapped a hand around the bin and shoved it between Stacey's feet. "Coney and quail," she said. "Rangers killed 'em fresh this morning."

"Outstanding!" The squire peeled back the retaining cloth. "Who else will be joining us?" She fell silent, instantly regretting the question.

Tamarah sat up and her eyes grew unfocused.

"I mean, is there anyone else in the tents?" Inwardly she cursed, she was only digging the hole deeper. "Uh, that is to say, how much food should we cook?"

"Vashal, Ector, and Ancel," the knight recited dimly. "They are all who made it."

"Oh." Stacey's throat tightened.

"You won't need to set a place for them," Tamarah shook her head and spoke more clearly. "Ancel has refused the lampyr for now and is recovering over yonder," she gestured with her chin toward the furthest of the three Benwick tents. "Ector was keeping watch over his brother, but I do not know where he has gone off to. And Vashal is with the dragoons, I believe."

"Lord Ancel is right over there?" Stacey whispered. "Wait, did you say *dragoons?!*"

"Do you need a moment?" Tamarah chuckled, color returning to her cheeks.

Carlysle returned lugging a heavy cooking rack, and without any urging, she heaved it atop the flames. "If anyone asks," she said primly, "an archer from Garlot said it would be alright if we borrowed this contraption."

The women seared and devoured the game, greedily inhaling the meat as Tamarah regaled them of all she had witnessed. Carlysle and Stacey stared in rapt attention while their hands continuously hoisted food to their waiting mouths. The pair was enthralled by the tale and nearly forgot their goal, but when Tamarah mentioned the swift arrival of the werewolves, Carlysle nearly choked on her current mouthful.

"A bit of gristle," she gasped in a husky baritone. "That's all, really."

Tamarah's eyes darted to Stacey. "Will she be alright?"

"Probably not," Stacey replied, handing her knight a skin of water.

Carlysle sputtered and choked anew. "What in the—?!" she cried out, spewing the clear liquid from her nostrils. "That's not wine!" Betrayal was plastered to her face.

"It's water," Stacey said calmly, snatching the soaked skin from her knight's trembling hand.

"Don't ever do that to me again!" the knight scolded before turning to Tamarah and smiling sweetly. "Now what was that you were saying about werewolves?"

"Uh, yes," Tamarah gave Stacey an apologetic look and continued, "the werewolves appeared seemingly from nowhere. And there was this massive one, and I mean *massive*, who broke right through the ice witch's barricade and shredded her apart. It was downright grisly, believe me, but it was also pretty satisfying."

Carlysle nodded her head and sucked the sticky meat juice from a finger. "Oh yeah, whoa, that's pretty crazy," she said. "So, tell me where we can find these werewolves, eh?"

Tamarah, not nearly through recounting her tale, was caught off-guard by the question. "I'm sorry, what?" she asked, reaching for a crispy haunch upon the grate.

"The werewolves," Carlysle clarified. "Can you point me to the nearest one?"

Stacey slapped her knight's wrist with a rabbit leg. "What Carlysle is trying to say is—"

"I'm not trying," Carlysle interrupted, pausing to choke back another swig from the water skin. Through a pained grimace, she turned to Tamarah. "My sister is one of those avenging werewolves," she admitted, swiping her mouth. "And any help you can give would be greatly appreciated." She flashed Tamarah her brightest smile once again.

Taking a second to chew, Tamarah raised a finger and swallowed. "Just like Benwick," she said at length, gesturing to their barren surroundings, "those who fought in the battle before the king arrived…" She did not need to finish her statement.

"The werewolves perished?" Carlysle repeated.

"Most of them, yes."

"Can you tell me where they are?" Carlysle asked, her eyes feverishly rooting through the ashes.

A male voice spoke from beyond the group. "Corbin has been attached to Arthur's hip," Ancel said, freeing himself from his tent. "You may want to check with him," he added, ambling toward the fire with a crutch fused under his armpit.

Tamarah and Stacey shot to their feet. Carlysle gaped as if struck dumb.

"My Lord, you should not be up!" Tamarah blurted, rushing to his side. "Don't put any weight on it!"

"I'm bleeding famished," Ancel said, surveying the food upon the grate as Stacey rolled a stump over to him. "Is that quail?"

"Easy, easy," Tamarah cautioned, guiding the wounded knight down onto the seat. "That's quail, and that bit on the side is what's left of the coney."

Amidst the swirling movements to accommodate the Lord of Benwick, Carlysle remained fixed in place, looking very much like one caught in the petrifying glare of a cockatrice.

"My Lord," Stacey said, standing over his shoulder with her hands folded behind her back. The sight of him had suddenly uprooted all of her years of formal servant's training that she had thought buried years ago.

"Please, sit," Ancel stated, indicating the stump next to him with his heavily splinted leg. "There is no need for formality here. I will serve myself." He reached toward the grate, gritting his teeth, but the pain was too much.

Stacey collected a few morsels of quail, extricated the biggest hunks of rabbit, and bestowed the assortment upon her Lord with a dignified grace that surprised even herself.

"Gramercy," Ancel said, saluting the squire with a floppy bit of quail. He bit down and wrenched the flesh from the bone and paused as saliva flooded his mouth. With a predator's voracity, he ravenously picked the bones clean. "What?" he asked the staring women. "I haven't eaten in three days."

"Would you like more, my Lord?" inquired Stacey. The meager remnants upon the fire were now only a laughable offering.

Ancel leaned back and winced. "I believe restraint would be appropriate at the moment," he said, though his hunger had not been satisfied. "If I indulge any further, I fear I will break this crutch when I stand again."

Carlysle snorted and made a series of noises that resembled giggling.

Displaying the grace of a liege, Ancel pretended not to notice. Stacey, however, fixed her knight with a glare and snarled under her breath.

"Lord Ancel," Stacey said formally, while her lip steadily uncurled. "May I introduce my knight, Sir Carlysle, a knight born of your realm, who now bears the title of errant."

An elbow from her squire urged Carlysle to her feet.

"Please," Ancel interrupted Carlysle's movement and waved her back down. "No formalities here." He took a sip from the water skin and choked. "Is there no wine?"

"I know, right?" Carlysle muttered, meeting Ancel's eyes and instantly shying away from them.

"Tamarah," Ancel beckoned the knight. "I would fetch it myself, but current circumstances..." he looked to the crutch leaning against his shoulder. "I believe Lowthean's pavilion is well stocked. Can you see about procuring a few bottles?"

Before Tamarah could nod at her Lord's request, Stacey materialized next to her. "I will go with her, my Lord," she announced, smiling and hooking her wrist under Tamarah's elbow. "Four arms are better than two."

Ancel's brows knitted in amusement. "As you wish," he said. "Be sure to bring back at least one bottle of mead, if you please? If their seneschal, Sir Doncus, tries to tell you they have none, don't believe him. He pays their smithy to hide a spare locker of the nectar near his forge."

The pair set off toward the Lowthean banners, walking arm-in-arm, and Ancel turned his attention to Carlysle. "Sir Carlysle," he recounted her name as if in reprimand, folding his arms across his chest. "I owe my life to those werewolves. I would be more than happy to use my *limitless* resources to reunite the two of you." His use of the term "limitless," was, of course in jest, seeing as Benwick had been reduced to less than a pinky finger on the king's fist of war. He continued, "I have spent much of my time being unconscious, but I was almost fully awake yesterday when I received a field report, though, now that I think on it, it is more of a haze actually." He scratched his jaw and closed his eyes. "For now, as I am, I cannot offer much help, but when my brother returns, perhaps he will be able to lend a bit of clarity."

Ancel smiled at the knight, awaiting a response, but received only an awkward stillness instead. Fidgeting with the crossguard on her longsword, Carlysle stared into the flames. Her lips began to move but no sound came forth.

"I'm sorry," Ancel said, carefully adjusting his seat. "Did you say something?"

Carlysle gripped the collar of her tabard. "It's—it's hot," she stammered. "Daytime fires make me sweaty." She offered a frail smile and ducked her head, wishing she could evaporate with the smoke. "But, yes, yes, I look forward to meeting your brother..." she trailed off, "what's keeping that squire?"

A look of concern graced Ancel's face. "Are you going to be alright?"

"I shall, I shall," Carlysle returned, nodding.

Before yet another awkward silence could begin, Ector strode into the encampment. Beside him walked Flya, who seemed almost fully recovered from her wounds. The only field dressing on display was a clean bandage wrapped from her sword palm to her elbow. Otherwise, the laif appeared as fresh as usual. It was hard to believe that she and Ancel had partaken in the same battle, much less that she had been nearly as gravely injured.

"Oh, Ancel," the laif cooed. "When are you going to accept a lampyr?" She tilted her head, taking in the scratches and wounds that still marred his face. "And when are you going to get fitted for a proper helm?"

Ancel dismissed the second question and favored the first. "Once the lampyrs have tended to the rest of the wounded, I'll accept their service."

"How noble," Flya responded, tisking and shaking her head. The laif quickly averted her attention to their guest. "And who might you be?" she asked, plunking down on the stump next to Carlysle. "New here?"

"This is Sir Carlysle, an errant," Ancel introduced the knight, sensing her reluctance. "She is seeking her sister." Looking to Ector, he spoke again, "Perhaps you may provide her some assistance?"

"I would be delighted," Ector bowed slightly, inclining his head. "But first, let's get some more meat on this fire." He rubbed his hands together and retrieved another container of fresh meat, pausing to introduce himself and his laif companion.

The laif extended her wounded hand in greeting and Carlysle moved to lock wrists, but hesitated. "Um," she said, trying to maneuver her hand above the bandage.

"Just take it," Flya smiled, "you can't cause any more harm."

Carlysle gripped the cloth and tightened her grip. "I wouldn't be too sure about that."

Flya returned an equal squeeze and relinquished her hold on the other woman's wrist. "I like you," she admitted. "And she's pretty! Isn't she, Ancel?"

Ancel did not skip a beat. "Quite," he replied, not taking the laif's bait.

Not to be out-played, Flya continued. "But not your type, eh?"

"Not necessarily."

The tips of Carlysle's ears were growing hot.

Luckily, before Flya's games could incite any further discomfort, Tamarah and Stacey returned.

Tamarah lowered a massive crate onto the grass next to her tent. "Pretty decent harvest, ya wager?" she said to Ancel with a smirk.

"Did you manage to—" Ancel began.

"Get the mead?" Stacey interrupted, prying at a crate with her dagger. The lid released, sending yellowy bits flying, revealing a diverse arrangement of bottles enshrouded in hay. Brushing the fodder aside, Stacey fished around for a few moments.

"Here you are, my Lord," she said grandly, offering the saffron bottle. With a double take, she noticed Ector tending the grill. "Oh, hello there!" she blurted. "I did not see you there, and—" she stopped short, noticing the laif who was sitting uncomfortably close to her knight. "And hello to you as well. Pardon me," she straightened her tunic, "the crate blocked my view, and—"

"I am Ector," the young knight greeted her with a smile. "And this is Flya."

The laif leaned back and assessed the squire. "Charmed," she said finally. Her scrutinizing gaze suddenly shifted brightly. "Tamarah!"

"It's good to see you up and about!" Tamarah returned, moving to embrace the laif.

The fire licked up at the grease droplets as Ector rotated the meat. "These three, he said, gesturing at the knight, his brother, and the laif, "were on the field when the werewolves slew the witch. And if it had not been for the dragoons..." he was suddenly caught up in thought for a moment. "That reminds me!" He raised a finger in urgency and disappeared into his tent. "Found it!" he announced. From the between the flaps, the knight emerged brandishing an ominous spear. The bladed tip was an onyx that dimmed midnight, and the handle exuded an aura that caused Flya to shift uneasily. "Bactaal wanted you to have this," Ector declared, extending the weapon to his brother.

Ancel received the gift thoughtfully. "I assume the dragoons have moved on?" he asked, running a hand along the wooden haft, assessing the weapon.

"There are dragons assailing Ruma, to the east. They were merely passing through," he explained. "You like it?"

"I do," Ancel said, though his tone seemed to say otherwise. "Did Bactaal mention why he wanted me to accept such a token?"

"He did not," Ector said, returning to the grilled meat. "This food looks ready. Please, friends, help yourselves." He snagged a portion and backed away, allowing space for the others.

20

"You were gawking like a ghoul who had just discovered a shovel," Stacey said as they walked down the stone road toward fort Navarene. "I mean, I admit he's pretty handsome, but to act like *that*? Really, Carlysle?"

"He's pretty," Carlysle mumbled.

"What did you say?"

"Nothing!" the knight replied quickly, lifting empty palms.

"If you ask me, I think his brother has him beat," Stacey said. "That is, if we're discussing which brother is comelier, which we are not."

"Why not?"

Stacey crinkled her nose. "I suppose I don't know," she said after a few moments. "Ector is the most handsome man I have ever seen."

"Then you need to travel more," Carlysle scoffed.

Stacey felt heat rising under her collar, then the ridiculousness of the conversation made her smile. "To each her own, I suppose." These were the lords of Benwick that they were discussing. They may as well have been formulating plans to make themselves fly. She did have to admit that she liked the wistful air about her knight. It was a welcome change to the constant mutterings about a stiff drink or the lack of taverns in the forest.

"Have you ever been to this fort before?" Stacey asked.

Almost imperceptibly, Carlysle's shoulders sagged. "Just once," the knight whispered.

Stacey would not be requesting the details of her knight's singular visit. Whenever she had inquired of Carlysle's past before, it never ended on a good note. "Oh, lovely," the squire said. "Then you're familiar with the layout."

Carlysle shrugged her satchel.

The squire took that as a yes. "Perfect," she said, "Ector said we should check the soldier's quarters first. It's where he thought the big silver werewolf would be. And if he's not there, then anyone else around should have a good idea as to his whereabouts."

"Perfect," Carlysle echoed.

The fort's gates were already open when the knight and squire arrived. Red knights and soldiers were about their duties: hewing lumber, restructuring the outer balustrades, and securing the damaged interior supports.

Rows and columns of bodies were arranged on the outer grounds just outside the gates. They had been organized with enemies to the left and friends to the right. Scores of unfortunate red knights had been employed for that particular job.

At first, Stacey believed that she heard a great woodpecker working away on some pines, but, to her dismay, found that one red knight had been given a mallet and chisel to break apart the petrified corpses. She inspected the archenlaif corpses to the left, suddenly shuddering.

"Who removed all their tongues?" she asked Carlysle, a horrified look on her face. "And why?"

"Good questions," Carlysle answered, "but not all have had their tongues freed. See that lot over there?"

The squire looked to the leaning figures against the stonewall. Arrows protruded skillfully from the gaps of their armour, but their jaws were completely intact and bereft of the telltale blood trail that indicated a tongue extraction.

"I don't think that we'll ever fully know what happened here," Stacey murmured. Despite the heat of the afternoon sun, a string of shivers passed through her.

"Sir Carlysle!" a familiar voice broke through the moment. "Stacey!"

Jekar approached the pair in his human form. "I'm glad you found me," he said, beckoning them to follow. "The thought of trying to find you two among all those banners and pavilions was beyond daunting."

"Do you have word on Lanaelle?" Stacey asked, catching up to Jekar. Carlysle flanked the werewolf's other side. "Is she safe?"

"Yes." Jekar nodded at Stacey, "and *maybe...*" he said to Carlysle.

The knight recoiled. "Wait, what do you mean 'maybe'?"

Jekar pointed at the rampart they were walking toward. "A more suitable explanation can be found from Corbin," he said. "Sir Corbin, I should say."

A vast werewolf stood deep in conversation with two royal knights, his hands clutching the parapet as he leaned out. Jekar strode directly into the group, venturing much further than Stacey or Carlysle dared. The knight and squire lingered several steps behind, feeling very much out of place.

A tap on Corbin's upper arm paused the seemingly heated debate. Stacey could not make out the first part of the discourse between Jekar and Corbin, but she did see Corbin whirl around and ask about the women's location.

"Right there," Jekar said, unnecessarily. Corbin had already locked his eyes on them.

The royal knights, clearly not in favor of this intrusion, craned their heads toward the women, folding their arms in displeasure. "Sir Corbin," one said, placing a hand on the werewolf's shoulder. "The king has instructions that—"

Corbin shrugged free from the knight's grip.

As she faltered backward, her meticulously braided hair swung from under her helm and brushed against her chin. "I must insist," she stated calmly, though her eyes were steely. Gently pushing the braid behind her pauldron, the knight collected herself. "We are not architects."

Wearily, Corbin pinned his fingers to the bridge of his snout. "Must I hold your hands along every step?" He shook his head in dismay. "Give me one moment, please," he implored, "and then I will return to discuss the finer points of gussets." Without waiting for a reply, the werewolf made his way toward his new guests.

"Come," he said, "I need a reprieve. Let us adjourn to the stables where directions are understood the first time they are given." The royal knights acknowledged the insult with matching scowls as the group descended the stairway.

"We are not really going to the stables," Corbin whispered once they reached the ground level. "I know that they will come looking for me if I do not return soon, and I wish to prolong that distasteful activity as much as long as possible." By the time he finished speaking, Corbin had transformed into his human form without breaking stride. He was completely naked, and Stacey struggled against snatching glances at his nether bits. Her knight, however, was openly regarding the man's dark places.

With an encouraging wave, Corbin led them toward the underground barracks reserved for the common soldiers, though under the current circumstances, it was where the red knights were residing.

The room was deep and wide, and hosted a heavy scent of earth and sweat. It was an interesting bouquet that Stacey found strangely appealing. A slew of cots, arranged side-by-side, stretched from wall to wall. The claimed cots were marked by the owner's sack and helm, neatly placed atop the thinly stretched blanket that spanned the pallet.

Corbin plucked a torch from a wall sconce and continued toward the furthest corner. The shadows receded as he walked, and as he passed a support beam, his hand flashed out between the lapping flames. By the time they finally reached the corner, Corbin was adorned in a simple red knight's tunic. How he managed to achieve such a feat was beyond Stacey's comprehension, though honestly, she did not really care. To her it was a mystery better left unsolved. Carlysle, however, clearly felt differently. The knight gaped at her squire, gesturing to Corbin as if he had suddenly upturned a table displaying the rarest wines and cheeses.

Stacey glared at Carlysle in response.

Corbin latched the torch to a sconce overlooking a tall wine cask.

"Your sister," he began, heaving himself up to sit upon the cask. His heels clipped the container, dangling a few inches from the dirt floor, and he continued, "was *not* involved in the battle, which I am sure comes as a relief to you."

Carlysle returned an audible sigh.

"She arrived late," Corbin explained, "along with the rest of the party that had stayed behind." He leaned back against the wall, pillowing his head with his hands. "But they did not arrive too late to give chase," he said. "Arthur's forces swept through, sending the archenlaives to flight. The pack and I had deserted the field by then to count our losses and lick our wounds, so to speak, *and* that's when Lanaelle arrived," he paused, "the stupid fool."

"So you're saying..." Carlysle trailed off to perform the proper mental mathematics.

Stacey finished the statement. "She is somewhere in the forest in pursuit of what remains of the archenlaives?"

Corbin looked toward the ceiling. "Correct," he said, clearly irked.

"Did anyone else give chase?" Stacey asked. "Perhaps some red knights or maybe even a few overeager knights?"

"No," Jekar answered for his alpha. "Once the fort was reclaimed, the king ordered a halt."

Shifting her weight, Carlysle turned away. "Let me guess," she groaned. "And you haven't heard word since?"

No one spoke for a few moments, the silence seemed to be an apt reply.

"Correct," Corbin said at length, dispelling any doubt.

"Are you forming a party to go after her?"

"Most assuredly not."

"Are you all craven?" Carlysle spat, curling her top lip.

If Corbin had been in his werewolf skin, his hackles would have heaved upward. "There is a distinct line between cowardice and good sense," he snarled, his low growl continuing well after he had finished speaking.

"Our orders are directly from the King's mouth, we are to rebuild and refortify," Jekar explained. "Make this fort as impenetrable as possible. The armies of the realm do not wish to tarry any longer than is necessary."

Carlysle whirled back to face them. "That means—"

"That means we await your sister's return," Corbin interrupted. "You may pursue her if you wish, I can not stop you. But know this: no one *can* provide you aid if you choose to do so."

Jekar adjusted his spectacles. "Many of the Lords and Dukes are eager to return to their—"

"Oh, fuck the Dukes and their smarmy households!" Carlysle said, stalking over to Corbin and looking up at him. "You mean to tell me that not one member of your pack feels just a hint of guilt? Four of their own are out there fending for themselves! What's the point of having a pack in the first place if you're just going to abandon them when it's convenient?"

"The King—"

"Oh, fuck the King too!"

Stacey balked. "Carlysle..." she whispered desperately, gauging the werewolf's reaction. The King had recently knighted Corbin, and such a statement could be considered treason. If he had any concerns over the outburst, it was immediately overlooked. Above ground, a royal horn could be heard issuing a tremendous blast, causing dirt from the ceiling to fall onto their shoulders in tiny, harmless streams.

"The gates!" Corbin shouted, vaulting from the cask and pushing past Carlysle.

"Which ones?" Stacey asked.

"The north gates!" Jekar called, hurrying after Corbin.

Carlysle and Stacey looked at one another. Neither was assured by the implications but they were certainly hopeful. They chased after Jekar, rushing past the cots, miraculously making it through with nary a bashed shin.

From the open stairway over their heads, voices could be heard relaying news. Another blast from the horn drowned the voices for a moment.

Stacey's face met the sunlight and her eyes slowly adjusted. The blurry shapes turned into soldiers rushing around, not frantic, but definitely in a hurry.

"Wolves!" several shouted. "Wolves at the gate!"

Before Stacey could even turn, Carlysle became a blur heading to the nearest stairway leading to the upper battlement. The squire darted after her, but found it impossible to keep up. A few wary soldiers made space for the knight's furious course, but if not for the merlons, one or two would have taken a headlong plunge.

"Sorry, sorry," Stacey apologized as she pushed past. "It's a family sort of matter," she hurriedly explained to an offended soldier who still clung, rather dazed, to the parapet.

Even fifty strides behind, Stacey could easily make out her knight's booming voice demanding that the gates be opened immediately. The shouting abruptly cut off. A captain, whose face wrinkled with youthful ignorance, was absorbed in a heated disagreement with the knight.

"I don't take orders," the captain sneered, prodding Carlysle's chest plate with a finger, "from you." He turned, assuming the debate was resolved. "Do not release the gates!" he bellowed to the soldiers below. "Await *my* orders!"

Carlysle was fidgeting with the cross-guard on her sheathed longsword.

"Don't," Stacey warned, finally reaching her knight. She was about to say more, but the view from the north wall stole her words along with her breath. She stared out into the rolling hills that heaved upward, undulating like a kite string amidst the tumbles of flight. The forest beyond appeared regal, bringing to mind a battalion of staunch warriors who would dismiss an artist begging to paint their likeness. Beyond Navarene was a wilderness that most mortals did not dare venture. It was rumored to harbor monsters that preferred the taste of human flesh to anything else, and who would hunt the scent for miles. In addition, the archenlaives had claimed much of the land north of Lake Humiel, and the closer one drew to the lake, the closer one drew to death.

"Open the bleeding gates!" Carlysle seethed, gripping the captain by his gorget and heaving him upward to meet her eyes.

The captain struggled, trying to release himself from the knight's gauntlets, but his attempt proved fruitless. His head was turtled into his armour, and the back of his neck became locked to the rim of his back plate. "There is nothing to open them for!" he squealed helplessly, flinging an arm toward the northern wilds. "The scout reported were-wolves, but do you see any?"

Lowering the captain down to his proper level, Carlysle brusquely let him go. He bustled backward and adjusted his armour, tugging at his gorget with contempt in his eyes.

Carlysle rushed to the parapet and leaned out. "But the horn!" she insisted. "Why would you sound the horn *twice* for nothing?" To her disappointment, the captain appeared to be correct, and the only activity was the breeze meandering through the tall grass.

The captain shrugged. "The scout seemed sure," he said, employing a cloth to scrub Carlysle's fingerprints from his plate armour.

"Where do you think Corbin went?" Stacey asked, joining her knight in surveying the landscape.

"*Sir* Corbin should be overseeing the builders," the captain said airily, pausing as he noticed another smudge on his gorget. "If he is elsewhere then I shall recommend that—"

"Alright!" Carlysle snapped, rounding on the captain. "Shouldn't you be overseeing a frilly dinner party somewhere else?" She huffed out a frustrated sigh that tousled the shorter man's hair. He gaped in shock, and heatedly shot his fingers through his disheveled mop.

"This is my post," he declared, stamping a foot onto the unwavering stone. "I'm going to have to request that you leave."

Carlysle's hand found her longsword's pommel. "And I'm going to have to ask—"

"Carlysle!" Stacey said, spinning her knight around, veiling the captain's view of the threatening gesture. "It was a false alarm," she said, inches from Carlysle's face. She looked over at the captain. "Happens all the time, right?" she asked, obviously urging the captain to agree.

The captain did not pick up on the subtlety. "Actually, false alarms are very few and far between..." he trailed off, noticing the murderous glare in Stacey's eye. "I mean to say, yes, yes, this fort is riddled with incompetence," he spoke woodenly, as if he was reciting a script. "Why, just the other day, a red knight was startled enough to blow the horn when a rather large toad happened to cross her path," he concluded with an apologetic smile.

"See?" Stacey said, leading her knight away. "It's a common occurrence and we should not—"

The sudden rumbling baritone of a royal horn consumed whatever the squire was about to say. This blast, however, was accompanied by shouting beyond the north gate.

"Open the gates!" the unmistakable voice of Corbin demanded.

The knight and squire bolted back to the parapet.

Making their way toward the fort, parting the grass with each hurried step was a small group of werewolves. Their fur rustled in the breeze as they drew closer. A tall, lean werewolf appeared heavily wounded, and was not walking on its own accord. Corbin had the beast locked to his shoulder and was heaving most of its weight as he continued to call for the gates to open.

Stacey recognized Jekar and the fiery red fur of Ren instantly. The shortest of the bunch was obviously that simpering toad who shadowed Lanaelle wherever she went. But it took the screaming of Carlysle for her to realize who the one draped lifelessly to Corbin's side was.

"Lanaelle!" Carlysle shrieked in desperation. Her steel fingers crumbled the face of the stone into powder.

Stacey flared a murderous look toward the captain, and he immediately picked up on her meaning this time, jumping into his role.

"Open the fucking gates!"

21

"Can we keep him?" Kenna asked his daughter hopefully, then blinked and shook his head. "I mean, would you mind if we kept him around?"

After a long deliberate pause, Linette began to scribble down her reply.

Kenna tried to remain casual, but his rhythmic drumming on the porch rail gave away his excitement. The man loved dogs, but his family had never been overly fond of them. In the past whenever a stray had happened upon their doorstep begging for scraps, whoever was the first to spot the mutt would shoo the poor creature away. More often than not, it had been Liesel or Natalia who would jump at the opportunity, but the other sisters had partaken in the activity at least once. Except for Linette, that is, who did not disfavor the animals in the least, although, generally speaking, she was not overly excited by the prospect of pet ownership.

"Should we ask Perla?" Kenna recited the words on the tablet. "Oh, come now, Netty!" he scraped a balled fist over his scalp. "She doesn't even live here anymore! Why should she get a say in—" the man paused, taking in the grin spreading across his daughter's face. "You're putting me on, you little hob!"

Linette bounced away from her father's sweeping arm, hugging the slate to her chest. What resembled a series of hiccups tittered up from her chest, her shoulders shaking in silent laughter.

The dog in question had arrived early that morning as Kenna was preparing for another day of toil. The middle-aged canine had appeared in the barn, startling the man so much that he soiled his trousers. To Kenna's delight, the dog had waited patiently as he crab-walked back inside to clean himself. For the rest of the morning, the mutt had clung to the farmer's side as a proper companion, and now, with tongue draping and tail beating, it stood next to the man, eagerly awaiting the daughter's verdict.

Sensing footsteps, the dog cocked its head to the side, as dogs do, and looked to the door.

"Oh, no, no, no," Perla walked onto the porch, sipping a cup of hot tea. "You can't possibly be considering this?" she asked while scowling at the dog, who began to sink under her glare.

"Stay out of this Perl!" Kenna snapped. He ruffled the fur on the top of the dog's head, flipping the pointy ears between his fingers. "This is between me and Linette," he paused, giving the dog a hearty pat on his shoulder, "and Gomer, here."

Perla spat out her tea. "Gomer?!" she laughed, her eyes darting to Linette, seeking confirmation of the sheer absurdity.

With the slate still pressed to her chest, Linette only smirked a smile at her sister. She had already written down her decision.

"Well?" Perla continued, "Haven't we been invaded by enough mongrels as of late? Haven't we only just gotten the scent of wet dog out of our nostrils?"

Linette and Kenna exchanged a look, warning each other not to mention the fact that Perla's husband was now just as much canine as human. Clearly, the woman still needed a bit of time to adjust, and she was putting her frustrations on poor old Gomer. It had been several days since Corbin and the werewolves had set out into the forest, and tidings of their fate had yet to be received.

While the tension was not slackening, it had been manageable, and Kenna and Linette had gone out of their way to avoid bringing up any topics remotely associated with wolves. Gomer's arrival had fallen at perhaps the poorest of timing.

Perla mumbled something under her breath.

Kenna's hand froze atop the dog's head. "What did you just say?" he asked lightly.

Regret flooded Perla's eyes, and she shook her head. "Nothing, Papa," she said, looking everywhere but at her father. "It's just that... well... what do you think Mama would say?"

"That's what I thought you said," Kenna lifted his hand from the dog's fur, and drew up to his full height. "Come on, Gomer," he said icily. "We have work to do."

Linette's shoulders drooped for second before she rounded on her sister, shaking her fists, pantomiming frustration.

"What?" was all Perla could offer in defense.

Chasing after her father, Linette caught up and displayed what she had written on her tablet. She beamed at him while lifting the slate, hoping to brighten his mood. When Kenna read the words, he only nodded and gave her a gentle pat on the head. With a sunken brow, Kenna made his way to the fields.

From the lawn, Linette stared daggers toward the porch. Angrily she approached her sister, scrubbing the tablet clean, and, without averting her gaze, began to inscribe a new message.

Perla's eyes scanned the tablet. *Apologize, you dirty skunk!* She recoiled indignantly. "He knows I'm right!" She pointed her cup toward the shape of her dejected father, somberly trudging from the barn, and instantly felt remorse. "Ah, hekk," she said, "I suppose you're right."

Linette backed up and leaned against the railing, waiting for her sister to continue.

"What?" she asked. "I'll apologize when he returns for supper. Ever since I became pregnant," she indicated her belly, "my emotions have been rather difficult to rein in."

Tapping her toe, Linette began to write another note.

"*Gomer stays,*" Perla read aloud. "Yes, of course," she sighed. "Just look at how that mutt shadows his every move. It's as if they've known each other for years."

Linette turned to admire the budding relationship between her father and the dog. At that moment, keeping a safe distance from her father's scythe, Gomer was keenly tracking a mysterious scent.

Joining her sister, Perla set her tea on the railing. "Want to hear some *official* Benwick gossip?" she asked, changing the subject, and poking a teasing elbow into Linette's ribs.

Brushing aside the invasion of her space, Linette nodded in reply and gazed back expectantly.

"Well," Perla retrieved her cup and took a sip. "You remember my friend Tawny? The one with the shimmering hair."

Linette shook her head, but Perla disregarded the response.

"You do," she said, tapping Linette's wrist. "Well, she was a scullery in the kitchens for years under Lord Ban, and eventually worked her way up in the household. Now she tends the estate in some capacity, I'm not sure in what way exactly, but she is privy to healthy doses of scandalous information. Anyway, Lord Ancel is now the new Lord, seeing as Ban has died, as you know."

At this point, the other woman would customarily chime in with some sort of comment regarding the late Lord's passing or something along those lines. Linette simply blinked and inclined her head, as if to say *go on...*

Perla took another sip and curtly dabbed the corner of her mouth. "So, Lord Ancel has been betrothed to Kurrva of Rhionydd for what, five years now?" She squinted thoughtfully. "Something like that. Anyhow, word is that ever since their betrothal, she has been having an affair behind his back."

Reeling back a few dramatic inches, Linette covered her mouth in feigned shock.

It was not quite the response that Perla had desired. "Oh, come now," she sighed, "I haven't even reached the most shocking bit yet!"

Linette gestured an apology, rotating her fist against her chest, urging Perla to continue.

"Personally, I think the gallows are what should await that cur *and* her skulking little partner. Sir Ancel is such a distinguished and intelligent sort of man, and such a lovely man hardly deserves to be made an unwilling cuckold."

Linette raised her tablet.

Perla skimmed the words. "Ah," she said, taking another sip. "I will get to that. I will get to that. Do not fret. You see, the news reached Ancel of his betrothed's *indiscretions* only days before Ban gave up the ghost. And now he's off to war and—" she stopped, clearing her throat and biting her lip. "We don't need to get into that right now, do we?" She wrapped both hands around her cup and gazed off toward the fields.

After a few moments, she gathered herself and continued, as if nothing had upset her to begin with. "By ancient law, Lord Ancel has the right to charge Kurrva with treason, and thereby require her to make the Walk of Atonement."

This time, Linette did not have to fake her astonishment.

"I know!" Perla squealed, fluttering her eyelashes. "Incredible, right? It's very rare, but that's why we sometimes hear of nobles killing themselves after committing adultery."

Biting her tongue, Linette fervently began to scratch down a question. Even though Perla paused to allow her sister time to write, she did not slow her frantic scribbling.

Perla studied the tablet. *"No one has ever survived the Walk of Atonement, right? And it hasn't been invoked in ages?"* She recounted the questions and tapped her chin. "No, that's not quite correct," she replied. "There are folks who have survived. Very, very occasionally though. But it has been quite a long time since anyone has been sentenced to make the Walk." She paused, "Wait, what was your question earlier? *How did Kurrva get discovered?"*

Linette slowly nodded, having already forgotten that she had asked. She quickly changed direction and began to shake her head, not wishing for a diversion from the Walk of Atonement business. She waved her hand at her sister, trying to encourage her to stay the current course.

"Alright, I'll get back to that," Perla fanned the air. "Tawny, my friend with the shiny hair and clear skin, she told me personally that Ancel is planning on carrying out the sentence. But..." she held a moment to lift her eyebrows dramatically. "He is going to send a laif with them."

Taking a step back, Perla folded her arms, watching with satisfaction as her sister digested the information.

"Yep," she said, already guessing what Linette was going to write. "Yep!" she said once again after reading it.

Linette lowered the tablet with the phrase *Get out!* inscribed on it. The Walk of Atonement was meant to be a death sentence, for the unfaithful. Hitching a laif to its charge was akin to scoring a notch in the hangman's noose before stringing it to a guilty neck.

"Why would he do that?" Perla asked, causing the screeching of Linette's chalk to abruptly stop. "I don't know," she admitted, not waiting for a response. "I don't think anyone knows. Before he left for

Navarene, his final orders were that a laif would accompany Kurrva and her swain, and that the sentence would be carried out upon his return."

"I have so many questions," Perla read the upheld board.

"You and me both," Perla replied. "Now *how* they were discovered is quite a tale unto its own..." She trailed off, suddenly noticing their father waving and trying to draw their attention. Gomer was at his feet lifting a busy nose in the direction he was indicating.

"What's he saying?" Perla leaned out as far as she could. "If he's going on about the whistling ducks again, I'm going to—"

Linette tugged at Perla's shoulder and fervently waved the tablet before her, tapping a finger on the single word she had inscribed.

"Riders?" Perla read. It took a moment for the implication to set in. "Riders!" She backed up against the railing, one hand bracing her stomach. "They may have tidings! Quick, Linny! Run! Be off!"

Before Perla finished her command, Linette had already rolled up onto the balls of her feet. She tore off for the road, hearing the faint clinking of armour gradually grow louder as she drew near. From the direction of the great forest, she could see knights, resplendent in their heraldry, making their way forward on the Benwick highway. She rotated her heels in the soil, correcting her route, and darted directly toward their flapping banners.

Linette easily picked out the grays of Orkney and the reds and blues of Rhionydd among the throng of riders. She peered harder, hoping to spy the colors of Benwick, but no other lands seemed to be in their midst. Bending at the waist, she placed her tablet on her thighs and began to write. While she was admittedly the worst candidate to relay news, she was the nimblest between her sister and her father. The two of them would make it to the road just in time to greet the dust left in the horses' wake.

The exposed steel around the knights' tabards was almost blinding, and Linette had to shield her eyes from the scorching rays with one hand. She wagered that she appeared a bit foolish, standing in her simple work dress on the wayside, hoisting a feeble sign, and awaiting these glorious knights on their purebred chargers. Until that very moment, she had never actually felt the expansive distance in the class structure. She was fully aware of it, but it was altogether different when facing her station's inferiority in broad daylight. Some of these knights were even the same age as her, or at the very least, were only a few years older.

To hekk with it! she thought, then raised the sign with both hands.

She foisted it into one particular knight's line of sight, waving it like a pennant. The man locked eyes on the message and squinted beneath his lifted visor. Giving the knight to his right a swat on the thigh, he pointed, indicating the girl by the roadside. The other knight nodded his agreement, and the first man broke formation and headed toward Linette.

"Hallo!" the knight said, saluting the girl and bringing his charger to a halt.

Linette returned a smile and strode to the horse's flank. Reaching down, the knight accepted the offered tablet with an amused look, awkwardly weighing the object between his armoured fingers, careful not to snap it.

"What do we have here?" He skimmed Linette's message. *"How goes the war?"* he read aloud before returning the slate. He placed both of his hands on the pommel of his saddle, chewing over an apt response.

A great discordance of spurs jangled beside them as the knights of Orkney and Rhionydd continued their journey, appearing to be in high spirits. A few were smoking pipes and swilling dark liquid from ivory drinking horns, while others were absorbed in cheerful conversation. Linette's eyes darted to the rear of the procession, searching for the injured soldiers. There was indeed a cart tagging along, pulled by two broad chested draft horses and overflowing with straw to cushion the bumps along the road. But the fragile occupants of the wagon were not wounded knights, they were casks of spirits.

"We did not see any war," the knight admitted, shrugging in his pristine armour. "But I can tell you that the King has routed the archenlaives and driven them back toward the great lake. But if it is a brother, or father, or husband you seek news of, then I must confess that I cannot be of service."

Wanting the knight to wait for another moment, Linette hastily wrote her next question. While the knight did not seem impatient, his mount was beginning to grow restless.

"*Werewolves?*" he said, reading the chalk. The horse pranced to the left and the knight clicked his tongue, bringing the animal to heel. "There were rumors that werewolves made an appearance early on, but I do not know anything for certain." His youthful eyes crinkled about their edges, staring toward the other knights, his gaze avoiding Linette. "But among those rumors, it has been said that none of them survived."

Soundlessly, the tablet slipped from Linette's fingers, lost in the tall summer grass.

When the knight finally looked at the girl, he saw the dreadful impact his statement had made, and he raised his hands in surrender. "These are only rumors, mind you," the knight said apologetically. "I do not know anything for certain."

A dull whine followed by a gentle brushing against her hand stirred Linette's attention to her right. Gomer had retrieved her tablet and was offering it back to her with hopeful eyes.

The knight offered her a wistful, courteous smile. "If that is all, my lady?"

Linette bowed and waved, releasing the knight from her service.

With an affectionate pat to Gomer's solid head, Linette nodded toward the farm, prompting the dog to return home with her. And Gomer readily trotted behind the disheartened girl.

22

Famyl rolled onto his belly and stretched his forepaws toward the hearth. The pads had started to grow chilly with his back to the flames.

Gomer! he thought, yawning and stretching for a second time. *What a ridiculous name.* A firm hand stroked his rib cage, startling him, and he looked back at the owner of the hand.

Kenna leaned back in his chair with a satisfied smile. "You gettin' tired, boy?"

The First Laif in the dog's body snapped at the air in reply and returned his chin to the carpet with a groan.

The last few hours had been tense. Famyl had nearly forgotten what it was like to be among mortals and forgotten the noise that their emotions wrought. With so much in their short lives at stake, he could not blame them for acting as they did. Freedom from the degradation of time had given Famyl an alternate view of life, and Perla's grief-stricken collapse after hearing that perhaps Avalon had claimed her husband, had been a sudden, sharp reminder. After all, it was not a definite fact that Corbin was dead, which only made the scene more painful. It was the unknown, a frightening concept for both mortals and immortals alike.

After a retreat to her quarters to bargain with the Creator, Perla finally rejoined her family in the warmest room of the house, much more calm and serene.

"Corbin is not dead," she announced. "I can accept many things, but I cannot accept that."

Her claim was returned with complete silence. Kenna and Linette glanced at one another, then to Perla, finally bowing their heads in agreement.

A string of time passed with nary a murmur, not including when Kenna coughed several times before quickly assuring his daughters that he was simply trying to clear his throat. Several moments later, Kenna rose to his feet and gazed out the window.

"Well, I think I'm off for an ale," he said, admiring the sunset. "Perla?"

She roused as if from a stupor. "Yes?" she replied. The puffiness under her eyes had deflated and dark circles now crept in their place.

"Up for a trip to the pub?"

"Oh, Father," she scowled. "You only just bathed! And then you'll come home late reeking of smoke and piss." Discord seemed to flood the life back into her.

"Bah!" Kenna waved away her concerns. "The sun has only just retired. There's plenty of time for me to be back at a decent hour." He turned to his youngest. "Linette?" he asked playfully, already knowing the answer.

Wrinkling her nose, Linette shook her head.

"Suit yourself," he said. "Gomer, tend the ramparts whilst I'm away."

Famyl lifted his head and huffed, watching his master shrug a mantle over his tunic and depart. The door snapped shut and Famyl closed his eyes. He had a night involving weird dreams of open fields and low flying birds to look forward to.

Early the next morning Kenna decided to take the day off. Behind bloodshot eyes and a sagging countenance, he explained to Gomer that it was an uncommon occurrence, but he was a few days ahead on the harvest anyhow. After making his unnecessary excuse to the dog, he slunk back to his darkened room to hunker down until living no longer hurt.

Though he could not voice it, would not have even if he could, Famyl was grossly aware of how seldom Kenna abandoned his morning work. After all, he had been monitoring this household for many years. His mind was still adjusting to the fact that he was no longer observing life taking place from the Hold, he was actually among them, able to intervene.

Famyl inhabited an adult dog, and he knew that he would always curse himself for stealing the identity of a fully formed creature. Not only fully formed, but mature. It was a forbidden practice, but not impossible. And he knew he would pay the consequences someday, but it would not be this day. *This* day would be spent with Linette.

The girl had fallen asleep on the couch, curled into a shivering ball, until Famyl had discreetly placed a blanket over her. Learning to use his mouth to perform such a task had proved unexpectedly taxing. As he eased the final inches over her shoulders, he feared a drop of slaver would fall upon her forehead, but if one had, it did not rouse her. And when she woke an hour before sunrise, she flung the blanket aside without sparing a second to recognize its existence. Admittedly, this bothered Famyl a bit, but he would not let it get him down. As soon as her feet touched the floor, he bolted up to a stand, regretting the movement instantly. Whimpering back a dose of pain that emanated from somewhere behind his hip, Famyl clenched his jaw and tried his best to wag his tail.

Old dog, old bones, he thought. It was a portion of the price for his breach of the rules.

Not wishing to disturb the still-slumbering Perla, Linette fixed a quiet breakfast of cheese and day-old bread before beginning her daily routine. Tossing a heel of bread over her shoulder as she retreated to her room, she was amused to find that Famyl was able to snatch the food right out of the air.

He sat outside her door patiently, and each time her footfalls drew near, his tail cheerfully battered the floor, though it was unintentional.

Soon they walked in the sunrise, spending the first hours of the day performing Kenna's chores. Well, Linette did the work while Famyl tracked woodchucks and chased goblins. The girl grinned each time the dog suddenly froze, bewildered, rattling out a sneeze caused by snuffling up the morning dew. Seeing the joy he brought to her face made his transgressions all worth it. In a sense, Famyl had died over a dozen times just to see the corners of her lips rise. All his previous dog bodies had been taken at birth, but had been killed and eaten rather quickly. It was actually rather remarkable how many pups managed to survive those first stages with the overwhelming predation in the forest.

Their chores eventually led them to the barn. Before the werewolves had arrived, a single mare had occupied the stables. Now six more had been added to the fold as part of the agreement between Corbin and Kenna. Ultimately, the contract would prove quite profitable, but in the meantime, the beasts required fodder and care. One at a time, Linette lifted the latches on each horse gate, granting free-range access to the pasture. The first two palfreys strode out hesitantly, their eyes plastered to the sky as if expecting it to fall down upon them. The third, however, refused to leave her stall altogether. When Linette tried to coax it out with a carrot, the beast ratcheted backward and screamed, nearly splitting the girl's face with its hooves. This enraged Famyl, and as he was about to bound over the gate and tear into the horse's flanks, the strangled shriek of a wyvern overhead abruptly stole all his attention.

Protecting Linette was Famyl's first priority. He prodded her ankles, shepherding her to an empty stall. She relented to the dog's guidance, but her eyes kept darting back to the barn where Kenna kept a longbow handy. Its purpose was relegated for goblins or foxes, or even the occasional ghoul. Kenna had employed it on many occasions for minor confrontations, but a pair of circling wyverns was not what he had in mind when he placed the weapon there decades ago. This was the sort of encounter that, if you survived, you merrily counted your losses afterward.

With terrified eyes and frothing mouths, the palfreys booked it across the pasture. They were very fast, Famyl thought, admiring their nimble limbs and ferocious gait. Unfortunately, he had seen this sort of theatre play out thousands of times and could foretell the outcome. The sky wyrms swooped, their bellies mere feet from the grassland, easily matching the speed of their prey. With apex voracity, the female wyvern struck first, snatching up one horse, and the male followed suit after. There was hardly even a waver in their upward flight toward Fenrirfang. Just like that, they were gone, and the faint echo of frantic horses, far off in the distance, provided the only evidence of what happened.

There are only so many things that a person can prepare themselves for when they wake in the morning. And, judging by the expression on Linette's face, witnessing two prize-worthy palfreys being stolen by a pair of wyverns was not one of those things.

War tends to uproot and shake the world just a bit. Famyl wagered that the wyverns had been pushed from their usual hunting grounds due to the conflict, and he would have comforted Linette with this theory if he had been able. Although he would not have informed her that without any resistance a monster was liable to return. In his current form, with all its verbal limitations, all he could do was boldly re-enter the pasture.

He sniffed the ground, pretending to trace the same scent for several minutes, hoping that the casual display would assure Linette that the danger had passed. With his snout intently pressed to the ground, he did not notice that she had already made her way from the shelter. A solid thump against the side of the barn made Famyl look up and take notice. And with a leap, he scurried to join her.

The rest of the day carried on as normal for Linette, but for Famyl, it was a dream finally realized.

Once the daily burdens were completed, he accompanied her to check on the progress of her silver shadesgill. While she could not voice it, Famyl knew that the small patch held much more value to her now. It was made clear in the way her feet seemed to leave the ground and the manner in which she held her chin, all conveying pages of gratitude toward the werewolves. And another page jotted full of the hopes and prospects that her flowers could win for her and her father. For their future.

Famyl knew these things. He had seen the secret messages that she erased, the messages not intended for the eyes of others. He had read the tablet when no one else was there to read it. When she wrote replies that she quickly erased before others could see what she truly thought, replacing them with more cordial words, he saw those too.

The flowers looked glorious, emanating a glow akin to fae magics. Famyl had seen a great many plants in his wanderings, but for some reason, they all seemed to pale in comparison to the shadesgill before him.

Gently, Linette peered between the petals and pitchers, careful not to spill any of the nectar. She worked for an hour or so, but it felt like ages to Famyl. He knew what came after, and that was what he was awaiting. More often than not on warm days like this, she would curl up around her tiny garden and steal a brief nap. And he would watch over her, protect her.

But then—"Is that *silver shadesgill?*" an astonished voice dashed the moment.

Famyl sprang to his feet, hackles jutting like a spiked mace. So intent on Linette's activity, he had failed to monitor their surroundings. A retinue of an army was passing on the road, and he had not noticed the pennants and heraldry fluttering in the wind, nor had his pointy ears paid any heed to the sounds kicked up by the armoured knights.

Such failure! he thought, growling loudly.

The man—the laif—seemed to regard Famyl as an oddity, and was clearly not threatened by the dog's attitude. "That *is* silver shadesgill!" the laif exclaimed, extolling the girl's skill with a salute. Before he could introduce himself, Famyl, with a jolt of horror, recognized the laif.

"Allow me to introduce myself," the stranger said grandly, performing a sweeping bow, "my name is—"

Amyr! Famyl thought, baring his teeth.

"Amyr," concluded the laif, dispelling any uncertainty. "Please excuse my interruption. You see, my knights and I were happening by when I sensed a bit of magic in the air." Amyr was adorned in a magnificent slim-fitting suit of armour that was as elegant as it was practical. Remarkably, the steel seemed joined to his flesh, and it glided along as he gestured toward the road. "From the thoroughfare, I spied such an exquisite beauty, and I bid my knights halt."

With a mix of uncertainty and awe, Linette stood regarding the laif, hugging her slate to her chest. Famyl's hackles had yet to settle, and his growl lingered with each breath, instilling a menacing baritone beneath Amyr's speech.

"And then I noticed the flowers," he said, sweeping his eyes upward to meet Linette's.

Having never been courted in the past, the girl was not quick to recognize his flirtation. But Famyl caught the message instantly.

Begone! Famyl snarled.

Amyr did not even flinch. "Your dog does not seem to favor me," he said coolly.

Linette began to write down a reply, and the sight of it caused a flicker to pass behind Amyr's eyes that Famyl did not like.

"He doesn't like you," Amyr read aloud, shaking his head dispassionately. His attention shifted back to the girl, and he did not care at all about the dog. "Can you not speak?" he inquired, inclining his head.

"*No*," he read from the slate, an almost imperceptible tremor passing under his armour. "How dreadful," he offered, but Famyl discerned falsehood behind his tone. "I do not wish to impose, but may I know your name, my lady?"

Scribbling the reply, Linette shifted her feet and raised the tablet.

Amyr almost hummed her name as he lowered himself down to admire the garden. "That is an exceptional name," he said. "Linette," he repeated, reaching toward one of the flowers.

The girl flinched, causing the laif to draw up short.

"My apologies!" he said, his hand frozen, "I have an extensive history with these particular plants. Please trust me." In this, Famyl knew him to be true.

Relenting with a tentative nod, Linette gave the laif her approval.

Warily he began to inspect the stems, delicate fingers pressing shoots, and he murmured cheerily after lightly tapping the underside of a dewlap.

"Fascinating," he intoned, rising. "I would like to make you an offer."

Famyl's lips curled.

In a display of interest, Linette raised her chin, encouraging the laif to continue with his pitch.

"First, I will need to confer with my counsel," he said. The laif paused to gaze at his sentinels adorned in the azure of the Church before continuing slowly. "You have an exceedingly rare talent, my lady." Turning and locking one hand to his vambrace, Amyr focused on the shadesgill beneath him. "This plot, though insignificant in size, harbors quite the opposite in potential."

Linette simply raised her eyebrows.

A smile crept across the laif's lips. "We will be in touch," he said.

"There were soldiers from the forest," Perla seethed, staring darkly at her dinner while strangling her napkin, "and you did not think to ask them about my husband's whereabouts?"

The joy in Linette's demeanor receded immediately.

"Now, Perla," Kenna said, reaching across the table and placing a hand over his daughter's trembling fist. "Your sister did not intend—"

She jerked her hand away and released a pent-up sigh. "I just, I'm just not..." she stammered.

"There will be more soldiers," Kenna promised.

Linette raised her tablet with the words *I'm sorry* written on it.

"It's alright," Perla said, dabbing her eyes with the throttled napkin, which now had the appearance of a ridged fan.

"*Please eat,*" Perla read, squinting at the new message on the tablet. "I have no appetite."

Scribbling sounds ensued, and then a third message appeared.

"*Maybe your baby is hungry?*"

Kenna chewed his moustache. "Your sister is right," he said, lifting her plate and walking toward the hearth. "I'll give this meat to the fire for a few moments to warm it back up."

Perla was not paying attention, and her lips began to move wordlessly as if in a trance. "Wait," she said, her watery eyes focused on Linette. "Did you say *Amyr?*" she asked, her voice husky. "As in *Lord Amyr*—the Arbiter—one of the first laives?" She spoke in an accusatory manner that Linette found unsettling.

Adjusting her seat, Linette avoided her sister's gaze, and offered a solitary nod in reply. A warm chin suddenly appeared in her lap. Looking down, she saw the comforting eyes of Gomer staring back at her.

"And he wants to confer with you, correct?" Perla asked. "Over some stupid flowers?" Her voice softened and she seemed to be speaking to someone else. Someone far away. "I never wanted to marry a warrior. Warriors are expendable. They are mere fodder for kings and lands, sent to defend courts and slay monsters. Whenever a warrior's offer of courtship was extended toward me, I dismissed it as if it were offal from a slaughterhouse."

A log in the fire snapped, sending sparks up into the smoke.

"And so I married an architect. I married someone who I could grow old with," she said, returning to the present. "You will go to the city tomorrow and speak with the Arbiter. And you will only return when you have tidings about my Corbin." Perla blinked, acting as if a spell had suddenly lifted.

"Now, where's that lamb?" she asked, "I'm famished."

23

Lanaelle woke to muffled voices just beyond her feet. The rumbling of the male was indecipherable and unfamiliar, but the female was unmistakably the voice of her sister's squire. The afternoon heat was stifling, leaving her feeling sweaty and uncomfortable. With a groan, she kicked herself free of the blankets. The voices halted their conversation midsentence, and Lanaelle was wary to stir again.

"She's awake," the squire said. "Want to come with me to fetch Jekar?"

The male must have agreed, and Lanaelle heard two sets of boots crunch across the grass, and steadily fade.

Where exactly am I? she wondered. The scent of smoke permeated the air, an angry plover thumped steel somewhere to her left, swords crossed and scraped behind her, and she winced at the sound of someone screeching chalk on a slate tablet to her right. The noise caused the skin beneath her fingernails to crawl, and she wanted nothing more than to sheer that person's hand from their wrist. Suddenly her jaw clenched, and her fangs began to extend. She curled up and hugged her knees to chest, trying to fight the beast back down. Transforming without willing it was not something she had experienced before, and she was quite alarmed by the event.

She covered her ears, feeling fur bristling up and the cartilage morph into pointy tips. The more she fought, the more she seemed to change. Fighting and praying, Lanaelle tried thinking of other things,

things that did not piss her off. This change in tactics seemed to work and the morphing of her hands and feet gradually diminished. Calm, even breathing brought her ears back down to rest behind her temples, and the thought of meat roasting on a spit melted her jutting snout back into her human jawline.

"Fuck me running!" she said, sitting up and wiping her brow. "What a terrible way to start the day." Rolling forward, she made her way out of the tent. On the positive side, she noticed that the aches she had experienced upon waking had resolved themselves, and she no longer felt as if an archenlaif knight had nearly bludgeoned her to death.

"Well, hello there—" a voice said.

Lanaelle cut the scrawny man off. "Where am I?" she demanded. Her senses had betrayed her. She hadn't realized anyone was still outside the tent.

The man was alone, occupying one of the stumps circled around the fire. He prodded the smoldering logs with a bone white sycamore branch. "Uh," he said. "To a regular person, you're in Fenrirfang Forest, but to a cartographer, you'd be in Irphen's Downfall, and to a—"

"Jackass," Lanaelle interrupted. "Whose camp is this?"

The man continued on as if he had not been rudely disrupted. "And to a *simpleton*," he said, inclining his head at Lanaelle, "this would be the site dedicated to Benwick's army." He waved his stick around in a circular pattern. "Or what remains of it."

Selecting a stump several lengths from the man, Lanaelle plunked down. "I'm famished," she admitted with a sigh, scratching her stomach. As her fingernails grazed the fabric, she noticed with a start that she was wearing an entirely foreign sleeping shift.

"No surprise there," the man said. Lanaelle was not sure if he was commenting on her nightgown or the fact that she was hungry. "You've been sleeping in that tent for two days now." He tucked his stick under his armpit and began to rub his hands toward the flames.

"Two days?"

"You were in rough shape when Corbin and Stacey brought you back," he said. "Quite a head wound."

Stacey! Lanaelle thought. *That's her squire's name! It was right on the tip of my tongue!* She began to recall the events leading up to getting her bell soundly rung. Archenlaives had surrounded them in the dark and Grandy had disappeared within the mess of it all...

Meanwhile the man had been speaking while her thoughts had drifted, and she was just now realizing it.

"What was that?" she said.

His head sunk between his shoulders like a battered turtle. "You have a nasty habit of interrupting me."

"Apologies..." she said, trailing off in a way that suggested that he fill in his name.

"Raymond," he supplied, and took a deep breath. "And I was saying that we have coney, venison, and there's a bit of quail left, I believe," he recited the options while tapping the sycamore branch rhythmically against his chin. Lanaelle listened intently as he offered her well over a dozen options. "And the brace of squirrel is surprisingly less greasy than I recall squirrel being," he concluded.

Saliva had been welling in Lanaelle's mouth for the duration of the man's speech. "That sounds good," she said, fighting back the urge to lick her lips. Having already lost her composure once this morning, she resolved to favor her more human characteristics for the remainder of the day. Or at least until she could get a handle on what had gone awry.

"Which would you like?" Raymond asked, blinking politely.

Lanaelle incrementally swiveled her head in disbelief. "All of it."

"Lanaelle!" Stacey returned to the camp with Jekar in his human form and an unfamiliar knight in tow. "It's great to see you back on your feet and..." she hesitated, unsure of her next words. From mouth to chest, Lanaelle was completely soaked with meat juice, the strands of her hair tainted slick as well. "Healthy!" she concluded brightly.

Lanaelle responded with a grunt and continued using her teeth to strip the meat from a femur bone.

"Hold still," Jekar ordered, approaching the woman. "I want to see how that gash on your head is healing." Using his thumb and forefinger, he gently parted a few strands of greasy hair above her left ear, and peered closely. Lanaelle stared into the flames and chewed, her face showing a little irritated from the probing fingers upon her scalp. But she obeyed and did not move.

"Ah." Jekar nodded and returned the sticky tress back to its place. "It seems to have healed rather well," he said, wiping his fingers on his tunic.

Greedily, Lanaelle resumed eating.

"Lanaelle," Stacey said, interrupting the werewolf's meal once again. "You have missed some news, and if you're well enough to hear, I'd like to fill you in."

Lanaelle garbled an incoherent response.

"What did she say?" she asked, looking to Jekar. He shrugged and smirked in reply.

Raymond leaned forward. "She said to give her a moment."

Stacey blinked, noticing the red knight for the first time. The man was utterly forgettable and she often lost track of him in even the blandest of surroundings. "Thank you, Richards," she said, dropping onto a stump.

The young knight who had accompanied the group assumed the seat next to the squire. "While you dine," the knight began, as Lanaelle continued to slurp and chomp, "allow me to introduce myself. My name is Sir Ector of Benwick, son of the late Lord Ban. And your sister has requested that—"

A barking sound issued from Lanaelle's packed mouth. She hastily swallowed and swiped one forearm across her glistening chin. "What news of my sister?" she demanded.

Ector could not discern whether the woman was angry or intensely concerned.

"Sir Carlysle is well," the knight said cautiously, gauging the woman's reaction. When she did not display a change in her disposition, he continued. "And she is very concerned about you."

A flint struck behind Lanaelle's eyes. She sprung to her feet, fur bristling from every limb, and when her gaze focused back on the knight, she was wholly transformed. "Where is she?" she said, her voice unrealistically calm.

"Whoa, whoa!" Stacey stood abruptly, causing her stump to topple. "Carlysle is only trying to help! She is doing some—"

Lanaelle cut toward the squire. "Where is she?" she repeated, now devoid of calm. The werewolf was standing in the remnants of the fire, ankle deep in ash and embers, ignoring the burning, clenching the squire's collar between her claws.

"She's, she's," Stacey stammered as her feet left the ground.

Ector rose, placing a cautioning hand to his sword pommel. "She's at the fort," he said rigidly, "with Corbin."

Lanaelle's eyes flicked warily to the knight's sword. "Very well," she said, returning Stacey's heels to the earth.

"Do not go there as a wolf," Jekar warned. "Please, Lanaelle, I implore you."

Stacey was suffering through a bout of coughs. "Yes, please don't do that," she said between hacks. "We will go with you, if you wish."

"Is the rest of the pack at the fort?" she asked Jekar, stepping out of the coals.

Jekar nodded. "Most of them, yes." He cleared his throat as one preparing to bestow ill tidings. "Bryndon has actually become quite the caregiver. He has been tending the ill and wounded with meticulous care for the last few days."

Lanaelle grunted in response. "That explains why he hasn't been hovering over me all afternoon."

"Yes, it's rather surprising. But he seems to have found his calling," said Jekar. "Anyhow, the pack has been commissioned for service to the crown." He waited for the news to sink in before daring to continue. "We have finally received the recognition that we were seeking."

The fur along Lanaelle's arms and legs began to recede, and she took a faltering step back, nearly tripping over Raymond.

A pained smile adorned Jekar's face. "We did it, Lanaelle."

She stumbled back a few more paces, reverting to her human form. "Why didn't you, why didn't—" she stuttered, searching for words. "Why didn't you wake me?" she asked finally, sounding betrayed.

"We feared that rousing you could cause permanent harm," Jekar offered as defense. "There was so much blood. Forgive us."

Part of her felt like rejoicing. After all, her life's dream, what she had been longing for for so long, had finally been achieved. Meanwhile, she had been sleeping alone in a tent, recovering from wounds sustained in a scuffle that had proved ridiculously insignificant. Twice now, she had been convalescing in a tent while others went on to receive the accolades that she desired above all else. While she understood that snuffing another's candle would not make hers burn the brighter, still, that other part of her—the part that was not rejoicing—wanted penance.

With a sudden, unexpected smile, Lanaelle faced Stacey. "I'm sorry for all of that," she said merrily. Her smile continued to spread. *A penance that I intend to reap!* she thought, extending a friendly palm toward the squire. "Please forgive me."

"I simply do not trust her, Carlysle." Corbin placed both hands upon the table. The man never seemed to sit. "I understand she is your sister... but that night in the forest... you were not there, you did not see."

Carlysle leaned back in her chair. "Did not see what?" Untouched whiskey sat in a snifter before the knight.

The underground captain's quarters were tight and tawdry and smelled of moss and cheap liquor. After growing agitated with the errant knight's line of questions, Corbin had excused himself from the "planning board" and led her down to his quarters for a private discussion.

"She is still alive," he said. "Can you not be satisfied with that? I cannot say the same for the rest of my knights."

"Oh, they're *knights* now? A few days ago they were a *pack*," Carlysle scoffed, her top lip twitching. "And before that, what were you?"

The werewolf stood to his full height. "I see where you are going with this," he said with a wan smile that quickly came and went. "Without Lanaelle, we would not have earned our belts."

"Royal belts," Carlysle interjected. "Which, as I understand it, is the highest honor a Warrior-born can possibly achieve, no?"

Returning his hands to the table and hanging his head, Corbin's long hair splayed across the tabletop. The solitary torch danced shadows on the opposite wall, and the gloom deceptively led one to believe that night had fallen. Slowly, the werewolf leader began to shake his head.

"It is true," he said at length. "We owe her a debt. Without her discovery of the decoction, we would not have made it here." He looked up at Carlysle, and she could see the toll that the last days had wrought upon him. "But I cannot in good conscience welcome her back."

Carlysle winced. "Come now, you don't need to be all dramatic about it," she said. "Look, I'm not asking you to get the warm fuzzies over her or anything, I only ask that you sleep on it. I can tell that you're exhausted."

Corbin appeared ready to object.

"Just!" she pronounced, thrusting a finger toward the ceiling, "one night!"

"Alright," he said reluctantly, scratching the back of his neck.

Carlysle chewed her bottom lip. "And..." she began, but trailed off.

Corbin looked up at her, his eyes encouraging her to continue.

"I will personally vouch for her," she said more assuredly. "Anything goes wrong with her, you can hold me responsible."

Corbin scratched his temple. "Why?" he snorted. "If she disobeys a direct order, you will be culpable. You will receive her punishment."

"Is that so hard to grasp?"

"No," he admitted, his chest swelling around a sigh. "I will sleep on it." He released the pent-up air, and laughed as if he had lost a heavy wager.

The day hurried past just as the others had. Life after battle was strange, and Raymond was attempting to learn how to savor a moment.

Everyone else had abandoned the fire, retreating to their tents or grabbing a drink and wandering about. Tents and pavilions went up then went down, and each day brought more blank spaces on the meadow. Trampled grass and wildflowers were the only evidence that anyone had been there at all. Raymond sighed as he looked around. He was beyond reluctant to join the fresh red knights stationed at the fort. None of them had gone through what he had gone through. None of them could relate.

He smiled in spite of his sadness. Vashal and Tamarah would be returning to their homes at daybreak. At some point tomorrow, Saeva and Flya were planning to disperse themselves into the forest, as laives do, and go back to whatever secret villages they hailed from. They both agreed to return to the spire someday, but it would not be anytime soon.

The Lords of Benwick would be the last to depart, though the precise time had yet to be determined. Once they pulled up their stakes, Raymond had decided that he would then make for his post once again.

After the last fires of war had been smothered, a band of laives had emerged from the trees and walked about the meadow bestowing gifts to select fighters. A few received ornate sleep garments, while others were given weapons and trinkets. Saeva had explained that it was some form of debt repayment, and he had divulged the name of the ritual, but Raymond had forgotten it. One of the laif children had even approached him the night before and offered an outrageously handsome suit of armour. Believing it was a prank, Raymond had turned the gift down, waiting for Flya and Tamarah to pop out from the shrubs and share a laugh at his expense. They did not, and the crestfallen child had sulked away.

A sudden tap on his shoulder roused him from his thoughts.

The laif child had returned. Raymond had not heard the squeaking wheels approach. An elder laif was hovering behind and the firelight painted a dour expression on her face.

"These are for you," said the child sullenly, indicating the cart with a sweeping hand. Last night the gesture had held much more excitement.

The elder cleared her throat, urging the girl to go on.

"If you decline this gift again," the youth continued, "then I will kill you."

Raymond expected the elder to correct the child by clearing her throat again, but she did not. The armour reminded him of Elithiel's exquisite plate, and he truly did want to take it. And apparently, if he did not accept the gift, he would die. But he was fairly certain that the red knights would forbid him from sporting such a set of arms. Shitty armour was part of the punishment.

He rotated on his stump to face the elder. "I don't have a place to keep it," he said dejectedly. "And my commanders would not allow me to wear it." He shook his head. "It goes against the dress code."

The elder's attention flitted over Raymond's shoulder.

"Tell me." Flya was suddenly occupying a stump across the fire. The flames tousled the contours of her portrait, and Raymond nearly choked on his spit at her arrival. "Why did you steal that child?" she asked, gazing down her nose at him and dragging a finger over her throat.

"I'm sorry, what?"

"You mentioned to me before," Flya went on, "that you landed yourself in the service of the red knights for being a child thief. And I want to know why."

"Well, quite plainly, it's against the law to steal a child," he said.

"Try not to make this any more difficult," a new voice said. Raymond whirled over his left shoulder, popping several joints in his neck.

Saeva stepped into the light. "Please tell us the story behind the abduction."

Raymond rubbed his neck and worked his jaw. "Sure thing," he said, watching the lampyr swing a leg over a stump and take a seat. "This may take a while. How familiar are you with the Duke of Celliwig, Harold

Pemberton?" He paused to see if the name garnered a reaction. "Judging by your shared blank expressions, you are not familiar in the least."

The red knight settled back, withdrawing his smoking pipe and filling it.

"Will this take all night?" Flya asked Saeva.

The lampyr smiled and cocked an eyebrow, encouraging her to exude a bit of patience.

"Alright," Raymond said, flicking his match into the fire. "Well, Duke Harold Pemberton is well known for being a—" he cut himself short and warily appraised the laif child. "For being a... *distrustful* man when it came to the ladies." Raymond batted his eyelashes salaciously, hoping to curtail the need to delve any deeper with young ears present.

"We get it." Flya sat back and grinned. "Now stop doing that."

"Such indiscretions were about to come to light with the poorest of timing," Raymond explained. "You see, Duke Harry's wife, after many trying years, was finally pregnant with an heir. And she was not wise to the Duke's *working abroad,* and he aimed to keep it that way. So he commissioned a company of thieves to go about the realm discretely gathering up the children that had fallen from his tree, so to speak."

Flya folded her arms across her chest. "You were arrested for following the orders of a Duke?" she asked.

"That's preposterous," Saeva added.

Raymond drew from his pipe, and exhaled a cloud. "Allow me to finish," he said, tapping the stem to his teeth. "You see, I am no professional thief. One of Harold's mistresses was extremely distraught when she awoke to find her cradle empty. And this particular babe was born gifted." He slid the stem to the side of his neck. "A warrior!" he added with a furrowed brow. "Likely one to change the game for this woman."

"And this is where you come into play?" Flya asked.

He leveled the stem at Flya. "Precisely."

"You stole a baby that had previously been stolen?"

"Precisely."

"For a price, I assume?"

"Precisely."

"Stop saying that!" Flya said, then turned to Saeva. "It's not quite as bad as it sounded on the surface."

Saeva leaned back and turned toward the elder that lingered in the shadows. Raymond had forgotten that she even existed.

"Care to weigh in?" Saeva asked the elder.

She nodded solemnly. "Firstly, he must accept the gift," she said, easing a palm out from between her floor-length cloak.

With his pipe perched between his teeth, Raymond smirked at the conclave of laives, waiting for them to continue with whatever game they were playing.

The elder cleared her throat.

"Oh!" Raymond uncrossed his legs and jolted upright. "I accept, I accept," he said quickly, just now understanding that it was a verbal response they required. "Of course, I accept the gift."

"Then we may proceed," the elder said solemnly, entering the circle. "This mantle is not often offered to mortals." Her voice sounded ancient as the firmament, but her face showed the wear of only twenty winters. "The forest will accept him."

"What is happening?" Raymond asked warily, extending his arms as the elder and the child worked in unison to secure the chest plate to his torso.

Flya only grinned in response.

Luckily for Raymond, Saeva was present. "You have been made a Jatel," he said, placing a reassuring hand on the red knight's shoulder.

The confounded expression on Raymond's face did not register with the lampyr, and he turned away without offering further explanation. The child only beamed up at him while snapping a greave into place.

"Say good-bye to the red knights, dummy," Flya said, standing and flinging the remainder of her drink into the fire. "You're coming home with us."

24

Linette had spent two days on her horse, and as she rocked in the saddle all she could think of was a nice warm bath. The road dust had become one with her skin, and when she tried to brush it off, it only burrowed deeper.

What a waste of time, she thought as she steered toward the farm.

Aside from the desire to get clean, her thoughts continuously returned to her shadesgill. They should be ripe for harvest tomorrow or the day after, she wagered. She had rushed her time in the city, just a bit, because of this knowledge. She could always make another trip if need be, but hopefully word of Corbin would reach Perla's ears without the need to return.

The late afternoon's limited light struck the shadesgill at the perfect angle, arcing rich beams every which way.

Linette stopped several feet from the flowers and hopped down from the saddle. Her legs were stiff from hours spent in the saddle, and she staggered the first step before pausing to work out the soreness. The magical aura beckoned to her and she obliged, delightedly hurrying forward. Time slipped by as water over glass when she was with her garden, and soon the day was drawing to a close.

"Linette!" Her father's harsh voice sounded off next to her. She reeled and looked up to see his rough countenance hanging above a lantern. In the dark, his recessed eyebrows shadowed his eyes into

255

crevices. "Your sister has been waiting for your return with bated breath!"

In a rush, Linette gathered herself and bolted for her horse.

"She's in the stables!" Kenna said, scowling so deeply that Linette thought that she could almost see bone as she galloped past.

The paddock was silent when Linette approached the lantern-lit stables. She dismounted, and led the horse toward his pen. The sounds of crunching and shifting animals would ordinarily greet Linette when she entered, but the stables were still and silent.

Perla materialized from an empty stall. "What of my husband?" she demanded, appearing sunken and haunted. "What of Corbin?" Her dry lips seemed as if they had not seen water in days.

Linette withdrew her tablet and presented her report.

Perla rushed to her and snatched the slate. *"No news,"* she read. "No news?!" She pitched the slate and stalked toward Linette. "Two days I have been waiting, and this is what you bring me?"

Shifting her weight, Linette extracted herself from her sister's grip and began to root for her tablet in the straw.

"Tell me!" Perla continued her tirade, seizing Linette by her wrist. "Tell me what they said!" She dragged Linette to her feet. "How hard did you try?"

When Linette tried to go back to the floor to search for her slate, Perla once again heaved her up. "Tell me!" she shouted, almost crazed.

Linette shoved her sister away with unintentional force. Perla rolled back on her heels, nearly falling to the earth. When she maintained her footing, Linette offered a silent thank you to the builders for planting the support beam where they had, for if they had not, her pregnant sister would have taken a rather violent tumble.

An unearthly sound emanated from deep within Perla as she righted herself. It was ragged and shrill and piercing all at the same time. The noise sent the animals into an uproar, banging and clamoring against their stalls.

Linette was sore from the saddle, and on top of that, very tired and hungry. She was not in a state to defend herself against the frenzy that her sister was sure to bring. She prepared to dart away, but from the corner of her eye, she saw Perla crumple to her knees.

"Forgive me," Perla said as Linette drew beside her. "This is all too much. Please, I just need to sit for a spell." Guiding her to the floor, Linette was struck by how light her sister had become. *She feels hollow as a bird,* she thought.

Once Perla was secure, Linette leaned forward and began to sketch on the dirt floor.

"Amyr was not receiving visitors," Perla read, still teetering a bit, *"and no one knew anything about werewolves."* Hope suddenly lifted Perla's countenance. "No news is sometimes good news, right?" she asked.

Linette nodded, and began to write again.

"I was told to ask the Lord of Benwick." Perla leaned back against the beam, beaten and exhausted. "This is such a fun game that the Creator is playing with us, isn't it?" she said, gazing at the rafters.

The sisters sat in silence while determined moths battered against the lanterns above their heads. Eventually, Linette stood and offered a hand to Perla, and wished, not for the first time, that she could actually *speak* comforting words.

"Maybe I should just wait patiently for news?" Perla said, accepting Linette's hand. "I'm sorry, Linny. I know you tried your best."

* * *

"But they must make the Walk!" the advisor insisted. He would have stood to protest, but his knees were not what they once were. Instead, he pounded the arm of the chair. "You will appear weak in the eyes of the realm!"

Ancel sat behind a grand bureau in the Lord of Benwick's quarters, hands folded, taking in the missives and reports that had arrived in his absence.

"Byron," he said, shifting his gaze between the two advisors, "Bilka." He rose and selected one of the many trinkets on the desktop. The quarters had yet to be cleared of Ban's personal affects, but it did not bother Ancel in the least. In truth, he was rather glad to return to his father's quarters and see them unchanged. "You served my father faithfully for many years," he continued, rolling the carved songbird in his hand. "I do not aim to create a revolution here, nor any manner of upheaval. But there are some matters that Lord Ban and I never saw eye to eye on."

"Lord Ancel," Bilka began, rustling uncomfortably on her cushioned seat. "There are rumblings that you have decided to send a laif to accompany Kurrva and Basva, which is a sign of weakness. Dismissing the charges will only plant those seeds deeper in the people's minds."

Carefully, Ancel placed the trinket back in its place. "What seeds?" he asked, regarding the woman with somber curiosity. Since his return, he could not even enjoy a drink without choking on the pulp of rumors.

Bilka cleared her throat and looked to Byron.

"That your *wrists* are frail," said Byron at length. "The decision to allow such treachery to go unpunished will only solidify what your dissenters believe to be true, and cause those who have yet to make up their minds to question your mettle."

Ancel leveled his gaze at the pair. "What a strange world we inhabit, eh?" he said, cracking a grim smile. The horrors that he had faced were mere figments and nightmares to the commonfolk.

"The people of Benwick like to see justice served," Bilka pressed. "They like outright displays of power, all else is craven in their eyes."

Byron spoke next. "It may sound simple, yes," he drawled, rubbing the darkened purple flesh beneath his eye. "But it is a simple that *we* understand. A simple that your *father* understood." Bridging the space between the chairs, Byron offered a reassuring hand to his fellow advisor, kindly patting her hand. "And now that our knights are only a fraction of what they were when your father took his seat—your seat now—the people are feeling even more insecure."

Bilka squeezed Byron's wrist and returned her hand to the arm of her chair. "A showing of justice, a showing of vengeance, a showing of..." she paused, scanning the window dressings and searching for the appropriate word. "Righteousness," she finally said. "A distinct showing of this nature will assuage their fears," she concluded with finality, a satisfied look in her eyes.

"Well said," Byron breathed. He turned to Ancel. "Please, Lord Ancel, I ask you," he paused to amend the statement. "No, we *beg* you to reconsider your decision."

"For how long?"

Byron leaned forward, shading an ear with his hand. "What was that, my Lord?"

"How long will their fears be abated?" Ancel asked, calmly brushing a lock of hair behind his ear. "A week? A month? And when they begin to grow restless again, should I fling open the jails and slaughter the prisoners in the courtyard like pigs? When will it end?" He eased himself down from the desk and strode to the window. "Since when has a showing of grace been defined as cowardice?" he asked.

Behind Ancel's back, Byron and Bilka exchanged a contemptuous smirk that they believed was in secret. They did not realize that the window's reflection clearly played out their insolence.

"My Lord," Byron said, feigning reverence, "they *must* make the Walk."

"Then have it through the gardens," Ancel said, staring at the advisor's flippant reflection on the pane of glass. "I do not condone revenge."

"My Lord, if there is any way that we can change your mind…"

Ancel turned to face them. "Is there anything else that needs my attention?"

The advisors' fidgeting conveyed to Ancel that they were not ready to move along yet. "My patience wears thin," he warned.

Defeated, Byron shifted the parchments in his lap.

Ancel lifted his hand to dismiss them, but Bilka suddenly sat upright.

"Oh, yes!" she said, "I almost forgot about a report from Sir Desdemona."

Over the sound of his own shuffling, Byron spoke. "I didn't see any such reports…" he trailed off.

Bilka ignored the muttering man next to her. "This was a testimony she gave to me personally," she admitted. This detail seemed to satisfy Byron and he stopped sorting through his stack of vellum. After a moment, Bilka continued. "Apparently, she lost well over a dozen horses to an unprovoked werewolf attack."

With narrowed eyes, Ancel gestured for her to go on.

"It happened perhaps a week ago, I believe. The poor woman was still shaking as she regaled me of the story. She told me that she was out collecting taxes in the northeast." Bilka rolled her eyes to the ceiling in thought. "Yes, I believe it was in the northeast. Well, anyhow—"

"Would that not be a bit early for the collection of taxes?" Ancel mused. "Especially in the northern reaches."

The statement interrupted Bilka's chain of memory, and she balked for a moment.

"Perhaps she was out in the fields surveying?" Byron offered, buying his peer time to collect her thoughts.

A shadow of doubt passed across Ancel's face.

"Yes, perhaps." Bilka fixed Byron with a grateful smile. "You will need to take that line of questioning up with Desdemona. The manner or reason as to why she was out there is hardly of great import. If you would like, my Lord, I can commission an agent to investigate the farm on which this event took place."

"And to hold the landowner responsible for the losses," Byron added.

Ancel swiped an aggravated hand over his face. "You will do neither of those actions," he said, perplexed at his council. "*Werewolves*, you say?" he squinted at Bilka and she nodded in agreement. Locking his hands onto the back of his chair, he rocked forward on the balls of his feet and sunk back down. "This is a matter that I will see to personally."

Struggling to stand, Byron wished to offer protest. "My Lord, there are other matters that need your attention," he interjected. "We need to recruit more knights, and our alliance with Rhionydd is in question, and need I go on about the recent resurgence of ghouls in—"

"Dismissed," Ancel said, taking his seat.

The advisors reacted as cats awash beneath an upturned bucket. "But! But!" they objected. Finally, Byron mastered gravity and clambered to his feet.

"There are tourney preparations, and a great many—"

Lesser men might have punched their desks, demanding that their wishes be adhered to, or they might shoot up and scream, clarifying their sentiments. Ancel was not like most men, and only glared in response. His glare seemed to calculate a thousand ways to disembowel the older man, which abruptly drew Byron up short.

"I am loath to repeat myself," said the Lord of Benwick casually, as calm as if he were inviting them to tea.

* * *

Amyr awaited a response.

The young woman knew that Amyr's chambers morphed into whatever surroundings pleased him at the moment. And at the moment, he was in a marsh.

"I'm sorry," she said, stumbling to find the correct words. Growing up in the service of the Church, she had attempted to be truthful most of the time, but when speaking to the Arbiter, well, it was an entirely different affair. An untruth spelled immediate death. "I did not know," she continued, slowly and carefully, "that she was important to you."

"Mallory was it?" Amyr asked, carelessly inclining his head away. A nearby egret, with a crayfish latched in its beak, rattled its wings and took flight. The laif followed the bird with his eyes alone. "I want you to do me a favor."

"Anything," she replied hastily. Immediately the lights fled her eyes and she dropped from the shore, tumbling into the murky bog, lost for all time.

The most aggravated sigh scraped against the ancient laif's throat.

A youthful-looking opossum trundled past, skillfully avoiding the prickers on a thorn bush. From behind his back, Amyr produced a green apple and snickered, encouraging the creature to approach. Reluctant at first, the opossum seemed to point to his chest and look around, as if to ask *is that apple for me?* With a renewed confidence, it walked toward Amyr's feet.

"Perhaps you can do me a favor," Amyr said, bending a knee and offering the fruit. The opossum snatched it from his hand and began to gnaw at the fruit. Withdrawing a small patch of vellum and a quill, Amyr wrote a brief message.

"There," he said, dotting the period. "Now, if you would be so kind." He twirled a finger, asking the creature to rotate. With the semblance of a nod, the opossum obliged, still crunching on its apple, and spun around with its tail facing the laif. "Take this message yonder," Amyr directed, placing the rolled parchment into the creature's tail and pointing toward a disruption in the trees.

The opossum fixed Amyr with a look that clearly conveyed, "in a moment."

"Oh, yes. Please take your time. I wouldn't want you to suffer a cramp."

Soon the apple core disappeared down the opossum's gullet, and it turned to face the odd tree. With another nod, the creature heaved the message upward in its tail and marched forward.

As Amyr waited patiently for the door to open and the animal to step beyond, his mind rushed once again to that girl, the girl with the shadesgill and the inability to lie. At least, she was unable to lie with her tongue. The ancient laif knew all too well that deceit could arrive in many different packages, curried in a vast selection of flavors.

Another page or squire would be arriving soon, and he grew bored of the marshlands. He mindfully delayed the transition, allowing the opossum time to amble back into the marsh before changing the décor. Winking and smiling, Amyr bid farewell to the creature before turning his face to the sky while everything around him whirled, shredding the world elastic for a glimmering second, before settling back into place.

He had returned the room to his living chambers. A fire sputtered to life in the hearth, his collection of arms and armour stood on display, and a vast expanse adorned with colorful tapestries stretched between himself and the empty space where a bed had once resided. Flicking his wrist, a crater opened in its stead, opening an expanse to nowhere.

Much better, he thought. Immediately after, a shaft of light spread across the stone floor. The door creaked open, and the shaft became a widening cone.

"Lord Amyr," a refreshingly bold voice said. "You requested a messenger."

The laif turned to see a belted knight standing in the doorway.

This is a first. Amyr smiled, fractionally intrigued.

"Ordinarily, my requests yield a young page. And other times, I am hailed by a first or second year squire."

"You have me in their stead."

Amyr tilted his head back and scratched the pale side of his chin. "May I interest you in some wine, Sir Knight?" he asked, gesturing at a bottle on a nearby sill.

The knight simply eased the door shut behind her.

Not lingering for a response, the laif poured a second cup. Amyr had grown accustomed to mortals opting to remain silent in response to basic questions.

"Let's stick to simple answers then," he said, releasing the cup into the knight's hand. "May I have your name?"

The knight raised her cup in salute. "Sir Esther," she replied, but did not place to cup to her mouth.

"Do you not wish to drink?"

"I wish to survive."

Amyr feigned a puzzled expression. "It's not poisoned, I assure you," he said, taking a seat and crossing his legs. He began to swirl the red liquid in his cup while resting his chin expectantly in his other hand.

Esther responded to the laif with silence.

"How prudential," Amyr commented, then slugged his wine back in one splash. "Prudential, but uninteresting." He sighed.

Suddenly, the opossum scurried up from the crater in the far corner of the room. In its cocked tail was a parchment of a different shade than the one placed by Amyr earlier. The laif reached down from his chair and received the offered note.

THE PAGE HAS BEEN DELAYED.

HE WILL ARRIVE SHORTLY.

—CLERIC ELLA

"How *interesting*," he said with relish. Esther's blade was suddenly a hair's breadth from his left clavicle, but he merely winked at his small messenger. Instantly the knight's appearance altered and her essence tightened. It cascaded in a fine downward mist and settled into a mottled gray appearance. Before her sword could strike a spark on the stone, Esther had assumed the form of a rather confused marsupial.

She looked up at Amyr and displayed the most bewildered expression an opossum could muster.

"I have my suspicions," Amyr explained, retrieving the fallen sword. "Squeak once if I am correct."

Esther, from the floor, bobbed her head while offering a wary eye to the other creature inhabiting the floor.

"Are you, perchance, a sibling of the squire that recently perished in my presence?"

The messenger opossum crept closer to Esther and she stiffened, remaining silent at the question. Amyr was certain that he was correct, and with his boot, he nudged the encroaching creature back, giving Esther more space.

"Are you Mallory's sister?" he asked.

A blank expression was the only reply.

"Fine." Amyr scraped his finger across his chest as if striking a match.

Gagging and rasping, Esther curled up on the floor. In a jarring turn, distinctly human sounds now issued from her throat. "Gah! Fack!" she cursed and clutched her neck. The other opossum reared back on its haunches in horrified concern.

"I can speak," Esther said in disbelief. "I can speak," repeated the furry knight, more assertively.

Amyr, still seated with his legs crossed, casually refreshed his wine cup. "For the moment," he said. "Explain yourself."

Returning to all fours after scratching her cheek with her hind leg, Esther worked her jaw. "I am Mallory's mother, and she—"

"That's enough," Amyr interrupted. His mild curiosity had been satiated. "Depart. Both of you." Immediately the creatures disappeared.

Leaning back, Amyr enjoyed the renewed silence. He lifted his eyes to the ceiling, and spidery vines began to spread behind the wake of his gaze. Moths with skulls adorning each of their powdery wings began to spring up from the tangled mass. In contrast, butterflies bearing the mark of the warrior came forth from the darkness as a rebuttal.

Odd, Amyr thought, screwing his eyes at the warrior butterflies. *Those symbols are upside down.*

The hinges on his door suddenly squealed, alerting him to the arrival of the promised page.

A small boy's face peeked into the room. "Hullo, Lord Amyr," said the page tentatively. "You need a message delivered today?"

"Yes," Amyr admired his cup. "I would offer you some wine, lad, but," he looked the boy up and down. "Please, close the door. Thank you."

The page folded his hands, awaiting his next instruction.

"If given a swift palfrey, how fast could you ride to Benwick?"

25

"Why would they cut out their tongues?" Stacey cocked her head in confusion. She had grown accustomed to Jekar having an answer for everything.

"I don't know," he admitted, tossing a pebble into the pond.

Stacey watched the little rock skip across the glassy surface, waiting for her turn. "Nice one," she said, rummaging through the assortment of stones in her hand.

Several days prior, she and Ector had stumbled upon this peaceful retreat just southeast of the fort. He had left for Benwick the other day, and the squire could not stop thinking about him, and had visited this spot every day since his departure.

"Aside from their proclivity for extracting tongues," Jekar continued, "I have recently come to understand that dragoons are very strange laives."

"Says the werewolf," muttered Stacey.

Jekar pitched another pebble. "I heard that," he said, tapping his ear. "I hear *everything* now."

A frog darted from the cordgrass on the bank and lunged into the pool, carving a smooth course on the surface before disappearing beneath a host of cattails. On the opposing bank, a clutch of goblins peered from beneath the shadows of the trees, tentatively approaching the still water with pilfered canteens held tight to their chests. Jekar's recently flung pebble splashed nearby, showering the embankment in a brief mist, and the monsters recoiled, sharing a startled flinch.

The werewolf felt a soft touch on his arm.

"Let's hold for a moment, eh?" Stacey said gently, nodding toward the goblins.

His ears flushed hot. "Of course, of course," he nodded, lowering his readied arm.

"How do they survive winters?" Stacey inquired, stepping over the embankment and taking a seat in the grass.

Jekar dropped the pebbles in his hand and followed the squire.

"Goblins?" Sitting down, he shuffled his boots off and placed his feet in the cool water. "Goblins are hearty little ruffians, to be sure. The ones without a clan will seek shelter, but just like mortals born without a mark, they survive better in groups."

"The ones on their own probably don't live long, do they?"

The werewolf watched the goblins frolicking and splashing, having totally forgotten their empty canteens. His eyes steadily grew unfocused.

"No," he replied after a drawn pause. "No, they do not."

"So," Stacey began, plucking a frond and stripping its tendrils, "speaking of packs. What do you think you'll do, *Sir* Jekar? Will you stay with your fellow knights at the fort or will you be setting off on your own?"

Jekar skimmed a knuckle along his prickly chin. Since his transformation, the stubble on his face had been growing faster and much coarser. He was finding it more and more difficult to maintain a clean-shaven complexion.

"I will stay with Corbin," he stated with calm assurance.

"You're a royal knight now," Stacey said, the frond clenched between her teeth like a pipe stem. "You have options."

Jekar's torso swayed as he buried his feet deeper into the silt. "You say that as if it is true."

"Because it is."

"It is not that simple."

"Look." Stacey plucked the stalk from her teeth and waved it toward the trees across the pond. "It's not like you're a goblin."

"That is flattering." Jekar leaned back, propping himself up with both arms. He closed his eyes and lifted his chin to the sun. "It is not duty to me. I *want* to stay with my pack."

The squire scratched at a nostril, weighing the werewolf's words. "Sounds simple enough to me," she said, returning the frond to her mouth.

"What about you?" Jekar asked. "How long until you are belted?"

"Well, not all of us are lucky enough to become werewolves one day, and thwart an evil army the next, *and then* receive the king's favor, *and then* get a swift field knighting ceremony." Stacey bundled her knees to her chest and placed her chin atop them. "For some of us, it takes years," she said, not a hint of bitterness in her voice.

"You know," Jekar began, a rare glimmer of mischief streaking behind his eyes, "I could knight you. Right here, right now."

Standing to her feet, Stacey inclined her head at the werewolf. "I don't care what Bryndon says about you," she said, grinning as she turned to leave. "I think you have a very keen sense of humor. It doesn't rise to the surface often, but when it does..."

Stacey and Jekar could hear the argument before they even approached the fort's south gate.

"Sounds like the sisters are at it again," she commented to Jekar as she waved at a sentinel. The man nodded, and passed along the signal to the guards below him. A few seconds later the gates opened and the two traversed into the fort.

The fort was still a mess of toil. Soldiers and red knights worked congruently to erect new fortifications and render support to the existing ones. Noticing the heat radiating from a nearby red knight's armour, Stacey whistled to herself. The others had been granted leave from their plate under the hot sun, but the red knights were held to a different standard.

"I am off to find Corbin," Jekar said, splitting off, "good luck with the *sisters*," he added, rolling his eyes. He twirled around and set off for the captain's underground lair.

As of late it was not very difficult for Stacey to find her knight. She would simply follow her ears toward the sounds of sibling discord. Between the ringing hammers and shouts of constructive guidance, she paused to listen for Carlysle's voice. Though she did not will it, within every pause, within any stillness, her mind would wander to *him*. Her mind was just beginning to reminisce on their good-bye scene when a screaming accusation shattered the picture.

"And you're such an inspiration?!"

Yep. "There they are."

As Stacey grew closer, she was able to pinpoint exactly where the current row was taking place. Approaching a shop, she saw a discontented blacksmith standing outside, leaning against the wall. His coal darkened forehead furrowed as he inclined his head at the squire.

"You know I survived this entire siege, Stacey," he said bitterly. "From start to finish, here I was, working away, keeping my head down and staying useful."

They both winced at the sound of something shattering inside the shop. Stacey was not sure how to respond, but she knew where he was going with this.

"But your knight," he said, thumbing toward the clamor, "and her sideways talking sister are the worst of it!" Flinging his hands up, the smithy stalked away, clearly only interested in grumbling about his recent misfortunes. For that, Stacey could not blame him one bit.

"I'm going for an ale, to hekk with this!" the smith called out when he reached the main path. "You with me?" he asked, startling a passing red knight who ducked his head and scurried off, pretending that he did not hear the offer.

I wonder what sort of ale Sir Ector enjoys... "Gah!" Stacey shook her head, banishing such thoughts. "Focus, squire," she said to herself. Pressing a hand to the door of the shop, she walked inside. The space was exceptionally hot even though the unattended forge was not waging its usual battle with the air.

"Irphen's Downfall is empty," Carlysle explained to her sister, speaking at a reasonable volume. "Everyone has gone home. You are going to need all the help you can get."

Lanaelle was seething. She was in her human shape, but her fangs seemed unwilling to retract. "As I have said a thousand times," she retorted, chest heaving, "we have more than enough *help*. A drunken jester would do better in the court of some lickspittle duke, not surveying the ramparts on the edge of war." Though the clarity of her words were impeded by the unnatural state of her mouth, they were understood all the same.

"Oh, so we're going *there* now, are we?"

"Where else are we going to go?" Lanaelle rose and surveyed the room with her hands upturned. "Drunks are more liable to fall from a parapet. Everyone knows that," she snapped. "It's a fact."

Sensing the hackles about to rise, Stacey cleared her throat, redirecting the ire. "Carlysle," she called. "I'm in need of a sparring partner."

"Just grab a red knight or whatever," Carlysle said, and rounded back to her sister. "I am staying, Lanaelle. I swore an oath. I am honor bound."

Though Stacey, as Carlysle's squire was always in her corner, in this instance, she wished for Lanaelle to win the argument. A return to Benwick would mean a return to Ector.

Lanaelle turned and smacked a gauntlet from a shelf. "Honor?! You want to discuss *honor?*" The piece of armour rattled to a stop somewhere beneath a bureau. "Just fucking leave already!" Lanaelle spat. "Get a laif and go back to whatever tavern you crawled out from!"

"I haven't touched a drink since I made my oath!" Carlysle protested.

Stacey rolled her eyes. It was as if these two were reading from a script. She had heard this exact argument a hundred times.

"Oh! Light an effigy! *Sir Carlysle* has sworn an oath!"

Stepping between the two, Stacey attempted to intercede again. "Carlysle, let's go get something to eat, eh?" she begged her eyebrows raising hopefully.

The knight recoiled. "You're still here?" She shoved the squire aside as if she were an invasive shrub. "Lanaelle, you should understand that I either fulfill my oath, or it's death. There is no way around this! And if not for me, Corbin would have banished you!"

By the look on Lanaelle's face, this was a new revelation and quite off-script.

"Corbin wanted me gone?" The werewolf sunk down onto a cask. Her words grew more distinct as her fangs receded. "Why would he want that?" she asked quietly, leveling her gaze out a small open window.

Carlysle smiled, knowing that she had finally struck a solid blow.

"I'm not sure," she lied, cutting across the room to recover her sister's hand. "But I want you to know that I trust you, sister," the knight said, feeling victory closer than it had ever been. "And I love you."

Lanaelle's eyes had not left the window as her sister grasped her. And Stacey sensed a renewal of rage was coming from the werewolf, wagering that Carlysle had overplayed her hand.

Before she could allow another outburst, Stacey stepped forward. "Carlysle, I was wondering—"

With an unexpected wrath, Carlysle whirled around, and clutched her squire about the collar. Violently, the knight dropped her shoulders and rendered Stacey to her knees before freeing her sword. A humming confusion filled Stacey's ears as she gaped in horror at the knight standing above her, brandishing the sword that she had spent countless hours maintaining. Before she had time to contemplate much else, Carlysle flicked the flat of the blade upon each shoulder, nearly grazing the squire's scalp as she did so.

"I dub thee Sir Stacey Cadfael of Benwick," Carlysle gasped angrily. "I release you of service!" she said, heaving another dry round of gasps. "Now fuck off back to that whelp you have been obsessing over for the last fortnight!" She seized Stacey by the collar once again and rushed her out of the door and into the daylight.

A myriad of emotions battered the newly minted knight as she watched Carlysle retreat back into the dark of the shop. Hatred, shock, relief, and terror stormed through her, and she staggered as reality crested into view.

"Whoa, hey!" A passing soldier caught Stacey as she teetered into him. "Have another round, why don't ya," he joked. He strode away with a mallet in his hand, returning to his labor.

She had not absorbed a drop all day, but she certainly felt a bit tipsy. The ground tilted and rolled with each unsteady footfall. As she stumbled toward her next destination, she left her past behind with each step.

The door she entered was surprisingly light. It opened quite easily and slammed excessively hard against the wall.

Corbin and Jekar balked as if lightning had just struck the tree they were sheltered beneath.

"Bite me!" Stacey demanded.

The werewolves gawked, sharing the same bewildered expression.

"There are no laives to get me past the wards. They have all gone home," she hurriedly explained, sensing the apprehension rising in the room. "And I am going home. Turning me into a monster would make that possible for me—" Her parched throat made it difficult to swallow.

For an awkward spell, she simply stared at the werewolves. Suddenly her mind caught up to her mouth. "Possible for me to return home without a laif," she said, brushing a stray hair behind her ear, finding her composure. "So please, one of you... kindly, bite me."

The early morning fog brushed along the grass, leaving its damp footprints upon each blade of grass and stalk that it reached. Lanaelle gazed out from above the north gate, and imagined the brume furtively glancing over its shoulder, readying itself for the sun's arrival.

She was trying to work through a conversation that she had held with Ren the previous night. She had this nagging feeling that she was missing something important. Like when someone told a joke that you did not understand at the onset, but you laugh because everyone else is laughing. That was how she felt.

"He will not be forgotten," she had said to Ren. "We will avenge your brother, rest assured." Her promise had been met with a contorted look of confusion on the red wolf's face.

"If you say so," he had replied. He tipped his cup of ale and measured her with a glance, then strolled away.

It was that *look*, the way he seemed to survey her as if she had made a joke that landed poorly. *What am I missing,* she wondered as she peered into her cup of beer. Just beyond the fringe of her memory, something loomed, some fragment of consequence. If she could only...

"It's one of those misty moist mornings, eh?" Carlysle chirped. Somehow her sister had appeared without her noticing.

"It is indeed," Lanaelle agreed flatly.

Carlysle placed her bare hand atop the nearby crenellation and removed it instantly. "Very moist," she muttered to herself, waving her hand. She placed her dry hand on Lanaelle's shoulder. "Today is the day, little sister."

Lanaelle nodded and took a loud sip from her cup.

"I only wish that I could be the one to do it."

"Yeah," Lanaelle said. "If only you were a royal knight—" She cut herself short. It had become habitual to pick fights with Carlysle, but after yesterday, she no longer wished to bicker.

Growing up, her older sister, the warrior, had been her hero. But as time had gone on, and disappointment piled atop disappointment, Lanaelle grew to despise her drunk, disgraceful sister. She had always renewed her bitterness by remembering the nights that her parents had spent in disappointed sorrow. While they had wept, she sat alone, wishing. She wished that she had been given the gift, a gift that had been wasted on Carlysle. A gift wasted *by* Carlysle.

Those days were behind her now. And Carlysle was right for once. *Today is the day.*

"*Sir* Lanaelle Trovac of Benwick!" Carlysle announced to the northern fields. "It has a rather knightly jaunt to it."

"Well, it's preceded by 'Sir,'" Lanaelle said. "Which dictates that it is actually knightly."

Carlysle beamed at her sister. "You know what I mean," she said.

"And," Lanaelle added, "it's not 'of Benwick.'"

Carlysle tilted her head inquisitively.

"It's 'of Fenrirfang,'" Lanaelle amended. "I no longer hail from our birthplace."

"Makes sense, I suppose," Carlysle said. "Which knight is going to be doing the dubbing?"

The sun, meanwhile, was lancing the mist below and setting the hill to a glimmer. The reoccurring cycle suddenly brought comfort to Lanaelle.

"Uh," she said tightening her jaw. "Sir Kenneth of Lowthean, I believe."

Carlysle blinked at the horizon. "Is he the bloke with the heavy eyebrows and the heroic chin?" she asked, puffing out her cheeks.

Lanaelle laughed. "Yes," she replied. "One and the same."

Carlysle joined her sister, laughing from the ramparts and ignoring the odd glances from the patrolling sentinels. "There are worse people to get knighted by, I suppose," she said, wiping a tear from her eye.

"Really?" Lanaelle said, arching an eyebrow. "Who knighted you?"

"You were there," Carlysle began, her tone suddenly dour. "Don't you recall?"

The younger sister contemplated the occasion for a moment. "I don't remember her name..." she said. "But I do remember that she was tall and handsome and very regal."

"Sir Lillian of Orkney," Carlysle stated, staring a thousand miles ahead. "The first knight I ever killed."

Lanaelle choked on her beer and spewed it into her cupped hand. She obviously knew that her sister had a past, but she had believed it to be filled with frivolity and nonsense. "The *first?*" she asked, wide-eyed.

Carlysle lowered her chin to nod, and all the joy seemed to drain downward, leaving behind a mask of heartache. "They tell you that the life of a knight is filled with glory, and that the soft road beneath your feet will be paved by warm gratitude." She sniffed and swiped a thumb across her nose. "For some, I'm sure that happens. But my first year as a knight, well..." She suddenly smiled and fixed bold, hopeful eyes on her sister. "It will be unlike yours. I'm sure of it."

"What happened to you, Carlysle?"

"A great many things," the world-weary knight replied. "But!" She brightened, "we will discuss such horrid things on a later date! Today we celebrate!"

It took a moment for Lanaelle to raise her cup in salute. She was not as gifted as her sister when it came to shifting emotions quickly.

"Do you wager that you'll be allowed to tilt in tourneys?" Carlysle mused.

Lanaelle had never contemplated such a notion. "I doubt it," she said. "I'm fairly certain that Camelot's first werewolf battalion will be relegated to the forest at all times. Our existence will probably become the subject of lore and fable to the common man." In secret, Lanaelle knew that would not be true. She would make certain of that.

"You're probably right," Carlysle agreed, moving her face toward the sun as the warmth of the new day began to overtake the chill. "Such a shame, really."

26

"Just where are you off to so early?"

Ancel started and turned toward the unexpected voice in the dark, having only stepped a single foot outside the keep.

"Ector?" he asked, peering into the darkness.

The younger knight drew into the light. "Aye," Ector replied. "Who else would it be?"

Within seconds, Ancel's eyes adjusted and he noticed a pair of murky orbs glimmering beyond Ector's shoulder. "Is anyone else with you?" he whispered. The morning fog was so thick Ancel could feel the moisture dripping behind his ears.

"Yes," Ector said, gesturing behind him. "Nolan and Gabriel and I have been drinking mulled wine and talking of father."

"You have been awake this entire night?"

With a frown, Ector shrugged. "I suppose so," he said, a tinge of wine still glazing his eyes. "We would have asked you to join but we—"

Ancel raised a hand. "No need to explain yourselves," he said, walking toward the stables. "I will see you later."

"Wait!" Ector chased after him, swaying just a bit. He drew close to his brother and gripped his shoulders. "You're the Lord of Benwick now," he stated emphatically. "And things are different..." he trailed off as he noticed Ancel's garb, the plain outfit of a Benwick courier.

"Hold another moment." Ector stepped back with his hands still locked on his brother's shoulders. Sobriety crept into the corners of his eyes. "I must return to my original query—where exactly are you off to, brother?" he asked, placing a finger to his chin. "I'm sensing a bit of subterfuge."

With very mild force, Ancel removed the remaining hand on his shoulder and returned it to its owner. "There are matters that require an impartial investigation," he said, clearly dismissing his sibling. "I must depart now."

Ector watched his brother head to the stables. "Next time let me in on your secret missions!" he called. "But I know you won't," he muttered to himself, "because that's just how you are. And how you will always be."

Ancel crumpled the map and shoved it into a pouch on his saddle, laughing to himself. *Of course,* he thought, giving his horse a firm pat on her neck, *the farm I am searching for would be decorated with horse skeletons.*

"This is it," he said, feeling his horse tense as he steered him to the left. "Do not worry though, you will not become werewolf food this day." The horse's gait remained stiff and jarring as they abandoned the road and overtook the lawn. Ancel rocked uncomfortably in the saddle. "Or any day, really. I promise," he added, alleviating the tension.

A magnificent palfrey with a black sheen that appeared blue in the sunlight was standing unattended next to the porch. Voices could be heard both inside the small house and also from the barn. Ancel swiveled his head, unsure of which building to attempt first.

Deciding on the house, he approached the building, curling his mantle to cover the mark on his neck.

"Hello," he called, rapping on the loosely hung door. It rattled on its weather-beaten hinges, creating a confusing noise and drowning out his initial greeting. Before he could take a breath to repeat himself, an overjoyed squeal issued from somewhere within. Rushing feet scuffed along the floor and the door was flung open.

The face that greeted him was plastered with hope.

"I am looking for—" Ancel began.

"Tell me!" The woman seemed ecstatic, and was also quite pregnant. "Please!" she exclaimed, bouncing on her feet, keeping balance by holding onto the doorframe.

Ancel was at a loss. This woman must have mistaken him for someone else.

"It's a messenger from Benwick, Father!" she called over her shoulder.

She is not confused.

An older male voice returned a shout of joy, and quickly joined the woman at the threshold. "What do they say?" he asked, swinging into the frame. Seeing the confounded look on Ancel's face, the man deflated. "You're not here about her husband, are you?"

The woman shot a bewildered look at her father, then gaped at Ancel as if he had thrust a dagger into her chest.

Ancel hesitated, wavered for a fleeting moment. Within that moment, the woman's knees buckled. She wailed, reaching out to the air, flinging her arms upward, but both men managed to catch her before she struck the floor.

"Who is her husband?" Ancel asked as they guided the woman out onto the porch to a nearby chair. They worked in concerted effort, lowering her down as a fragile ornament.

"Easy now, easy now," the man said, and gently released his daughter into the chair. After he was satisfied that she would remain upright, he turned to Ancel, his hands on his hips. "He's an architect," he finally replied, wiping his brow, sweaty from the dense and humid air moving through the porch. "Well, he was born an architect. But right now, if he is still alive—" this statement caused the woman to shudder and heave, almost as if she was about to vomit. The man cast a wary glance at his daughter and stepped a careful arc around her.

Leading the messenger aside, the man continued at a lowered volume. "If he is still alive, then he would also be a werewolf," he said, biting his knuckle.

Intrigued, Ancel closed a thoughtful eye. "What is this werewolf's name?"

The tone of the messenger's voice had rekindled hope and before the man could answer, he was cut off. "Corbin!" the woman yelled.

Ancel faltered a step back.

The woman bundled her hands beneath her chin.

"Oh, he lives," Ancel assured them.

As sudden as a storm, the woman rushed Ancel and clung to him, burying her face in his greens and blacks. He could do nothing else but wrap her up in his arms, and console her as she cried, *or laughed?* He could not tell the difference.

Her father sunk down and toppled onto his rear. "Oh, my. Oh, my," he murmured after he was finally able to sit up. "Perla, we must tell your sister," he said, returning to his feet in a messy display.

Perla eased her tear-streaked chin from Ancel's chest. "She's in the barn," she said, fighting back a tearful tremor, "with Amyr."

"And just like that?" Amyr asked, snapping his fingers. "Your horses were gone?"

Linette returned a half-smile, leaning against the first empty stall's gate.

"Wyverns can be nasty," said the laif, resting his forearms on the other stall. "Does it cause your father any concern," he paused, taking a step back and sweeping a graceful pirouette, concluding the brief rotation with a gesture over his shoulder, "being this close to the forest?"

The girl found the laif's odd mannerisms to be rather charming.

Her dog, meanwhile, was disgusted. Gomer, a name Famyl had grown accustomed to, was not impressed by Amyr's second appearance at the farm, and, frankly wished the first had never taken place at all.

Each of the other first laives had been willingly gathered up, himself included, their spirits taken to Avalon or other places. But Amyr had remained, and that fact alone held the origin of Famyl's initial distrust.

"He loves living here," Amyr read the tablet, arching a speculative eyebrow. "But do you love living here?" he countered, scuffing the stall's gate with his boot.

Famyl did not appreciate where this was headed.

"Your dog seems to be broken," Amyr commented. "He growls incessantly like a kettle."

Covering her mouth, Linette gasped laughter and gave Gomer a pat on his head. She had nearly tripped over the relentless dog several times that afternoon.

"And he has yet to leave your side," Amyr added. His eyes remained, unwaveringly fixed on Linette. "So, do you?" he asked, returning to the original question.

Biting her bottom lip, Linette tapped her chalk to the tablet. Even though her reply would be written, she knew that lying would be the death of her. Amyr had advised her that she keep her answers short and concise, and that if he asked anything that may promote a problem, she should avoid answering altogether.

After a period of rhythmic tapping, Amyr called a halt. "I retract my question," he said, turning his back to conjure another.

"Linette!" Kenna stumbled breathlessly into the stables. With his hands on his thighs, staring at the straw riddled floor, the man wheezed out another phrase. "A messenger arrived!" He squinted at Linette and thumbed toward the house. "He brings news," he said, sucking in another gasp, "Corbin yet lives."

Gomer tailed the elated girl as she took off toward her sister. While he was pleased that Corbin was alive, he was more grateful for the chance to abandon Amyr.

Odd, Famyl thought as he maintained a gallop behind Linette, careful not to become entangled in her feet. *Most couriers are born under the Runner, not the Warrior.* It was clear to Famyl that the man standing beside Perla was obviously not a simple message boy.

The sisters rocked back and forth in their embrace, and Linette struggled to remain upright. "When Amyr said that he did not know his fate," Perla confessed into her sister's hair, "I thought surely he must be dead."

Gomer cavorted about their heels, and once space was created, he placed his forepaws onto Perla's thigh. She received his thick head and began to rummage through his fur, fawning over him and murmuring. "Yes, yes, you're a good boy," she said, and, "My husband is alive, yes, yes," and also, "Such a good boy..."

After releasing her sister, Linette noticed the messenger for the first time. She approached him, extending a hand in greeting.

"This is my sister, Linette," Perla made the introduction while Gomer writhed happily on the ground. "She is without speech," she added, resuming scratching the excited dog's belly.

The man clasped her hand. "My name is," he began, and cleared his throat. "Launcelot," he concluded, releasing his grip to scratch his neck. After all, he technically was not lying. He was merely hedging his bets that these folks did not know his given name. Seeing as there had been no sudden intakes of breath or any formal bows at his admission, he believed his identity secure.

Linette began to scribble on her tablet, then lifted it up for his review.

"Have we met before? he read, *"you look familiar."*

"I do not believe so, my lady," he replied, adjusting his stance, and formally clasping his hands behind his back. "But I do travel frequently."

Rolling to his feet, Gomer appraised the rider by sniffing the hem of his tunic. "And that is Gomer," Perla announced. She went on speaking in a higher octave, "he's a good boy!"

Launcelot greeted the dog with a sincere pat upon his haunch. "So I have heard," he said, offering a palm to the busy snout. Though this man was exuding a deceptive scent, Famyl could not sense anything else to dislike about him.

"Do you know any further news of my husband?" Perla asked, rising to her feet.

"Only from what I have read in the missives, my lady," Launcelot replied, holding his stance as a soldier. "He has been—" the man turned his chin and coughed into his fist. "I feel ill-suited to inform you of such happenings."

"Just bloody tell me!"

Linette lowered her tablet. Her sister had expressed the exact same sentiment that she was about to convey—only a great deal quicker.

"Tell her what?" Kenna had returned, lips pale with exhaustion.

In stark contrast to the heavier man, Amyr seemed to have glided the same distance. He stood next to Kenna and placed a steadying hand atop the man's bent back, his mouth forming a quizzical shape while surveying the messenger.

Perla, one hand caressing her belly, lightly crossed to her father and added a reassuring hand to his back. "The messenger, Launcelot, has more news of Corbin, but he—"

"Well, then!" Kenna surged upward, sending the hands flying. "Spit it out, man!"

Appraising the messenger still, Amyr appeared ready to speak but stayed silent. With a brief flash of contempt, he noticed Gomer cheerfully sitting at the stranger's feet.

"Corbin," Launcelot began, "is no longer referred to as merely Corbin. You see, the King saw fit to reward your husband's valor with a royal knighting."

Clutching her collar in surprise, Perla was rendered speechless.

"*Sir* Corbin!" Kenna clapped with glee. "How wonderful!" He and Linette shared an embrace and reached for Perla to join them. The shocked wife eased into the group with crossed arms.

At length, Perla stepped free, staring at the ground. "Will he be returning home for the ceremony then?" she asked timidly.

Launcelot shook his head. "He was knighted on the battlefield," he explained. "Which is partly the reason that I am reticent to report this to you."

"What do you mean?" Kenna asked.

"The werewolves have been commissioned by the royal knights, and are stationed at Fort Navarene indefinitely. Their existence is not meant for common knowledge."

Kenna only seemed more confused. "What does that mean?" he asked, swiveling his head around.

"It means," Amyr cut in, lowering his chin and glowering at Launcelot, "that your son-in-law will not be returning for a long while," he paused to swat an insect on his neck, "if at all."

"That's not—!" Perla flushed and reeled, cradling her belly. The others believed another dramatic bout was about to burst, but looking at Linette, she summoned a measure of unexpected resolve. "We can send a bird, can we not?" she asked with marked composure.

The messenger bowed. "I would be honored to carry your letter to Benwick and employ our finest flyer."

"My gratitude," Perla said, hurrying inside. "Please don't leave, I will not be long."

Amyr stepped toward the messenger, brushing in front of Linette. "Launcelot?" he began, "if that is, indeed, your true name. What brings you to this humble corner of the countryside?"

Gomer's hackles raised, but the dog remained seated. A deep growl gurgled for a few moments before intensifying to a hearty thrum.

"Launcelot is my true name," he said without batting an eye. "And I am here in respect to the slain horses on the roadside. An investigation may commence, and I was sent to place eyes upon it first."

"Sent by *whom?*"

"The Lord of Benwick."

Amyr turned around like a victorious advocate in court. "*Who* else would have sent you, I suppose." He whirled back and fixed the messenger with a hard look. "Who else but *him?*"

The exchange was rather odd for Kenna and Linette, as they could not see where the laif was heading with his questions, or with his inflections.

For Launcelot it seemed natural. "Who else," he stated in agreement.

"Ah!" Amyr swung back around and retrieved Linette's hand. "My lady," he began, lifting her hand to his lips, "I must take my leave for now, but with your father's blessing, I would like to come calling again soon?"

Kenna bristled at that, whether from surprise or disfavor, none could tell. And perhaps neither could he. After all, who was he to turn Lord Amyr, the Arbiter, away? In a wise display of fatherly obligation, he remained silent, and simply folded his arms across his chest.

Amyr sent Kenna a solemn nod, and as he strode past Launcelot, he hooked the messenger's arm. "A word, if you please, good sir," he said, escorting him away. "Good Sir Ancel," he hissed under his breath into the man's ear. Gomer shot to his feet and snarled a warning that was completely ignored. Heedless of this, the dog followed behind, rushing to remain at Launcelot's side.

As soon as they reached Amyr's palfrey, far from earshot, the laif relinquished his grip. "I wish to make my intentions clear," the laif said, nudging a stray lock of hair aside. "You appear confused, but I am not easily fooled. In fact, it is almost impossible to fool me, as you are well aware." With a jerk, Amyr secured his saddle, before hastily rocking back to face the man. "You think you're so clever. Appearing here, from out of nowhere, with a tale of *investigation.* I know what you are seeking."

The bewilderment on Ancel's face only deepened.

Amyr gathered a sudden fury. "She is meant for me!" he seethed through grinding teeth. "It would be wise to keep your distance." Leaping onto his mount, the laif, with venomous eyes, gazed down. "I see nothing," he spat. Clicking his teeth, the laif turned his horse around to face the man head on.

"Farewell, Lord of Benwick," he concluded, an ominous tone in his voice.

Ancel and Gomer watched in stunned silence as the laif's horse tore across the lawn. When Amyr reached the road, he pressed his courser, driving her at an impossible rate of speed.

Turning to Gomer, Ancel raised his eyebrows. "What do you suppose was the source of that display?" he asked the dog.

Famyl knew Amyr could be a bit eccentric at times, but this was out of character, even for him. If the dog could have responded to this Lord of Benwick with a shrug, he would have, but instead he thumped his tail on the grass. Outwardly, he displayed merry canine ignorance, but inside there was a pitched battle of fiery indignation.

Linette is not meant for him, he promised himself, bouncing as he trailed Ancel's return to the house.

Kenna and Linette had retreated onto the porch. Leaning back in his chair, the broad farmer laughed uproariously at something written upon his daughter's tablet. Once he caught sight of Ancel from the side of his eyes, he straightened and waved for him to come and join them.

"So please, Launcelot," he said, wiping a tear from the corner of his eye. "Please stay for supper. You must have been riding all morning to reach us." Kenna caught the messenger's hesitation. "Linette here made her famous flayed grouse stew. It's really good..." he added.

Since Ancel first set foot on this farm, everything that transpired had been strange.

A welcome sort of strange, he thought. *And strange is far better than war.*

Launcelot shrugged. "How can I refuse?"

27

Ancel's eyes darkened. "These tax collectors have been taking your shadesgill for how long?" he asked, setting his fork aside.

Kenna had been speaking for his daughter. "For going on nearly ten years now, perhaps?" he said, turning to Linette. She gave a confirming nod while swirling a spoon in her tea.

"That is an expensive harvest!" Ancel exclaimed. "How many plants do they take as tax?"

"All of them," Kenna dabbed his moustache with a cloth. "They claim that it's necessary for the realm."

How many more tales of this nature will I uncover? Ancel wondered. *Oh, Father, did you know?* Taking a measured breath, Ancel tried to focus in order to maintain his veneer of a simple courier. A nuzzle against his thigh spun his attention downward. Gomer was gazing up at him, panting and smiling in the way only a dog is capable of.

"Interesting," he noted calmly, looking away as he slipped a hunk of meat down to Gomer.

Linette caught the gesture, a smile tugging her lips.

"And these tax collectors," Ancel continued, "were coming to claim the tax that day?"

Perla looked up from her second helping of stew. "More like *coming to torment*," she said. The color had returned to her cheeks, and along with it, her appetite. "And, for the record, if you're keeping one—those assholes got what they deserved!"

"Perla!" Kenna scolded his daughter, waving a spoon and scowling at her.

Perla wilted.

"Come now," Kenna said gently, settling back into his bowl. "We have a guest here... and we all know that was only a fraction of what they deserved." The man could never maintain a jest, and it was not long before his frown cracked and fractured into a vast grin.

"Oh, Father." Perla flung a napkin at the chortling man. "Oh, father!" She jarred the table as she shot to her feet. Something beyond the window sucked the humor from her face. She raised a trembling finger and pointed. "Father! Those... those men in the field!"

With a clattering of utensils, the table jolted once again as Kenna stood and rounded toward the window. "Those aren't men!" he cried, looking back at Ancel.

"Those are ogres," Ancel stated, as calm as if he was simply identifying an insect. He was still seated, enjoying his meal. Sensing that Kenna was about to flinch toward the door, he halted him by lifting his fork. "I will take care of them."

A simple messenger would not exhibit such a mild demeanor in this situation, and although he recognized this, he disregarded the ruse. This was his realm, and he would not allow suffering if he could help it.

Ancel walked out into the daylight.

"Your sword!" Kenna shouted, watching from the window. "He forgot his sword!" He stumbled about the room, drunk with fear, searching for the blade. Upending a chair, he paused as a thought occurred to him.

"Who is going to bring it out to him?" he mumbled. Carefully reaching down, Kenna picked up the fallen chair and set it back in its place. "Certainly not going to be me..." he muttered, walking between his daughters and returning his elbows to the window.

With rapt attention they observed the bold messenger striding out to meet the monsters, unarmed and seemingly unafraid. Keeping a safe distance, Gomer barked from the porch. The ogres traversed the hem of the forest, skirting several yards into Kenna's fields, an acre shy of the dog's challenging reproach. Beneath the heavy whispers filled with fear and awe, the scratching of chalk to slate could be heard.

Tapping Kenna on the shoulder, Linette offered up the tablet.

"That was the direction the wyverns came," he read, flitting his eyes out the window. "Creator preserve us. What is happening in that forest?"

Famyl paced back and forth on the porch shouting at the incursion.

"Get out of here!" and "Make yourselves scarce!" were among the phrases he had selected, but when they reached the air, they merely sounded as barks and shrill yips.

I have made it all the way here. Finally, I am exactly where I want to be! He lamented to himself, recalling the deaths that had befallen him on his journey thus far. *I really do not want this to end.*

"To hekk with it!" he cursed, and set his jaw. However, to the ears of those nearby, it sounded as only a howl. He set off from the porch, sprinting to aid the young Lord. No harm would ever come to Linette as long as he could help it, and what kind of protector would that make him if he sat idly by.

Within moments he caught up to the man.

Ancel paused to turn, parting shafts of wheat, and looked at the dog as if he had been expecting him to join him all along.

This lad is either daft or beyond gallant, Famyl thought, slowing his run to match the man's measured gait. It could not be long before an ogre would spy the two of them and inform his mates. Just as Famyl was making this speculation, one of the spindlier ogres started and turned toward them.

So it begins, Famyl snarled, mustering generations of rage that he hoped this vessel could contain.

Grunting and pointing, the ogre made the alert, and the others shifted their trajectory toward the man and the dog. Not that it would make a lick of difference, but there did not seem to be an alpha among the ogres.

Famyl noticed that Ancel was not slowing in the least. The man was unwavering. *Yes,* Famyl thought, shaking his head, *it seems likely that he is quite daft.*

"You can go back now," Ancel said discreetly, addressing the dog as if they were equals. If he was about to say any more, he did not get the chance. Breaking from the others, the spindly ogre released a yelp and charged headlong toward them. His gangly limbs sputtered in the tilled earth, ratcheting his body in a crooked manner that might be humorous in other situations.

An arrow hissed over their heads, a clear warning, and Ancel heeded it, finally coming to a stop. Famyl was waiting for the man to brandish a hidden weapon, guessing if he were to do so, he should do it soon. The spindly ogre was only twenty paces away and closing.

Crooked teeth and crooked spine wrenched to a halt right before Ancel. The ogre's lower lip quivered, damp and pitiful, as if he was staring his own death fully in the face. Hardly seeming to even register the ogre's existence, Ancel retained his relaxed posture. Impatient lines began to crease the corner of his eyes as he waited for the others to approach.

"Can any of you speak?" he queried, passing his eyes over the monsters.

Famyl knew that ogres and other monsters were occasionally gifted with laif speech. It was an oddity and, more often than not, the misfit was slaughtered for the gift. This Lord, this Ancel of Benwick, was somehow aware of monster culture.

He's neither daft nor bold. Famyl viewed the man with new eyes. *He's prepared.*

After a few moments of stillness, an ogre stepped forward. "I am able," he said, the words creaking forth like scraping boughs. Bashfully, the ogre scratched at his wrists and stared at the grain wavering in the breeze.

"There is no shame in your gift," said Ancel. The ogre's eyes surfaced for an instant, then fell. "You are far from your lands," he continued, "I ask that you go back."

Once the ogre interpreted what Ancel had said, the clan began to grow restless. The spindly fellow had shuffled back into their shadows, unnervingly pacing like he had been afflicted with a spirit. A stout ogre hefting a broad axe to his shoulder offered a series of grunts to the interpreter.

"They own the tilled earth," the ogre recounted in a strange accent. "We own the trees of shadow." He concluded with a knowing nod, as if he had spoken a secret code that Ancel was privy to.

"I do not know what that means," Ancel replied, shaking his head and looking to the axe-wielding ogre. "If you stay here," he said, gesturing downward, "then you will be met with your death." Drawing a line across one's throat was a signal that was fairly universal, and Ancel employed the motion. "You must return."

All of the ogres reeled at once. The interpreter and the axe ogre were the only members that did not quaver. "But where should we go?" the ogre. "We do not fit anymore."

Ancel approached and the archers nocked. "Easy," he said, raising palms of surrender. "Go back into the trees. Stay off the tilled earth. That is all that I can offer."

"You welcome us," the ogre's face wrinkled. "Why do the others not?"

Disappointment was clearly written on Ancel's face. "The others prefer blood over words," He pointed over their heads toward the forest. "Go back and travel under the trees. You do not need to venture far inside, but just stay in the forest."

Acknowledging the advice, the ogre bobbed his head and conveyed the message to the others.

"Please," Ancel pleaded, fanning them back. "Please."

As if the word contained an incantation, the ogres spun in unison on heavy heels and returned to the forest. The interpreter remained briefly, standing with folded hands. "An evil comes," he warned. "Stay safe."

"They're going back," Kenna said in disbelief, looking between his equally awestruck daughters. "They're going back!" he repeated, clapping his hands.

The knee-high grain seemed to bid the messenger farewell, receding behind his return. As he swiveled his head to look down at Gomer, trotting faithfully next to him, Linette felt a shock of remembrance. *That profile,* she thought. *I know where I've seen it before!* For a fleeting moment, she wanted to tell her family who the man really was. If her tablet had been nearer, she very well may have. In the end, she decided that she wished to see how his game would play out. Akin to all of her favorite stories, she hoped that this one had a happy ending.

Kenna hurtled toward Launcelot, appearing ready to wrap the taller man in a hug, but at the last moment decided against it. "How did you do that?" he asked, instead vigorously shaking the man's hand. "That was brilliant!"

"*That* did not happen," Launcelot replied sternly, freeing his hand. "No one must know of this."

"Yes..." Kenna was a bit startled by the severity in the man's voice. "Yes, of course," he agreed, looking to Linette. "Not a word." He turned to Perla, who was already nodding in agreement.

Launcelot closed his eyes. "Gramercy," he said. He unfolded his hands and peered at Kenna. "Now, about those tax collectors?"

After Launcelot had heard the tale, Linette asked if he had any interest in seeing her garden. She led him outside, under gathering clouds and retreating daylight, waiting for his eyes to see what was taken from her each year. The pair stood outside in the humid evening as the thrum of forest frogs listlessly invaded the air.

"This has," Launcelot began, taking a deep breath, "this has taken an unexpected turn." The shadesgill before him was brilliantly maintained, and his heart ached looking at it.

Tucking the tablet under her folded arms, Linette gave the man her full attention.

"The harvest of these plants alone would fetch..." he covered his mouth and started an internal tally. "Quite a sum," he finally said. "If what you say is true," his mouth snapped shut, suddenly finding himself at a loss, "it is just that, well, it would be difficult to quantify your damages."

Without torch or flame, Launcelot needed to draw close in order to read the woman's message.

"Just let me keep this one," he read. When he realized how closely he was standing to the woman, he stepped back quickly. "Are you sure?" he asked, fascinated. "You have lost so much."

Linette wrote a reply and moved close.

Launcelot inclined his head and narrowed his eyes, the scent of balsam and hyacinth drifted past him. *"I am sure. This one is my favorite anyhow,"* he read the words and a pit began to form in his stomach. His realm had been stealing from this small farm for years, and this woman had no interest in negotiating. She shouldered all the leverage in the world against him. If she had requested to be free from taxes for the rest of her life, he would have obliged.

"You humble me," he said, dropping the issue. But inside, he swore that he would make amends to her someday.

A swelling chorus of insects resonated from the field across the road, brawling with the other singers of the night. Linette coughed a laugh at their sudden outburst.

Launcelot squinted into the beyond. "Katydids," he said, smiling at her. Beneath his line of sight was the horse graveyard that had brought him to this farm in the first place. "You know, I came here to see about a werewolf attack on some horses, and now I find that those horses were, more than likely, purchased with the profits from stolen crops."

Speculative eyebrows appeared on Linette's forehead.

"I think it best that the realm drop any further inquiry."

Linette's chalk scraped the tablet, and she drew closer. Hyacinth and pine swept past again.

"Can a simple message boy make that call?" Launcelot staggered back, feigning affront. "I'll have you know that despite my simple raiment," he said, plucking his shoulders, "my family is actually rather well-off, and all three of my brothers are Warrior born, so my word holds a bit

of sway." Nothing in his statement was false, but the parcel it was borne in was not entirely wrapped in truth.

Fanning her face, Linette pretended to be on the verge of swooning.

"It's true," Launcelot continued. "We own a small keep where silver shadesgill grows wild. A shame that no one maintains the poor flowers. They are not very healthy, but their shoots agree with the soil there, most assuredly. Faewort sprouts from the boughs overhanging the plot—"

Abruptly the collar of his mantle was wrapped in a fist and pressed painfully to the underside of his chin. "My lady!" he croaked with amusement. The ferocity in her eyes gave the man pause, but he did not fear her. "Perhaps I can take you there someday?"

Linette's feigned aggression gave way to a playful smirk. A thought breached her mind and the dim evening sun was not very helpful with the search for her recently flung tablet. She probed the grass with her fingers, hoping to brush against the familiar slate. Several steps behind her, Launcelot noticed a stark flatness against the contour of the lawn.

"Found it," he said, reaching down and wiping the mist from the smooth tablet's face. He passed the slate back to her and peered into the dwindling light on the horizon.

Chalk was already in her hand and she set to work, scribbling away.

Dropping his vision to Linette's message, the man read, *"You understand shadesgill?"* He nodded in reply, but she hardly noticed and was already inscribing another phrase. *"You must take me there,"* the upraised slate said. Launcelot's nose nearly touched the tablet in his effort to see. The words had become a bit more difficult to decipher with the slickness from the grass mixed with the powdery dust that had clung and gathered with each erasure.

Locking both hands behind his back, Launcelot did his finest servant impersonation. "I would be happy to escort you there someday," he stated with a courtly nod. "Alas, this day is waning, and I have a long, dark ride ahead of me."

As he prepared to leave, he noticed another message that had been written without his notice. *"Will you come back soon?"* The tablet was hastily withdrawn upon his recital of the question.

"Yes," he replied. "In three days I will return," he promised. "That should allow ample time for the Lord to render his decision."

His horse was hobbled near the porch, but before he crossed the lawn, he turned back to the woman. "If that is all right with you?" he asked then, shyly, hitching the hood of his mantle over his head. His long hair poured from the sides of the hood, draping over his chest and further concealing his Warrior mark.

The woman rose on her tiptoes, ardently nodding. After she descended to her heels, she offered a single wave of good-bye.

"Sleep well," the messenger said, and departed into the gloom.

28

"How was I supposed to know that they would react that way?" Jekar asked over quick suctions of breath. While continuing to sprint, he looked over his shoulder for a brief instant to make sure that another axe was not being lobbed in his direction.

"Oh, I don't know," Stacey argued, crouching beneath a thick branch and springing back into a run, "maybe the fact that they're *rat people* and we're *wolf people,* could have told you?"

"But how did they *know* we're wolf people?" Jekar lunged between a crevice dividing a rising pair of elm. "We're in our human skins."

"Smell, maybe? Hey, try to keep up."

"I am keeping up."

"No, I'm slowing down—"

Stacey had only glanced back for a moment, and in that gap of time somehow a mischief of victus had formed ahead, blocking their escape. The rat folk apparently knew this patch of the forest pretty well. Stacey wagered the fleet-footed rat-like people were hunters, judging by their bows and slim blades. They looked like hunters to her, all wrapped in animal furs piled atop their own fur. Their leader stepped forth, adorned in a crag lion pelt, the hood of which bore fangs that dangled a wary inch from his snout. It seemed a bit impractical to Stacey, but if he made it work, who was she to judge?

"Your weapons and satchels," the leader whined, twisting his head curiously.

Jekar and Stacey were averse to giving up their belongings, and it did occur to both of them that if they were to transform, the altercation would come to a swift end. A swift, but brutal end. Secretly each hoped that the other would change, and they would follow suit. But being the first to bring carnage was something neither wanted to be held responsible for. They were werewolves, but they weren't without scruples.

The leader was growing impatient. "Now!" he demanded, scraping claws into his open palm. The hunters at his flank began to raise their bows menacingly. "Wait for them to alter into wolves," he said. "Think of the pelts, boys." A delighted hiss whistled past his buckteeth. "They'll be magnificent."

Carefully Jekar began to loosen his belt with one hand, keeping his other raised in surrender. "No need for that," he said, complying to the demands. "Here." He dropped the belt and scabbard, then looped his satchel over his head and added it to the pile. Following suit, Stacey begrudgingly did the same.

"A pity," the victus leader gestured for his hunters to retrieve the items. "Your pelts would have made handsome conversation starters." In a matter of moments, everything Stacey owned was swept up, bundled, and carried away. As the victus began to dissipate into the shadows, the leader turned back. The slender tail of his lion mantle swung around, corkscrewing and winding around his shins.

"One last thing," he moaned, slowly leaning to the side at a dreadful angle. "Why did you approach us in the first place? If you had waited, you would have passed undetected by our scouts."

"I am a physician," Jekar began, adjusting his spectacles. The bridge pieces were slick from sweat and sliding down his nose. "I merely wished to offer aid to your people."

The victus sniffed the wind and abruptly wrenched up. "A bit of advice," he said with whistle at the end, "commit to one life or the other." He walked backwards into obscurity, and called out from the darkness, "you'll find life much simpler after you do." Red eyes inset in the gloom hovered facing the werewolves for a moment, then vanished.

"Well, that was unfortunate," Jekar remarked, his tunic billowing at the hips where his belt had been. "We have a decision to make."

Stacey was already seated on a knoll, unbuckling her boots.

"It seems you have already decided?" said Jekar. "Understand that traveling in the forest as werewolves will be much swifter and easier. But traveling outside the forest among the humans in Benwick, I fear will not be as simple. We will need to find clothing as soon as we can. A pair of naked humans will draw attention just as swiftly as a pair of skulking werewolves."

After a few moments of contemplation, Stacey resumed her unbuckling. "I'm more concerned with the immediate dangers we face," she said, setting a freed boot aside. "We won't need to worry about finding a change of clothes if we're cut down by a victus arrow, or plucked from the path by an aspweaver, or whatever else, before we even make it out."

The physician appreciated Stacey's chain of logic. He was glad that Corbin had granted him leave to escort the knight back to her home, though Jekar recalled that the captain had seemed quite distracted when he had made the request. Jekar felt that growing up poor had given him a keen insight on how people behaved when they were concealing pain or sadness. On the rare occasion he would ask his mother for permission to buy a toy or sweets, she would relent with a pained smile that he could recall to this day. Even though his family had been of meager means, his parents did not want their children to go without.

That smile, the sort of beleaguered smile that his mother would bear on those dreary afternoons was the same that had crested Corbin's face.

"I agree," he said at length. "And let's avoid helping any monsters that we may stumble upon."

Standing barefoot atop the knoll, Stacey stretched and yawned. "That was on you, my friend," she reminded him. "I only want to go home and comfort my aunt, take a nice long bath, and eventually make my way to the manor—" She was about to mention Ector, but felt awkward about it in Jekar's presence.

"In that particular order?"

Stacey laughed as she continued her routine; limbering up before transformation was a bit of advice that she had found extremely helpful. "No, I believe the bath will come first."

* * *

"Isn't it rather late to be sending a bird?" Tamarah asked, peering through the torchlight surrounding the aviary. Both of her hands were buried in the thick sleeves of her coat, avoiding the late night's chill. Sleep had been elusive since her return from war, and she found a stroll often eased her mind. And some of the things she had stumbled upon in this castle when everyone was considered to be asleep had been *remarkable*.

The flapping of the bird's wings were steadily consumed by distance. "Good evening, Sir Tamarah," the hooded figure said, wiping residue from his fingers before lowering his cowl.

"Oh," Tamarah drew a startled breath. "My Lord, I apologize. If I had known it was you..."

"No need," said Ancel, unconcerned.

Tamarah noticed the telltale dark circles inhabiting the skin beneath his eyes, and her heart lurched into her throat.

"Is there cause for worry?" she inquired, expecting the worst.

Striding out from the light and to the parapet, Ancel leaned out and was swallowed by the purple skies. "Nothing that should give you any concern," he finally replied.

"That missive is heading north," she said, hitching a torch from a nearby sconce and approaching Ancel. "I assume it's bound for Fort Navarene."

"You would be correct."

"And you just sent Nocky, the realm's finest harrier, into the dead of night. My Lord, he's a war bird—that doesn't inspire comfort."

Glancing over his shoulder at Nocky's empty pen required more effort than Ancel could gather, and his shoulders sagged into the crenellation. "It is nothing of grave import, I assure you," he said, fighting back the waves of fatigue.

"Tell me then." Tamarah pressed an elbow into the merlon beside Ancel. Her torch exaggerated the scars on his face. "What's this message on the wings?" she demanded, breaking several codes of knightly conduct.

Notoriously, Ancel ignored hierarchy, especially in the manner he treated his knights. But on this night, Tamarah received a *look* from her Lord that she had never received before. The manner of look that was usually reserved for his foes. Many a knight had fallen before the tide of his blade while fixed in that same glare.

For a brief instant, the night began to tunnel around her.

"Until the morrow," Ancel said, heaving himself to a stand.

Without knowing, Tamarah had almost dropped her torch. Reflexively, her fingers snapped tight and the torch corrected itself in her hands, sending papery fragments adrift. Between a barrage of painful blinks, the crenellation had emptied and Tamarah found herself alone on the tower. She knuckled the eye that had been struck by the embers.

"I'm sorry, Ancel," she whispered to the emptiness. "I just can't go back so soon."

At night, the Benwick keep had a face entirely different from the one it presented under the sun. During the daylight hours, there was a happy bustle that consistently pervaded the many corridors and halls. Clattering plates and sloshing tankards were emptied and refilled well after the sun grazed the horizon keeping the servants in magnificent physical shape. Beyond the gates, in the courtyards and gardens, the dwindling number of squires and knights trained. They trained not only for themselves and their lands, but for the knights recently fallen, evidently forgotten by Camelot, but not forgotten by them. Seemingly without end, the crash of steel upon steel could be heard through the apertures in the stonewall of the training grounds, and only when it paused did one recognize the existence of the din.

Back inside, in the galleries and sitting rooms and in the apartments and kitchens, men and women studied and stitched, spun looms and repaired armour, baked bread and triumphed in games. It was not a large castle, but it was full, filled with passionate people who would collapse at the end of the day, onto their beds, hardly sparing a moment to recognize the clean sheets they had fallen upon.

For these reasons, the keep felt solemn and cavernous as Ancel lowered his weary head, gazing at the floor as he pressed on toward his chambers. Without a steadying arm to the corridor wall, the Lord would not have been able to make the distance, and in the morn, his sleeping form would have provided an unexpected nifty tripping hazard for the scurrying feet of some hapless servant.

Ancel pressed against his door, feeling the wood flex beneath his hands, then slapped the latch, swinging the door violently open. He staggered into a room he had believed would be welcomingly dark, save for the light splashing from the roiling hearth, but, to his chagrin, it was illuminated and occupied.

"Ancel," said the woman seated at the foot of his bed. She rose to her feet in greeting, using one hand to smooth her riding dress and red and blue traveler's mantle as she stood. The worn dollop on the bed indicated that she had been waiting for a long stretch of time. Ancel noticed his gifted dragoon spear in her hands. She was casually rolling it into her fingers, then bouncing it back onto her wrist in a clearly practiced motion. "You're back late."

Ancel found it remarkable the way anger effects the body, even a weary one. "If I would have known that *this* is what would greet me," Ancel snarled, "then I would have lingered until the end of harvest."

"There's that sense of humor that I missed so much," said the woman, leaning the spear against a shuttered window. "And people wonder why I decided not to wed you."

"Get out, Kurrva."

"Aren't you curious as to what brings me to your chambers?"

"I am more interested in what will remove you."

She playfully pranced toward him. "I wanted to express mine and Basva's gratitude," she said, pouting her lips, "for relinquishing us of our sentence. Entering the forest without a laif is certain death, and the Walk requires a crossing of several wards, which would have been our end for certain."

Ancel had not moved an inch. "Get out," he repeated, emphasizing the statement by pointing at the threshold.

"Other Lords would have discarded us as waste," she continued, un-afraid. "Please accept our gratitude. Your mercy was as welcome as it was unexpected."

Ancel knew that she was baiting him, but he relented into the trap. "You were never cruel to me," he sighed, finding the back of a chair to rest his hand. "You were aloof. I do not think that justifies execution."

"I stepped out behind your back," Kurrva goaded, caging accusatory fingers to her collar. "But you were always pre-occupied with study and learning about the sleeping habits of goblins in heat, or how many cycles a lapsucker could live inside its host, or how a ghoul selects a grave-yard, or some such nonsense." She paused to collect herself, then jutted a finger at Ancel. "You were continuously absent."

"You're saying that I am to blame for your deception?"

"No," she said, returning her hands to her side, drawing a deep breath. "We share equal blame in this," she stated quickly, releasing a heavy sigh.

"I was never unfaithful," Ancel said curtly, "and I accepted this union as paramount, beyond my personal desires. I accepted it as a lasting bond between our lands, Benwick and Rhionydd. Our children would secure that bond, and it was a burden that I was willing to bear."

"You see?"

"See what?"

"The way you say such things!" Kurrva spun to face the window. "That *we* were nothing but a *burden.* Admit it, you have yet to rid your-self of *her* memory. What you believe Arthur stole from you—"

"It was never a choice," Ancel interjected, ignoring the path that she was leading him down. She knew his past with the king was not a topic he discussed freely. "Our fathers—"

Venomously, Kurrva suddenly rounded on him, unsettling the sheaves of parchment atop a nearby bureau. "Our fathers were selfish!" she spat. "It is a selfish practice to use children as pawns in schemes."

"I would not deem unification as a *scheme*," Ancel objected. "They were seeking an alliance for our realms, for our people. It is not an uncommon practice."

"Common or not, I still find it quite selfish."

Ancel was too weary to point out the obvious irony in her words. Prolonging this exchange would only see him asleep on his feet. "Very well," he said. His eyelids were caving in, and he tried his best to gracefully cross the room without falling on his face. Whether he was successful in appearing coherent to Kurrva, he neither knew nor cared. "Is there anything else?" he asked, bent over the bed frame, his hands beginning to sink into the welcoming velvet resistance of the mattress.

"Only gramercy from Basva and myself," she said, sounding miles away. "And one of your old scholars came by several hours ago with that scary-looking spear—" she cut herself off. "You look exhausted," she said sourly. "Well, he left you a note telling you all about it, along with the details of an upcoming tournament. But I won't keep you any longer."

The gentle breeze that drifted in her wake was the last thing that Ancel remembered, asleep before the door even closed.

29

The line for judgment stretched from inside the basilica, out through the great doors, and beyond, out to where the ground gave way to the flagstone thoroughfare of the central road. Common folk stood alongside royalty, waiting anxiously for their chance to speak with the Arbiter. One could observe shifty landowners and prudential businessmen seeking to garner favor over their rival in a squabble, and also watch the more destitute begging for the Church's blessing on an expectant newborn. No one was barred from entering the basilica to stand at the dais of judgment. It was the singular location in all of Camelot where the lowliest of peasants could rub crusted elbows with the grandest of dukes. That is, if they were bold enough.

Between trembling lips, some mumbled practiced lines to themselves, while others restlessly reviewed written scripts on palm-sized parchment. All were welcome, indeed, but it was understood and clearly cautioned that uttering a single falsehood would mean instant death.

This day, however, Amyr hurried through the week's judgments. He was draped sideways on his throne, one leg kinked over an armrest. His mind wandered elsewhere, and it showed.

"R-Really, Lord Amyr?" the thatcher stammered in shock at the yawning laif. He rocked the dais in excitement. "Oh, thank you so much!" Not wanting to exclaim a jest that could be perceived as a lie, the man wisely skipped away from the dais and ran out into the early afternoon sun.

"My Lord," a crone-like voice invaded Amyr's left ear. "That is the second person who has requested an endless supply of breadsticks," she sighed reprovingly before adding, "and dipping sauce."

Amyr peered at the withery corn stalk of a deacon. "I am aware of this. I was the one who suggested to the first man to make the request," he said, distractedly twirling a lock of his hair. "Has it been three days already?"

The deacon's mouth rumpled in confusion. "Three days since what, my Lord?"

"Since I have seen my Linette, you ditzy drake."

"Ditzy drake...?" The deacon squared herself to the throne, her thin frame barely impeding the onlookers' view. "My Lord, this line has diminished more expediently than any I have ever witnessed. If you have other pressing matters to mind, then—"

Rounding as a serpent to a shrew, Amyr faced the deacon.

"You know what," he said, tracing her wrinkles with his eyes. "You're correct." He surged to his feet, causing the deacon to reel backward. He surveyed the folk comprising the remainder of the expectants, noting that they all appeared to be solitary requests. Disputes brought at least two parties and witnesses along with them, which tended to draw things out.

Huddled before the dais was a solitary woman overripe with child. Behind her was yet another woman afflicted with the same condition. It did not take a diviner's wand to surmise what request they brought.

"Granted!" Amyr shouted in a whirl of movement, racing for the door to his right. "Both of you, granted!" The sentinels, who had never been seen breaking more than a marching stride, dashed to converge on the Arbiter's retreat.

The women wrung their hands together and rejoiced, their distended bellies bouncing together, knocking them back. If not for the lock on each other's wrists, they likely would have been flung to the stone from their own rapture.

The deacon plucked at her long sleeves and bustled to the front of the audience. She shared a look with the pages and squires attending the perimeter, and heaved her arms upward, calling for an impossible silence.

"Dismissed!" she announced. The discussions and remarks drowned out her words. "Dismissed!" she yelled again. Where she failed to be louder, she succeeded in being more grating. With a shrug that caused her bony shoulders to spike around her ears, the deacon bustled away, leaving the basilica, for the first time in her memory, in confounded turmoil.

"Who is this Linette?" the squire leading Amyr's courser from the stables blurted. He tried to seem indifferent, but only came across as terrified. Yet another squire who had drawn the short straw, though the Arbiter had not beckoned this one.

Amyr accepted the offered reins with a furrow upon his brow. "Who put you up to this?" he asked the squire, skimming a finger along the animal's cheek.

The blood drained from the young man's face as he took a step back. His head swiveled back and forth, and his eyes darted and tumbled across the pasture.

"It's a rather simple question," said Amyr, now atop his mount. "Here, let me help you. Take a deep breath and picture whoever it was that spoke to you. Then simply say their name." The horse pranced, turning once round. "I'm sure whoever it is will understand."

Yanking at his bottom lip over and over, the boy held a heated debate in his mind that finally concluded with another outburst. "Deacon Kendall and Magistrate Valencia!"

"Thank you," Amyr replied soothingly, watching the squire's face return to its proper shade. "That wasn't so hard, was it?"

Before Amyr could retract his offhanded remark, the squire replied, "No, not really," and instantly dropped to the muck and straw floor, culled by death.

For the first time in a long while, Amyr felt the sharp sting of guilt latch behind his sternum. "I'm sorry, young lad." The Arbiter swung to the ground and propped the boy's corpse against a nearby bale of hay. "In answer to your question," he began, his voice breaking with emotion, "the reason I am feeling these *feelings* right now is because of the woman you inquired about. I wish you were still alive, and I wish that I had not asked that rhetorical question." He looked to the rafters and shook his head. "But the truth is, my friend, my mind has been absent. My critical mind, that is."

Hastening to his feet, Amyr paced, recounting to the dead young man the time he had spent with Linette. He went on for several minutes illustrating how her hair tumbled at just the right length against her cheeks, then meticulously described the way that she was delightfully imbued with the aromatic palette of pine, mixed with a decadent helping of hyacinth.

"And unlike yourself," Amyr continued, "her eyes do not constantly flit toward the nearest escape whenever she shares my presence. Well, when you were still drawing breath that's what you did. What I mean to say is that she does not exhibit fear. She's casual, but not to the irritating point of apathy. She listens and carefully responds." Presuming the boy would offer objection to that statement, Amyr lifted a finger for silence. "No, no, no, she does not respond carefully because she wants to avoid an early grave, though I'm sure that may be part of it. But, no, I get a sense that she wants to hold a *real* conversation with me."

Dropping to one knee, Amyr fixed the dead squire with a troubled look. "She is also exceedingly attractive. I'm sure you would have agreed. Don't mistake me for being naïve, I assure you," he held back a giggle with two fingers, "I have come across people afflicted with aphasia in the past, but none of them were so..." he paused, his tongue scouring the inside of his cheeks, searching for the proper word. "Pretty," he concluded with supreme satisfaction.

Amyr returned to the saddle. He sniffed the air and gave the organized stables a measured glare. The horse swung towards the open gateway and the rolling hills beyond, yearning to break into a canter. The impatient courser suddenly reared and tore for the fields, flinging fistfuls of debris upon the squire's body.

As Amyr shuttered his eyes from the piercing daylight, he called back toward the barn, "May the cup you raise in Avalon be clean before the wine forever invades it!"

* * *

As they wove through Fenrirfang, bounding fallen logs and evading limbs, Jekar spied a sliver of a tributary meandering through the underbrush. He drew beside his companion and flicked the back of her shoulder. The newly altered werewolf shifted her hips and locked her ankles sideways, churning the softer soil beneath her, and rending a pair of channels behind her heavily clawed feet.

Jekar, more accustomed to his nature, slowed to a trot, leaving the ground intact. "I thirst," he said, illustrating the fact by swiping the foam that had accumulated at the corners of his muzzle. The trickling stream was a leisurely five paces distant, and Stacey only caught sight of it when Jekar dropped to his elbows and began to greedily lap from its waters.

"How did you notice this stream?" she asked in astonishment. "I was so busy dodging branches and gnarled roots and trying not to get lynched by vines..." The other werewolf was loudly sputtering and heaving, drinking so voraciously that Stacey was sure he was not listening.

Where shadows grasped from the endless treetops toward a brief patch of daylight, the tiny waves sparkled cheerily along its course, inviting Stacey to come closer. Striding into the golden rays, Stacey closed her eyes and tilted her chin to the sky, trying to absorb as much light as she possibly could. Her new skin seemed to soak in the radiance like parched earth beneath drizzling rainwater. Without willing it, Stacey began to gently nudge the inner wolf aside, and her fur slowly receded.

As her coat withdrew to her tail, revealing more and more naked flesh, she heard a sharp intake of air from Jekar then a series of sputtering gags and coughs.

Stacey turned abruptly, covering her chest while her fur swiftly crept back upward like a shift, returning her to her werewolf body.

Tears gathered at the sides of Jekar's oval eyes. "You asked how I noticed the stream," he spoke with a husky voice, pummeling his chest and fighting back more coughs. Obviously, the man wished to ignore what had just transpired. "The more time spent in your new form, the more attuned your senses will become." As he spoke, his rasping gradually diminished. "It is something that just takes time," he concluded, not able to meet Stacey's eyes.

Stacey nodded, placing her hands to her hips. "Good to know," she said after an uncomfortable silence. Lowering herself down, she gracefully drank of the freely flowing refreshment. Water had become her most constant companion while traveling with Carlysle. Between the two of them, one needed to maintain a clear mind. And the countless mornings spent pulling her knight's hair back from vomit splashbacks had given Stacey a healthy aversion to stiff drink. Even now, whenever the scent of stale booze wafted past, she needed a moment to fight back the dry heaves.

After consuming her fill, Stacey shook the fur on the underside of her snout and looked toward the forest that lay ahead. "Well, Benwick won't rush to meet us, will it?" she said, glancing sideways at Jekar, who was still bashfully shying from her gaze. *Or was he?*

Jekar's ears were flat to his skull, and he was surveying the treetops as if flaming pumpkins were about to descend upon him.

"Fack!" the physician who never cursed suddenly took up the practice. "Do you hear that?" he asked, now unafraid to join eyes.

Recoiling at the faint clicking seeping through the stretch of forest they had recently left behind, Stacey's heel sunk into the spongy creek bed. "What is *that?*" her voice came hushed, terrified.

"Dullicha," Jekar replied, somehow sounding both reverent and frightened.

"What?!" Stacey reeled another step back, soaking her other foot. "Why?!"

"I don't know why! Stop moving!"

"We should run," Stacey hissed, staring at the forest ahead with fevered eyes. "We can't fight a single dullicha, let alone a host of them!"

"They pursue by sounds of their prey," Jekar explained, spitting out each word. "They're bloody blind."

The clicking grew in volume. "I know that!" Stacey whispered, sinking an inch into the creek.

"Stop. Talking." Jekar made his request through gritted fangs, without shifting a fraction.

At this point, even basic human ears would have been well equipped to pick up the intense clacking of the fabled predators' mandibles. But in an extremely unnerving shift, the clicking came to an abrupt halt a mere stone's throw from the werewolves. Overwhelming silence shaded by the faint tinkling stream infected the atmosphere. A wave of emerald moss that felted against the knees of a nearby tree crept toward a shade of purple, spreading slowly as a toppled vial of ink.

For all the world, Stacey wanted to call out to Jekar and draw his attention to their fate, but she shriveled and blanched instead. Ector's face flashed into her mind, and a dull ache selected a place in her gut, and without permission, took up residence.

I'll never see him again, she thought in desolation. The pain from those words was crippling, and the dull ache became a searing burn that brimmed up into her throat.

Not much was known of the dullicha, other than what little had been recounted by the survivors; folk who had somehow rendered their own bodies paralytic, and those were very few. The majority of those survivors had kept their eyes closed for the duration of the encounter. As with most rare creatures, their descriptions differed, but what was universally agreed upon was the distinct clicking sound that could be heard moments before an attack. For laives and werewolves, they held the advantage of superior hearing, but how one combated such a monster was rendered into the unknown.

The lack of knowledge or of any drawn imitation made it difficult for Stacey to discern exactly what she was witnessing. Though she knew there to be many dullicha, she could see only one. In the shrouded gloom, she strained her eyes, but all she could make out was a pair of great leathery wrinkled wings casually spreading beneath a middling bough. The monster's deepening shadow on the moss below revealed that her eyes were not playing tricks.

Just hold still and wait for them to pass, like a snake over a stone, Stacey told herself. *Or like a warm knife through butter,* she amended, shaking her head, disliking the connotation of the latter. But before she could think of another metaphor—

"Stay... see?" At first the voice sounded like a rock chipping along a craggy descent, broken and unnatural.

"Stacey?" the voice spoke again, this time better sculpted.

Ector? she thought with a swift intake of air. A series of clicks from the front facing trees resounded immediately after her faint sound, collecting into a focused torrent.

"Stacey where are you I am lost in this thicket," Ector said, sounding painfully weary or fall-down drunk. The knight must have wandered into the forest in search of her. Benwick was mere hours away, and there were no wards carving the leagues between, but Stacey was confused that neither werewolf had picked up his scent. Ector would have had to pass nearby, and Stacey could not detect his scent in the least. This all felt very wrong.

"Stacey I love you please *come here,*" the knight spoke again, and the manner in which he beckoned made her hackles stand and the flesh beneath tingle.

From the corners of their eyes, the werewolves peered at one another. Jekar shook his head in tiny agitated increments, begging her to keep silent. Nodding in stark understanding, Stacey assured him that she was not fooled by the daemons at play.

"Jekar," a demure feminine voice soared from the bracken to their right. The volume was unnatural and jarring, and Stacey's heel slipped another inch into the creek. The clicks arose once again, their vibrations fusing together as their proximity tightened. What had sounded as dozens now sounded as two.

"Jekar my skin itches," the female voice said from the same distance. "Jekar help me out of it please."

Oh what the hekk, Stacey fought the urge to shout. *That's my voice!*

Beneath Jekar's fur, he felt warmth flooding into his face in embarrassment.

When Stacey glanced at the other werewolf he was looking elsewhere, trembling in renewed fright. The dullicha on the tree nearby was craning downward, swiveling an orbital appendage that morphed with every twitch. Where once the conical visage of fox appeared, the flatter face of a bat replaced it, and after that a locust, then a creature that she recognized from one of her father's nautical maps. The appendage never settled and was in a perpetual state of change. Even when the monster bowed downward into the sunlight, the faces refused to remain fixed. They were an endless stream, and, as far as Stacey could tell, each was unique and did not repeat.

Stacey imagined stiff calluses developing on the pads of her wolf feet as they scraped against the creek bed. Unmoving and unflinching, she held her ground as the grotesque projection leveled itself to the ground. Slinking behind was the attached body, unfurling its vein-riddled wings and languidly dragging them across the brief distance. Invisible in the trees and thick protruding vegetation, the rest of the dullicha began to click with renewed spirit.

The solitary monster before the creek, lowering itself as if gathering a leap, was hauntingly silent. Its faces continued to endlessly contort and change, and the monster's body came to a halt several feet away, splitting the gap between the werewolves.

If Jekar chose that moment to run a hand through his scalp, his elbow would have grazed the snout of the appendage staring toward him with vacant, milky eyes.

"Jekar come over here I want to show you *something*," Stacey's voice said over the cacophonous clicks, and Jekar's fur began to climb on the back of his neck.

In seeming recognition of the unintentional movement, the facial appendage screwed itself at a keen angle, retracting several feet, and suddenly shot forward. Where the countenance of a llama had been at the wind-up, an almost mirror image depiction of Jekar now pressed inches from his. Snout to snout, the werewolf faces stood within lapping distance of the other, and the dullicha's wolf eyes snapped into focus, swirling toward the forest beyond before settling on what was before it. In that same instant, the monstrous clicking was abruptly drowned by silence.

In a display of dramatic repulsion, the dullicha's body pressed to the earth, and it violently withdrew its projection. Twirling in place, it sputtered and spat and carried on like a beheaded serpent. The monster hastily braced itself and reared up on what could be considered haunches, and ratcheted a stream of clicks into the skies. A tumult of cracking tree branches and scuffing husks returned the call, and the werewolves could sense the dullicha making a swift retreat. With a final glance, the disgusted monster heaved its body in their direction, revealing its true face.

"Werewolves!" the dullicha wheezed, disgruntled. "How revolting." With a single beat of its wings it sent the nearby flora into disarray, and the dullicha shot up toward the taller branches, disappearing from sight.

"Oh, dear," Stacey remarked to Jekar. For nearly a minute, neither wolf had dared make a single movement. "What would you say that looked like to you?"

As Jekar opened his mouth to offer his opinion, a cricket chirped nearby, and the werewolf nearly released the contents of his bowels into the stream.

30

Famyl's head swung like a short pendulum, following Kenna's pacing back and forth. The man had awoken with the thick meat of his palm pressed to his left eye, moaning of a headache. From his bedding on the floor, Famyl had been stirred from his sleep by the creaking floorboards beneath the window. At first, he believed it to be an intruder sneaking in under cover of darkness, but the distinct silhouette was most definitely Kenna. The thrashing candle on his nightstand cast monstrous shadows across the walls and ceiling, multiplying the farmer's agitated footsteps.

"She's my last daughter," he mumbled to himself, scratching beneath his collar. "And yes, I would like to see her married and happy, but..." Turning to his dog, he spoke again, "being courted by the Arbiter? How is a father supposed to respond to that?"

Famyl felt fortunate to be in his current form, for even if he was able to offer advice, he had no idea what to say. Instead, he simply inclined his head and huffed a slight whine.

"Besides, who will help me tend the farm?" Kenna continued, placing his hands on the windowsill and hanging his head. "She is an incredibly hard worker, and Creator knows I can't afford to hire hands." With a heavy sigh, he withdrew from the window and resumed his pacing.

The sun was not expected to crack the horizon for another few hours, so Famyl rested his chin back onto his forepaws and dozed. The idea of Amyr and Linette was disconcerting to him, but at the same

320

time, it was ridiculous. There was still plenty of time for something to go awry, and Famyl was fairly certain that it would. Like Kenna, he had a host of intertwining emotions concerning Linette. This sense of urgency, however, while one that he understood, was a feeling he could not share in. At least, not for now—not yet.

It seemed to Famyl that mere moments passed as he rested peacefully on Kenna's floor, but when he opened his eyes, he found the room was vacant. Sunlight poured through the window and the dull silence of midmorning filled his ears.

I feel as if I merely blinked, Famyl thought, working his joints as he rose. *But it appears as if I have slept much longer than I imagined.* Troublesome as they were, Famyl had grown accustomed to the aches and fragile stiffness. It was a harsh reminder of his transgression, but also a reminder that he had succeeded in his quest. Every day that he breathed the same air as Linette made it all worth it.

Carried in on the breeze, a tittering sound swept through the open window.

Linette! Famyl recognized the unique laughter. With a bowing stretch, he shook off the last shreds of sleep, and bounded for the outside. Every door was open to accept the fresh air, and as he passed through the house, he could hear a conversation beyond the porch.

"The scent was so foul that even the flies were retreating." A distinct male voice was speaking, relaying a tale that Famyl was clearly late for. Linette was gazing intently at the Lord of Benwick, shielding her mouth from the fits of laughter that her trembling shoulders betrayed. "And in that moment of clarity, I realized that ghoul tracking was not the trade for me," Ancel concluded, swiping invisible sweat from his brow.

Eyes brimming with joy, Linette caught sight of Gomer and immediately dropped to a knee to greet him. Drawing into her arms, Famyl nestled into her shoulder, and as she stood, he protectively pressed his flank to the side of her shin.

"Hello, old boy," Ancel said, placing his hands to his thighs. "Gomer, was it?"

Linette nodded and Gomer flicked his tail in acknowledgment.

"Do you remember me?"

The dog's tail perked up again and began to wave in excitement.

With a rough pat to Gomer's ribs, Ancel turned a heel toward the barn. "Are your father and sister nearby?" he asked. From inside the stables, sounds of iron striking iron resounded. "Not to be presumptive, but I believe I know your father's location."

"Is that so?" Linette's slate said. She arched a speculative eyebrow above the message.

"Far be it from me to make such a claim," Ancel said, stepping back and grinning. "But I find it difficult to entertain the image of your sister, in her current condition, waging war upon horse tack with such fervor."

Biting back more laughter, Linette began to write a reply while Ancel gave Gomer another round of stringent ruffles to the top of his head.

"Don't know where Perla is, but you could try calling for her."

"Ah," the messenger said. "With your leave, I will take a look around your dwelling."

Linette nodded.

As Ancel strode away, Gomer lurched his shoulders as if to follow, but forced himself to remain pressed to Linette. It was an involuntary response that Famyl found difficult to reconcile. There were qualities in the lad that the ancient laif found admirable, aside from the manner in which he quelled the potential ogre uprising. His overall bearing exuded a calm ferocity that was intriguing, yet beneath it all, Famyl could still detect hints of deception. Faint, indeed, but lingering, as disturbed sediment in a shallow pool. Why he concealed his true identity—Ancel, the Lord of Benwick —was puzzling to the First Laif.

Observing Ancel bounding the stairs to the porch, Linette's face held the purest look of admiration. She hugged her slate to her chest, and bit her bottom lip. Surprisingly, jealousy did not rise in Famyl's throat, as he had feared would happen when a day like this arrived. Instead, he felt displaced.

Leaving Linette's side, Famyl trotted away, unsure of his destination. He only sought an empty space in which he could properly spread his thoughts out to dissect them. A rasping sound caused his left ear to swivel as he passed the house, the noise like a rider freeing themself from a mount. Sure enough, alighting from a horse was another visitor. Before the stranger turned to reveal his identity, Famyl's instincts released an unmitigated snarl that morphed into a bark of forewarning.

Amyr! Famyl hissed inside his skull. The unexpected arrival felt like a punch to the gut. Although Ancel had not made his intentions toward Linette as clear as the Arbiter had, this sort of perceived rivalry was never good. Especially when it involved a laif who wielded such immense power as Amyr.

Rounding back, Famyl aimed to return to Linette. Before he left sight of the house, Perla and Ancel emerged onto the porch. The expectant mother walked behind the courier, beaming as she bounced along the floorboards and onto the lawn. Upon hearing Gomer's sharp voice, Kenna had freed himself of his mallet and tools, converging upon the group, wiping his blackened hands upon his deerskin apron.

"This is now twice I find you here, *courier*," Amyr said, dispensing any formal greetings. "What business brings you here *this* time?" The malice imbued in the laif's voice gave away his desire for a lie.

"Business that does not concern you," Ancel replied. He appeared unimpressed with the Arbiter's arrival, but indifferent beyond that.

With a severe intake of air, Amyr motioned as if to speak, but was cut short when Kenna drew a step closer, sealing the impromptu circle that had formed.

"Please, let us hear it," he said with folded hands. "If you'll excuse us for a moment, Lord Amyr." Kenna addressed the laif Lord meekly. "I don't want anyone here to die from a careless word..." beseeching Amyr with reverent eyes, he concluded apologetically, "you understand?"

The tension that followed clung to the air and seemed to quicken toward a dispute until Amyr took a step backward. "I honor your request," he stated. After existing for hundreds of years, the laif knew he was a liability, and once again was reminded why he never received invitations to dinner parties. Though the lie had to be expressed solely toward the Arbiter in order for the person to expire, he appreciated the nature of conversation and how careless one could become when engaged in any verbal exchange.

Kenna smiled affably and said no more to the laif.

"Now," he began, his eyes following Amyr's withdrawal, "I pray you have nothing but good news for us, eh?"

Ancel folded his hands behind his back. "Lord Ancel convened with his council regarding all the information that I provided. And from the evidence gathered, the council has decided to drop any further investigation into the matter. Ancel will accept the loss of horses as long as you accept his sincere apology."

Collectively, Kenna and Linette released pent up breaths.

"Additionally," Ancel continued, "concerning the silver shadesgill and the apparent theft, Ancel has decided to no longer accept taxation from this farmland. Effective this season and every season until the Culmination."

"Hold on," Kenna stepped forward and staggered. Linette took hold of her burly father's arm to steady him, more a display of affection than for actual stability. "You mean to tell me—" It was all the man could manage before his inevitable collapse.

At first it sounded like the man was bawling, hanging his head and shuddering, but suddenly the sounds of anguish swung into peals of exultant laughter. Linette pushed back up to her feet after becoming unwilling collateral in her father's deflation, covering her mouth in sheer joy. And without any aforethought, she rushed to Ancel and wrapped her arms around his neck. She swung from his broad shoulders, sending bits of grass and soil from her shoes as they kicked up from the earth.

Standing by with a look of pleasure on her face, Perla clapped, but her eyes were marked with a measure of misgiving. This news held a tremendous boon for her family, but the messenger had told her that he also carried tidings of Corbin. She wondered why would he not lead with that information. She knew that it was common practice to deliver good news first in order to soften the ensuing blow that the latter would bring. She looked to Launcelot, but his eyes betrayed nothing as he gazed back at her from around her sister's embrace.

Setting Linette down and patting her back, Launcelot courteously signaled for Linette to relinquish her hold. Without a hint of embarrassment, she backed up a step to give the messenger space to continue. The sisters stood together, each holding one of their father's arms, pressing next to him, their bones nearly crushing when he flexed his muscles in rushes of elation. His neck never stopped swiveling back and forth to bestow kisses upon each daughter's crown.

Launcelot coughed into his fist, realigning their focus. "The second message I bring is written on parchment, and if you would prefer—"

"Read it!" Perla blurted.

"Are you certain?" Launcelot inquired. The man's calm demeanor did not betray whether the news spelled ill or otherwise.

Kenna lovingly buried his chin into Perla's hair. "Go on, man!" he urged, giving his daughter's crown another kiss before turning his attention to the messenger.

After delicately unfurling the missive with the tips of his fingers, Launcelot began to read aloud. "To my precious wife Perla, I pray to the Creator that you are well and safe, and that our unborn child grows strong in your womb. You, no doubt, have heard word regarding my current station. Being both an Architect and a werewolf has made me quite valuable to the Crown, especially concerning the recent archenlaif invasion, and the resistance currently underway in the inevitable happenstance of another siege."

Perla snorted, and Ancel lifted his eyes.

"Go on," she said, fanning the air.

Returning to the parchment, Launcelot continued. "I fear that I do not know when I will be returning to you and to our home. It pains me to say this, but I do not think that I will be present for our child's birth. Crippling amounts of responsibility have been heaped upon me, and I hesitate to admit that I worry I may break beneath the burden. Aside from that, I cannot put into writing the suspicions that raise my hackles on a daily basis pertaining to my pack. Perhaps it is the pressure getting to me, and maybe I'm falsely envisioning the twisted glances and bared fangs focused in my direction as I pass. Phantasms and mirages are what Jekar says they are, and he may be right. But what I do know is that I need rest and I need a holiday. I need to be with you. Once this is over, I will be tearing straight for Benwick, and a force of ogres or gorgons would not be able slow me, not even a single pace, when that day comes. Join me in praying that the day comes soon. Though we are far apart, we will always be beneath the same night sky. All of my love, yours and forever, Corbin."

Kenna heaved a groan. "Well, fack," he said. Creases of disappointment rippled his forehead. Linette sagged a bit beneath her father's arm, but Perla remained steady.

"He... he..." she stumbled over her words as her mind reeled, combing through the conclusions. Suddenly she shouted, "he still loves me!" and rushed through the space to Launcelot, snatching the message from his hands. She wheeled toward her family with the parchment clutched to her chest. "He still loves me! Don't you see?"

Noticing that their countenances were still dismal, Perla tried to spread her optimism to her family. "Chins up! He still loves me!" she said, reaching for their hands. "Now, we have nothing left to do but pray for a swift end to this conflict."

The expressions on Kenna and Linette's face did not share her confidence, but to their credit, they managed to curl their tightened mouths into encouraging smiles.

"Yes," a soothing voice said approvingly. "Let us pray that good triumphs over evil, and that the rulers' heads are perpetually distant from their own arses." Amyr stepped from under the shadowy copse he had been occupying. "Will that be all, messenger boy?" the laif asked. His left eye narrowed and the opposite eyebrow arched in unison as he cast a withering glance toward Launcelot.

Knowing better than to reply directly, Launcelot took a casual step back and bowed. "I must take my leave," he said in a courtly voice. As he passed Amyr upon his exit, he paused to whisper, "Wait for it..."

The Arbiter was caught off-guard by the comment. "Wait for what?" he asked, incredulously tucking his chin. As the final syllable came from behind his teeth, Linette suddenly burst forth from her father's wing, aiming to join the messenger on his way out. Gomer bounded happily after, and whether by accident or design, the dog hitched his flank against Amyr's armoured shin as he passed, causing the laif to lurch forward.

"Shit hound!" hissed the laif, muttering a string of curses in long-forgotten tongues.

Gomer hurried toward the oak where Ancel's mount waited. The palfrey was tugging at the longer shoots of fescue, curling her lips in satisfaction upon each mouthful. From his periphery he noticed his master's return and issued a welcoming whinny as Ancel's shadow dissolved under the tree. Lagging a few paces behind, Gomer noticed that Linette and Ancel's hands would casually sweep near the other's, but the flesh never touched. Unbeknownst to the other, this bashful game played out for the duration of their walk, though it ended once they reached the tree and turned to face one another.

"*Will I see you again soon?*" Ancel read the displayed slate.

"Funny," he said, looking off toward the fields, a smile tugging at his lips. "I pondered the same question as we strode across your lawn."

Linette bounced on her toes as she scribbled a message.

A shiver trickled down Gomer's spine as he looked between the pair. The adoration they already shared lit his soul to a kindle, but with Amyr pummeling the backdrop, he knew simplicity would not be forthcoming.

"*A week from today, will you take me to your family's keep?*"

Ancel's eyes swept the farmland, pausing where the patch of gilly had grown, the landscape now flush to the earth. He smiled widely, knowing that she had harvested her flowers, and for the first time, would be allowed to pocket all of the earnings.

"Are you seeking my company, or are you vying for a means to get your hands on a few scraps of Faewort?" he joked.

Linette widened her mouth and returned the messenger a look of startled offense. *How dare you!* her eyes playfully countered, then she began to write a reply.

She held the plate up for Ancel's review.

"Maybe a bit of both columns," he read, and upon recital, the woman tucked the slate behind her back and darted behind Gomer. The dog bounded away, believing a game was afoot, and tucked himself behind Ancel's knees.

"It appears to be two against one," Ancel announced while Gomer growled playfully from the shelter of the tall man.

Bending at the waist, Linette pounced toward the dog, rooting the traitorous mutt out from hiding. An upraised root snared the woman's toe causing her to topple, but with the reflexes of a swordmaster, Ancel caught her, preserving her from the hard fall. Holding her in his arms, a jolt lanced up from their bent knees.

Snorting her laughter, Linette beamed at the man she knew to be the Lord of Benwick, as he gently placed her back on her feet. She flung a loose hank of hair behind her ear and blinked meaningfully at him, indicating she was still awaiting a reply. Gomer continued to bounce about their ankles expecting more chases to occur.

Ancel was the first to avert his gaze. "I do believe I have plans one week from this day," he said, running a palm through his loose locks and freeing a bundle that had collected beneath his collar. "But I do not quite recall what they are, and truthfully, I am beyond caring." His lips connected and contoured into a smile. "I will arrive *here* in one week from this day to take you to Joyous Garde."

31

"Trust me," Stacey said. "The blue matches your eyes much better."

The werewolves were well inside Benwick and had been very much naked upon their arrival. They had opted for their human skins over their monstrous counterparts, wagering that befuddled sneers would be more preferable than flaming arrows.

"I favored the gray," Jekar replied, fumbling with the overly long sleeves on the sky-blue tunic he had procured from a full and sagging clothesline. He hurried to catch up, walking straight and tall now that he was clothed. The past few hours had been spent lurking behind shrubs and ducking into alleys, trying to avoid detection, and this change in posture was quite a welcome adjustment. "Gray is more liable to blend in with a crowd," he added morosely.

Stacey halted at a crossroad lined with shops along all vertices. "These rags are only temporary," she said distractedly, peering down the bustling streets. "Once we reach the keep, I'm sure they'll be more than happy to wrap you in any shade of gray that your fuzzy little heart desires."

With a nod, Stacey decided which direction to traverse next. They passed a row of fruit stands where a long cloth banner was being skillfully unfurled overhead. The vendors craned their necks out to watch the men on ladders steadily plying their trade.

From one end Jekar could read *TOU*, and at the opposite length he saw between the smoothing hands of the workman the letters *NT*.

"Hold a moment, Stacey," he said, tapping a finger to his companion's elbow. "I believe..." he held his words, waiting for the men to reveal a few more letters. "Yes! There is a tournament coming to Benwick!" The man's eyes painstakingly followed the gradual unpeeling of the banner. "And it is five days hence!" he announced, sounding as triumphant as if he had just conquered an impossible riddle.

Stacey gawked at the ornate streamer for several moments. "I was a little girl the last time Benwick held a tourney," Stacey revealed, her face alight. "I remember watching the jousts while perched on my father's shoulders." Memories surged behind the knight's eyes and collected, simmering beneath her lower eyelids. "He told me that one day I would be one of those armoured warriors with the big sticks and shiny swords. He told me to pay attention and not to forget..."

Unsure of what to do, Jekar placed a hesitant arm across Stacey's shoulder. "What is stopping you from joining in this tournament?" he asked, returning his gaze to the banner.

"Ha!" Stacey barked, wiping away a thin tear that threatened to tumble down her cheek. "Carlysle never taught me to tilt. All the horsemanship I know was learned prior to my service to her."

Jekar jostled her against his side. "Well, you have five days to learn."

"I don't think that would be enough time," she admitted, swiping the last of the dampness from beneath her eyes. "I am more than happy to spectate this one."

"There will be other tourneys," Jekar said as he removed his arm from behind her neck. The locks of her soft hair pleasantly tickled the skin beneath his wrist. "There is still plenty of life remaining, Sir Stacey."

Just as the streets along the main concourse were a jumble of activity, Benwick's keep was a teeming hive of energy. The drawbridge sealed behind the entering werewolves with a slap and a misty sprinkle of water from the wood, damp from the overflowing moat. Rains from the karbaled had collected into the tributaries, more than doubling the winter's thaw, causing water to spill out from the lakes. Any additional precipitation only acted to increase the overabundance of moisture that the northern realms were now enduring.

The portcullis was wrenched open for their arrival and the pikes comprising the gate wobbled at the strain from the pulleys. Ropes had replaced the rusted chains, and they had to be frequently swapped out for fear that the wetness in the air would cause them to snap like cheap thread.

Across the expansive bailey, a flourish of green and black mantles rushed forward. At the center of the formation, the form of Sir Ector could be seen setting the brisk pace. A tabard clung loosely over his armour, cascading sideways with each step, revealing the prismatic sheen to his plate.

"Stacey!" he shouted, surging into a run.

"You!" Stacey shouted in reply, caught up in the moment.

The scene played through nearly silent, save for the rattle of Ector's armour and the slapping of Stacey's bare feet against the stone path as they sped toward one another. Their reunion was a delirium of happiness that was saccharine to the ladies-in-waiting spectating intently from the balconies, but a warm encouragement to the knights who were alone for the summer. For Jekar, however, the intensity of their display made him cower back as though he was caught up in the searing heat of a blistering forge.

After a particularly prolonged kiss, Stacey unlocked her lips and turned to face her companion. "Jekar! Come along now," she shouted across the expanse, waving encouragingly for the werewolf to join them.

As truly canine as Jekar was, he was nonetheless quite opposed to being summoned to heel, as a common housedog. Without urging, his top fangs began to augment themselves, extending beyond their natural length. Quickly, he sealed his mouth to draw attention away from the startling expansion occurring along his gum line.

"Yes, my lady," he murmured, crossing to join the radiant couple.

Ector squinted as he surveyed Jekar. "Don't tell me..." the lordling appeared thoughtful, rummaging through his brain for the werewolf's name. "Jekar!" he announced at length, pointing first to Jekar, then to his own temple. "I almost never forget a name! And if I may say, that tunic almost perfectly matches your eyes."

Stacey grimaced as she patted Ector's vambrace.

"Top notch, Sir Ector," Jekar replied formally, but with a slight twitch.

His mouth falling open, Ector fixed the werewolf with a look of concern, but before he could continue, Stacey cupped a hand to his cheek, shifting his attention.

"I'm starving!" she declared, hooking an arm into the crook of Ector's elbow.

Sparing only a single uneasy glance back at Jekar, Ector spun around. "Yes, yes," he stated, twirling a finger in the air. His company of knights responded by turning and accompanying them as they made their way back to the keep. "The kitchens have been firing at full tilt all week," he divulged, placing a hand atop Stacey's. "You may eat until you're bursting! How does that sound, Sir Jekar?"

Trailing several lengths behind and feeling like no more than an accessory, Jekar nearly missed the question. "Sounds lovely," he replied lightly. "I pray that ale will be served?" *Buckets and buckets of ale,* he continued to himself, sensing his fangs finally beginning to recede.

"I wish we could have made it back in time for the service," Stacey said to Ector, placing her cup of wine down on the long table. "Your father was a great man."

"Aye," Ector agreed, glassy-eyed. Whether it was from the three flagons he had recently pounded back or from the memory of his father's wake, none could be certain. "Yesterday was harder than I imagined it would be. While I was away at war, his death almost seemed like a false memory. But standing there at his gravesite yesterday..." His shoulders sank and his chin dipped down. Stacey began to rub his back consolingly, causing Jekar to shoot to his feet, making for the serving counter for an overdue refill.

The werewolf ignored the servant offering a jug of ale on his way to the tap. The dining hall was vast, yet Jekar felt cramped. Only Ector's knights and squires were dining with them, leaving hundreds of spaces open on the benches.

Why do I feel this way? Jekar wondered, though he knew the answer. He watched the amber liquid flow from the barrel into his cup. Ordinarily he avoided strong drink, but this day was not a day for caring. *When you close your eyes, she is all you see. That is why,* his mind explained to him, unnecessarily.

A faint breeze swept across the coarse hairs of his extended arm.

"I don't understand it," a familiar voice invaded the space over his shoulder. "But for whatever reason, I find comfort in seeing fellow survivors of the siege."

"To be honest," Jekar said to the speaker, "I did not actually engage in any of the combat." His misty eyes brightened when he spied the knight in front of him.

Sir Tamarah opened her arms and bundled the smaller man inside. "No matter to me," she said, resting her chin atop his scruffy head. "I'm glad to see you, healer."

"And I you," he replied from somewhere beneath her head. The unmistakable scent of knights filled his nostrils; steel, oil, and sweat.

Relaxing her hold, the pair stepped back from each other. Jekar took his spectacles off his nose and wiped at the newly acquired smudges with a cloth from a nearby table.

"What brings you out of the forest, Jekar?" Tamarah inquired. "Secret werewolf business?"

Before he could respond, another voice cut in from his back.

"I thought I smelled a dirty dog!"

As he wheeled to the man, Jekar caught the impish smirk creeping long Tamarah's face.

"Vashal!" Jekar shouted. His inebriation caused his thigh to strike against the corner of a table as he rushed toward the knight. He bet there would be a bruise to greet him in the morn, but he happily dismissed the diagnosis.

The men greeted one another by clasping each other's wrists, but Vashal was not one to settle for such a modest reception. Suddenly the werewolf found himself wrapped up in the hearty embrace of yet another Benwick knight. Aside from the usual knightly smells, Jekar detected, to his amusement, a hint of sunshine on the knight's attire. An element noticeably absent on Tamarah.

"So yes, what does bring you here, friend?" Vashal repeated, sweeping his flagon up and draining it in two gulps.

Jekar wriggled the hinges on his spectacles, struggling to focus on the task. "I am merely an escort for *Sir* Stacey," he said, pointing the wiry tips toward the table. At that very moment, Stacey and Ector were once again locked at the mouth.

"Oh," Tamarah said, widening her eyes at Vashal in a knowing manner. "So she's been belted, eh?"

"Indeed," Jekar seethed. "And it appears that she will be *bedded* soon as well."

"Ohhh," said Tamarah again. She placed her hands on Jekar's shoulders and steered him toward a bench, one strategically facing a wall. Tamarah snapped a finger at a servant passing by, stopping him short. "A tankard of water," she requested, and the servant returned a bow and bustled away.

"Water?" Jekar slurred, swiveling his head. "Are we entertaining fish now?"

Straddling the seat next to his drunken friend, Vashal rested his elbow on the knurled surface. "The water is for you, mate. You've had enough for one day."

"Who cares!" Jekar blurted. He appeared to be growing more and more intoxicated as time passed. "It's ale! It's mostly concocted of poison anyhow!"

Ector's mind appeared entirely untainted by the amount of alcohol that had passed his throat. He engaged in conversation as one who had long ago made peace with the spirits. There was only one other knight that Stacey knew who could handle such large quantities of drink: Carlysle. The increasing concern she felt was quickly subsumed by the joy and elation that she was experiencing as an effect of her reunion with Ector.

She banished the unpleasant notion to the recesses of her mind. *Another day*, she told herself, *another day*.

"Beneath your knight's dotty exterior," Ector explained, pointing a meaty drumstick toward Stacey's chin, "was a cold, iron-like understanding. As if she truly knew how the world *really* works."

By degrees, Stacey leaned back. "Carlysle was a puzzle for sure," she admitted, watching the drumstick arc safely away. "But she is no longer my knight."

Ector blinked and folded his hands. "I misspoke," he said. "I meant no offense. This news of your ascension to knighthood is still fresh."

Abandoning words, she tilted forward to bestow another kiss on Ector's mouth as ample assurance that she held no grudge. After all, she had only given him half the tale. He was well versed on her knighting, but was unaware of the *other* change that had taken place since last they had been together.

Surveying the hall, Stacey realized she had yet to see the Lord of Benwick. "Where is your brother?" she inquired, dabbing the corners of her mouth. Their most recent kiss had been a bit damp from his end.

"Nolan and Gabriel are right there," Ector replied, indicating the knights across the table before filling his mouth with a wedge of bread sopping with gravy.

"No, no." Stacey shook her head with a laugh and set her palm atop Ector's hand. "I mean Ancel."

The energy in the hall suddenly sapped away. All chewing ceased and every eye creaked toward Stacey at the mention of the name.

Sloping his head back, Ector swallowed the lump of bread. "Every day, I feel as a cat with its fur rubbed the wrong way. And every time that name is spoken, I feel another stroke against the grain," he growled.

"I was un-informed," Stacey said apologetically, leaning into Ector's view. "Is he not Lord anymore?"

Ector snorted. "In title alone."

"What," Stacey began cautiously, meeting the host of eyes staring at her, "what happened that makes you feel that way... the way you said?"

Gabriel inclined his head, his eyes tight slits. "He has been absent as of late."

"Absent," Ector echoed dryly, "doesn't properly describe his in-activity and willful abandonment of his kith and kin."

Clearing his throat, Nolan felt the need to add to the conversation. "He was not at Father's wake today," he said, glancing between his brothers. "It's a pattern with him, you see, sometimes—"

"Sometimes he grows preoccupied with *other* matters," Ector concluded.

From across the hall, the subject matter had attracted the attention of Sir Tamarah and Sir Vashal, two of the few remaining Benwick knights that Stacey had been acquainted with at Irphen's Downfall. She had noticed that Jekar had found company near the casks of ale, but had not realized their identities until now.

Stacey's eyes intently followed the approaching knights. "What are these other matters?" she inquired, meeting Jekar's lethargic eyes as he rounded on his seat. The werewolf did not bother to approach the group. His ears were well equipped to hear the goings on without risking an unsteady trek across the hall.

"Some matters involve a woman, of course, but other dealings are more suspicious," Nolan spit with presumptuous zeal.

"More severe," Gabriel added, and the brothers locked eyes and nodded as wartime comrades. "Probably back door dealing with those filthy mongrels at Navarene."

For a fleeting second Stacey believed that the brothers, sitting side-by-side, were about to clink their cups together in celebration. And in that brief moment, she understood why these chaps had been absent of Benwick's wartime force.

Two separate tankard filled fists slammed onto the table, flanking Gabriel and Nolan, snapping their attention to the fists' owners. The foamy ale roiled out and spilled out onto the table and began to spread toward Ector, but the lordling deftly produced a cloth and dammed the flow.

"Tamarah, Vashal," Ector murmured without glancing up, "welcome."

"I do not believe that our Lord is *back door* dealing with werewolves," Tamarah thundered, staring a hole into Gabriel's forehead causing the lordling to squirm. Though also born a Warrior, Gabriel was leagues behind Tamarah in training and talent. "And any more talk like this is treason."

Hatching a smile, Ector folded his arms and made a show of admiring the knight. "Come now, Tamarah," he cooed. "You must hold theories of your own. Lurking in the shadows at night, scouring the castle for wraiths and goblins. You must have stumbled upon something of note regarding this most recent scandal?"

Vashal twitched his chin aversely when she looked to him.

"I knew it," Ector said, shoring his elbows to the table and resting his cheek onto his fist. "Spill it," his tone twisted to a command.

Tamarah slowly brought her flagon to her lips and took a heavy draught. She aggravatingly swiped away the filaments of froth that threatened to trickle down her chin.

"One night," she began, but was interrupted by Vashal rushing to his feet in a huff and storming off, muttering phrases filled with hard consonants. When his words had dwindled into silence, she spoke again. "One night, I was walking near the aviary..."

The tenants of the table sat in complete silence after Tamarah completed her peculiar tale.

Ector finally spoke, breaching the pervading stillness. "And who do you believe that message was meant for?"

This was met with another wave of silence.

"Tell me more of this woman who Ancel is fancying," Stacey said, interrupting the dense air, trying to steer the subject toward seemingly less treacherous waters.

An irritated sigh escaped Nolan, who clearly wished to remain on topic.

"In brief," Ector said, turning to Stacey, "the enmity between Arthur begins and ends with a particular woman. The details aren't commonly known, which means that if I tell you what I know, which, admittedly, isn't much, it can't leave this hall."

Slowly and reverently, Stacey nodded her head. "I understand. Not a word."

Ector took a measured breath and began. "Ancel was courting a maid of Astolat—"

"An arranged courtship," Nolan interrupted.

Ector's chest deflated in irritation. Gabriel sharply deployed an elbow into Nolan's upper rib cage, acting as an emissary for quiet. Groaning and groping at his side, Nolan gathered his brother's meaning and kept his mouth shut.

"Elayne, I believe was her name. Her family still grieves her to this day," said Ector sadly. "Lovely girl. In any case, she was enamored with Ancel to an almost unhealthy height. And Ancel returned her affections, becoming enraptured with her as well. Not to the same level, mind you, but it did come to the point where Ancel was rather derelict in his duties. He would wander off at all hours of the day, and sometimes entertain a journey after dusk. Honestly, their devotion to one another was admirable, especially considering their union was…" he trailed off and smiled stiffly at Nolan, "arranged."

Nolan returned a nod, gripping his ale with both hands.

"The details afterward are hazy," Ector continued with a smirk. "All we know is that Arthur met Elayne after a tourney, and shortly afterward she was dead."

Recoiling as if waking from a nightmare, Stacey stared at her companions. "W-Wait! That's all?!" she stammered in disbelief. "You mean to tell me that she died mysteriously?" Easing back and clamping a breath within her lungs, Stacey's eyes widened. "Did *the King* steal her? Did he kill her?" she whispered, hunching her shoulders suspiciously.

"No one knows," Tamarah replied, ignoring the traitorous implications. "Well, save for Ancel and Arthur. And neither has spoken to the other in a long while."

Ector rose, blinking wearily, and offered a hand to Stacey. "It's perhaps a query we will not resolve until we ourselves arrive in Avalon," he said. "Now, I'm for a piss and a walk. Would you care to join me?"

Receiving his hand and rising eagerly, Stacey agreed with a terse affirmative smile. Before she exited the hall, she scanned the room, hoping to spot Jekar. The table he had occupied with Vashal was empty. Only a pair of abandoned wooden cups sat upright, desolate, punctuating her friend's absence.

32

The room continued to shift, flashing figments, the surroundings never sticking to one theme. Desolation, craggy mountains, a lush forest, more desolation, an abandoned cathedral, a cliff overlooking the sea, a window view within a tower, a marshland with its shores enclosed by massive birds with stilts for legs, a *familiar* farm...

A firm shake of his head and the surroundings melted and shaped back into the elegant but static atmosphere of Amyr's chambers. The First Laif wrung his hands in frustration. "Never!" he seethed between clenched teeth. "I will not humiliate myself! I will not become a baseless voyeur, an ogler, a wretched pinecone of perversion!"

Amyr fluttered an eyelash and the room became a dull, placid pond.

"I may go wherever I please," he said, scouring the moonlit banks for a dry place to sit, "but I will never visit my Linette *that* way. I must court her as if I were mortal, as she is." Amyr huddled his knees to his chest and gazed at the glassy water. He watched a yellow spotted salamander as it crept from between the reeds and struggled to overcome the ridge of a large stone.

"There are ways to prolong the lives of mortals," said Amyr to the salamander. He offered a finger to the creature's forelimbs, creating a slope to reach the desired plateau. "And there are even ways to bestow immortality. Although, I must admit that the aging process grows quite disturbing as time passes and flesh erodes." He smiled, gazing at the salamander wandering aimlessly to its destination. "But those are decisions for other days, my little friend. Right now, I must focus on bolstering the meager particles of her father's affection toward me."

The salamander settled down, its bulbous eyes reflecting Amyr's face as it gazed in seeming understanding of the plain speech.

"Do you rest here often?" Amyr inquired, scrubbing his chin with a thumb.

The creature bobbed its head once before settling it against the chipped stone surface. Aside from the glittering quartz, the stone was a slab of plain gray, and after sunset, daytime stalkers would fail to discern the creature as a meal. Night stalkers, however, would immediately recognize the salamander as easy, vulnerable prey.

Amyr peered at the trees, fervently sweeping up from their latched roots and across their exposed trunks. Looking toward the treeline that rimmed the backdrop of this favorable oasis, he saw a particular wooded copse carrying precisely what he was seeking.

Gliding up to his feet, Amyr bent his head earthward. "Stay here," he instructed the salamander. "Don't move," he added, shooting toward the deepening shadows of the forest.

Lashed to the trunks were thick cords of vine, wrapped and coiled tight with the years of the trees' expansive growth. With a series of successive snaps, the vines tension released, and soon Amyr was returning to the pond with what appeared to be a bundle of lifeless serpents clutched to his chest.

Amyr spent the next several hours seated upon the bank, bent over with his legs crossed, weaving a basket from the stripped flesh of the vines. Night gave way to morning, and yet the laif continued to interlace the canes.

"Ah!" Amyr exclaimed in triumph, placing the upturned basket over the sleeping salamander. The fabricated cave blotted out the creeping daylight that threatened to overtake the stone slab. Placing a hand to the basket, Amyr closed his eyes and thin tendrils swept up from the stone and began to mingle into the spaces between the weaving, permanently fastening the minerals of the stone to the basket.

"A roof for the faithful," said Amyr. He leaned back and stared unblinking at the rising sun. His mind wandered once again to Linette, an increasingly regular pastime that he did not forbid himself. "Too much beauty," he said, framing his thoughts.

Inspiration slammed into his mind.

Amyr closed his eyes. The salamander basket, within his mind, grew in breadth and stature, becoming much, much more. Fertile soil began to unravel, flooding his mindscape and continuing beyond the horizon. The basket was no longer a basket, but now a farming manor complete with servant's quarters. Fresh, clean water surged beneath the layers of productive earth, flowing freely, begging to be tapped. Stables, granaries, a smith shop, and several other outbuildings for storage or shade would rise from the earth.

A smile wreathed Amyr's face. "And one particular acre will be enchanted," he said, easing his eyes open. "An entire field that will accept silver shadesgill."

* * *

Stacey rose early, frustrated. Sleep was not behaving as the welcome companion she had grown accustomed to. Elusive and dodgy, her tired mind would not settle. It felt as a sparring partner who refused to strike and ceaselessly evaded.

She was briefly startled and confused upon waking in a luxurious bedchamber, but the moment quickly passed. Finding herself in a soft bed surrounded by tapestries draped along the posts seemed almost like a waking dream. The stiffness that greeted her after sleeping on the ground or on a soldier's pallet was gratefully absent. Ector had thoughtfully gifted her these guest quarters, which not only offered lush accommodations, but was also situated in the quietest corner of the keep. Far from the servants and other tenants, this section was cordoned off for the unwell or wounded who required undisturbed tranquility.

Looking around the room, her eyes fell upon a large mirror, its reflection displaying the changes her body had endured. Her cheekbones were sliced tighter to her face, and she discovered a foreign hardness that had developed behind her eyes. When she leaned closely, gazing deeper, her round pupils flickered crescent. Shooting back upright with a start, Stacey wished to fold and discard the mirror. She desperately wanted to tell Ector *everything*, but she feared rejection. She also worried he would learn the truth on his own before she was ready to reveal her true nature to him personally. Such a breach of trust would prove a difficult hurdle for their blossoming relationship to recover from.

Perhaps this is a topic that Jekar might... her thoughts involuntarily trailed off.

Over the past few weeks, Jekar had turned into the person she had regularly found herself beseeching for guidance, both before and after her transformation. He had become her most trusted and reliable friend, but only a friend and nothing more. Though exceedingly kind and wise, Jekar was not the person she should discuss the subject of her romance with.

Bumping her fist into the center of her forehead, the young knight scolded herself for her sheer stupidity. *How could I not have noticed it before?* While she had sought his council, only wishing for advice and an ear to listen, he had falsely believed a romantic attachment was developing.

Integrity began to needle at her, urging her to seek him out and make amends somehow. His quarters shared an adjoining wall, the same wall she was fixated upon. Her mind spun a placating scenario; the perfect conversation-starter that could ease her into the perfect apology that would set everything right. Set everything the way she wanted it to be. The way she had believed it to be.

The stonework hall was vacant and cold despite the summer heat. Stacey strode to Jekar's door and hesitated. The apologetic script was teetered on the forefront of her mind, fragile and vulnerable, quickly to be forgotten if she did not utter it soon. Tentatively, she rapped the door with her knuckles, though a portion of her wished that she could return the sound to silence. From beyond the thick wooden door, nothing responded to her knocks. She tapped again, this time with more fervor. The surface felt as unyielding as if the door was suctioned to the frame by mysterious means.

Still nothing.

She knocked louder.

Nothing again.

She balled her hand into a fist and battered the door.

Stillness, complete silence.

"Jekar!" she shouted.

Taking a step back, Stacey noticed a speck of light sprouting from below her chest. An iron inlay crafted in the shape of a kestrel adorned the center of the door, and something about its eye appeared peculiar. Waving a hand in front of the raptor erased the speck, depleting the rays funneling from within the room. She quickly thrust her head toward the ornament, pressing her nose into the smooth door planks, and focused her vision into the chamber beyond the pinhole.

Nothing. Still nothing.

The silence relieved her of any residual guilt she was feeling for what she was about to do. Hefting the latch with a flick, she stormed into the room, foregoing any further announcements. Dust fragments gilded by sunlight wafted above a bed that was undisturbed, the space surrounding it completely void of life. It appeared as though no one had invaded the chamber in quite some time. Cobwebs congregated in the corners, and a film of dust coated every flat surface.

A mirror, almost an exact replica of the mirror in her room, framed the shared wall, lending this smaller room a false sense of depth. She could almost see the knot forming in her stomach as she scowled at the reflection of a woman who she hardly even recognized anymore.

* * *

Another unexpected advantage of being a werewolf, Jekar discovered to his amusement, was the body's swift demission of hangovers. He had pried his eyes open, expecting a poisonous sludge to be roiling in his skull, but lucidity greeted him in its stead.

Apparently in his inebriated state, he had decided that the finest place for his head to rest was upon a straw-mounded rafter in some poor sod's barn. Dangling from the wooden girder at an unknown height, his left foot twirled the air as he sat up to take in his surroundings. The creatures inhabiting the stables below were either dead or out to pasture, thankfully. Jekar sincerely hoped that they were indeed alive and breathing and out to pasture. With a shake of his head, he dispelled the notion of consuming another man's livestock without payment.

Such urges needed to be checked, needed to be reined in at every turn. Last night had been a regrettable mistake. He had learned long ago to control his emotions, but these new abilities brought him curses along with gifts. One of the more unfavorable being rash petulance and a rapid surge into rage. The previous night, he had made a plain demonstration of such behavior.

In truth, he regretted his actions, but the wounds that had motivated his behavior were far from healed.

A rumbling in his stomach urged him to find new surroundings. Preferably one that contained hearty morsels of the breakfast kind. Leaping from the rafter, his feet struck the hay-riddled floor, and soon he was shoving the massive barn doors wide.

"How far did I rush from the keep?"

Hillsides shrugged and rolled before him, bathed in the tangerine whispers of dawn. Fenrirfang's doorstep was within view, but just barely, beveling the horizon with its treetops. The barren barn was the only structure within eyeshot, bereft of the usual farmhouse that would rise in accompaniment. Not a single human, laif, or creature stirred the calm within the range, and judging by the gashes in his tunic, his distant trek had been enhanced through werewolf means. Which explained *how* he had gained so much ground this far north. The *why* was obvious to him; an envy fueled return to Fort Navarene.

The peace of the morning was suddenly breached as the wind carried an abrupt yelp to his ears. At first, he believed it was the shrieking of a tree bough scraping upon another, jostled by the wind, but the landscape spreading before him did not support that thought. The trees dappling the slopes were not within reach of one another and were spaced at nearly half acre increments.

Another yelp lanced the air, this one joined with a trailing whimper, stilling Jekar's hunger and replacing it with curiosity. The sounds had originated further north, over the hillside, toward the forest. He thought, rather optimistically, that perhaps the cries were the sounds of someone preparing a meat enhanced breakfast. His stomach wished it to be so, but his mind concocted far more troubling theories. The voice that had lifted upon the air seemed far too tremulous for simple livestock. The notion of devouring an articulate chicken was rather unappetizing to Jekar, even famished as he was.

The morning breeze tousled his hair as he crested the gentle hill that overlooked a sparsely populated valley. The settlement congregated toward the middle of the valley's curvature, seeming to have been initially placed around the rim only to slip downward, unbidden, as the years flowed.

Unnoticed at first, the dark circling pattern imprinting against the clouds drew the werewolf's eyes to the skies. Vultures. A host of the carrion fowl simmered, drafting the gusts above a solitary hut plunked far across the valley's expanse, where, despite the pervading gloom, Jekar detected further movement. Smoke funneled upward, intertwining with the ensuing daybreak.

Setting off at a jog, he navigated the grade with concentrated focus, but once he reached the base of the hill, another shrill cry arose from the smoking ridgeline. If any folk still lived inside the dilapidated cottages that Jekar hurtled past, they were still asleep or deaf to the vivid notes of distress.

Something is amiss.

The scent of despair struck Jekar's nostrils.

Rising over the rim of the hillside, Jekar was met with a gruesome spectacle. Strapped into wooden chairs, looking much like a macabre outdoor classroom, were about fifty forest creatures of varying races. Their eyes flicked toward him at his intrusion, and held onto him, pleading, setting their restrained bodies trembling all at once.

As he drew nearer, he noticed a pile of ogre tusks—immature ogre tusks, worthless to any collector or tradesman. Separate from the tusks were other piles of assorted juvenile monster harvests: teeth, fangs, skulls, bones, claws, and even a few pelts. To his left, where the smoke swirled into the skies punctuating the vultures staring down in flight, broken bodies were piled, most rendered to cinders. There were hundreds upon hundreds of bodies. Rib cages protruded from the ash, cloth fabrics still clinging to the tapered bone fragments, a reminder of the lives disposed of in the flames.

"What manner of evil..." Jekar muttered, locking eyes with an exceedingly young danegust. Her reptilian feet barely reached the edge of her seat, and above her gagged snout, the werewolf noticed that her egg tooth had yet to detach.

The hut door suddenly swung open. "The trick is, ya see, ya gotta pour the soup while it's still a-roilin'," a top-heavy human with a generous belly issued forth, carrying a bubbling cauldron of hot liquid. A single step behind, cutting through the steam billowing from the cauldron, a smartly dressed man and woman intently followed, hanging hungrily on his every word. "Spin it around nice and even, ya don't wanna get all crazy—" The cook bit himself off, noticing an unusual tangle of movement in his periphery.

Just as the door had creaked open, Jekar had flung himself onto his stomach. A forest of bound ankles and chair legs obscured him from the trio's sight. In the moment before the trio had emerged from the house, Jekar had managed to loosen the scarf that bound the danegust mouth.

"They, they, they," she stammered. Her scarf tumbled and snagged on the budding barbs sprouting from the back of her neck. In a movement inherent with the stupidity that comes with youth, the danegust rotated her head to speak to the man prostrate below her. "They have a wizard!"

Footsteps hastily plodded a course for the wedge of seats near the pile of ogre tusks. The cauldron had been set aside, and Jekar could make out the shuffling steps that followed a few panting breaths behind the man and woman.

Which of them is a wizard? Jekar wondered, trying in vain to divine the spellcaster. He knew from experience that magic could often detect other magic. Not a single hair on his arm sprung up in alarm, nor did his hackles jut from an encroaching aura.

"Now how did your gag get so low, missy?" said the woman, shaking her head at the danegust. "Who tied this one?"

"I think you did," replied the gentleman.

Jekar wriggled between the chairs and pressed a finger to his lips, signaling the frantic children to remain still and quiet.

"I want to see my parents, please," the danegust begged, glancing between her captors.

The pair shared a sorrowful look, seeming to offer sympathy, but their demeanors cracked quickly. Peals of mocking laughter drenched the air, drowning out the voice of the danegust who faintly murmured, "I miss my mommy." The appeal was lost to the ether, but Jekar heard every syllable.

A haunting silence advanced, the sort of silence that murder often filled. And judging by the notes of startled terror upon the surrounding youngling faces, Jekar knew that some manner of cruelty must be happening. The scent of panic and fear flooded his nostrils, making it impossible to pinpoint what the danegust was experiencing. Events were moving much faster than he wished.

Jekar rose.

The man and woman, dressed in fineries, held the hatchling near a festering burn pile with their backs facing him. The cook was off to the right, milling about the ground, and Jekar knew that it was only a matter of seconds before the greasy man spotted him.

"Make sure to save her talons," the cook called, brushing off his hands and rising to his feet. "They make good broth, and—" his words ceased, his lips began to quiver as if they wanted to offer remark.

Fortunately for Jekar, the cook's abrupt muteness caused a brief moment of confusion. The lady turned her head to look, and within that breath, Jekar surged forward and overtook her male companion. The gentleman's trachea popped like a cheap trinket, surprising Jekar with the ease of the act.

"My lady!" the cook managed to shout, his lips finally in concert with his brain.

The lady rotated just in time to see her partner fold upon the grass, his neck flopping unseemly. Standing above his body, a slight but ferocious sort of man glared at her, the danegust huddling behind his hip. His spectacles were fogged with sweat, but the eyes behind were sharp with vengeful intent. She drew the slim sabre at her hip far too late. Cutting the short distance between them, Jekar grabbed her drawing elbow, stopping the movement, and engaged her, nose to nose.

"What, what," stammered the lady, struggling to pull her weapon. Jekar's grip on her arm was unyielding.

From the corner of his eye, Jekar noticed the cook had composed himself and was stumbling toward them, a rescue clearly on his agenda.

Jekar abruptly released his hold. Hope flashed in the lady's eyes as the scraping of her scabbard rang in the air. Clasping both of her shoulders, Jekar administered a firm shove, fully extending his arms. The hope fled from the lady's eyes as her heels caught on a stray slab. She toppled backward, her sword brandished uselessly, and she fell onto the smoldering ashes. She screamed and writhed as if she was being burned alive, which, technically, she was. The ornate fiber of her gown eagerly welcomed the flames, blanketing her in fiery tongues. If Jekar had had the time, he would have put her out of her misery, but he had another foe to contend with at the moment.

Watching the lady roll around, slowly burning in the cinders sent the cook into a rage. He redoubled his pace, and an enraged scream gargled out from his mouth as he loped toward Jekar, sword whipping above his head.

The danegust shrank, whimpering at the sight of the man's charge, and her talons latched onto Jekar like a series of thorns, burrowing deep into his thigh. Without removing his gaze from the cook, Jekar herded the scared child with one arm, urging her away from the flames. The smoke carried the scent of burning flesh, tainting the air with the sickly aroma. The lady continued to wail, death taking his time to reach her, seeming to savor each passing moment.

Rushing through the gray screen, the cook's eyes were shut when he emerged on the other side. The smoke proved to be an unexpected adversary, assailing his eyes and throat. Assuming full advantage of his disorientation, Jekar simply stepped to the right, and eased a log across the big man's path with his foot. When the cook opened his bleary eyes, he did not have the agility to avert his momentum. Where he believed Jekar would be, he instead found an open rift, and his toes unexpectedly collided with a fallen trunk. Falling belly first, the man yelped once before flopping atop of the still-wriggling lady, dampening the flames for a split second, silencing her howls. Wondering if the cook's great heft had squelched the fire, Jekar could not help but smile when the fire pit answered his query by abruptly surging into a roiling inferno.

Until this day, Jekar had only worked to preserve and save lives, and had never taken one. Now he had taken three, and it was not yet midday.

The tips of his fingers trembled, overflowing with ardor as he began to release the prisoners. He fumbled and cursed, avoiding the pleading face of the goblin that wriggled in the bondage, making release leagues more difficult. The grateful danegust had extracted herself from behind his back and had employed her talons, releasing six to Jekar's one. It was slow going and much less expedient than he desired, and he scoured the ground for a sharp implement.

The distinct pommel of a sword jutted out from the dead gentleman's hip. As unwieldy as a longsword could be, Jekar decided that he would prefer the steel edge to trying to untangle these wretched triple knots.

The two-handed blade was much longer and thinner than he had anticipated, and the crossguard extended a garish several inches further than the average knight's sword. Clumsy and foolish as he felt handling such a floppy ornamental weapon, he had to admit that it worked much more efficiently than his stubby fingernails. Swept up in the urgency of the situation, one eye glued to the wizard's cabin door, Jekar had forgotten that he too owned a set of claws.

A creature with the intelligent eyes of a serpent and the bearing of a sloth heartily thanked Jekar as the remnants of his bonds fell away. It was an unusual beast, to be sure, and one of which the physician had never encountered in life or in his studies.

"Where are your parents?" Jekar asked, helping the beast to his feet. The exceptionally long limbs had been restricted for so long that it caused the creature to nearly collapse into Jekar's chest.

Bracing himself against Jekar's sternum, the creature looked up, desolation marring his face. "We fled far from home," he said, still unsteady and leaning heavily on Jekar. "The archenlaives breached the wards and our elders told us to flee to the south." He paused, his emotions welling. A translucent membrane blinked horizontally across his eyes, squeezing tears down his furry face. "They told us we would be *safe*. We would be *welcome*." The creature buried his face into Jekar's midsection, clinging to the man's waist with the remainder of his strength.

By this time, a crowd of the displaced creatures had gathered around their savior. None of them had yet to depart for the safety of the forest, and even a few were still in their seats. Jekar surveyed the throng, feeling a strange tinge of guilt. The wizard's existence needled at the back of his mind.

The children were not yet safe. He was not yet safe.

"Fly to the trees!" Jekar urged hoarsely, gesturing toward the forest. "You will be safe there."

Not one child stirred.

"I will go with you."

Every head snapped up at the statement. Beaks brightened and fanged maws coiled into hopeful smiles.

"With me, then!" Jekar roared, thrusting his sword forward.

The newly assembled host began to rush for the welcoming embrace of Fenrirfang, swaddled in shadows and absent of humanity. To his delight, Jekar felt the sunlight impeded briefly as several creatures took his advice directly, making use of their wings and taking flight. He slowed his clip to see each child safe into the forest, and soon Jekar found himself standing on the precipice of Benwick.

The final current of children hurtled toward him. The little danegust had been trying to wrench the fearfully tentative captives from their chairs, and when they saw Jekar leading the flock to safety, all despair was discarded.

"They were afraid!" the danegust said, panting and holding her sides. "But I told them you would—" Whatever she was about to announce was lost for all time.

A searing bolt of crimson licked out, originating from a window on the cabin, striking the danegust in the back, throttling her against Jekar's shins. When Jekar reached down to pick up his fallen friend, his hands found nothing but ash. In disbelief, he sifted through the coarse powder, searching for the bright-eyed child—who had unexpectedly grown very dear to him within a very short span of time. The gray sands poured between his fists as his claws began to grow, puncturing the flesh of his palms.

Jekar could see a silhouette gracing the window of the cabin. The coward hiding within the sanctuary issued a second flaming dart, this one arcing directly toward Jekar's chin. His tendons acted of their own accord, averting the deadly projectile with ease. Stifling heat trailed in the bolt's wake, cauterizing and curling the loose threads on his tunic. An innocent cedar caught the entire impact several feet above its roots, bursting it asunder, spraying needles into the air.

Tracing a wide crescent to the front door to avoid the angle offered by the window, Jekar felt his emotions taking over once again. Before he knew it, he found himself before the door. The scent of the wizard's hatred emanated from between the wall planks, intermixed with notes of panic. Tendrils of smoke were creeping from beneath the door's lower frame, hinting to Jekar that a trap lay just beyond.

The aura of magic was powerful, causing the underside of Jekar's tongue to grow numb. He noticed, to his grave dismay, that the children were gathering along the hem of the treeline, wishing to see what was happening. As they approached the pile of ash, well within the wizard's range, Jekar quickly flung his shoulder into the door, rendering it to splinters. A scorching wave of heat washed over him, but the man drove forward.

The wizard was at the window, leveling her braided wand toward the children. She clearly believed that her incantation would melt any trespasser who endeavored to violate her threshold. Her confidence in her prowess nearly prevented her from glancing at the charred remains that, no doubt, were now commencing to settle upon her floor. Her single fleeting glance became a double take, and the double take funneled into a gaping stare.

With longsword in hand, a soot-faced Jekar closed the gap, pressing the spellcaster to the wall. He crushed the flat of the blade across her chest, pinning her in place. His right hand was firmly balanced on the slender blade, bowing the pliable steel around the wizard as he throttled his weight forward.

"We can split the profits!" the wizard offered as all the blood receded from her face. When she shook her head, Jekar noticed the delicate points adorning the tops of her ears. For some unknown and seeming instinctual reason, the fact that she was a laif jolted the physician further into an unseeing rage.

"Please!" she continued to plead. "There is so much—"

Bristling with fur, Jekar engaged every muscle of his arms, every tendon. The slim blade surged up the wizard's chest, never leaving the fabric surface. The werewolf leaned every fiber of his being on its trajectory, grotesquely shearing her head, leaving her pointy ears intact, and displaying the ivory spine still attached to a portion of the halved brain.

A morbid mannequin, the wizard remained on her feet. The bisection of her skull sloughed face down on the floor and rocked slightly against her nose before halting, the space subsumed by the blood collecting around it.

His fury spent, Jekar abandoned the longsword, leaving it, tangled in the gore and strands of torn hair. Decked in his werewolf skin, Jekar strode from the cabin, fixed for Fort Navarene. All notions that he had held of a life in Benwick now dissipated as Fenrirfang rushed to meet him.

33

"No, no," Ancel insisted, lifting his hood and turning from the stoop, "that is all for you."

The widow stood in the doorway gaping at the sack of gold that her youngest child was struggling to contain.

"It's far *too* generous, my Lord," she protested.

Halting his steps, Ancel peered back at the woman. "Your husband. The boy's father gave all at Navarene without hesitation. This is the very least I can do."

"I don't know what to say."

"Say nothing," replied Ancel, heaving himself up onto his saddle. "Tell no one."

It was the last of the restitutions he would be dispensing in the aftermath of war. To avoid the council's anger, he had procured the gold from his personal accounts, nearly draining his coffers. It made little difference to him. No amount of gold could ever wipe away the memory of Sandrin's demise from behind his eyelids when he closed his eyes.

* * *

Procuring the land had been simple. Manifesting the structures from the existing ones was even simpler.

Amyr watched the craftsmen setting to work upon the skeletal scaffolding encasing the tremendous farmhouse, reinforcing the crumbling pockets and replacing the rain weary roof. It was well within the Arbiter's power to sweep the disruptions and structural impurities away with a single swipe of his hand, but he understood that love meant nothing without labor. Words were merely wind, but sweat and tears and blood *showed* intention. Though he would not be sharing in the stress and strain of the work involved, this gift would not come to fruition without his guidance and direction. This gift for his Linette.

* * *

As she had watched Launcelot depart, leaving a promise in his wake, Linette had scribbled a word onto her slate. Though three days had passed, she had yet to erase what she had written.

Never once before had her father been beseeched for her hand in courtship. The way Linette toiled in the fields and rarely attended social gatherings, her existence was hardly ever remarked upon. *Five daughters?* Men would query with their eyes narrowed in suspicion. *I thought Kenna had fathered only four?* The ensuing explanation usually indicated that Linette was much more interested in agriculture than anything else, and the men would nod their heads in the manner in which men did when they wished to move along to the next topic.

Linette snorted, thinking of Amyr. Such an absurd idea. In truth, it had the makings of a faery tale. A tale she was much more interested in reading than living. Her poor father seemed torn by the idea. The man's first encounter with a suitor for his youngest daughter was a First Laif.

Amyr was beautiful, she had to admit, in an exquisite, exotic sense. Certainly aesthetically pleasing, like that of a chiseled statue or an image upon a sweeping tapestry. But the notion of a romantic relationship with him was far from reality for the simple farm girl. Besides, if someday the desire for children caught her, human females were unable to reproduce with male laives. For as powerful and magical as Amyr was, even he was subject to the Creator's limitations concerning the womb.

On the other hand, Launcelot had yet to reveal his true identity to her, which she found slightly disconcerting, but not without some charm. At some point the man would have to come clean and reveal himself as the Lord of Benwick, of course. He was renowned throughout the realm for his wisdom, so the man must have a good reason for his deception, Linette rationalized. But then again, if Linette was as important as she believed she was to him, would he not have confessed his charade by now?

Placing her hand flat atop Gomer's head, she brought her fingers together. The fur sprung up from between the spaces in-between as parallel lines of overgrown grass. Shaking her hand, she stroked the dog, and the jutting fur vanished beneath the movement, brushing against her palm.

Every year, the days following the summer harvest held an adjustment period for her. Sitting on her porch during the growing season, Linette became accustomed to her view of the forest being limited by the stalks of corn bristling up from the soil. Now as she sat with Gomer enjoying the afternoon warmth, the satisfaction of another harvest in the books, she regarded the full majesty of Fenrirfang. A border she had never dared cross. For some unknown reason, she felt she could sense unrest behind the mysterious leaves and trunks. Perhaps her mind had developed a bias after witnessing the interloping wyverns and ogres on her property. Such images were not so easily dispelled as anomalies. And maybe it was nothing, but she would sometimes catch Gomer staring off toward the enveloping darkness in the endless trees, his ears craned as if he were discerning conversations underneath the thrum of nocturnal insects.

Was the siege of Navarene only the beginning? she wondered, scratching Gomer's snout. A smile cracked her lips as a shiver overtook her.

But what did she know?

She was merely the daughter of a poor farmer.

34

L inette wanted to shout for joy, but instead, flung her arms into the sky. The speck on the road grew into the shape of a solitary man on a horse, plodding along. Every burgeoning detail was exciting as it was revealed, from the meager trail of dust kicked up by the charger to the calm assurance borne in the rider's shoulders. At first, she had assumed it was only a local farmer making their way down her lane, for she had not been expecting Launcelot to arrive until tomorrow. But moment by moment, it became apparent just who the rider was.

She ran out to greet him, the grass slick under her feet, and their paths connected beneath a large oak tree.

Gomer yelped to alert every one of the arrival as he slowed to a trot below the cool of the boughs, recognizing the man as a friend.

Grinning broadly from his mount, Launcelot spread his hands and shrugged at Linette. "I hope that this does not send you into poor spirits," he said, "but I have arrived a day early."

Immediately, Linette scowled at him.

Launcelot pointed to the road over his shoulder. "I can simply leave, if that is your wish."

From behind her back, Linette produced her slate with the word she had written the week before still adorning it, faint but recognizable.

Stay.

Faithfully, Gomer trailed the horses for nearly two miles before he gave up. Launcelot seemed to sense the dog's resignation, and turned in his saddle to offer a farewell salute.

Seated on the wayside of the dirt lane, Gomer observed the pair disappear deep into a thicket, a path worn from years of mounted riders passing inside. He stared until his parched eyelids clicked when he finally blinked.

And just like that, she's gone, Famyl thought morosely, his tail stirring a dusty swath. *Not even a wave good-bye.* Feeling replaced and rejected, the ancient laif lowered his head sadly.

A shrill rattling call picked the dog's head up. *Kingfishers? Straying this far from a river?* Famyl pivoted his snout to the nearest range of trees. A concentration of fowl, resplendent in brilliant sapphire, arced overhead tracing a course opposite Fenrirfang. Famyl wagered that the solitary creatures must have banded together for this exodus from their home range. Of the meager host, one particular bird leveled his beak toward the dog and began a gentle descent, splitting from the others.

Believing the creature to be flight weary, Famyl returned his gaze to the source of his discontent: the bramble curtain.

"Of all the magnificent creatures," said a voice, feigning regret, "you decided upon an old graying mutt."

Famyl turned to see the tired kingfisher latched to a frond, clicking his beak and hunching his shoulders, as if he had suddenly caught a chill. "Are you addressing me, friend?" Famyl asked cautiously, fearing that his melancholy was instigating hallucinations.

"I have finally succumbed to my curiosity, big brother."

That voice! Famyl recognized it now that he was focused on the bird's mannerisms.

"Uljae," stated Famyl, devoid of elation.

From his perch, the kingfisher's beak followed the dog's shoulders as they sagged, defeated. "I seem to have caught up with you at a poor time," said Uljae. Such a statement would usually lead to the person's courteous departure, but Uljae lingered, gazing down at Famyl.

Famyl briefly wondered if he remained perfectly still for a great amount of time, the bird would lose interest or grow hungry and seek his pleasures elsewhere. But he knew in the back of his mind that Uljae had subsumed that form solely to obtain this discussion. *Let's get this over with,* thought Famyl with a resigned sigh.

"What are the happenings in Fenrirfang?" Famyl asked at length. His eyes etched the course from which the bird had flown.

Regally, the kingfisher reared back and tucked his chin, displaying the bright orange plumage on his belly. "Ah, yes," replied Uljae. "Where to begin? There is so much unrest in this world. Let's see, let's see." He thoughtfully tapped a primary feather against his beak. "I can merely retell what I have seen. The laif cantons are bolstering their defenses as if a massive storm is about to surge through them. I spied many creatures scurrying south, great and small. But I don't want to give everything away, now do I?"

"Of course not."

"Right so," the kingfisher nodded. "Two scrappy dragoons managed to bring down and summarily slay a greater dragon. You know the one—that big red bastard with centuries of humans fattening his ribs. He was a right mean sort, even to the very end." Uljae leveled his eyes to the east as if he had heard a voice calling for him, then snapped his beak beneath a wing and began to preen.

The sultry afternoon was advancing, and Famyl wished to move this nonsense along. "That all sounds very interesting—"

"It is," Uljae interrupted, "but not as interesting as what I seem to have stumbled upon *right here.*"

"I highly doubt that."

Hopping to another perch, Uljae fastened himself to the peak of a sapling, closer to the dog and also beneath a pocket of shade. His feet soaked up the coolness of the new texture. "I recall the great Famyl staring despondently down from the heights of the Hold, uninterested in immortality, uninterested in famine or war. And certainly not interested in the passage of time." A stiff breeze caused the sapling to bend down, bringing Uljae within the dog's snapping distance. If Famyl had not been distracted by the brief coolness that ruffled his fur, he may have ended the conversation with a mouthful of feathers.

"That is," Uljae continued, settling back as the sapling resumed its previous posture, "until Famyl's focus was captivated by a mortal. A *mortal* whose very being obeys the rules of time and eventual degradation. A fleeting figment in the laif's timeline. And for what reasons? Who can say."

Famyl was growing weary. "Get to the point, Uljae," he said, trotting beneath the shadows and slumping down into the trampled grass, pillowing his head with his forepaws.

"Oh, I'm sorry," said Uljae, cocking his head to the side. "Do you have other places to be?"

"The *point*," Famyl reiterated with hostility.

The kingfisher's eyes constricted. "That is my point," he stated. Cocking his head to the other side, Uljae observed the gravity of his words beginning to settle. "Is she not the reason you disobeyed the Creator's wishes?"

Ruminating for a moment, Famyl understood with stinging realization the truth in Uljae's words. Here he was, receiving what he had been longing after for so long, and how was he spending the time stolen? Moping like a scolded child. As reticent as he was to admit it, Uljae was correct. But Famyl would never concede such ground.

Without another word, the dog rose to his feet and loped under the oval gateway, following where Linette had tread.

Famyl thought he heard from behind, "Now that wasn't so difficult, was it?" but he refused to turn around now that he was making headway.

* * *

Not good, Jekar thought, *not good at all. During periods of unrest, stability is paramount to ambition.* As hard as he tried to remove the memories of yesterday from his mind, he could not. The manner in which Lord Ancel's knights had spat their Lord's name, dishonoring the very house they served. The very house that clothed their children and protected them, giving them the status they wallowed in. The status that imbued them with the privilege to speak at all.

"It's none of my concern anyhow," Jekar murmured to the tree he was pressing his forearm against. He shook his head and dropped it to the forest floor. Though his heart longed for Stacey to gaze at him in the way she gazed at Sir Ector, the werewolf knew it was not a road he would ever undertake. *She is not meant for you.*

"Did you say something?"

Jekar looked up at the small voice. "I thought you lot would never catch up." He beamed as the clearing filled with monster children. "I have been waiting for ages!" He barked a laugh and ruffled the head of a giggling victus youth.

Before returning to Fort Navarene, he promised that he would reunite the strays with their parents. Thus far, he had observed the reunions of well over half of the families. The first had been a clan of danegusts who had mustered a small force, marching toward the cabin at the same time that Jekar liberated it. As children ran to their parents,

Jekar's eyes settled on a mother and father whose faces never stopped searching, and he immediately knew who they were. The length of the mother's snout and the recesses of the father's eye sockets were dead giveaways. Reverently, Jekar approached the lizard folk. He did not speak, he only offered a vial that he had filled with the hatchling's ashes as a keepsake. They did not beg for explanation, they did not crumple in anguish.

"Thank you," the mother had said, her shoulders sagging. He recalled that he had nodded before shuffling off, ready to be anywhere but that spot in the forest.

After running his bristly forearm across his nose, Jekar regarded the children. "Let us be off," he said, "before the gloom of night overtakes us."

Over their heads, the branches rustled.

"Mater!" a gargoyle child shouted, rising to her tiptoes and flapping her wings in useless excitement. "Pater!" her brother shouted into the upper branches.

In a whirl of glistening scales and vibrant wings, a pair of gargoyles landed, sending Jekar and the children reeling, all of the children, save the gargoyle triplets at the epicenter of the tornado.

As Jekar heaved himself back up to his feet using a hemlock branch that had fortuitously grown at the perfect height for such an action, the werewolf thanked the Creator for this homecoming. After all, he had no clue where to find wild gargoyles and neither did any of their offspring.

His remaining concern lay with the young ogres. He feared that their clan had already moved so far east that he would not see his own return for a week or more.

Suddenly the mother gargoyle appeared in his vision. "There are victus seventy or so footpaces north east of here," she said sternly as her mouth tweaked the thick scarf obscuring the lower half of her face. Thumbing over her shoulder, the gargoyle clarified the direction. "If you would like, we can guide you from the trees."

"S-Sounds good," Jekar stammered. He had never shared such close proximity with a fabled creature like this before. He unwillingly imagined a feline face beneath the scarf, and the notion made him smile.

This must have been an eerie display for the gargoyle. "Are you unwell?" she inquired, lowering her chin in concern.

Realizing that the sight of a werewolf trying to suppress a grin must appear quite disconcerting, Jekar quickly opened his jaw and filled it with a yawn. "Oh yes, yes. I am fine, just tired is all," he said quickly, feigning another yawn.

"There are pirskis huddled high in trees further back," the gargoyle continued, "my mate can curry them back for you. As for the noctyms and the jikavos – I will scout ahead for their kin—those kinds are not difficult to find."

"What of the ogres?"

The gargoyle faltered with clear displeasure. "What of them?"

"I would see every child reunited with their families."

"It would be in the forest's best interest if you were to abandon them at your next juncture," the gargoyle drew a serrated breath. "Or better yet, dispose of them now." She spoke without a shred of irony, leveling her gaze at him, expecting him to agree.

The ground beneath Jekar seemed to harden, along with his resolve. "I *will* see every child reunited."

"Very well." The gargoyle waved dismissively and turned her back. "We will see the rest *reunited,*" she mimicked Jekar's accent. "But you are on your own concerning the ogres."

Seeing the noctym children reunited marked the final reunion, as well as the end of the gargoyles' aid.

Jekar followed the last of the noctyms' pink prehensile tails as they disappeared into the foliage, not needing to turn his head to know that the mother gargoyle was standing next him.

"We are indebted to you, werewolf," she said, nodding her head in gradual increments. "As I said before, we will be departing now. But the forest is in peril, and I would be remiss if I did not advise you a second time—"

"It's fine," Jekar cut off her words. "Take care of yourselves." He angled his shoulders toward the east, signaling the ogres to follow, and began his trek anew. "You stated before that you know where the gremlin village is, correct?" the gargoyle called to him, her voice carrying the question softly to Jekar's back.

The werewolf halted and craned his head toward her. "I do," he affirmed, then shouted to draw the ogre children's attention. He had forgotten about the gremlin younglings the adolescent ogres were carrying. Good sense told him that he should deliver the gremlins before setting off east. But that path lay to the north, brushing against Navarene's doorstep.

With a growl, Jekar course corrected by pointing left, toward north, toward Fort Navarene. Truthfully, the gargoyles had offered to spirit the gremlins to their village, but the small, shy creatures had vehemently disagreed with that plan. All gremlins were instilled with a healthy fear of heights, and the thought of leaving the earth at such heights sent the smallest gremlin into unceasing tremors until the ogre wrapped her in a cloth and soothingly stroked her tiny head. The tallest adult gremlin was hardly as long as a man's arm outstretched to its fullest extent, which meant that their offspring fit comfortably in the palm of Jekar's human hand. Delicate and fragile were apt words to describe them, yet against his pre-conceived notions regarding the clumsiness of ogres, Jekar had entrusted these small creatures into the eager juvenile ogres' care.

The internal map Jekar drew in his mind would skirt the forest just enough for him to glimpse the fort, but he hoped the distance would allow his greatly diminished party to remain concealed from the sentinel's eyes.

Five ogres and seven gremlins were all that remained. The gremlins clung tight to the ogres who shielded them against the slapping branches, displaying a great amount of care. Perhaps they were not the mindless brutes they were so often viewed as, but still, Jekar knew that would not stop a hail of arrows from lashing out at them if they were spotted.

Jekar slowly trod the spaces between the vast trunks while the ogres lumbered straight through, displacing saplings and scoring trackable footprints on the needle-ridden grounds of the evergreen sections. Caution was necessary when selecting the gaps to traverse, certain areas offered very little space, but the more open areas sometimes contained shrouded threats. The gargoyles had warned Jekar that the more single-minded predators were not fleeing from the evil invading the forest. Instead, they were weathering the incoming storm, using the fleeing creatures as opportunities for impromptu feasts. As far as aspweavers were concerned, Jekar's nose would alert him to their location, but the more subversive predators required a conjoining of the senses.

"Jekar?" a grumbling voice disrupted the momentary stillness. The group had taken a pause near a creek to cool their feet and refresh themselves.

"Yes," Jekar asked, his hands locked on his hips as he surveyed the crowding trees.

"How much farther?"

With a final glance at the boughs, Jekar squared his shoulders to the ogre. "We're almost there," he said, peering beyond the edge of the creek where the water was waist high on the gremlins. The little monsters were splashing and carrying on without a hint of a care.

"Do you... do you think that we could—" the ogre paused bashfully.

"What is it?" Jekar asked, scouring the ogre's face for some sort of clue, placing one hand on the monster's surprisingly broad shoulder. From behind, one of the female ogres scooped a gremlin up from the creek and spun around, flinging droplets and filling the air with the combined laughter of two very different races.

The ogre wrinkled his mouth, briefly displaying the fledgling tusks just beginning to grow. "Could we stay with the gremlins, ya think?"

Jekar's eyebrow shot up.

"I mean," the ogre continued, straightening his posture, "we could be their defenders, you know." He looked back at the creek. "They're so flimsy..." he trailed off, his eyes sinking to his feet.

A sudden silence overtook their sliver of ground as the ogre spoke. The young ogre who had been dancing with the gremlin had not moved in several moments, and the others were backing away from the stream as if it had turned to blood. Opposite Jekar, a vast tunnel began to open at the base of the trees. The female ogre, her back to the werewolf, was frozen staring into it, her hands still upraised and cupping the wriggling gremlin. The gray of her skin did not appear normal, now a more subtle shade of granite.

That's no tunnel! Jekar thought, his breath seizing in his chest.

"Basilisk!" Jekar screamed, senselessly rushing the creek to free the squirming gremlin from the ogre's stone grip. He arrested his third step onto the bank when he noticed that the gremlin no longer struggled against his confines. The poor creature had also succumbed to the basilisk's petrifying gaze.

Whirling and stumbling to a knee, his heels splashing in the stream, Jekar shouted for the children to flee. Thankfully, they did not require his urging and were already disappearing under the vast canopy. Burying his claws in the clay substrate of the bank, Jekar launched himself forward, darting into the anonymity of the bordering coppice.

In no time at all, Jekar reached the escapees. Moments before, the forest had rushed past him in streaks of auburn and green, but now he moved at less than half his full speed. Urgency drove him to encourage them to increase their pace, lest they meet the same fate as their sister. To his dismay, their current rate was the peak of their abilities, and any faster would be akin to asking a caterpillar to become a butterfly at the snap of a finger. Jekar bounded at the ogre column's flanks, signaling favorable paths to the group, all the while glancing back for any sign of their aggressor.

"The ground will sag ahead," Jekar called to the frontrunner.

The ogre replied with a defeated look, foam forming at the corner of his mouth.

"Slow just a bit and use the trees for stability."

A nod and a grunt came from the young monster. The gremlins he carried were latched to his shoulders, their shivering faces peeking up just enough to reveal their ears and eyes.

Standing at the peak of the ridge, Jekar signaled for the children to continue down the hill. He waved and encouraged them to bury their heels in the soil and cling to the saplings for support. "If you reach the end of the forest, do not leave it without me!" he shouted to their backs as the last ogre began to descend the steep grade. As horrifyingly dangerous as the basilisk was, the humans guarding the fort would prove equally as lethal.

The forest behind appeared vacant. Great serpents navigated the trees silently, and unless locked in repose, basilisks proved exceedingly difficult to detect. Their scales deadened sunlight, offering very little glimmer if a ray were to strike their hide. Not to mention that meeting their eyes caused almost instant petrification, for which a cure had yet to be discovered. All these facts rattled around in Jekar's mind as his eyes feathered the forest. He refused to allow them to settle for an instant.

A dark tendril drew his attention, snapping his head over his right shoulder. The spectre coasted down the gorge, sliding seamlessly over the flora and stones. Smooth as a skimmer upon the water, the creature flowed over every contour, every barrier, and weaved between the trees without losing an ounce of speed. A tremendous shock vaulted Jekar back to cognition: *the basilisk had been cutting off their escape the entire time!*

Turning to the children, Jekar lifted his eyes above and beyond, peering between the leaves. The banners of Fort Navarene beat against the pure blue skies in seeming defiance of the clouds that gathered behind its backdrop. The ogres with their clinging gremlin accessories were heedlessly stumbling right toward the fort's doorstep.

Bolting down the hill, ignoring the brambles and vines, Jekar caught up with the group. If perhaps he could break cover first, he could signal the knights not to fire on the ogres, and maybe, just maybe, they would open the gates fast enough for them to escape the basilisk.

"Keep your eyes on me!" he shouted as he rushed past the gaping children. "Do not look elsewhere! Follow me!"

Lowering his shoulders, Jekar burst through the trees, bounded the grasping hedges, and landed in the bright clear landscape. He waved his arms and screamed for the sentinels to stay their bows as the sunlight scorched his eyes.

Not a shout rang back. Not a signal horn was blown.

Jekar continued to scream and flail his arms. He looked back just as the ogres broke from the shadows, clearly flagging, tottering on the last of their strength.

"Open the gates!" his voice cracked. He yelled hoarsely over the blood beating in his ears, "For all that is sacred! Corbin! Open the gates!"

Looking back once again to the children, fearing the silhouette in his periphery to be the basilisk, Jekar's eyes finally adjusted to the brilliance of the unimpeded daylight.

The ramparts were vacant. He squinted up between the crenellations, believing that his eyes were erring. Beyond the spaces, leaning against the hearth-like stone, there was a dead man.

But before his mind could register such an impossibility, the labored creak of the gates groaned, rupturing the silence.

35

"Contrary to common assumptions," Launcelot began, swaying playfully in his saddle before leaping off, "Fenrirfang is not the only forest filled with magic."

A tree sprung from a rocky patch nearby, an impossible place for vegetation to grow, and yet, somehow it thrived here. Linette noticed with some alarm that the tree's bark did not appear entirely normal. She blinked and refocused only to find that her senses were not betraying her.

As if Launcelot could read her mind, he strode over to the strange plant and gave it a solid strike with his knuckles. "Sounds like marble, does it not?" he queried, looking up at Linette on her mare.

Wryly, she scrunched her lips at him.

"You doubt me?" he scoffed.

Leaning forward and placing her elbows onto her pommel, she rested her chin in her palms. She blew a lock of hair from her cheek and cast Launcelot a look that conveyed skepticism.

"Fair enough," said the man posing as a messenger. He moved, pointing a finger to the meadow below them. "To the uninformed among us, this appears to be a simple heath, but it may be more than what it appears..."

Drawing a dagger from beneath his mantle, Launcelot swiftly carved a red line across his palm. "Keep your eyes upon the heath," he advised, not faltering from the pain. Within two measured steps, fist closed to seal in the blood collecting, he reached the strange tree and slapped his open hand to its marbled flesh. Speckled droplets fanned out from the crimson imprint left behind, and Linette's eyes disobediently flickered to the blood stain. Tiny rivers ran down the smooth surface, not one intermixing with another. Her forearms were overtaken by gooseflesh, and the back of her neck tingled.

Then, with a sharp intake of air, the meadow no longer stretched ahead of her.

"As the blood of laives allow travelers to cross the wards of the forests," Launcelot explained, admiring the landscape while enjoying the awestruck expression on Linette's face, "so the blood of my family grants passage to Joyous Garde."

Somehow, Linette did not need to shield her eyes from the brilliance. The sunbeams shone as gently as moonbeams, white and radiant, brushing between the blossoms without stinging her eyes. The world was bright, but it was also soft, as if filtered through a fabric that spanned the skies. Curious plants with leaves of ivory joined with the waves of emerald covering the keep's stonework, save for the walkway leading to the gate.

Where the meadow had been flat, sharp hillocks now burst from the soil, creating hard angles that impeded her view and encouraged her to ride onward to what lay ahead. Her eyes locked upon the castle ahead. A colossus of a tree writhed toward the clouds above the castle, establishing itself as a canopy for the entire fortress. Its leaves, emboldened with ancient grace, clad the branches in wavering armour, sprinkling the path with shade and offering respite from the heat.

Unbeknownst to Linette, Launcelot had remounted and was now next to her.

"Shall we?" he asked.

With a start, Linette's head snapped to the left. Her eyes required a moment to refocus.

"There is more to see, I assure you."

She nodded eagerly in response.

They hardly needed to urge their horses forward; the beasts were just as keen to continue. Soundlessly they trod on the spongy turf, and when they reached the flagstone walkway, Launcelot alighted from his saddle. Linette did the same, and when her feet landed, she searched for a place to tether her mare.

"No need," Launcelot interjected, correctly interpreting her look as he unbuckled his saddle strap and looped the bridle free from his horse's head. "They will not wander. They have nothing to fear here, except for perhaps the ache from an overfilled stomach." He gave the horse a pat on the flank as it strode toward a generous patch of rye-grass. Linette's mare was eyeing the grass longingly and curling her lips with impatience. Once the beast was relieved of her burdens, she hastily joined her kin, chomping and tearing at the tender plants as if an equine feast did not surround them.

"Pace yourselves," chuckled Launcelot. "Welcome to Joyous Garde," he said to Linette. His accompanying shrug was almost embarrassed as if he were showing her a stubby paddleboat riddled with holes rather than a glorious wonder.

Standing beneath the keep gave Linette a broad perspective on the grandeur that was Joyous Garde. A host of questions churned behind her eyes. *How did your family come to own this spectacle, and how does it even exist?* was one such query. *Who created this?* and, *where exactly are we on a map?* were articles amongst the top of her brimming curiosities. Above all her other questions was, *just how long will the Lord of Benwick hide his true identity?*

She watched him as he waited for her response. *He thinks he's so clever.* Bringing her writing slate up, she began to scrape the surface with a hunk of chalk.

Launcelot placed his hands behind his back and leaned toward the slate.

"*I am hungry,*" he said, conveying the message aloud. He quirked a smile. "You are in luck! There are orchards along the eastern path that are overflowing with fruit, and if one were to scour further past..."

Excitement flowed up from Linette's heels and surged into her scalp.

"One may find quite a bit of *faewort* congregating upon certain over-hanging—" was all Launcelot managed to get out before the crook of his elbow was snatched and pulled, jolting his neck back.

The very first tree in the orchard that they passed beneath was stippled with brilliant crimson apples, and Linette grabbed one and took a bite.

"Good, eh?" asked Launcelot as they ventured further into the trees.

She shrugged and carelessly tossed the unspent fruit over her shoulder before reaching up for another. The next apple was green with golden stripes. Just as she had with the other, Linette took a single bite and pitched it aside.

Launcelot frowned. "Are they not to your liking?"

Pausing their trek, she met his eyes for a moment, shook her head, and opened her mouth as if she had forgotten that her voice was inoperable. Quickly, she brought her lips together and tapped her chin thoughtfully, before walking away.

Bemused, Launcelot viewed the woman with great interest as he followed her path.

The toe of her shoe met the shadow of a pear tree, and at once, she turned back as if she had forgotten something. Swinging her head to the left, she spied something that caused her to bounce back on her heels and spring forward. Plucking the fruit excitedly, Linette took a bite, and unlike the others, she set upon it until there was nothing but the pit remaining. She unstrung another from a branch and held it aloft to Launcelot as if to say, *these!*

"Nectarines?" Launcelot's eyebrow arched.

She arrested her feasting to nod, a blissful grin on her face. Swiping away the juices that had dribbled down onto her slate, she began to inscribe a message.

I loved these when I was a child, the slate said. She erased the words with her sleeve and etched a few more. *The market stopped selling them long ago.*

"Ah," said Launcelot. "Then I am glad that I was able to oblige you this small wonder." He paused, appraising the woman. "When you leave, you're free to take as many as you would like."

A slight scowl formed on Linette's mouth, before swiftly dissipating. The thought of leaving brought a flash of disappointment, but there was still so much yet to see and no need to focus on the eventual departure. An unseen force, akin to a tempest, seemed to overtake Linette, and before she realized it, she locked her hand with Launcelot's.

They walked in comfortable silence, only pausing to allow Linette to sample any of the fruit that caught her eye. Once she had eaten her fill, she turned to Launcelot and smiled, heaving her shoulders to her ears.

"The family crypt is quite lovely this time of year," he said, turning toward the keep. Two hands firmly crimped his arm and spun him back around. "Are you sure? I mean, the skeletons *are* quite impressive. The bone structures alone—"

Linette released her hands and abruptly ran toward the forest.

An unannounced figure entered the frame, running a course that would rapidly intersect with Linette's. Tightening his jaw with alarm, Launcelot surged forward. Recognizing the form running toward her,

Linette's face lit with a grin. Dropping to a knee, she received the excited dog, fervently scrubbing his head.

"Gomer!" Launcelot breathed in stark relief, releasing his anxiety with sagging shoulders. "Clever boy."

* * *

Amyr had been staring at the sunrise for far too long. The light had slowly flooded his chambers, and he wagered that now would be the proper time for his arrival.

Today will be the day that I win over her father, he thought, filled with the assurance that comes from ages of experience. *And after that, surely, she will be mine.*

With one glance over his shoulder, the room flashed into his stables. As he saddled his dappled mare and swung his leg over, the barn instantly blinked to a roadway. The stolid mare did not flinch at the sudden transformation and trotted forward as if nothing was amiss.

Ahead loomed the simple farm where his Linette currently lived, but not for long. His workmen had secured every beam, painted the last wall, and secured and sealed the final threshold of the new home less than one day ago. Amyr had visited the site the evening before, giving the foreman his final payment. A glorious homestead had stretched before him, nestled pleasantly at a gentle hitch along the rolling pastures.

"Soon," whispered Amyr, lifting his voice for his next words, "you will truly be *my* Linette." After all, how could any mortal woman resist him?

Amyr knocked twice.

A sleepy face greeted him, shuttering his eyes as he opened the door.

"Hello Arbiter," Kenna croaked, his voice as equally awake as the rest of him. "To what do I owe this timely visit?"

"The tournament in Benwick," stated Amyr, fastening both hands behind his back. "I would like to escort your daughter, Linette, to it. With your leave, of course?"

Blinking and squinting, Kenna did not appear to process the request.

"And afterward," Amyr continued, "I would like to present you with a gift."

The farmer's pinched eyelids were accentuated with heightened eyebrows. Drowsily, he parted his moustache with thumb and forefinger. "She is not here," he replied, carefully selecting his words. Even as unawake as he was, Kenna discarded pleasantries, knowing better than to convey false pleasure.

Clearly taken aback, Amyr wavered on his heels. "Is she afield?" the laif inquired hopefully. His throat began to tighten as he watched Kenna sort through his lexicon to produce a wholly honest reply.

"She left yesterday with that brave messenger boy."

Amyr gnashed his molars, at a loss for words. The choice in descriptor was gutting. Gutting that Kenna had decided to add such a word, which would have been his end had it been false. Since the man still teetered on his groggy legs, the needless adjective proved to be true, upending more salt onto the wound.

"But if you would like," Kenna began consolingly, "Perla and I wouldn't mind company to the tourney."

Oftentimes, problems can be plunged and twisted into opportunities.

The traces of disappointment immediately vanished from Amyr's face, replaced by hopeful optimism, reinforced with ambition.

"I would be delighted," he replied, closing his eyes and nodding.

* * *

Fortunately, the basilisk retreated at the grinding sounds of the gate activating. Not that the children noticed in that moment, hurtling forward on their last legs.

Jekar watched the monster slink back into the brush that hedged the forest, unsure of the finality in its departure, but immeasurably relieved all the same. He dashed to the gate and waved the children toward him, pretending that the danger had not receded for the time being.

"Yes! Yes!" he called, "you're almost here! Don't look back! Yes! Almost safe!"

In seemingly perfect timing, the gate rocked on its hinges, reaching the limits of its welcoming arc as the children poured in. Bringing up the rear, Jekar rushed inside the fort, his neck craned back toward the forest. *Perhaps the basilisk will be satisfied with the meal it had already secured, and will not—?* The werewolf's speculation was interrupted when he stumbled and nearly sprawled atop one of the young ogres.

"We need to keep moving if...!" Jekar began, quickly brought up short.

A massacre was spread out before them, broken bodies scattered all around. Some of the more whole remnants were draped on rails and crenellations, but the rest were torn and shredded. The armour of dead on the ground were shorn free or peeled upward in places, the steel marked with dried crimson. And there was not one archenlaif corpse among the dead.

From their backs, the gate groaned back to life, securing the north entry.

A trap! Jekar's head swam as he rounded. *Who is controlling the gate?!*

"Get behind me!" he shouted, backing away from the gate, closer to the dead. The children huddled as tightly together as they could manage, their eyes frantically tracing the parapets. The gremlin passengers were frozen, except for the arrhythmic twitching of their ears.

Flexing his claws and building a roar in his lungs, Jekar waited for whatever evil had befallen the fort. Not one of the defenders had died peacefully, and he held no intention of joining their ranks.

Holding his breath, Jekar waited for the engineer to reveal himself. The platform on the rampart where the gate operator worked was obscured by a brief protective segment of wall. Chips and dents from centuries of battles marred the surface of the bulwark. As Jekar stared, his mind began to pick through the possibilities, each building in severity, and as he started to reconcile himself to the return of a spellcaster, the gate slammed shut.

Silence splashed into the void, filling the fort to the brim, increasing the volume of the children's whimpering. High above in the clouds, a host of vultures gathered, awaiting the outcome. Their presence indicated that this slaughter was fresh, maybe a few hours old, which meant the perpetrators must still be close.

Stumbling out from behind the bulwark, an armour-clad knight fell and clung to the top of a parapet. A soldier of the fort; a survivor.

Relief flooded every vein inside Jekar. The children did not understand, and their whimpers turned to sobs.

"It's alright," said Jekar calmly. "That knight does not mean us harm."

A tear-soaked ogre face peered out through damp fingers. "How do you know?"

"Because I'm fairly certain that I know that knight. And as she helped us, we should help her. You understand?"

The ogre bit his lip and slowly nodded, feigning confidence.

Jekar regained his full height. "Not all humans wish your kind dead."

Nearby a stonework building stood, door agape, but Jekar could not smell any decay from within. "Go and rest in there," the werewolf instructed, pointing. Not one ogre shuffled a foot in that direction. "You will be safe, trust me," he continued, trying to soothe their fears as best he could. "I've gotten you this far haven't I?"

A gremlin tittered in the ear of the ogre that Jekar had previously deemed the bravest, though now he realized from whence the courage may have been springing.

"Alright," said the ogre, glancing sideways at his gremlin companion. "We trust you." With that, the ogre loped into the building. One by one, the three other ogres followed behind. The last to enter stopped at the threshold and offered Jekar her best attempt at a smile before disappearing inside.

As Jekar made for the knight upon the parapet, he could hear what sounded as great banners flapping in the wind, though it was, in reality, the vultures alighting to the ground. Soon the puckering and tearing of flesh would ensue, and Jekar was glad to make some space between himself and the feast.

The knight was in worse shape than she had seemed at first. Beneath her right armpit, the plate had been wrenched back, revealing hideous devastation to flesh and bone. Deep gouges were drawn across her neck, ending at the corner of her mouth. The armour on her lower limbs was completely soiled scarlet, and the cloth of her tunic grasped and sucked at the blood. Her eyes flicked to the encroaching werewolf, and she drew back a few painful inches.

"Jekar, right?" she said, struggling for air. The last segment of each drawn breath was accented with crackles from deep in her chest.

The beast nodded. "Sir Carlysle," he stated, hesitating.

"Looks worse than it is," she wheezed and coughed, doubling over the crenellation. For a moment Jekar was not sure if she would inhale again, but suddenly she straightened and laughed.

"We need to seek a lampyr," said Jekar, knowing full well that he was out of his depth when dealing with wounds of such severity. "Your lung has been pierced and there may be venoms at work that we don't—"

Harshly, Carlysle gulped a pocket of air. "Tell me something," she paused to heave, "that I don't know, doc."

"Who did this? What happened?"

Carlysle's spine stiffened as if she were receiving another lash. "Forget about lampyrs," she said. "Lampyrs can't heal werewolf attacks."

"Werewolves?!"

"Your pack," Carlysle coughed. The spittle was free from blood, Jekar noted.

"Why?!"

The knight shrugged. "They betrayed us and attacked without warning." She began to rise.

"Don't strain yourself," Jekar advised. His ears were craning, involuntarily, to the slurping of the vultures and he began to revert back into his human skin, hoping to lessen the distracting sounds with weaker ears.

"And the archenlaives marched right through," Carlysle looked Jekar full in the face, mustering the remaining ounces of her strength. "We need to alert the kingdom."

But how? Jekar wondered, his pulse quickening. The aviary must be in shambles.

As if she could read his mind, Carlysle said, "Corbin had a messenger bird in his quarters. She released a shudder and sank back down. "Creator abiding, it's still there," she blinked slowly, as one about to meet death, and placed her chin to the stone. "I need a drink. Go now."

Torn between wanting to offer comfort and send warning, Jekar wavered, but in the end, he whirled to the stairs and made for Corbin's quarters on clumsy human feet. Thankfully not far and not hard to find, he arrived in his old friend's space. The room was completely vacant, and to his relief did not display any of the carnage from outside. A generous cage hung in the corner above the bureau, just as empty as its surrounding, save for a few stray feathers adorning the bottom. Curiously, the cage had been closed.

Hurrying around the disheveled bureau, Jekar discovered an incomplete missive that Corbin had been scribing. A few of the letters were smeared.

Lord Ancel,
As I feared, the pack has revolted and

Jekar snatched the parchment and flipped it around. "That's it? Oh, Corbin…"

Retrieving a feather from the cage, Jekar stabbed the sea of spilled ink and continued where his friend had left off. "And they have killed everyone in Fort Navarene. They are marching south, joined by another archenlaif army. Do not think to meet them at Irphen's Downfall, they will have passed by the time you read this. Alert the King. Alert the kingdom." He paused in his transcription. "The war is not yet over."

He signed his name at the bottom and pressed a hand to his forehead, scouring the room for a way to get this into Ancel's hands.

Breaking from the cool musty underground chambers, Jekar had no other option. He would need to run this message to Benwick. The transformation overtook his body in a matter of seconds, and soon he was bounding past the bodies and vultures, every sense heightened.

A commotion in the mass of carrion birds stole his attention for a fleeting second. The disruption was caused by a bird that displayed maturity greater than that of a fledgling vulture and was strikingly more regal and well-groomed. Jekar skidded to a halt and turned back to the creature that was clearly out of place.

Narrowing his eyes, Jekar approached carefully, treading on foreclaws.

Adorning the bird's amber colored leg was a double latched clasp.

The messenger harrier!

36

Now that Stacey was grown and more experienced from the turmoil of life, she found her perspectives on many things had greatly changed from when she was a little girl. Seated in the stands, observing the gathering tournament, she reflected on her changing outlook.

Ector, in a gesture of providence, had provided her with a pillowed chair in the central viewing box reserved for royals. The seat beside her was reserved for Ancel and sat vacant, fortifying the notion that caused many courtiers to now refer to him as "Lord Absent" from behind closed doors. Feeling awkward, Stacey sat in the grandstand alone, waiting for more prominent people to fill their seats. As Benwick was hosting the tourney, she had not had far to travel, which afforded her this spacious room of silence, for the time being, at least.

The dew dried on Stacey's thin leather shoes as the morning advanced. With a snort, she suddenly recalled the last time she had donned such fineries. She had been a mere child attending a tournament with her father the summer before she took her oaths to become a page. The frills ornamenting her neck and wrists were reminiscent of the dress she had worn back then. The current gown, a gift from Ector, was immeasurably more elegant, and certainly much more pleasant against the skin than that itchy fabric from her childhood.

The solid red banners of Ghore passed before the deck, bringing her attention back to the present, and a retinue of two knights with their accompaniment followed behind; a meager showing in comparison to the other realms. Well, aside from Tintagil, who had matched Ghore's showing, also providing only two knights.

A few familiar faces glided before Stacey, recognizable as the bannermen at Irphen's Downfall in the closure of that final battle. But only very few could she identify; the rest were residents in the sea of the unknown.

Rumors swirled, as they often did at such events, that King Arthur would be present today. Stacey immediately dismissed such a notion, as did most level-headed folk who encountered a person delusional enough to believe, insist upon, and spread such information.

An intermittent breeze from the side brushed one of the frills against Stacey's cheek. Without fanfare, a luxurious entourage from Lowthean filed into the space, their brilliant regalia paling the ornamentation in the booth considerably. The duchess rested her palm to the duke's fist as she entered, surveying the new surroundings, expressionless. Both duke and duchess carried a curly long-stemmed pipe in their offhand, wisps of smoke issuing from the triangular bowls, smelling of saccharine pastries. Sweeping into the room, their attendants entered behind and overtook the dark orchid seats set aside for Lowthean. The duke, thin and elegant, wafted along the rear perimeter of the space, drawing sips from his pipe, leaving clouds in his wake.

"What is that smell?" a crisp voice invaded Stacey's right ear. The duchess was seated beside her, gloved hands folded in her lap, dispensing of any introductions.

With a curled lip, Stacey casually obliged the question, making an audible sniff.

"All I smell is the duke's pipe smoke," she replied, "icing and caramel."

"No, no," the duchess' lips tightened without somehow forming a wrinkle. "When we first arrived in this carton, we were met by an unpleasant lingering aroma."

Cocking her head to the side, Stacey gave another sniff. "Sorry, I don't notice anything else in the air."

The duchess drew a finger across her eyebrow, smoothing the deftly groomed hairs. "It smelled oddly reminiscent of our hunting kennels back home on the Isle," she declared, lifting her chin. "Has a dog been present recently? A wet one perhaps?"

Not knowing whether to take affront or not, Stacey decided to play oblivious, replying with a shrug and a confused scowl.

The duchess did not appear contented, fixing Stacey's incredulous face with a focused glare. Fortunately, the doorway suddenly filled with the shadow of another entry. The duchess of Celliwig invaded the room, barreling toward her assigned section.

"When will the first meal be served?" she bellowed, taking her seat and dabbing the perspiration coursing down the bridge of her nose. Though tall and frail of frame, it was well known that the duchess was servant to an insatiable appetite. Jokes carried from other realms claimed that a portal to other worlds dwelt somewhere within her guts.

After Celliwig's entrance, a veritable floodgate was opened. The remainder of the realm's royals engulfed the booth within minutes, filling seats. The duchess of Lowthean had withdrawn to her section, but not before gifting Stacey with a withering stare that conveyed clearly, *I know what you are.*

As a child, Stacey had favored the Lowthean knights, finding their ornate, colorful armour to be *pretty and sparkly,* which had garnered shouts from her each time Lowthean was announced. Her father, a Benwick man through and through, had not been at all spurned by his daughter's favor of the rival realm. On the contrary, he had been immensely entertained by the looks of disdain transmitted by the die-hard Benwick fans whenever their knight was unhorsed by a Lowthean knight, although it was quite rare for a Lowthean knight to unhorse anyone. They were regarded as no more than a garnish for the aesthetics of the pageantry that went along with a grand tournament, and they seldom produced a knight that endured through even the first round. Her father would often joke with her, tilting his head to look up at his daughter perched upon his sturdy shoulders, "There is not doubt about it—your knights do make the loveliest of lawn ornaments."

Unintentionally, Stacey's eyes scanned the crowds. She found herself cramped in a paradox, wishing to see her father, but also at the same time, *not* wanting to see him. The death of his brother, Belfast, undoubtedly weighed heavy upon him and that uncomfortable conversation was something she wished to postpone as long as she could. On top of that, there was also the matter of her now being a werewolf, which was another horizon that she was not entirely excited about crossing with her family. In truth, the news that she had finally become a knight would bring them heaps of delight, but she felt that the wolf news would outshine the latter, and she thought it best to wait for another time to have a familial reunion rife with admissions.

The sputtering bleat of a horn ratcheted Stacey's attention to the tilt grounds. Standing beside the king of arms was a youth struggling to create a distinct note with his instrument. With his eyes pinned to the sky, the king of arms waited impatiently for the lad to complete his single duty. Bulging out his chest one final time, the youth slammed his lips to the mouthpiece and produced a tremendous blast that swung every head. The king of arms had been distractedly stroking his lengthy beard, and the sudden burst of sound startled him so much that he clenched his beard, almost yanking it from his face.

"Th-thank you, Wilfred," the king of arms stammered, patting the boy's shoulder. With his right hand sitting between the buttons of his gambeson, he rocked back on his heels and began the welcome statement. "Let me be the first to congratulate each and every one of you for having superior taste in your choice of entertainment on this fine day," he bellowed. "But it is with a heavy heart that I must first reveal to you, my fine people, that word has come from the Crown that our King will not be in attendance this day." He paused to allow for a heavy sigh of disappointment to escape from the sea of hopefuls, before continuing, "he sends his deepest regrets, and wishes all challengers the best, but says he'll gift a dozen gold pieces to any Lowthean knight who actually reaches the semi-finals."

A roar of laughter erupted from every corner of the grounds. Inside the royal box, in the wake of the involuntary outburst of laughter, anxious eyes danced toward the Lowthean royals who were scowling and scratching their respective necks in marked dismay. Covering her mouth in an attempt to conceal her amusement, Stacey flicked her eyes toward the duke and duchess. As fate would have it, the sour duchess happened to be glowering in her direction at that very same moment. With a guiltily contorted mouth, Stacey slowly readjusted her head, turning back toward the announcements.

"However!" the king of arms burst through the dwindling laughter. "We do have the privilege of being graced by the presence of our Holy Arbiter, Lord Amyr!" He swung an exuberant finger toward the royal box.

Stacey flinched back into her seat, briefly thinking the man was pointing directly at her. Royal heads craned toward the seats in the upper portion of the box, and Stacey rotated her torso to join them in peering that direction. A glorious laif rose, resplendent in cerulean and white, his shoulders and legs accented with pristine armour. He moved his arm from behind his back and saluted the king of arms. Offering a wave toward the crowd, he took his seat between a weathered man and noticeably pregnant woman. Amyr patted the man's leg and whispered in his ear before turning and whispering into the woman's ear. Both humans appeared to be ordinary mortals, and their attendance with the Arbiter piqued Stacey's curiosity—and no doubt the curiosity of most everyone else in attendance.

Guarded whispers began to weigh the air, speculations and estimations, Stacey caught the word *"who"* most prevalently throughout.

"Lords and Ladies!" The king of arms cut off the gossip. "Without further ado! It is my greatest pleasure to announce the first confrontation! The first tilt! The first scrum, if you will!" Flinging his arms into the air, the king of arms backed from the field, the vast audience roared their approval, and trumpeters along the fence raised their instruments and belted a triumphant melody.

Stepping onto a raised platform directly across from the royal box, the king of arms stood waiting for the crowd to settle. "From the court of black and red," he began, gesturing to the right side of the grounds. Voices lifted at the words, knowing exactly who was being ushered forth. The royal members of Garlot surged to their feet and began screaming in glee. "Sir Seyfried of Garlot!" the king of arms concluded, shouting to be heard. In a gallant display, Sir Seyfried reared her mount and gave a heroic salute.

Once the relative noise had returned to a reasonable racket, the king of arms resumed his duty. "And from the court of violet," he said pointing a finger toward the left as if it were a dueling saber. Clamorous shouts rang out, though not of the same sort that Sir Seyfried had been greeted with. The attendants from Lowthean remained in their seats, their faces flat, their spines proudly erect. Laughter peppered the wave of noise, and good-spirited jeers were tossed toward the purple knight as he approached his line. "Sir Lavenche of the Isle of Lowthean!"

With the visor open, the delicate face inside the helm appeared grim and determined, sizing up his opponent from Garlot with a curling sneer. To Stacey, Sir Lavenche appeared a hare to Sir Seyfried's lion. Even the slighter knight's lance seemed shorter compared to his opponent's.

"She's gonna fewkin' annihilate that little squeak!" the Duke of Garlot said to the duchess of Celliwig. She was otherwise occupied, heartily chomping on a leg of mutton, but lifted her head to reply with a fervent nod.

A viscount from Ghore put in, "Oh, most assuredly," which was received with a chorus of cheers. The Duke of Garlot and the viscount of Ghore bashed their tankards together in agreement.

"Would ya look at his lance?" a page of Tintagil jeered, nudging the squire beside her. "It's just as short and scrawny as he is!"

"I'd request a refund if I were you," the Duke of Garlot shouted to the Lowthean royals, "and drive that lance crafter from your lands as if he had a blight!"

The Lowthean attendants appeared unfazed by the din. Their eyes remained calm and steady, which to Stacey appeared much like a hawk before taking easy prey.

"Knights to their lines!" the king of arms announced, alerting the squires to lift their banners. A hush befell the grounds as soon as the banners reached their apex. The duke of Garlot gripped his seat, perching on the very front of the cushion. He was not alone in his eager anticipation, and Stacey could hear creaks and groans from the other chairs all over the box.

In a sudden arc, the king of arms dropped his upraised arm and the banners followed suit. The crowd ruptured into hysterics as the knights spurred their mounts, shredding soil and charging toward the tilt rail. At a discernibly swifter rate, Sir Lavenche reached his end of the rail before Sir Seyfried met hers, but this meant nothing, for the knight in black and red had a superior reach. A rending clap seared the air as Seyfried's lance shattered upon Lavenche's shield. With his lance flailing toward the skies, Lavenche reeled against his crupper, but miraculously remained in his saddle.

"What did I say?!" the Duke of Garlot shouted, surging to his feet. "What did I say?!" He spun around, flinging ale from his mouth while the contents of his tankard splashed over his knuckles.

In near frenzy, the crowd praised the skill of Seyfried. In contrast the knight quietly and calmly approached her starting line. Suddenly, taking Stacey by surprise, the knight reared her destrier once again; striking a pose that sent a shiver down her spine. "She's unreal!" Stacey muttered, unable to hold back her awe. Adulation swirled through the masses, and the floorboards trembled beneath her feet, causing her to fear that the box would be unable to sustain such fervor. This was merely the first tilt!

From the side of her eyes, Stacey glanced at the Duchess of Lowthean. She was reclining in her seat, appearing completely untroubled, and casually puffing from her pipe. The duke seated beside her, however, was hunched forward, gritting his pipe between his teeth, looking much like a criminal about to be handed a death sentence.

"Shoulda invested in a longer pole!" a shout came, practically punching the back of the duke's head. He winced at the jape, curling further into himself.

On the field, a page planted a black and red flag into the scoring framework next to the king at arm's platform. "That is one decisive round for Garlot!" the king of arms declared, beaming into the audience. "For a successful touch and a smartly shivered lance!" He swept his eyes to the empty Lowthean rack and heaved a breath. "Now! Knights at the ready!" His arm shot into the air.

Sir Lavenche was working his shoulder beneath the replacement shield his squire had handed him. The previous one had been scrapped after enduring such a blow; the steel caved in so much that it was nearly folded.

Both knights dropped their visors, and nearly simultaneously, the king of arms dropped his hand. The knights converged.

Stacey thought perhaps Lavenche was coursing at a slower clip than before but imagined the side swap may have affected her perspective. The sound of hundreds of lungs gasping at once filled the air as Lavenche lost grip of his shield, the protective implement falling to the freshly clipped grass below. Right before the second impact, Stacey almost covered her face at the ensuing thunderclap, but an unexpected flick of Lavenche's wrist popped her eyes wide. Subtly, the knight diverted the course of Seyfried's lance, ever so slightly, and managed to guide the lance beneath his shield-less arm. The expected crash was replaced by a disappointing scraping of wood to steel.

Stacey could not help but gasp when Lavenche unexpectedly locked Seyfried's lance beneath his armpit, and violently rotated his torso, springing his opponent from her saddle and onto the earth. Seyfried's iron grip—which had been the source of many victories—had now caused her downfall.

The sight of Seyfried's destrier running past, riderless, silenced every voice. The fallen knight tumbled to a halt and lay on her back staring at the clouds, a thick quiet pressing from all sides.

With Seyfried's lance still tucked under his arm, Lavenche leaned in his saddle toward Seyfried's squire. The wide-eyed lad retrieved his knight's weapon, moving as a sleepwalker.

The Duke of Garlot was frozen in place, save for the foamy trickle of ale still rounding his knuckles. Baffled and perplexed, the royals gawked, their eyes darting from Lavenche to Seyfried, unable to comprehend this turn of events.

Meanwhile, the king of arms, the first to recover his senses, beckoned Lowthean's page to plant his flags into the scoring stand. His booming voice, now seeming much louder in the silence, breached the calm.

"Lowthean wins!" he announced, shrugging unintentionally. Normally he would offer a bit of commentary after a victory, but he clearly was at a loss for words. Lowthean defeating Garlot was as unexpected as an afternoon snowfall in midsummer, but compounding the fact was that such a jousting maneuver had never been witnessed before.

"Well done!" Stacey was the first to offer congratulation. And after her, a trickle of applause and praise began to release.

Sir Lavenche, visor still locked, rode past the box to offer a nod toward his duchess. This simple gesture garnered a renewed response and a torrent of applause broke free, shaking the floorboards. Furtively, Stacey glanced at the Duchess, and as before, managed to make eye contact. This time, the werewolf was greeted with a squinty-eyed look of admiration that conveyed, *I still know what you are, but I suppose you're all right.*

* * *

Of all the days to be stuck in the palace...

From his post atop the rampart, Kasyan could hear the tournament clearly. The reverberations from the lance strikes carried very well even through the cheering of those lucky folks who had not been mandated to work aviary duty. Those many, many lucky folks.

Disappointedly being born under the sign of the observer, Kasyan had always been stationed far from action; his gifts more suited for great distances. Not only could he spot movement from leagues away, but also his periphery was unimpeded, allowing him to view the world before him without the need to swivel his head. This was quite advantageous for a garrison to have a spotter amongst their ranks, especially when pressing forward through unknown territories. But Kasyan was not yet of an age to earn a rank beyond *sentry*. While he stood alone leaning forward against the crenellation, far flung from the festivities, he felt that he would never see the sort of action that he longed for.

How could he earn any sort of renown just sitting around the palace, watching and waiting for messenger birds to arrive? Besides, most everyone in Camelot had traveled great distances to be here in Benwick for the tourney. What sort of messages would be sent from their lands on this day of all days?

To be accepted among the knights of Benwick, riding with them toward battle, rescuing them from unseen perils using his skills of perception... Kasyan imagined so many fantastical scenarios.

As his imagination started to formulate some sort of evil spectral machination, a speck on the horizon abruptly coaxed his attention back from the forest of make believe.

"Is that..." he whispered, adjusting the visor on his helm. His vision leapt distances in increments, bringing the shape into focus, as if it were right before his nose. "Nocky?" he concluded.

The aviary log did not register that the harrier had been sent out, and he should be in his enclosure. Kasyan had not bothered to check on the creatures before his shift, and now he kicked himself for his dereliction.

He spun toward the wired door of the aviary, and hurried into the feather-dappled atmosphere. A sign reading "Birds Only" wavered on its peg as he pulled the door closed behind him.

A dark silhouette was perched inside Nocky's generous cage. Drawing closer and plucking the torch from a nearby sconce, Kasyan threaded his eyes through the darkness. Indeed, the silhouette belonged to a harrier, but there were discrepancies along this bird's plumage.

"You're not Nocky," exhaled Kasyan at the imposter. The bird heaved its shoulders and glared back, seeming to say, "And you're not my dad."

Returning to the open air, Kasyan focused on the harrier that was now within fifteen breaths from the palace.

Maybe it's a routine missive or something, he reasoned, trying to dismiss the insidious feeling creeping up his spine. He had not awoken this morning with the intent of uncovering conspiracies or any manner of underhanded plots that had nothing to do with him. The business of lords and ladies and kings and dukes and any other members of the ruling class were far from his limited range of expertise, or quite plainly, his interest. And if this had anything to do with *them*, then he wanted to stay far, far away.

The great bird perched upon the crenellation before Kasyan. He strode on hesitant feet, telling himself over and over, "this is nothing bad, this is not out of the ordinary." Sure enough, a scroll was latched inside the message compartment, causing the creature's right leg to appear thicker than its mate.

In a few moments, Kasyan had unfurled the scroll though his eyes refused to press on after the first sentence. The initial words revealed a living nightmare. Returning to the start over and over again, as if he were standing on the edge of a tower, fearing to take the plunge. Finally after the fourth attempt, his eyes pierced the surface and he read the missive in its entirety.

With mouth gaping, Kasyan stared at Nocky.

"The war is not yet over..."

* * *

The tourney carried on in usual fashion, but the effects of the first tilt still pervaded the grounds. The sense that something was amiss lingered, almost as the bitterness from sour fruit tends to remain on the teeth. The mood finally stabilized only after a dozen contests rinsed their collective tongues.

Stacey's knight, Sir Ector, proved victorious in his contests, not relying on the tallying of scores; he unseated every opponent he faced. Afterward, he would pass her seat from the field, pausing his mount's canter to lift his visor and wink at her. Each time it would set her heart fluttering. She could not help it. She was completely enamored with the young knight.

At one point during the tournament, a newly minted Benwick knight named Sir Desdemona faced one of the knights of Tintagil, though his name escaped Stacey's recollection. An ordinary contest to be sure, the opponents appearing equally matched. The normal amount of cheering greeted them when they moved to their lines, but when the Tintagil knight rocked Desdemona from her saddle, securing victory, the screaming praise from Amyr's guests startled the royals. Heads snapped in all directions in alarm, the most concerned among them being the members of Tintagil.

"That was a sound thrashing!" the mustached man shouted, nodding fervently. "How did you like that?!" he taunted the knight who was splayed out on the pitch, counting birds.

In usual tournament fashion, the semi-finals gave way to the finals, which meant the best two knights would face off for the final tilt.

Stacey could barely remain seated right before the king of arms announced the combatants.

"In an unforeseen turn—from the isle of Lowthean," the king of arms began, "I present the first of our final competitors on this fine day: Sir Lavenche!"

A roar completed the announcement, allowing only the first syllable of Lavenche's name to be heard clearly. At this point, everyone in the crowd knew who this Lowthean knight was. Never before had a knight presented such prowess and cleverness, in spite of his lean build, and the audience knew that they were watching history unfold. A few of his matches had been determined by score, unlike his adversary, who had unseated each and every one of his opponents.

"And now, and now," the king of arms fluttered his hands, waiting for calm. "And now," he continued, "we have a knight who has displayed unparalleled skill this day!"

Stacey watched Sir Ector ride to his line.

"From this very land of Benwick," the king of arms shouted, his volume growing to meet the swelling crescendo of the crowd, "I present the son of Lord Ban, brother to Lord Ancel: Sir Ector!"

Her feet had been impatiently locked to the floor, and in a flurry, Stacey shot up and screamed, joining the upheaval.

A commotion from the crowds behind Ector disturbed the elation, causing silence to ripple throughout the masses. Leaping from his mount before it had even come to a halt, a young armoured sentinel rushed the stage. His hair was matted to his forehead, his helm somewhere forgotten along his journey. The look of grave concern on his face made Stacey reel back into her seat.

After reading the scroll that he had been roughly handed, the same hollow look was transferred to the king of arms. He clasped the sentinel by the shoulders and shook him, conveying a string of questions that

Stacey could not hear. The sentinel replied with a solemn shake of his head, and the king of arms looked toward the royal box.

"The tourney is off!" he boomed. The statement was not returned by the sounds of disappointment or groaning, as it seemed that all the people had guessed what was happening. "Muster your forces!" he shouted, his voice harshly becoming a scream. "Rouse the king! They have not been defeated yet! The enemy is marching to our gates! War has come!"

37

"Where is Ancel?!" Stacey suddenly found her voice, grappling Ector's vambraces. "We must tell him!"

The commotion of bodies and souls propelled by the king of arm's proclamation was disorienting and nigh deafening. The royal box had drained immediately, leaving Stacey by herself. Ector alighted from his mount and stumbled through a sea of scurrying pages and distressed common folk to reach her.

"Why?!" came Ector's brackish response. "For all we know, that sod is leading the enemy forces!"

Stacey released his wrists and recoiled in shock.

"*Where is he* is the perfect question," Ector continued. "Chasing wisps and puffing pan flutes, you think?" He shook his head, flinging sweat droplets. "I think not!"

"Then where—" began Stacey, but was interrupted by a stirring from behind.

Ector's eyes flashed to the movement.

"Tell me more of your Lord's treachery," commanded a silky voice.

After returning from the battle sites, Stacey had held Ancel in high regard, and this disloyal talk did not sit well with her. "Ector," she began, tugging the fabric protruding between his armour, "let's return to the keep, where—"

"Where to even begin!" Ector replied to the man, ignoring Stacey's pleas. "He's in league with—!" The son of Benwick's blood drained from his face when he recognized to whom he was speaking.

Rising from his seat, Amyr folded his arms and gave the knight an admonishing look. "In league with whom?" he asked, cocking an eyebrow at a dangerous angle.

From behind a fumbling tongue, Ector finally managed to reply. "I cannot be certain, but there is great suspicion running throughout the councils, and it trickles down to the knights and servants alike."

Relieved that she had not watched Ector pass right before her, Stacey heaved herself to her feet and rounded on the Arbiter. "These are matters that can be sorted after the evil is beaten back," she managed to state diplomatically, while urging Ector toward the most convenient exit.

Appearing greatly dissatisfied, Amyr's scowl deepened. His lips opened to continue his inquiry, but Stacey and Ector bowed and discreetly departed, avoiding further scrutiny.

Not wishing to be a stumbling block, Kenna had remained in his seat. He tipped his head back to look at Amyr. "Do you think that Lord Ancel has sided with the enemy?" he asked quietly.

Amyr was momentarily puzzled by the question, then realized that Kenna was still a player in Ancel's ruse; the simple farmer had no idea that his daughter was on the verge of courting the Lord of Benwick. Biting back the impulse to reveal this choice morsel, Amyr decided to reserve the revelation for another time.

"All good questions, my friend," replied Amyr, gladdening. "Where do you think your Lord is at this very moment?"

* * *

"You cannot appreciate a levelheaded man until idiots surround you," Ancel declared, seated in a bosk. The trees were not as old here, nor very tall, which was perhaps the reason why the faewort flocked there in such quantities. Like cave moths to a torch, the strange and rare plants encircled the area, growing vine-like across the saplings. The older trees had faewort falling only from their lower branches, as the plant was not inclined to leave the ground.

While filling baskets with as much faewort as she could reach, Linette listened intently as Ancel regaled her of his latest frustrations. With all the responsibilities that the man complained of, the woman wondered how he was able to shed his burdens to spend this time with her. Either he was too heavily laden to accomplish what he must, or it was not as bad as he quailed. But these thoughts were quickly dispelled, for thinking of such things while in a paradise, absent of evil, was a waste of time.

"They lack a basic understanding," he continued, "of human nature. How liable we are to selfishness, and none of them have ever spent a night without a full belly." Nodding in agreement, Linette felt she was beginning to get a handle on the characters that filled Benwick's council.

No wonder he has been avoiding them! Linette thought. *They seem stupid and awful.* She reached on her tiptoes for a knuckle sized mass atop a crook and her eyes flicked to her slate. Recognizing the look, Ancel retrieved her link to speech.

"Why can't they appoint a new panel?" Ancel read the words and coughed into his fist. "If only they could," he moaned, reaching toward another clump of faewort that was far from Linette's grasping fingers. "Councils serve seven-year terms, and Lord Ban re-enlisted this coven of whelps a few months before his death."

Linette heaved a sigh that conveyed more than words. The man was now ardently shaving the bark, filling her basket without regard.

"Yes," replied Ancel. "You see, we have a long road ahead of us—" Abruptly he noticed the faewort spilling onto the ground. "Apologies!" he said, hurriedly dropping to a knee and collecting the vagrants.

Off in the hedges, a harsh rustling caused Linette to start.

"If this doesn't just warm the cockles of my heartwood," a voice said from above, its timbre resembling a creaky branch. "Ah, young Lord Launcelot, it cheers me to see you this day."

The basket fell to the ground. Backing up a startled step, Linette lost a bit of wind when her ribs struck the trunk of the tree behind her. She looked to Ancel but saw the man appeared to be the opposite of frightened.

"Priraeda!" Ancel exclaimed, flinging his arms wide open and meeting the loping tree person with an embrace.

Feeling as if she were in a dream, Linette continued reeling. This *Priraeda* appeared to be as if the Creator plucked an immature elm and smashed a laif into it, before kneading the pair together like clay, then the creature aged and grew tall for many centuries.

"Linette," said Ancel, beaming at the woman with a congenial arm draped around the grinning tree person. "This is Priraeda." He paused to allow a nod to pass between his friends. "Have you heard tales of drevnigosts? Also called ancient guests by commonfolk."

Awareness dawned on Linette. Of course she *knew* what an ancient guest was, but their descriptions varied greatly between campfires, and she had had no idea what one would look like in real life.

"Your friend is speechless," remarked Priraeda, digging a finger into an ear-like protrusion. "I take no offense. This is a most common response."

Sharply, Ancel shook his head. "Even if she wanted to reply, my friend, she cannot."

"Oh," breathed Priraeda, grasping the meaning and covering his eyes with his gnarled spindly fingers. "Pardon my mistake, my lady."

The woman graciously smiled and bowed her head, recognizing the creature's contrition was genuine. Unfurling from the shade beneath her hip, a furry face curled and revealed a muzzle full of teeth.

"Who is this fellow?" inquired Priraeda, curiosity twitching his leaves.

"This is Gomer," Ancel replied above the dog's simmering growls. "Priraeda is a friend." The man approached Linette's protector, his voice softly placating. "He has served the Keepers of Joyous Garde since the beginning. We need fear him as much as we fear the branch that scrapes upon your window at night."

Priraeda took a step forward. "My Lord speaks the truth," he said.

The snarls had subsided, but Gomer's hairs were still on end.

After scratching a phrase upon her slate, Linette lifted it to the ancient guest. The bark above his eyes tightened as he peered at the words. Puzzled, he looked to Ancel for guidance.

"It says, *Gomer is always wary of the unknown,*" Ancel recited. Then to Linette, he said, "Priraeda does not understand our script."

The tree man began to ease downward, his gnarled limbs creaking. "Caution is a prudent measure," he stated, interlacing his hands atop his settled knee. "Your guardian is a wise beast."

While scratching the crown of Gomer's head between his ears, Linette smiled at Ancel. The simple gesture registered to the ancient guest as more than mere friendship. And the way Ancel received it suddenly caused Priraeda to feel uneasy.

"I fear that I am intruding!" Priraeda spat as if flinging a curse. Lithely and violently, he shot to a stand. "My deepest apologies!"

"Soft, Priraeda," Ancel spoke as if he were consoling a child. "You have not committed any such offense. Stay with us as long as you wish."

"I cannot!" returned Priraeda, swiveling his trunk to the forest behind. "I have many duties!"

"Honestly—"

Priraeda halted his Lord's assertion. "Apologies," he said curtly, lifting his arms to block the retreating sunlight, creating a crosshatch shadow over his eyes. "It was a pleasure meeting you, Linette." He gave Gomer a brisk nod before leveling his vision toward Ancel. Briefly, a pattering all around broke the tension. Raindrops began their introductions, gently at first, their intensity beginning to bloom.

"My Lord?!" Priraeda fixed Ancel with a look of grave concern.

The blood had drained from the man's face. With a hand locked to the hilt of his arming sword, his stance menacingly spread, endlessly turning in place, he frantically scanned the surrounding forest as if a daemonic host were about to descend.

"My Lord," Priraeda continued, "are you alright?" The placid falling of the raindrops in the calm setting caused the young Lord to appear crazed. He seemed to be elsewhere.

Penitently, the ancient guest backed away, inclining his upper half in remorse. As Priraeda conceded ground, Linette overtook the distance. The rain fell in driven sheets now, the monsoon passing over, accenting Ancel's whirling silhouette with great bursting droplets. Wrapping her arms about the haunted warrior's neck, the woman clung tight, her jaw clenched, embracing him while simultaneously bracing herself, expecting to be hurled aside.

A mask of sanity staggered across Ancel's face, flickering for an instant. Linette increased her grip and brushed his ear with her lips. What she could not whisper, she exuded with a touch.

Shoulders wilting, the spell seemingly broken, Ancel turned and held Linette. With their hair drenched and streaked across their features, the rain showing no sign of easing as they defied the storm together. Feeling even more as an intruder, Priraeda slunk back into the forest, disappearing, his departure completely unnoticed.

38

By the time Benwick reached the capital, the war had already been met. Sir Ector led the remnants of a force that had once been mighty, but was sadly dwindled over the centuries. Among the eleven knights with him, only two had been present for the re-taking of fort Navarene; Sir Tamarah and Sir Vashal. The rest had yet to experience battle.

The faintest chill from autumn's early whisper swept beneath Stacey's mantle, causing her to tug her hood over her head and shiver. She could see thick smoke pluming the dawn skies from the vast force gathered at the gates. The misty chains intermingled and joined into a single shaft of somber gray that tunneled upward into the gloomy skies.

It seemed, for perhaps the first time in memory, that Benwick was the last to join Camelot's army.

"It is just as I feared," said Tamarah, coming up behind Stacey.

"And what is that?"

"It's far from over."

Tamarah was correct. Now within view, the fields and meadows that stretched northward from the capital's front gates displayed clear evidence of recent battle. Beyond the fields, gathered at the edges of Fenrirfang, a bannerless army waited. Clouds of smoke surged upward, separate and many, lacking the unity that Camelot displayed. But how important was unity when your force vastly outnumbered your enemy?

"Creator guide our blades," Ector whispered. The enemy's dark armour fanned out for leagues, stretching at an insurmountable length. "You will have much to pay for when this is at its end, brother."

To Stacey's great disquiet, her beau had convinced himself that Ancel was behind the incursion. When she had gently offered other possible ideas the night before, she had been met with unflinching enmity. It was a subject to which Ector had committed and remained unwavering in his resolve.

"Do you think," Stacey began, trailing off as she waited for Ector to acknowledge her. Once he turned to her, she began again, "Do you think that your brother is among them?"

Jutting his chin toward the archenlaives, Ector narrowed his eyes. "Doubtful," he replied bitterly. "The coward is sure to be far from the fray, sipping some manner of vile brew and conspiring with his new lords."

"Ah," was all Stacey said in reply. She wanted to continue the conversation, but their trek was nearing its end.

Celliwig occupied the west flank. Bleary eyed and wrapped in a thick cloak, their general hailed Ector's arrival. "Benwick, at last!" he said with a measure of irony, taking in their numbers.

"What have we missed?" asked Ector, his upper lip twitching at the man's display of insolence.

The general swiveled his head at the Celliwig soldiers pressing around him. All appeared weary, their red and white tabards soiled, their armour caked in mud, but their spirits surprisingly light. "Sometime between supper and dusk the enemy sent a third of its numbers out," the general reported. "All were foot soldiers, none mounted or flying. The king dispatched over half of Camelot to meet them."

One of the nearby soldiers tugged at his general's sleeve and whispered into his ear. An irritated look passed across the general's bearded face. "Take it easy, Gerald, I'll get to that in a moment," he said to the eager man. Turning back to Ector, he continued his account. "Sheesh!" The man shook his head. "Cadets, am I right? Where was I? Oh yeah, so pretty much everyone except Tintagil and Ghore rode out. And of course, the royal army and the Church hung back as well."

"You prevailed, I presume?" Ector asked impatiently.

"More or less. We managed to drive them back—"

Ector suddenly urged his mount forward, tugging the reins sideways and lifting the beast's neck in a dismissive gesture. "That was all that needed to be said," he muttered, riding around the ring of soldiers.

Gerald, hopping excitedly, looked about ready to catapult into the sun. "We captured one of 'em!" he shouted, clapping his hands. "Brought her all the way back to our camp!"

This news stopped the Benwick knights in their path.

"What did he say?" Ector demanded, staring at the general.

The general slapped the beaming soldier in the gut. "Damn it, Gerald," he said. He turned to look at Ector. "It's true, yes, but—"

"May I speak with her?" Ector's eyes were ablaze.

"Would that you could, my lord, but we surrendered her to Sir Kay last night."

A scowl draped over Ector's chin.

"Yep!" Gerald added cheerfully, twisting a heel into the soft soil. "We received commendations for it too!"

Ector appeared ready to snap at the cadet, but Stacey nimbly interrupted before he could release his ire. "That's wonderful," she said, grinning broadly.

The young man rushed toward her and enthusiastically raised a medallion. "See? See?" he said, battering the air.

"Hold it still," Stacey cautioned, playfully recoiling. She held the token between her fingers and appraised it with a thoughtful frown. "Well done, Gerald."

"We haven't the time for this!" Ector growled and snatched the medallion from Stacey. "I'm sure this trinket will be such a great comfort to your mother when she places it atop your grave." Scornfully, he tossed the medallion over the unwary cadet's head, turned away as it splashed into a muddy recess at the feet of the Celliwig soldiers.

As bewildered sorrow melted Gerald's face, and Stacey began to offer an apology with deep contrition in her voice. "He is a good knight, he really is..." she stammered, beginning to doubt her own words. Her eyes darted to Ector who was already twenty paces hence. "It is a rather lovely medal!" she shouted before driving her spurs into her horse, hurrying to catch up with her fellow knights.

Once Stacey reached Ector, Tamarah was already beside him, speaking quietly. The muddy track allowed two horses to ride comfortably abreast, and Stacey found herself lingering behind, though still within earshot.

"We need to establish our place among the battalions first, my Lord," advised Tamarah, flicking a defiant glance back at Stacey. "The inquiry with the captive can wait."

Rising in his stirrups, Ector swiveled his torso to peer around. "Just where are the royal banners, you wager?" he asked, steadying a hand on his pommel. "Arthur's popinjay brother should not be far from them."

"Have you not heard a word I said?" Tamarah pressed.

"I have," replied Ector coolly, still surveying. "I merely wish to check the validity of that inbred commander's words."

"But that—"

"Won't take long," Ector overtook the knight's speech. "Ah," he said, lowering back down on his saddle, "there it is."

Swinging toward the gates, Ector led the knights off the path. An Orkney page scowled at the muck kicked up onto his gambeson as the horses filed through. Stacey attempted an apology as they passed, but the lad ran before she had the chance.

Alighting to the damp earth, Ector approached a pavilion with guards wandering about in royal livery.

"Hey!" A guard before the tent flap raised a pike, barring passage. "State your business!"

Ector palmed the guard's face and gave it a substantial push. The man tottered backward and nearly fell onto the pitched canvas. "Is Kay within?" inquired Ector, turning to another guardsman.

"He is," came the swift reply.

Inclining his head and flexing his hand, Ector gave a curt nod and pressed inside. Hustling from her mount, Stacey trailed a few paces behind and entered the tent shoulder to shoulder with Tamarah.

"Why don't you wait outside," the elder knight advised. "This is an audience for seasoned warriors."

"Look," Stacey began, rounding on the knight, "I've never seen war, but I've seen my share of—"

Bumping blindly into their backs, Yaval was held up at the entrance. "Keep it moving, ladies," he urged. "C'mon now."

Tamarah hissed between her teeth and sauntered forward to obtain her place in Ector's shadow.

A gentle hand pressed Stacey's shoulder. "Don't mind her," said Yaval. "She's just nervous."

"Well, she's not alone."

"I know," Yaval lifted his hand and swept it before them in a lordly gesture. "After you."

Lanterns lit a circular table topped with a neatly arranged map. The outskirts of the heavy parchment were held by hands belonging to a laif with a troubled expression on his face. The most colorful of tabards hung over his armour, brushing against the edge of the table as he leaned heavily upon it. He did not look up at Ector's approach.

"Arthur is elsewhere," said the laif wearily.

"I am not looking for Arthur."

The laif whom Stacey assumed was Sir Kay lifted his chin. "Then what can I do for you?" he asked. "Benwick, I presume?" He wrinkled his nose at the outfits before him, muttering to himself as he looked at his map, "green and black are such dismal colors when paired..."

"The captive," Ector interjected. "Where is she?"

"Why, she is gone," Kay replied, straightening in surprise. The arrangement of wildflowers adorning his hair bobbed at his movement. "What does Benwick want with an archenlaif?" He looked over each of their faces again. "And where is Sir Ancel?"

Ector leaned onto the table and glared at the laif. "Where is she?" he repeated with malice. "And if you speak—"

"Out," Kay leveled his eyes at Ector. "Now."

Ector knew better than to challenge this laif any further. He had already overplayed his empty hand. Folding his arms across his chestplate, the lordling offered a pained smile and moved to depart.

"Hold a moment," Kay's statement froze Ector several steps shy of the exit. "We have set aside a patch of earth for you between Tintagil and Orkney."

"Gramercy," replied Ector stiffly.

"And I hope you don't mind," Kay continued, shooting a sly look at Ector, "we have bolstered your numbers with the remnants of the red knights. Congratulations. They are now under your command."

Ector's fists curled and uncurled. Within the brief stillness, Stacey feared that she would bear witness to an irrational assault on the king's brother. Fortunately, nothing of the sort played out. With a courtly bow, Ector returned Kay's statement with silence, and resumed his departure.

"What's that smell?" Yaval asked, stepping beside Stacey as they surveyed the battlefield.

Immediately, she thought he was making another dog joke, but then realized that his nostrils had finally picked up what she had detected leagues before. And besides, her werewolf identity was yet unknown to her comrades.

"I'm not sure," returned Stacey, "but it smells like grease."

"Yeah." Yaval nodded. "Sorta like breakfast meat and arming oil, I guess."

Stacey nodded her agreement, squinting against the rising daylight as they made their way forward. The field stretched north for several acres, littered with battlements, but to the west, the space was practically boundless. Eastward lay a bit of territory for a fray, but the Patreka River created a barrier that rendered any meaningful flanking run utterly moot. The real threat was before them, straight ahead. She had overheard a few conversations that highlighted such a layout. The knights embroiled in the discussions seemed delighted at the prospect of a pitched battle with the opportunity for cowardly tactics removed.

"We're in for a knock-down-drag-out battle, friends!" the stout Tintagil knight announced to his comrades. "A real slobberknocker!" he concluded, slugging back a tankard of early morning ale. Stacey received an affable wink from the knight as he swiped the froth from his thick beard.

"Have you seen any werewolves?" Yaval inquired, startling Stacey.

Joining the knight in gazing across the expanse, Stacey tried to make out any familiar silhouettes, but she failed. "It's too far to really tell."

"You're right," Yaval agreed before abruptly changing the subject. "It was clever of the archenlaives to send out a smaller force last night. They're testing us."

"That is a new tactic," Stacey added. "In the past, they tended to batter us with their numbers, until we eventually repelled them."

Yaval turned to leave. "That's history for ya," he said, walking away.

"And what's the point of history, if you don't learn from it?" Stacey murmured, standing alone in the field.

The afternoon passed and the horns of war had yet to sound.

"The louts are probably waiting for dusk," wagered Yaval, flicking a match into the flames. "At least it doesn't look like rain."

Seated next to him, Tamarah shivered in spite of the day's warmth. "Please don't mention rain," she said. "Every time I hear raindrops, I lose my mind a little bit."

Fixing the woman with a rueful look, Yaval eased the stem of his pipe from his bottom lip. "Same thing happens to me," he admitted to Tamarah. "That sorceress did a number on us didn't she?"

"Do you think the archenlaives have another spellcaster?" Stacey interjected. Blank expressions were all that answered her question.

"Word from command," Ector stated, breaking the silence, "is that *we* have another caster on our side, in addition to the royal mage."

"Come now," said Yaval in disbelief. "Where are they from?"

Ector looked over his shoulder at the adjoining camp. "Apparently Orkney has an apprentice. He's young, but they assured us that he would be ready."

"Any other details that bear repeating?" Tamarah inquired, carefully peeling the skin from a singed haunch of rabbit.

Ector remained silent, glancing at their newest recruits. The band of red knights that now filled the empty Benwick ranks were in their smallclothes, performing stretching exercises. Their captain was barking orders, and the ragtag bunch actually displayed a semblance of discipline.

Turning back from surveying the red knights, Ector shrugged. "When battle is sounded, our pals in red are going in first," he divulged. "And we may join them at our own peril, but the Crown has advised that we stay back until our banners are waved, if we wish."

"Oh, forget that, brother," Gabriel leaned back interlocking his fingers over one knee. "Me and Nolan have no wish to die with those cads."

After weighing his brother's words, Ector heaved a sigh. "Do as you wish," he said. "I plan on doing the same."

"But aren't they Benwick now?" Stacey said quietly, fixing Ector with a scrutinous look.

Gabriel and Nolan snorted.

"Only on parchment," Ector scoffed, peering between his brothers. "I hold no allegiance to them." He turned to Stacey and softened, "I would rather you stay near me."

"We in agreement then?" Tamarah asked. "None of us will be joining the red knights?"

Despite her great discomfort, Stacey reluctantly nodded in agreement with the rest of the knights. She did not owe any fealty to those convicts, but still, the decision did not sit right with her. Yaval's sunken shoulders conveyed the same conviction. As the two shared an apprehensive look, the horns of war sounded.

Stacey found herself fully armoured, standing atop a central tower some forty paces behind the frontlines. The tide of soldiers beneath teemed and shifted as they adjusted straps and secured their footing.

Beyond the battlefield, the archenlaif army was positioned across the hem of Fenrirfang, spreading at a great length along the border. Camelot attempted to mimic the formation, but could not match their numbers. Even a novice commander could easily recognize what the enemy formation represented. The central point of battle would be enclosed by the flanks, creating a death bowl in the center, from which there would be no escape.

"You know what to do," a stern knight said to the Orkney apprentice. "Many lives depend on you, my friend. No pressure or anything."

The young man in a gray mantle placed a foot on the embrasure and gazed out. His hood was still drawn, and Stacey could only see his stubbled chin move when he spoke. "Do you think they have a karbaled, Subin?"

The stern knight clenched her jaw and said nothing. It never boded well to make such guesses right before war.

A sliver of crimson shuffled forward, the vanguard of Camelot's host. The archenlaif army echoed the movement, blasting horns that could be heard for miles around. Ushering from the center of the enemy line, werewolves burst forth overtaking ground at a drastically faster rate than the red knights' march.

Stacey reeled a step backward, shocked by the sudden appearance of her beastly kin. "They're going to be slaughtered," she gasped, meeting Ector's eyes. The apprentice and Sir Subin looked to her but said nothing.

The werewolves invaded the field, meeting the red knights well across the midway. To the red knights' credit, not one of them fled. But neither did any of them survive. As a claw lashing out, the werewolves struck and killed, then retreated back to their haven, rendering the red knights' sacrifice seemingly useless.

"What did that prove?" asked Stacey.

"You'll see," came Ector's reply.

"We now have an accounting of the werewolf numbers," Sir Subin said dryly, revealing what Ector was withholding.

"There is great concern hovering over those disgusting beasts," Ector spat, shooting an irritated look at Sir Subin. "And they have just unwittingly revealed a bit of their hand."

From all around, a sudden shuddering blast rent the air. The blast was met with a myriad of other blasts, each varying in timbre and volume, and voices of human and laif joined their song. The initial blast ended, but in its wake, a cacophony of pure outrage swelled from the knights.

Surging forward into the gathering twilight, the colors of the realm streamed forward, the colors a flurry of bitter pageantry. In response, the archenlaives signaled their charge. If they lifted a trumpet to the skies, Stacey could not hear it. The world around her was awash in sound, her tower rattling from Camelot's response.

The archenlaives, along with the enemy werewolves, sprinted forward in a massive wave. Almost simultaneously, Camelot archers suddenly rose from the towers on the battlefield. Their arrows already nocked, they released volleys into the dark horde, dropping their numbers. Werewolves and archenlaives alike fell over their dead comrades. The archers, whom Stacey assumed were laives, relentlessly struck the enemy, notching and firing with blistering speed.

A patch in the gloomy skies flickered. Swelling into the heavens, what appeared to be a sinister cloud of bats took the field. Within moments, the Camelot archers were flailing and swinging their arms, fighting back the oppressive force.

Winds overhead abraded the back of Stacey's skull. Before she could turn to look, the skies at the top of her vision revealed an unexpected ally.

"Gargoyles!" the apprentice shouted, his voice cracking in elation.

The war was waged on two fronts now.

The armoured knights in flight soared toward the archer posts and began to decimate the evil batlike creatures assailing them. Beneath that battle, the ground forces met in a cataclysm of roars and screams. The few surviving archers continued to pelt the enemy, though some were taken by werewolves keen to climb. To great effect, gargoyles retrieved foes from the ground and soared into the skies before spiking them back to the earth. Crevices in the enemy line began to form from this tactic, and from where Stacey stood, it appeared that the archenlaif force was dwindling at a marked rate. The skies flickered again, and the battle was once again bathed in bats. This rapidly replaced the gargoyle's attention, and they shifted their focus once again.

Poleaxes and halberds rose and fell along the contour of the battle horizon. Stacey could not determine who was giving more ground, and looking behind her, she noticed that the Crown and the Church had yet to enter.

Turning back, Stacey noticed many things happening at once. Gargoyles began to drop. The outer flanks of the archenlaif force started to close in a wicked embrace. And night was collapsing over the battlefield.

Beside her, Ector sucked in a harsh breath.

Stacey abruptly shifted her focus to the change taking place on Subin's helm. Tiny splashes accompanied by faint tings.

It was raining.

39

I do not know what comes over me," Ancel mumbled, seeming at his wit's end. "Facing that karbaled day after day... and when it rains, my mind is transported back..."

Ignited with a single spark, the freshly lit flames in the hearth lashed and roiled. Linette and Ancel were seated upon a rug made from a sadhuzag, felled by skilled hunters from centuries past. Running her fingers through the brindle patterns on the luxurious pelt, Linette altered the shades, bending the strands down while lifting others up. She found contentment by simply being near this man, even when he was distressed. She wished she could retrieve each hour that slipped past and bring it back to spend again. Without saying as much, she *knew* that Ancel felt the same. It was in the way they had retreated for the keep under the pelting raindrops, fingers interlaced, and when Ancel needed to free his hand to release a machination on the gates, his reluctance to do so was quite apparent.

Now in dry clothes, their hair no longer dripping, Linette listened to the Lord of Benwick speak, continuing his charade. Every statement from his lips was wholly honest, but the pretense that brought them here was based in falsehood. Linette wondered, as time ticked by, just when Ancel would reveal his true identity. He had discussed matters of House and detailed disputes with specific council members that a silly messenger boy would not be privy to. He had even carelessly mentioned his father several times in passing, not by name, but in station.

It seemed that he would often forget the lie, but other times, he seemed painfully aware; like the way he guarded the warrior's mark upon his neck with a scarf, never removing it in Linette's view.

"I wonder if anyone else reacts to rain the way I do," said Ancel. "I suppose I could ask my brother..." he trailed off, suddenly deep in thought.

Retrieving her slate that still held the letters from her last statement written upon it, Linette erased it with the hem of her borrowed gown and began to write.

Casually, Ancel grazed the statement with his eyes. *"Is your brother a messenger as well?"* He furrowed his brow, biting something back. "No," he replied at length, scratching the side of his nostril. "My brother... dabbles in many things but is the master of none."

Linette scribbled another question. *"Is he brave?"*

Turning to the flames, Ancel contemplated a response. A smile eventually elevated his face. "Insurmountably," he replied.

* * *

"Cast the spell!" Sir Ector gripped the young spellcaster's shoulder. "Light the oil!" The momentum from his hand caused the novice to fall forward against the apron of the tower.

Ice spires were rupturing the battlefield, piercing soldiers and sending their gored bodies heaving toward the dying light. Entrails burst in rapid succession, littering the survivors. Mindful of the new peril, the gargoyles above the battlefield dispersed, careening higher into the air. Towers of ice decorated the grounds, displaying the corpses of horse, laif, and human alike. Some still clung to life and were striving to wrench themselves free to helpless avail.

Rain and spittle burst from Ector's lips. "Cast your spell!" he screamed, turning to Sir Subin. "Unfuck your wizard!"

Subin's face was awash in bewilderment, totally vacant and useless.

The forces of Camelot were falling back toward the gates. The golden banners of Tintagil remained at the forefront, seeming to ignore the call to escape. Ector rushed to the tower's edge and leaned out, calculating their withdrawal. Stacey joined him, rocking forward against the crenellation and staring at the horrors beyond.

That smell from earlier, she realized with a jolt of understanding, *the scent of breakfast and grease... is oil!* And now their flint stone, the feckless spellcaster, was curled up on the floor, shielding himself from the rain with his mantle pulled well over his head.

"You must rise, Earon!" Subin knelt over the writhing shape of her charge. "The field needs to be lit by your spell, or else—"

"Aw, fuck this!" Ector stormed past the quailing apprentice. He retrieved a lance with a pennant attached, and revealed it with an upward thrust, pointing toward the heavens.

Subin appeared frantic. "No!" She reached toward Ector, while her other hand lingered upon Earon. "Tintagil is still afield, and the army is only midway through retreat!"

A frigid smile kinked one corner of Ector's mouth. Ignoring her, he turned back toward the gates and began to wave the pennant.

Flints could be seen sparking in response, and flickering arrows lit the periphery.

"NO!" Subin was on her feet and charging Ector. With inhuman speed, Stacey cut the distance and yanked the knight backward. Watching Subin fall, Stacey felt her jaw beginning to expand. Whipping her head back and forth, she tried to expel the transformation.

The arrows streaked the skies, leaving molten trails behind. A whir of light flickered at first, then all of a sudden, a portion of the field burst into flame. The fire's intensity roared, billowing as each successive volley struck. An untamed inferno overtook the battlefield, consuming the ice pikes and devouring all living flesh within its influence.

"What have you done?" Subin asked, breathless. The flames painted her armour a roiling crimson.

Camelot fled, and beyond, the archenlaives were doing the same. The fire was purging the combatants from the field, driving them back to their origins. The waves of Camelot's force were streaming around the barriers, circumventing obstacles as best they could, all while the fiery wall nipped their heels, swallowing those cursed with limping wounds. Banners had long since been discarded, and now the realms intermixed, all colors joining together in their frantic flight.

The rain ceased. A hush fell before being battered and broken by voices plagued with desperation. The spreading fire had run to its boundary and held in place. The fortunate souls who had escaped were unaware, and continued their retreat without slowing.

"Creator forgive you," said Subin, her shoulders sunk, "for what you have done this day."

The entire host of the royal knights of Camelot waited, mounted before the gates, and they had been joined by the Church's holy knights. It should be noted that Amyr's personal guard, his trusted sentinels, also filled a bit of the ranks. The entire realm's forces had been spread in front of them before the horns of war had shuddered the earth. And now, the army was racing back toward the gates on a return course of retreat.

"It seems the apprentice from Orkney has failed," said Amyr with an appraising smirk. He turned to Arthur with his hands casually resting atop the pommel on his saddle.

The destriers among the royal knights shied at the sound of the laif's voice, but Arthur's stolid horse remained unaffected.

"If he could have managed to conjure his spell," Amyr explained, "the holy flames would have left our soldiers fully intact..." he trailed off for a moment, lost in thought. "An excellent strategic measure, *if it would have been implemented*, but now we must contend with the unfortunate results brought by the contingency."

Arthur dourly nodded his agreement.

The flame wall created an irksome barrier for Amyr. From his current vantage point, he could not make out the archenlaives' withdrawal. The casualties exacted upon the friendly forces by the flames were obvious from his side of the field, but he wanted to see the other side to see how they were faring. Had the fire decimated their numbers just as much? Or perhaps even more?

Amyr's eyes lifted toward the gargoyles embroiled in battle, still facing those wretched bat-like gwythin, above the skirling embers. How the archenlaives managed to earn those fiends to their side was a mystery that the Arbiter would have to investigate later.

This whole war was growing tiresome. It had completely ruined the surprise he had in store for his Linette. All that work! And now she was off with—

Without warning, the immense churning flames were quenched. The field went utterly dark, all the light gleaming from steel dropping from sight. Ash listed across the charred remains, billowing toward the river. The knights surrounding Amyr reeled in amazement.

"What manner of force?" screamed Kay. His voice was almost drowned out amidst the tumult of armour and whinnying equine. "How many spellcasters do they have?!"

The firelight was devoured by darkness, a rich darkness that had not been present before the flaming arrows. Warmth fled from Stacey's cheeks and was consumed by the night's chill.

Sir Subin managed to coax Earon onto his feet, and the mage apprentice was huddled at the rear of the parapet, refusing to face the battlefield. The lad seemed unaccustomed to the elements. The sound of his teeth chattering broke the silence, distracting Stacey from the field for a moment.

An alteration in the blowing ash garnered her full focus. "Ector!" she shouted in urgency. "Is that what—" All power for further speech died in her throat.

The knight was beside her in an instant. He was not gifted with the same strength in her eyes, and it took several moments for what she had detected to enter his view. As he opened his mouth to speak, his voice was overtaken by Subin's screaming.

Hurtling to the tower floor, Ector rummaged through the lances while Subin shrieked at the retreating knights on the ground. Earon remained tightly hugging himself, trying his best to be invisible.

"Found it!" Ector clamped his teeth and bounded to the peak of a crenellation and began to wave the pennant. In the torchlight of the city wall, the knight was a vision of valor, defying exhaustion, raising the banner of last resorts; for Ector was indeed signaling the cloth and the crown to unite upon the field.

Stacey cradled the apprentice's face gently in her hands. "If you ever felt the need," she said quietly, trying to garner his full attention, "to do something, to bring aid," she paused, seeing Ector's murderous expression as he approached them. She hurried to her conclusion, "*Now* would be the time!"

"They are pressing!" Subin's voice suddenly pierced the skies. "They are right behind you!" The knight clutched a single fist to a balustrade, her entire torso angling off the tower. She waved her free hand, striving to funnel the forces back into the fight. "They will be at the gates! Turn and fight! TURN AND FIGHT!"

Not one soldier seemed to acknowledge the knight's cries from above.

Though Subin's efforts appeared to be in vain, Ector's had not been. A single breath after hoisting his signal, horns had bellowed a reassuring response. And now Ector was throttling Earon, shaking him so hard that Stacey feared the lad's neck would break.

"Just one fireball!" Ector demanded, marching the apprentice to the ledge with one hand pressed fast to the back of his skull. "A single cinder! Do something! Ignite a scrap of coal!" The incoming archenlaif horde caused Earon to turn his face away in terror. "Fucking cast something!"

Subin's face hardened as she took in the sight. "Release him!" she screamed, striding toward Ector. Just as fast as she had started, her body stopped and clattered to the stone. Her head was kinked at a drastic angle, and an ebon fletching sprung from her throat just below her helm.

"Down! Now!" Ector screamed, forcing Earon to the ground.

Sliding to join them, Stacey rocked her back against the battlement. Her movement seemed much easier than she thought it should have been. And that's when she noticed that it had begun raining again.

"Laives to the front!" Sir Kay directed. The royal knights shifted masterfully, and the holy knights joined their ranks without urging. Twilight battles were not meant for humans, bereft of the night vision the laives possessed. The gathered clouds effectively impeded any scrap of the moon's favor. Torches sputtered against the damp, kicking fitfully.

Arthur turned to Kay, a slant of wet hair veiling one eye, and he spoke quietly, for only his brother to hear. With a bleak nod, Kay turned and moved to the vanguard. Horses parted silently, allowing the knight seamless passage.

"Royal knights!" Kay addressed the mounted warriors of varying armour, all unified with gray and black tabards. Helmets turned to regard their field commander. "Drive the incursion to the west!" Swiveling his head and locking eyes with Amyr, Kay spoke again. "Holy knights! Drive them into the depths of the river and beyond, if you can!" Raising a sword, Kay's horse bolted forward, signaling each regiment to follow.

Enraged cries tore from the holy knights as they surged behind, aiming east. The royal knights held a moment, their tabards undulating while the riders remained stagnant. The opening created for Kay was penetrated by a single rider, rushing through the crevice, and bursting out the other end. King Arthur had joined the battle. And now the voices of every royal knight joined the cacophony.

The karbaled needs to be brought down! Stacey thought, bouncing the back of her head against the unyielding stone of the parapet. She was drenched, completely exposed to the skies on the terrace.

"We must kill their caster!" Ector said through clenched teeth, meeting Stacey's eyes through the pervading raindrops. "If only this worthless whelp could pull just a bit of his weight—" he drove an elbow into Earon's ribs.

"There's no use counting on him," Stacey replied, scowling at the apprentice.

Working the meat of his hand into his eye socket, Earon spoke up. "They have more than one mage."

"More than one?" Ector leaned closer to hear. "How do you know?"

"They have a windcaster," Earon offered tentatively. "It's how they put out the fires."

The mage attempted to peer over the embrasure, but Ector forced him back down. "Don't put your hands on me again!" warned Earon.

"Do you wish to end up like your knight?" Ector snapped, jabbing the mage in the sternum and gesturing at Sir Subin's body. "Those archenlaives are just waiting for us—"

Ector's speech was drowned out by a host of voices emanating from the gates. Like a wave, they spread across the ground beneath the tower, and swept off toward the enemy. This time when Earon rose to look, Ector and Stacey joined him.

An illumination spell cracked the sky, exploding radiance in a vast circle. Both royal knights and holy knights were bathed in a spectral light, and for the duration of the spell, the field was bright as day.

Beyond the knights, Stacey could see the archenlaif force for the first time. Before she could even process what she had seen, the battle was met once again. As a magnificent joust, the front line of the royal and holy knights met the mounted archenlaives. In a shuddering impact, lances exploded and horses reared. Unseated warriors toppled over their cruppers, falling from sight into the muddy earth. A renewed wave rode behind the forefront of the Camelot forces, and before the archenlaives could adjust from the initial assault, the opposing forces worked to divide the field in half.

Gargoyles, their glittery scales reflecting the spectral light, fought in the air. Below, azure clad knights pressed to the right toward the river, while the royal grays ushered a dire cut to the left. Between the parting, perhaps a stone's throw from the back of the last archenlaives, hovered two unsettling entities.

An arrow cracked upon the stone beneath Stacey's chin, causing her to fall back onto her rear. "There are two casters!" she shouted as she clambered onto her hands and knees. A series of arrows followed suit, smattering harmlessly somewhere behind.

"You were right," Ector commented to Earon. He watched Stacey crawl toward a different merlon to hide behind. "If only we had some way to combat their magics..." he trailed off, ironically thumbing his chin.

An idea bloomed in Stacey's mind as she thought back on how Corbin had overthrown the karbaled at Navarene. The sorceress there had been horrified when she had seen the silver werewolf, and had seemingly melted beneath his gaze alone.

The radiance spell abruptly went out, cloaking the field in night once again. Inside the forest, the turncoat werewolves howled ominously. The royal mage crested another spell into the skies, shattering the darkness just as he had before.

The howls continued to oppress the air.

Disturbed, Stacey stared out into the woods. "What are they waiting for?"

Sir Derathane had received his belt at the cusp of winter, a royal knight for merely three seasons now. One year prior, he had been a squire, practicing the arts of war all the while being told that war was beyond his lifetime. The promise had been solidified by the notion that as long as Arthur wore the crown, the archenlaives would remain banished. Now, he found himself locked within a battle, where the space between his destrier's ears showed armoured archenlaives rushing him as he rushed them.

He couched his lance, just as he had done so many times before, and amid the moments before impact, Derathane eased his chin down. The meager eye slits showed only a landscape of black armour. He was no laif, and yet he was among the vanguard. Sir Evaline had been riding ahead of him, but a spear hucked from an impossible distance had felled her mount.

Derathane aimed his lance tip low and timed the strike to perfection. His archenlaif foe was maneuvering a pike, drastically heavier than Derathane's lance, and had yet to bring it up. Catching the foe beneath his helm and slaying him in his saddle, the royal knight's horse hardly registering the event.

A sizable portion of the archenlaif's neck flesh, adorned the tip of Derathane's unbroken lance. The sight cheered Derathane, but his joy was short-lived. As he broke through the fray, he slowed to find his king. His fellow knights were pressing west, spectacularly driving back the archenlaives as they staggered on their haunches. The field before him was empty, and he swept his gaze toward the forest just as the lights went out.

The werewolves who had withdrawn early in the battle cried out, howling to the skies, but their position remained static. The royal mage, Kravit, released another incantation, sundering clouds and bringing day to night.

Steering his mount back toward the combat, Derathane suddenly found it difficult to draw a breath. At first, he thought that his chest plate had shifted, pressing a hard edge into his upper rib cage. Each breath grew taut, his lungs felt trapped in a snare. The more he breathed, the less space he was afforded to exhale. The lance fell from his grasp without his knowledge, and his horse slowed to a canter. He tried to swallow, but a coppery liquid came out of his mouth.

A translucent tip smeared in crimson, appeared at the hem of his eye slit. Its origin seemed to be from beneath his right pectoral. Derathane worked his chin to get a better view, but to no avail. And with the last remaining ounces of his strength, he worked his visor free. Teetering in his saddle, the knight's hand wrapped around an icicle fashioned into a spear.

Then another ice spear emerged from his clavicle, rocking the knight forward against his pommel, and as he rose up, another struck, then another. And that was the last that Derathane saw of the world.

40

Amyr held his position at the gates, watching as the king and his knights flung themselves through a most perilous avenue. He sat alone, waiting for a *stillness*. Lifting a finger to conduct a silent orchestra in his mind, the First Laif remained.

The bannermen had fled the field in defeat and scattered around the charging knights of Camelot, both royal and holy. Their eyes did not concern him. Let them talk: an activity that humans so heavily favored. Though it would be in his best interest if no one saw him before, or during, his escape. Opening his eyes, Amyr felt a gentle pressure in the space behind his tongue. *Now*, the pull told him.

"Now," he echoed, and his mount responded, wheeling toward the royal encampment.

Earon inched upward, trying to hazard another look over the tower wall.

"Let's not," Ector advised, hunched forward.

"I can still see the gargoyles," said Earon, lowering back down. "I wonder what it is they're fighting against."

"Evil fae, I'd wager."

"I think they're pirskis," Earon offered. "Or a bevy of rare bats."

Fearing the men were beginning to give up or lose focus, Stacey quickly poked her head over the embrasure.

"Eh!" Ector shouted. "Careful!"

In great haste, Stacey dropped down, crawling on elbows and knees to reach the lifeless form of Sir Subin. She released the chinstrap on the knight's helm before racing back to the wall.

Ector's eyes widened. "What are you—" he started, but was interrupted by a rapturous ting.

Holding the helm aloft, Stacey drew the enemy archers' attention. "Get ready to make for the steps!" she urged, scrambling to another embrasure. "We need to put that ice witch down!"

"That's a dumb idea!" Ector said.

"We need to get off this tower!" Stacey gestured toward the stairs.

"No, not that!" Ector batted the air. "The helm! There are too many archers! We'll be cut down by that simple diversion!"

As the lovers quarreled, an idea occurred to Earon. Working his way around Ector, he laid down on his back with his neck awkwardly stacked against the stonework. Tentatively, he placed the palm of his hand to the top surface of the embrasure.

"We would need a dozen hands and a dozen helms!" Ector was loudly pleading his case, and Earon tried to silence the noise, squeezing his eyes tight as the rain drizzled down over his face.

"It's not as if we have any other options!" Stacey spat.

Focusing every ounce of magic, from the soles of his feet to the tips of his sideburns, Earon looked to the prostrate body of Sir Subin. Above the quiet, he heard Ector complain, "If our wizard wasn't so fucking useless!" And finally something sparked deep in Earon's core. He felt the damp stone beneath his palm begin to roil and fizz.

"We can't change—" Stacey's voice broke off in utter amazement. A mist was rising from the novice's hand. "Keep doing that!" she shouted.

"Then slide back just a pinch," replied Earon, rolling onto his belly to ensorcell the next section. He worked his magic, rolling from one station to the next, and soon a steamy veil barred the view of the tower's parapet. A few arrows arced through the cloud, flying aimlessly, illustrating the enemy's frustration.

"Wait for the next volley," said Ector, eyes panning the scene with his palms flat to the floor, "then break for it."

No sooner than he spoke, strands of fog half-heartedly groped the fletching of a handful of arrows as they lanced through the mist.

Stacey was the first to react, leaping for the stairs, her claws tearing through her boots. From behind, Ector gripped the novice behind the neck and ripped him from the stone, forcing him down the steps, shielding his every step.

Rushing from the tower, Stacey could feel her transformation taking place.

Ector did not notice at first. His attention was held by the events on the still-lit battlefield.

As the knights divided the field, their flanks were left exposed, and the spellcasters were exploiting this. Working in tandem, the karbaled formed massive ice shards while the windcaster flicked a tornado into the midst of the workings, blasting missiles into the vulnerable knights. The accuracy and precision were remarkably terrifying. It was only a matter of time before all the knights would be impaled, defeated.

Ector whirled to Earon. "Let's get you closer, mate!" he shouted. Mustering the momentum for a headlong charge, his mouth suddenly fell open. Where he had believed Stacey to be, now stood a savage-looking werewolf adorned in a Benwick knight's tabard.

"I'm sorry, Ector!" the werewolf began. The voice resembled Stacey's. "I wanted to tell you sooner, but I—"

Appearing gutted by horror, Ector trailed the werewolf's tabard from top to bottom, concluding where the night breezes twirled it between the monster's ankles.

"But I..." continued Stacey, spreading her hands, unable to read Ector's expression. She paused for a lingering moment before speaking again. "But this is—"

"Perfect," Ector said.

The spectral light of the battlefield flickered, and Sir Kay's night vision kicked in again.

"Kravit!" he shouted to the mage, rounding in his saddle. The spellcaster was busy at the moment, withdrawing the spear end of his halberd from the collar of an archenlaif bowman. Looking up, Kravit nodded and leapt from his saddle.

Bellowing for the nearby knights to cover Kravit, Sir Kay realized that their numbers had noticeably thinned. The seven knights assigned protective detail over the mage had dwindled to two. Kay squinted at the remaining knights, trying to see if either of them was the lampyr.

Kay's vision registered an ice pike bearing on a direct course for the kneeling mage. Within the time it took for him to blink, the weapon impaled Kravit. The man would have been struck flat on his back, if not for the length of the protruding weapon. Instead, Kravit reclined at a grisly angle, arms dangling, propped up by the pike buried in the soil. The hood of his mantle bobbed, grazing the grass below it as the mage turned his head toward the knights rushing around him.

"Lampyr!" Kay nearly toppled the nearest knight. "Lampyr!" he shouted again, this time over the knight's head, beseeching the heavens.

"Sir!" the knight regained his footing. "I am your lampyr!"

Kay did not understand the admission and continued calling for aid.

Blood was leaving Kravit in torrents, inky scarlet spilling down the pike and dissolving into the soil. The muscles in his legs were failing, and he was sliding down the icy haft, his body curling backwards in excruciating increments.

Raising his kite shield in resignation, Kay turned toward the direction from which the pike had issued. Through the rain, he could see strands of ephemeral light flashing, one casting a pale blue, the other a murky, soft yellow.

Everything suddenly flared brighter, causing Kay to reel back.

"My lord," a voice said from behind Kay, "that is the fourth time."

Kay pivoted to face the familiar voice. "Kravit!" he shouted in disbelief, drawing to the man's shoulder. "I thought we had seen your last spell!"

"Nay, my lord," replied Kravit, tucking behind the taller knight's shield. "But I must admit, I feel quite weary." A series of fang marks adorned the man's neck. The fresh pricks were weeping, discolored with the rainwater funneling beneath his mantle.

"Of all the dead men I have revived," another voice joined, thrusting his shield to Kravit's front, "he is by far the *deadest*, if that is even a word."

An ice spear hurtled toward them. "How many does he have left?" Kay questioned as he deflected the spear into the ground. The shuddering impact rattled his molars.

"Tough to say," the lampyr grunted, defying another ice lance and shrugging it harmlessly to the side. "This dead man has a gargoyle's resolve."

To their right, a third shield was added to the barricade around the mage, but almost instantly subtracted. The knight holding it crumpled against the lampyr's ankle, devoid of life. Ice shards were embedded from her throat to her heels, spanning across her flank.

"They need to see," said Kravit, lifting his gaze from the fallen knight.

"Need to see what?" The lampyr peered at the mage. "Their demise?"

Kay knew that a rush into the battle at this point would be folly. But he hated just standing here deflecting magical missiles. Arthur's entire plan, the bisecting maneuver, had been halted by the unexpected insurgence of ice and wind. Kay watched as destriers reared across his vision, rising onto their hind legs before tumbling to the ground. The lucky riders were thrown free, but the less fortunate were crumpled beneath their steeds. If their constricting armour did not suffocate them, then the boggy ground would see them drowned. Either option was a horrible way for a knight to die.

Wave after wave of ice spears flew, finding flesh where they could. And wave after wave of knights fell beneath the unending battering.

"There is no clear victory here!" Kay shouted to his companions. He could not see Arthur's golden armour anywhere on the field. "What say we join?! Shall we make the best of this?!"

Discreetly, Kay attempted to pass his dagger to Kravit.

The mage refused. "Get me to those sorcerers," he said, menace leaking into his faint voice.

"What will that—?" Kay began, interrupted by yet another ice lance breaking against his shield, "accomplish," he concluded through gritted teeth.

A horn blast on the edge of Fenrirfang sounded, and vying to overtake its volume, a pack of werewolves howled in response.

"Oh, no." Kay felt death drawing his coffin nails. "The beasts are taking the field!"

"Get me to the casters!" Kravit demanded. "Now!"

The lampyr nodded, taut lips visible before he locked his visor down.

Kay cocked his head to the side, cracking his neck. "What have we got to lose?"

The two laives and the mage pressed toward the blue and yellow radiance on the *other* side of the battle. There would be no parting of the proverbial sea for them, such as Arthur had received earlier. The knights would need to fight for every step to make it through to their comrades alive.

After freeing his blade from a downed holy knight, an archenlaif suddenly noticed the small group approaching, and began to sprint, running swiftly toward Kay's exposed left side. No sooner had the enemy knight managed half a dozen steps than he was snatched up by a gargoyle, who rent the archenlaif in half.

Kay's sigh of relief was short-lived. The lampyr's shield began to waver as the lampyr buckled, nearly collapsing. An ice dagger had struck just above the laif's knee, shattering upon impact.

"It's alright!" the lampyr wheezed. "None of it managed to even break the skin!"

The unmistakable melody of claw rending steel could be heard ahead, confirming that the werewolves had joined the fight. *It's all just a matter of time,* Kay thought dismally, tucking his chin and shouldering aside a dying, stumbling archenlaif that crossed his path.

They carried on, though Kay understood that as soon as they entered the thick of the battle, their rear flank would be utterly compromised. He nearly voiced this concern, but as he made to speak, a cry went up behind him. Faceless archenlaif helms swiveled at the sound.

"Into the flames!" a voice screamed the Benwick battle cry.

Something told Kay to step to the right. Whether it was a vibration in the earth or air or some unknown sense, the knight only knew he needed to make space.

"When did we get a werewolf?" Kravit's small voice asked, penetrating the downpour.

Kay cast a glance to the mage who was staring behind them, following whatever it was with eyes lit with elation.

A keen gargoyle took notice as well. Both Kay and the lampyr shifted their gaze to a sudden movement directly over their heads. Kay nearly faltered at what he beheld. Within the hardened grip of a gargoyle was a werewolf adorned in the greens and blacks of Benwick. He wished that he had more time to gape.

"Into the flames!" The shout was closer. Perhaps only ten paces back.

Ice spears issued in a concentrated volley, prompting Kay to shrink behind his shield as ice flew directly toward the Benwick battle cries. Kay was hesitant to turn around, fearing to see the carnage wrought by the hail fire, fearing to see his allies impaled all around him. But he was wrong.

A surging of hoofed beasts pounded past Kay, mere inches from his left shoulder. Greens and blacks stained with fresh crimson washed the scene before his eyes. The knights of Benwick simply refused to die.

The lampyr recognized the opportunity a moment before Kay. "Move!" he shouted with a stumbled step. "Press behind their wake!"

Keeping the mage between them, Kay and the lampyr ushered Kravit onward with their sword hands firm upon his back, not once allowing their shields to fall. A Benwick knight, dead from the focused volley, had somehow remained seated, but was jostled from her mount as they passed. She fell before them and was consumed by the muddy pools. With no other route, they tread upon the quickly submerging body. The lampyr paused to withdraw a wooden seax from under his mantle.

"We can't slow down!" Kay angled his shield to compensate for the gap created by the lampyr's stalling movement.

"Just a moment!" The lampyr plunged the seax directly between the dead knight's shoulder blades. "Alright! Let's end this!" he spat, returning to a stand.

There was no time for explanations.

Trudging forward, the mage was approaching the end of his presumed final stroll. The sources of the blue and yellow auras were nearly within sight, demoralizing lights at the end of a long tunnel. Ahead the werewolves were savagely leaping atop the knights who had preceded them. The riderless destriers reared, striking with their steel shod hooves. Ice spears found many of these faithful beasts' exposed chests and brought them down shrieking.

Benwick's already small force was thinning to nothing on the fringes of the battle. When the last valiant knight was swept from her saddle, Kay noticed that he was now able to make out the face of the ice caster with perfect clarity. Right before her were two werewolves embroiled in bitter combat with one another.

"Their powers wane!" Kravit shouted, answering the unspoken question stirring within Kay's head. *Why were the casters entertaining this display right before their feet?* It made little difference at this point. Camelot was all but lost now that the werewolves had joined the enemy. And where was Arthur in all this?

Kravit's previously cast spell began to dim and darkness descended once again, save for the glow from the spellcasters ahead. Kay felt the mage drop to his knees for his next conjuring, and he and the lampyr angled their shields to compensate.

A roar from the left of the field fractured all other sound, a roar that was clearly not a werewolf.

"Oh, Arthur!" Kay rotated toward the west, mindlessly leaving a void in the shield barrier. *Brother, what has befallen you?!*

"Hey!" The lampyr reached behind Kravit to grab hold of Kay's mantle. "Don't break the cover!"

"Forgive me!" murmured Kay as he turned back, sounding as if the admission was meant for someone other than his current companions.

With the shield curtain restored, his gaze continued to linger toward the west.

Heartbeats earlier...

One moment Stacey was bearing down upon the mystic lights, leading the Benwick charge, and the next, she was weightless. She rose in drastic measures into the sky as clusters of tiny fae attacked her, spattering violently against her face. From sheer surprise, she inhaled harshly and swallowed one of the evil little beings. Sharp protrusions lashed inside her windpipe, but with a hearty swallow, the movements ceased.

The gargoyle shouted something to her that she could not quite make out. And suddenly the battleground rocketed up to meet her and she struck the rain-saturated soil, instinctively tucking her chin and rolling. When she rose, her tabard soaked and clinging to her fur, the spellcasters were before her while the gargoyle who had been carrying her hurtled to the earth somewhere beyond the light.

The two mages balked at the werewolf's unforeseen arrival.

Swiping the damp from her lips, Stacey strode forward with a menacing smile.

An ice wall erupted, barring passage. Lowering her shoulder and crashing forward, Stacey shattered the brittle working almost instantly. Where she imagined she would find the casters huddling in fear, she instead found a mirror reflecting the savage face of a werewolf. Too late, she realized it was not her face looking back at her and there was no mirror.

The other werewolf attacked, blood and spittle burst from Stacey's jaw, and she believed that her tongue had been sheared free. A tremendous force barreled into the cavity right beneath her heart, immediately followed by what felt like hardened steel cables enveloping her arms.

Pain seared the left side of her face as she grappled the opposing werewolf, trying desperately to free one arm. She had no idea how she managed to maintain her footing, but she did know that if she did not manage to free herself of this entanglement, the soggy earth below her would serve as her grave. Using the slick ground to her advantage, Stacey dropped low, her fangs scraping against her enemy's ribs as she ratcheted herself loose. Her trailing arm was almost dislocated at the shoulder as she folded and the other werewolf tried at gripping her wrist, but Stacey prevailed.

"You're on the wrong side!" the werewolf growled, appearing like a dark void in the mages' glow. "Strip off those colors and join us."

Stacey recognized that voice. She had heard it plenty of times before. "Lanaelle?" she gasped.

"My reputation precedes me?" the other werewolf asked coyly, striding into plain view. The black of her fur seemed to absorb all the light. "In your new form, they will always see you as beneath them. You know it's true. The archenlaives have offered us a place in their new world, a place to call our own." She took a cordial stance, clawed hand outstretched. "So what will it be? Will you join us?"

Werewolves emerged from the forest and rushed past, overtaking riders, shifting the tide. Stacey glared at the offered hand. With the multitudes of bannermen dying behind her, the hundreds of knights barely clinging to life, all of it in defense of the realm, such a gesture of treatise felt like a slap to the face.

Not wishing to betray her intention, Stacey shifted her weight by fractions.

"Well?" demanded Lanaelle.

Surprising even herself, Stacey darted past the werewolf and headed for the casters. Lanaelle's grunt of disappointment shifted to a growl as she rolled forward on the balls of her feet, giving chase. The muddy terrain proved a hindrance, and the taller werewolf quickly overtook Stacey by the time she was three paces shy of her quarry.

The world devolved into mud, claws, and fangs. The two werewolves tore at one another as blue and yellow radiance knitted together around them. Without warning, the battlefield collapsed into darkness once again and the eerie green mage light was all that pierced the gloom. Stacey fell onto her back as Lanaelle throttled her. She idly wondered which would claim her first, death by claws or death by drowning.

A roar from off the battlefield consumed all sound, diverting Lanaelle's focus for one glorious moment. With claws extended, Stacey deployed a single strike to her enemy's throat. A pennant of blood sailed from Lanaelle's backward arc, and the werewolf fell to the earth, grievously wounded.

Stacey buried her front claws into the sediment and sprang toward the spellcasters. As she focused her charge on the karbaled, the blue aura began to pale. It seemed the ice caster's magic reserves were nearly spent.

A teeming mass of shadows loomed beyond the karbaled.

From somewhere behind her, the royal light mage flung another casting into the sky, but it proved frail upon bursting. The illumination wavered, momentarily flickering clarity. A mass of teeth and horns came into view, the steel from armour glittering like stars in an overcast night sky.

Then the dark held.

Oh, Creator! Another enemy wave?!

41

He could feel her. She was somewhere near. Somewhere just beyond his sight.

Amyr sniffed the air, inhaling deeply in spite of the falling rain. *Where are they keeping her?*

The square cordoned off for the royal knights was completely devoid of life. Not one guard stood waiting, not one gargoyle prowled the skies above. The banners hung limp, soaked to capacity. All bodies, able or otherwise, had been called to the war.

Amyr sniffed again, taking in the dismal scene.

A great tree with spreading branches stood behind Arthur's tent. He swung his laifhorse in that direction, and the Arbiter felt unexpected anxiety welling. As they turned the corner, his mount surveyed the scene first, and the laifhorse's premature snicker spoiled any surprise.

Clasping the trunk of the tree in a reverse embrace, arms bound behind her, the archenlaif prisoner sat hunched, chin firmly pointed toward the roots. Long unbound hair draped over her face, droplets falling from the ends. Her armour had been stripped and she wore a simple undertunic, which was now plastered to her skin.

"Pitiful," remarked Amyr, still in the saddle.

The archenlaif said nothing.

"Such a proud race reduced to this."

The statement garnered yet more silence.

Amyr rode beneath the canopy that the tree provided, hunching to avoid the dripping foliage. "Remember, if you will, if you can, the humans that once were shackled in a similar fashion," said Amyr in a pleased tone, admiring the archenlaif. "All of this," the laif began, inclining in his saddle, "all of this because you want the humans under your thumbs once again."

"There is more to it than that." The archenlaif spoke without looking up from the ground. "You know that better than any other." Her voice cracked as if she had not spoken in days.

"I beg to differ," Amyr argued, rolling his shoulders. "I believe it's fairly simple. You had slaves once, and now you want your slaves back."

The archenlaif dug a heel into the earth and rocked against the trunk that held her. "There is a matter of penance as well," she said, glancing from the laifhorse to the rider. "And a return to order. Your world has been in chaos since we departed from beneath the eye of the Creator. You know this to be true, rodaek."

"I am your rodaek no longer," Amyr's eyes flashed. "The rift that divides us only increases."

"Say what you will." The archenlaif attempted a shrug. "Is there something you want, or have you simply come to gloat?" She paused, glaring at the laif before continuing, "Out with it, then. But you will be choking on your words soon enough."

"How do you imagine that will come about?"

"As long as the rain continues to fall," the archenlaif squinted toward the sky, "I fear your warriors will continue to do so as well."

A laugh burst from the back of Amyr's throat. "You're very sure of yourself," he scoffed. "You are correct on one thing, though."

The archenlaif tensed.

"I do want something from you," stated Amyr, pinching his fingers to a lock of his hair, purging the water from it. "And in exchange, I can give you the *penance* you are so desperately seeking."

"What difference will it make?" the archenlaif sneered. "Your kingdom will fall this night."

"You appear confused as to the situation."

The prisoner faced the Arbiter with the resolve of a mountain, not one crack visible in her foundation.

Amyr continued, ignoring the glare fixed upon him. "Honestly, you believe that I would allow such a thing to happen?" He turned his head and spat. "Let's pretend you did not utter such foolishness, and thus, allow us to discuss our arrangement."

The rain battered the tents behind them, filling the silence.

"Alright," the archenlaif said at length. "But you do understand that I am no longer beneath the Creator, and not liable to die if I speak falsehood to you."

"Oh, I am aware," said Amyr with a deepening grin. "I am *very* aware."

Ector knew that leading such a charge held its inherent perils. He had lifted his shield to allay the ice spears, but as soon as he let his shield drop, a frenzied werewolf latched herself to his chest. The beast nearly removed him from his saddle, and it may have succeeded, if Earon had not been seated directly behind him. The lad's frail frame acted as adequate leverage for the knight who, dropping his lance, rebounded with a dirk in his hand.

Sloughing the weight of the werewolf from his saddle, Ector could feel blood leaking from the side of his neck. He wanted to staunch the flow, but his hands were occupied. A dizzying flock of werewolves launched upon him, driving him sideways from the saddle and leaving Earon exposed.

Curse you, Ancel, ran through his mind, *you traitor!* He plunged into the mud and scraped his armour upon the stones beneath. During his fall, he had been gouging the closest cluster of fur with his dirk, and by the time he concluded the tumble, the beast was quite dead. However, the beast's companions were unharmed, emboldened by the scent of blood.

Ector could feel the cold burn of claws rending his skin. Yet all he could do was continue to stab blindly, trying to exact as much damage as he could before he expired. The mud was freezing, and his wrist was cramping. The muscle on his left leg was weakening as well. When he felt he could hold no longer, Ector saw one of the werewolves' eyes suddenly widen in fright. The beast began to flail uncontrollably, moving out of his view as a searing heat swept over the knight. The pressure trapping him released when the other werewolf finally dislodged itself and scampered away. A peaceful pattering of rain tapping his helm lasted only a brief second before a hand found his vambrace and tugged.

"On your feet!" Earon yelled. "Come now, Sir Ector!"

Surging to his feet, surprisingly spry in spite of his injuries, Ector met the mage's eyes. "You wasted a casting on me!" he accused. "Save your strength for the other wizards!" Casting aside his dirk, the knight drew the longsword at his hip. "Shall we?" Ushering the apprentice to his back, Ector headed toward the hues of yellow and blue.

"Quick! Tilt the tip of your sword back to me!" Earon shouted.

Ector obliged, searching the field around him. Benwick knights were being picked off one by one, though he seemed to have found a blind pocket. The gauntlet on his right hand abruptly felt hot and he heard the raindrops sizzling above it. Ignoring it, he moved toward his friends.

"Hold! Just another—" Earon blurted out, rooting the knight in place with a firm hand. "Moment! Ah!" The mage relinquished his grip. "All set!" announced Earon, striking Ector's pauldron in triumph.

"What have you done?" Ector cried, bringing the sword back around. The weapon was engulfed in flame, lapping tongues spouting up toward the orbiting gargoyles.

"Well... I... well..." Earon stammered. A werewolf stumbled from the melee, blood pouring from her gasping jaws, unfortunately not her own blood. A knight lay behind her, clearly in the throes of death. The were-wolf's eyes fell upon Ector's sword, and she tried to retract her steps, but fell in her haste as she spun. Ector was upon her in an instant.

Upon withdrawing the blade from the nape of the beast's neck, the damp fur caught flame. "What have you done," Ector repeated, grinning. The downed werewolf became a pyre, burning into writhing ash. As the flames died and ash became ember, darkness once again flooded the field. Ector quickly lowered the flaming sword parallel to the ground, hoping not to draw too much attention to himself.

From his left, Ector heard voices that were clearly not archenlaif or werewolf. With Earon in tow, the knight worked his way toward the voices, hoping to find safety in numbers.

The light from his blade spread across the ground, reflecting off the vast pools of water agitated by the endless rainfall. Along its course, his torchlight revealed the forms of two laif knights protecting something. The knights swung their heads at the sudden illumination.

Not wishing to startle them further, "Friend!" Ector announced quickly, and urging Earon to lead.

Whoever was kneeling between the knights had apparently never seen a flame-engulfed sword before, and when he saw the blade, the man faltered. A half completed working shot out from his hands, leap-ing up as an arrow. Somehow, the working regained a bit of vigor partway up its skyward climb and managed to lodge itself at a decent height before a rather disappointing explosion. The battlefield flickered in and out, then went dark.

"Kravit!" one of the knights shouted to the terrified mage. "Can you conjure another?"

Appearing as if he had endured a punch to the gut, Kravit nodded his head slowly, his hollow eyes never leaving Ector's sword.

"Come!" the other knight beckoned to Ector, "Cover our rear, will you?"

Ector stepped into the space, heaving Earon back to his feet along the way. A gargoyle smashed to the earth to Ector's right, the beast's wings devoured by fae. The gargoyle's face was filled with agony, and then it was out of sight.

"We're so close!" one of the knights shouted, flinging blood from his blade. "See the lights?" he pointed his sword toward the haze beyond the wreckage. "Once Kravit here sets the world alight again, we're pushing for them!"

"Aye!" Ector tucked his chin and leaned sharp, avoiding the downward slash from a black knight. He struck back, tagging his opponent below the hauberk and instantly igniting the armour. The archenlaif screamed and swatted at his fiery plate, flinging himself into the mud. "We aim to do the same!" Ector replied. "How long does it take—" his statement halted by a loud groan immediately followed by a flare erupting ahead of him.

This missile was more robust than the previous one, and Ector needed to shield his eyes to avoid being blinded.

"We must move!" one of the knights placed a hand to Kravit's back. The mage was quite unsteady, and Earon stepped in to support him.

"Gramercy," Kravit said to Earon. Leaning close, he spoke again, "Would you like to make an end to all this?"

Stacey was frozen in disbelief.

Out of the dark obscurity, a gray werewolf was upon the windcaster, making short work of his neck. The yellow aura flickered upon the fall.

Jekar?!

When the wizard's neck hung on by only single pieces of flesh, the werewolf pitched the corpse aside. The body bounced upon the ground, and where blood should have flowed, instead a gust of wind billowed forth. Easy at first, like a shallow leak, then suddenly a tremendous gale issued forth. The corpse could only manage to hold on for a single breath before the terrible energy discarded the husk, hurtling the spell-caster's body somewhere into the treetops far from sight.

Towers, battlements, and anything else inside the area of the final working could not stand. The single gust created complete desolation. Standing in the aftermath, Stacey stared briefly, but could not afford to spend the time thinking about the chaos that had been created.

Rounding toward the karbaled, Stacey felt a pain shiver up her leg, jarring her all the way from heel to hip. Jekar had already set his sights on the karbaled, and was tearing through an ice bulwark. Stacey tried to ignore the seemingly insignificant pain shooting through her leg and join her friend.

"Stacey!" Jekar shouted, spotting her as she sagged toward the ground. The pain had proven to be too much and her leg seized. As she plunged her hands into the mud, a weight bore down on her back and a snarl erupted in her left ear.

"You die here!" spat Lanaelle.

Stacey felt her flesh tear and claws sunk into her. Her world devolved into ice, then fire as more of her became exposed. All she could hear was Lanaelle cackling and howling into her ears. Helpless, Stacey sunk another inch, then her elbows gave way, and her chin plunged into the mire. Foul water filled her mouth as she heard a pause in Lanaelle's maniacal laughter. The enemy wolf howled in pain, but then was abruptly silent.

A pressure encased Stacey's upper arm and wrenched her from her despair. The weight of the Lanaelle's corpse fell away from her as she rose.

"Can you stand?" An unknown knight spoke. In answer to his question, Stacey slumped back down toward the ground. "I will be back for you," the knight said, easing her onto her side. "Try not to drown."

Beyond him she caught the unmistakable form of Ector approaching, and her eyes widened in disbelief. But he was not coming for her, he did not see her. He was focused elsewhere.

With the plan in mind, Ector briefly recoiled when he crested the grade to find that a werewolf had nearly made it through the ice palisade. A werewolf that was not Stacey. This beast had accomplished almost everything for them. And the werewolf managed to take down the ice caster, there would be no need...

The lampyr, having broken formation to render aid elsewhere, was now converging with the werewolf. He jammed his blade into a fissure in the barrier and began to wrench with all his might. The werewolf beside him smashed a lowered shoulder into the wall, increasing the cleft. As Kay appeared and ran to the lampyr's side, Ector stood guard before Kravit and Earon, acting as their shield. The fire from his blade presented a slight deterrent at the very least. The ice spears had ceased, but he knew it did not mean that his mages were safe. And besides, he would need to be near them, when the time came...

A horn wailed in the darkness beyond the tent of light.

"Get behind us!" Kravit commanded Ector.

"Is that another—?" Ector stared in disbelief. "How many armies did they muster?!" He cursed his brother once again. *Only Ancel is clever enough to create such a contingency—if the archenlaif mages were to fall.*

Kravit and Earon stepped out in front of Ector. "Kay!" shouted Kravit. "Drop to the ground after you clear the ice!"

Pausing a moment, Kay turned to the mage and nodded, before passing the phrase along to the lampyr and werewolf. The lampyr acknowledged the knight's words, but the werewolf was now moving as if in a frenzy. The incoming wave had acted as quite the motivating force.

"You know what must be done!" Kravit called out to Ector. Earon said nothing as he shifted into line with Kravit.

Ector lifted his visor. "I don't know if I can!"

"When that karbaled shows her ugly face," Kravit yelled, his voice sounding strained, "you must do it!"

At that moment, the werewolf latched himself to the top of the ice wall. "Pull my tail!" he shouted to the knights below, heaving all his weight. The wall seemed up to the challenge until Kay grabbed hold of the werewolf and braced it to his pauldron, dragged it backwards with all his might while the werewolf shrieked in agony. The wall cracked beneath his hands, and all the fissures burst at once. Standing helpless inside the encasement, the exposed karbaled thrust her hands up for one final working. The raindrops burst into mist. The lampyr and Kay abandoned their feet, dropping headlong to the earth.

"Ector!" Kravit screamed. "Now!"

The mages before him dropped their chins in perfect synchronicity.

Forgive me. Ector inhaled. Bending a knee to launch, the knight gathered all his remaining strength, focusing it, tensing every muscle. He ignored the werewolf flailing his arms. Filled with sorrow, he plunged his ensorcelled blade into Earon's back, and pressed harder, skewering

Kravit as well. The mages arched in anguish, parting their arms, and released an overwhelming flash of light.

Stacey could not believe her eyes.

"Hold! Please!" Jekar had shouted, waving frantically. "They are with me!" he pointed to the approaching horde. Stacey had turned to see the ogres en masse rushing the field. How Jekar had managed such a feat was beyond her. It was brilliant. Truly. But messengers did exist for reasons such as these.

The werewolf's cries had not been heard. And after Ector had pierced poor Earon and the other mage with his fiery sword...

At first only a focused beam of crimson sprang from the tip of the sword. The ray culled the karbaled in an instant. The witch hardly had time to realize what was happening, watching her limbs melt beneath wild eyes. Immediately after, the world before Ector and the mages went white. The flanking ogres, rushing to bring aid to Camelot, were there and gone in an instant. Everything standing before the great flare was rendered to shadow, traces of their bodies picked up as ash in the wind.

The rain had ceased.

"There you have it," said Amyr, relishing the manner in which the archenlaif withered before him. "Ready to strike that deal?"

42

After the magic flash culled the karbaled and the ogres, Stacey tried grappling to her feet, but she found the pain in her leg made standing impossible. As her hand worked a course down her limb to assess the damage, she could feel her fur falling away in clumps, leaving only bare flesh behind. She winced when her hand found the raw gouge that Lanaelle had left on the tendon that connected her heel to calf.

The war continued off to the west. The tremendous, mysterious roar she had heard carried itself through the hollows of her ears, and she knew that Camelot would prevail.

She looked around and saw a werewolf plodding a course toward her on his elbows and knees. Ashy tendrils lifted from the scattered patches of fur that still clung to his skin. Stacey, recognizing Jekar, began to crawl toward him.

"I am so sorry," said Jekar as they met. The flesh around his snout bunched into crags. "I should have come for you when that werewolf..." His eyes were glazed and Stacey knew he was struggling to stay focused.

"Think nothing of it," Stacey cooed, placing her friend's head on her lap. Sitting upright proved painful, but she bore it nonetheless. "We only need a lampyr's kiss and you'll be back on your feet in no time."

How Jekar managed to laugh, Stacey did not know. His exposed bones clacked against one another. "Lampyrs cannot heal werewolves," he craned his head, shuddering, concluding in a retching a series of dry

456

coughs. "You know, Camelot can burn for all I care..." his voice trailed off. He tried to speak, but death had crept his way up into his voice box.

Stacey leaned down and pressed her forehead onto Jekar's furry temple. "You were coming to save me."

"Arthur drives them west!" Sir Kay cheered, thrusting a fist into the air. The lampyr joined him at his side and lifted his visor, his sharp eyes cutting through the gloom. The laives rocked back on their heels, laughing almost hysterically.

The words hardly registered to Ector. His hands were full of ash. The remnants of Earon filtered through his fingers, lost to the wind.

"We shifted the stream!" shouted Kay in triumph.

Upon their casters' defeat, the werewolves had split westward for the forest, the archenlaives fleeing with them. Camelot gave chase, unrelenting at the enemy's retreat, King Arthur leading the charge.

"We even managed to decimate their ogres!" Kay declared, regarding the army of shadows burnt into the soil. "The seers could not have predicted such a turn!"

The lampyr appeared in front of Ector, pausing to unclasp and remove his helm. Ector had not even noticed his approach, his thoughts still fixed on Earon's final moments. "Rejoice now, friend," the lampyr said, lowering his stance to meet Ector's eyes. "Mourn later."

A ribbed wail caught their attention. Stacey, back in human form, was keening while cradling the head of that heroic werewolf.

Looking down at the powder in his hands, Ector wavered. Unexpectedly, an overwhelming sense of revulsion overtook him. The sight of Stacey grieving for that beast, her kin, made the knight swallow down the bile accumulating in his throat. She was not like him anymore. She was something else entirely and had moved beyond.

"We have no future," mumbled Ector, swiping the last bits of Earon off onto his chest plate. He met the lampyr's eyes. "Come, let us rejoice."

* * *

Thrumming rain had kept Ancel awake for most of the night. Their fingers had been steepled together throughout.

Sleep, the first night, had found Linette by the hearth. This second evening, after a day of joy, had found her retired to Ancel's master suite. Ancel had led her through the winding corridors, past resplendent antechambers, and up a twirling staircase. When at last they reached the end of the hallway, they gazed out a window overlooking the gardens. Directly to the right, a wooden door comprised of planks sat hunched, as the gateway to a child's play chamber.

"You first," Ancel coaxed.

Ducking to avoid striking her forehead against the doorframe, Linette discovered a room that filled her with wonder. Gomer immediately pushed through between her legs and hurried to the hearthstone. A fire sat already kindled, so perfect it almost seemed an illusion. Tapestries flowed along the walls, weaving across the expansive chamber that did not quite feel as ordinary. The walls felt heavily layered as if a tremendous pressure encased them, preventing a leak from the outside. She often imagined what it would feel like to live under the waters of a lake. And with her limited knowledge of such things, this room seemed to be just that. The room gave her a feeling of indescribable security and a sense of total concealment.

There was rainfall on and off throughout her stay, and each time it rained, Ancel seemed to shrivel into himself. Linette found she could help calm him by touching the space beneath his eyes, just above the beard, mouthing silent words. The haunted man was grateful, and once the spell broke, he would gradually rebound to his usual demeanor.

This night, however, he was inconsolable. The walls of the room retained silence, but the windows were not as gracious. The raindrops battered the glass like lead-filled hornets. Ceaseless and unending. White light occasionally illuminated the room as lightning rent the skies, further fraying the knight's nerves.

Unable to sleep through the storm, Linette passed the time reflecting on the joyful day spent. She and Ancel had set to work developing a language that required neither slate nor tongue. Ancel shared with her his knowledge of monsters who communicated through only gesticulations and grunts. The nockbogle, for instance, could not vocalize at all, but used pantomime and dance as a means for communication. She had giggled at the thought of the strange little creatures waving their spindly appendages at one another, turning somersaults and performing pirouettes. Ancel had laughed and assured her that they would create something less ostentatious with no need for her to twirl and flex. Before she knew it, the hours had dwindled and the daylight had drawn to a close.

Bringing her mind back to the present, she focused on Ancel. Beside her, he pulled gently at the air, finally drawing even breaths that no longer shuddered.

The drevnigost had been oddly absent yesterday, and today the forest seemed to strangely lean.

Famyl scoured the treeline, snout to dirt, but could not detect a hint of the ancient guest's scent. When they had first arrived, Priraeda's essence had permeated the forest like an oppressive veil. The humans were seemingly unconcerned at his absence, laughing in the orchard as they continued to create a language of their own.

Perhaps the persistent rains had scrubbed the air and vegetation of his scent? Not even a trace lingers...

"No," Ancel beamed, shaking his head with amusement. "I think we should tuck the thumb inside the fist when we point down," he said, taking Linette's hand into his. "See, that way 'stay' distinguishes itself from 'down,' where we allow the thumb a bit of freedom." They sat opposite each other upon benches, a table dividing them.

Linette watched as a brief gust from the forest played with the ends of Ancel's hair. She desperately did not want to leave this place, or this man.

A harsh, violent clamor disturbed their peace, beginning in the trees and rapidly suffusing the orchard. Linette was shocked to see the sound was coming from Gomer. She had never heard him make such noises before. They sounded *otherworldly*. Ancel immediately leapt to his feet. The thicket roiled before them, and although Gomer's voice could still be heard somewhere beyond, he sounded muffled. From the mass of beating branches and twirling vines, a solitary figure emerged.

"Priraeda." Ancel shifted his jaw, looking up with surprise. "What is this?"

The ancient guest stood with his hands interlocked, the picture of an ever-faithful servant. He did not speak, but lowered his chin with a brief nod, then stepped to the side as if to reveal a gift.

A cerulean clad laif stepped into view, armour shimmering beneath his cloak. "Ask me how," he instructed. Upon his words, ten holy sentinels breached the treeline directly to his left and right.

"Leave," said Ancel firmly.

"I'm sorry." Amyr signaled for his sentinels to form a ring around the couple. "That didn't sound like a question to me."

Amyr's eyes softened when they fell upon Linette. She placed a finger to the side of her mouth then traced the finger outward in a downward arc.

The laif's neck muscles tightened. "What does that mean?" he asked, glancing at Ancel.

"How," replied Ancel. "She wants to know how."

"Ah." Amyr panned his gaze between the humans. "I'm glad someone knows how to play the game properly." He licked his thumb and scrubbed at a scuff on a vambrace. "In due time, I'm afraid. All will be revealed in due time. But if I were you, Linette, I would be more concerned with the *who*."

Fearfully, Linette inched closer to Ancel. The man extended one arm and she gratefully huddled beneath it.

"I fear that this has all been a grand jape," Amyr announced. Acid seemed drip from his tongue. "This *Launcelot* is no mere messenger from Benwick's roost. He is the *who* that you should be inquiring of." Amyr paused, glancing once again at Linette. "You don't seem addled by my admission."

A sentinel crept a bit too close for Ancel's liking. The crunching of his boot halted when Ancel flinched in his direction, violence in his eyes.

"Now, now, there is no need for physical confrontation," stated Amyr, his palms lifted in mock sincerity. "No blood need be shed here today. Lord Ancel of Benwick, you stand accused of treason by kinsmen, Crown, and Cloth." His statement did not garner the response he had desired. "Ancel, the Lord of Benwick." He repeated the title, staring at Linette as if in fierce concentration.

Linette removed herself from Ancel's arm and retrieved her slate. She began to write, scribbling her words aggressively.

Rocking back on his heels, Amyr rolled his eyes. "How long must we—" but she cut him off by holding up her slate.

"I knew," Amyr read in disbelief. He had believed that this revelation would leave Linette enraged at the farce, and would see her rushing into *his* embrace. What a delusional oaf he had been! A First Laif made the fool by a mere mortal!

Lashing out with all the waves of hatred brewing in his depths, Amyr commanded the sentinels to take them. "If you resist," Amyr shrieked at Ancel, his usual control nearly spent, "I will snap her neck like a paltry trinket!"

The sentinels began to fill the orchard, and in the distance, Gomer could be heard loudly braying, sounding gravely wounded. Priraeda whirled toward the sounds of misery.

"Drevnigost." Amyr lifted his forefinger, stopping the ancient guest from moving toward the sound. "You have earned your freedom this day."

Priraeda dipped his gnarled chin.

"Now," the Arbiter paused before lifting his eyes, "see that hound slain."

Each cylindrical hardwood that sprung from the ground laughed at Famyl as he raced through the forest, searching for an opening. Their derisive cackling punctuated the hopelessness teeming within his chest.

Too late, he had realized what was to occur. Seeking the source, he had run through the forest, only to find Amyr and the ancient guest standing in a clearing. He had arrived just in time to see a retinue of the Arbiter's personal sentinels rushing toward the orchard.

I should have seen this coming all along! Famyl cursed himself, barking and bounding into a sprint. *No good can come when too many hearts become intertwined...* A serpent-like tree erupted in front of him, barring his passage. He wheeled, skidding to get past, but another such working materialized. It seemed that every side-step he took created another tree. They sprung up, one after another, each tree hurling insults and jeers.

Breathing heavily but continuing to bark his warnings, Famyl abruptly found himself before a copse. The trees spoke scornfully, mocking him in a long-forgotten language that he had not heard in ages.

Between the tightly packed tree limbs, Famyl could not see where Amyr had gone. He was suddenly grabbed by fear. He cried out to the Creator, begging for his laif body. If he was only the first Healer once again, a well-balanced blade in hand, he would gladly reap Priraeda's spawn as a ripe harvest.

The bleating dog leapt onto his hind legs, fervently pleading for the Creator's blessing. His jaw would not form the words, could not form the words.

Creator! Grant me this one boon! Why do you abandon me at the hour of my greatest need?! Famyl tried to shout but it came out as a grievous howl.

The trees shouted insults as he cried out, using uninspired titles, calling him stupid, pathetic, and ugly. One proclaimed he would put the dog out of his misery, if only he had working limbs. Alas, he was merely a picket of a fence.

Famyl was losing hope, bashing his shoulder against the trees again and again. *Creator! Help me!*

As he launched himself forward for the hundredth time, the trees produced an opening, and the canine found air where obstinate solid had been a moment prior. After a few breaths laying on his side, he rose unsteadily, looking up to see the knotted face of Priraeda peering down upon him.

"I sense a language somewhere underneath your frantic ululations," the ancient guest mused. His uppermost sprigs groaned as he bent down. "Your masters are gone, little one." He paused, winding a vine between his fists. "What was it you were trying to say?"

Famyl did not bother to reply. He only lowered his hindquarters and sat.

"Before you meet thy end," said Priraeda. "Would you not like to say something that could be accepted and understood?" The ancient guest lurched close, angling the vine toward Famyl's neck.

There was nothing pertaining to the ancient guest which weighed heavy upon Famyl's tongue. He continued to remain silent, his chin inclined upward. Only the Creator was privy to his words. He would not deign to give this lumbering traitor a response.

"Very well."

The ancient guest was preparing to cinch the vine around the dog's neck when a shadow suddenly absorbed the clearing. The chill it brought swept between Famyl's ears and concluded midway down his spine. The deep grumbling that accompanied it from beyond the mountains signaled a storm. And from what Famyl could sense, it smelled furious.

Filaments of light lashed overhead, causing Priraeda to shy away from the skies. The clouds opened upon them, weeping in torrents. Famyl galloped away, but he could not outrun the impending flood. His fur was drenched, weighing him down. He angled his rush toward the orchard and out of the forest, searching for a place free from Priraeda's influence.

The trees that burst up around him were no longer laughing. They cursed and swore, calling down evil oaths that would prove ill if even one prevailed. Fortunately, the water saturating his fur worked as an effective lubricant. He slipped between the trunks, evading capture.

Priraeda's voice broke through the downpour. "Slay that hound!" he shrieked, his voice frantic. "See it done!" But it was no use. The dog had already slid through the boundary.

43

Amyr had mentioned the *how* when he had emerged from the brambles. But as Linette rocked forward, the cart finding yet another rut in the road, she wondered in disbelief about the *where* and the *why*.

His wrists and ankles bound together with rusty shackles, Ancel was unable to regain his balance as quickly as Linette. They had been plucked from paradise and thrust into this cart, placed as far from one another as possible. Linette imagined Amyr must have worked some sort of incantation, because before she knew it, they were far from Joyous Garde, too far to have traveled naturally.

As the cart trundled up a hill, she recognized this road as one in Benwick. *That answers the where, at least,* Linette thought, eyeing another sentinel as he stepped away from Ancel.

The faceless guard resumed his gait alongside the cart, muttering a string of muffled phrases beneath his helm. A recurring theme between the curses was the word "traitor." While Linette understood what a charge of treason stood for, she could not for the life of her understand how Ancel could be involved in such a plot.

The Lord of Benwick's face was blackened and swollen from the alarmingly regular pommel strikes and gauntleted backhands he had endured since their capture. And the cart driver seemed to have an avid lust for furrows, which he displayed passionately, finding and angling for each and every painful gap on the cobbled route.

Riding at the forefront was Amyr upon his laif-bred destrier, riding with all the confidence of a holy man. He had wisely positioned his sentinels within tight proximity to Ancel, knowing that while Ancel exemplified the common traits of physical power and strength, he was also exceptionally clever and resourceful. Perhaps it was for this reason Ancel's mouth had been bound as well.

"I had wished to hold the tribunal in my basilica," began Amyr, now riding beside the prisoners. "It is, after all, a place designed for judgment. But the fervency with which your landsmen argued to hold it within your court compelled me to relent."

Ancel was jolted to his left and slammed his shoulder into a solid rail. He struggled to sit up, all while defiantly staring at Amyr.

"I hope this news is satisfactory to you," Amyr continued, "as we will be arriving shortly."

Linette wished she could be by Ancel's side, but each time she made a move closer to him, a severe hand would find her shoulder and thrust her back into place. If she had her slate and chalk then perhaps she would be able to reason with Amyr, or at the very least, discover what this was all about. For within Ancel's rather threatening frame there did not reside one treasonous bone. She *knew* this to be true beyond all doubt. And she knew if she were capable of voicing this to Amyr, she would survive the telling.

"Tell me." Amyr flung one leg across his pommel, easily riding sidesaddle. "How comfortable are your dungeons? What sort of amenities do you offer your detainees? Are the rats well-fed or kept in check?" The laif crossed his legs and his left heel clipped the flank of his mount. The laifhorse did not react in the least. "Do I detect the hint of a question percolating in that head of yours?"

Ancel rolled his eyes. Whether from Amyr's words or the fact that the driver had just lodged a wheel in an ogre-sized crater, Linette could not tell. The horse drawing the cart heaved forward, failing to remove the sunken wheel from its lodging. The sentinels, all at once, placed firm hands to the rim of the box and began to shove, tossing the prisoners back and forth. Each time Ancel reeled toward a sentinel, he received a swat, which did nothing to prevent his swaying.

Finally, with great groans, the cart was free and their doddering resumed.

A trickle of blood slid down Ancel's right eye. One of the most recent rebuffs had opened a coin sized slit just above his eyebrow. Linette failed once again as she tried to reach him, soundly shoved onto her rear by one of the sentinels for her effort.

Urging his laifhorse forward a bit, Amyr almost seemed to float next to the woman. "Do not fear," he said, repositioning his legs, the right now atop the left. "Your quarters will be well above the ground."

The cart crested a grade, and the barbed towers of Benwick Castle appeared in Linette's vision. They would indeed be arriving shortly.

"Now hold still," advised Amyr, nodding at the sentinel just beyond her shoulder. A sudden jarring sting overtook the side of her face, flinging her hair across her eyes. Searing pain settled on her cheekbone, and as she lifted a hand to feel the space, another gauntlet strike caught her on the other cheek.

"One more," Amyr ordered, signaling to the lower part of his jaw.

After the third clout, Linette fell forward, spitting a bloody mist from her mouth. A dislodged tooth joined the spray, falling between the planks. Hovering above the ringing in her ears, she could hear Ancel writhing against his fetters, receiving a hearty pummeling to his face and neck.

"I do not want him rendered unconscious!" Amyr shouted. The blows abated, and the laif leaned down into Linette's view. "This will all make sense soon enough, my dear one," he murmured. "Oh, how excited your father will be to see you."

* * *

Rumors seemed to gush from every open mouth. The words spilled from windows and poured out into the streets through which Stacey waded. War had exacted many casualties, many final results, but the gossip was a welcome guest, it seemed. A comforting distraction.

"Who would have thought *he* would do such a thing?" one woman said, clutching the medallion around her neck. She furtively glanced at Stacey, realizing abruptly that her words had been spoken perhaps a bit too loudly on the well-trod avenue.

This war had ravaged nearly all of Benwick's knights. No other realm had paid even close to such a heavy cost. *But, yes,* Stacey thought angrily, *let us speak of dubious claims and baseless accusations.*

Passing a leather workman's cart, Stacey caught another ridiculous snippet. "Yes, I know! That's where he has been all along! I have it on good terms that he was in league with them before the first assault." A burly man spoke with folded arms. He rocked onto his other foot when he noticed Stacey. "Can I help you?" he said, eyebrows furrowed. The man and woman he had been speaking to also turned and glowered at her.

Stacey apologetically raised her makeshift cane, fashioned from a shattered spear, and shook her head.

"Anyway..." the workman continued, pausing to allow Stacey time to walk on.

For all that she sacrificed and all that she lost, these people should be thanking her, not scorning her.

In the aftermath, Ector had abandoned her. The lampyr who had rescued her from Lanaelle was a kind laif and had done all he could to mend her body. But the most grievous wound she had sustained could not simply be healed with a tincture. She had laid in the recovery tent, closely watching every crease in the flap when someone passed by. She had expected at any moment that Ector's face would punch through, and he would hold her and clothe her in kisses. But it had never happened. It was not meant to be.

"Aye," a fruit purveyor said as she secured her cart, "I heard it from Belinda that they are to keep him in his own dungeons!"

"Oh, what a pity."

"Pity?" the vendor spat, placing her hands on hips. "Reserve your pity for those souls lost from Lord Ancel's treachery."

The scolded woman ducked her chin apologetically. "You're right, you're right, of course," she mumbled. "This is just so much to take in... and you said that they *actually* captured an archenlaif who will testify?"

"Don't you worry, the Arbiter will sort it all out on the morrow..." The rest of the conversation was lost to Stacey. She was deeply bothered by it all, but did not stop to listen. She had heard more than enough.

* * *

"My girl!" Kenna sent his chair flying as he shot to his feet.

After recent events, Linette did not feel quite herself, and she shied back from her gleeful father. The hurt he displayed, stumbling back, pained her more than the bumps on her head.

"What, what," Kenna sputtered, finding his feet. "What has he done to you?"

The soft carpet beneath Linette's shoes had a springy texture that she was unaccustomed to. If she weren't so rattled, the lavish suite that had been provided for her father may have impressed her. A suite all his own, she distantly registered. Perla was nowhere to be seen.

The man scurried around the room, seeking a writing parchment.

"Oh, forgive me," he muttered, flinging towels from a dresser. "I seem to have lost my head…" His frantic search proved fruitless. Shrugging in resignation, Kenna walked to the door and eased it open. "Excuse me, sir!" He called to the guard beyond the door.

The guard's husky voice was impossible for Linette to discern. It merely sounded as a low grumble to her. She could, however, hear that her father was growing more and more flustered with each returned grumbling.

"Ah, well!" wailed Kenna, flinging the door closed. "That seals it! Gah! I'm a witness, so they won't allow me paper and ink before the trial!"

The carpet absorbed each of Kenna's heated stomps. The resiliency seemed to fuel the man's ill temper. After all, a satisfying stomp has been proven to help cool the heels of the disgruntled, especially when performed in rapid succession.

Kenna approached his daughter again, this time with a dose of apprehension. "My dear," he said, slowly winding his fingers around her shoulders. "My little cob, what has that deceiver done to you?"

Linette swiped her father's hands loose and grabbed hold of his shoulders, locking eyes, and emphatically mouthed the word "nothing."

Kenna's forehead rumpled. His eyes moved away from hers and began vigorously searching for something below. "That's not possible!" His lips tightened in resolve. "He must have cast a spell—"

A light gust of air rolled against the back of Linette's neck.

"Linette," a solemn voice said.

Linette started at the sound of her name. Turning, she saw a laif sporting a healer's white surcoat standing before her.

"My name is Laevephen," he said. "And I am here to escort you to your chambers." He stepped toward the entryway, beckoning her to follow "And, of course, to tend to your wounds once you are settled. I will await you." The laif exited, but left the door enticingly ajar.

Kenna appeared to be working figures in his head. He retreated to his spilled chair and returned it to its feet. The meal he had abandoned was cold now, but he sat to dine regardless.

Raising a tentative hand in farewell, Linette beseeched her father's attention.

The man appeared beyond distracted, almost haunted. From the corner of his eye, he caught her simple gesture. "Good-night, little tiller..." he mumbled. His moustache hairs billowed as he exhaled a sigh. Slowly, he jammed a forkful of soggy greens into his mouth.

* * *

The servants swirled throughout the keep, performing their usual nightly functions as well as a host of other assignments. Then afterward, for most, it was time to hit the bunks. Tomorrow would prove more than just a trial for the Lord of Benwick. Royals and scriveners, Lords and laymen, knights errant and knights-a-squire—all would be in attendance. Such an event had not been seen in ages, and the ensuing excitement had spun the glaring spotlight from the battlefields of war directly to Benwick's doorstep. And who would be ensuring the comforts of those in attendance, and additionally, needed to maintain proper gloss for the courtroom? Why, the servants, of course.

A discussion that had begun in a corridor was now fanning into the armour gallery. The servants set to preserving the aged steel, some upon ladders, wearily swiveled their heads at the sudden invasion.

"Should we wait for the King?" The cleric's stumpy legs struggled to keep up with the Arbiter's clip. "I, mean, is this not something he should be present for?"

The fringes of Amyr's mantle swirled as he came to an abrupt halt. His exhausted gaze set the servants back to work. "Dispatches were sent," he said calmly to the woman. "We have yet to receive a response, and I do not believe that Arthur needs to sully himself with this business. And furthermore, the Cloth does not require its hands to be held."

"I, I understand that, Lord Amyr," the cleric persisted, "but this is *treason* we are trying Lord Ancel with, and he and Arthur have quite a history. I'm sure you—"

"Enough!" Amyr's hand shot up, deflecting the words. "Listen..." the laif trailed off, waiting for the cleric to supply her name.

"Credence, my Lord," the cleric said with a nod.

Amyr's lip quivered. "Such a name... anyhow, Credence, I sincerely believe that time is of the essence here. This Lord Ancel is quite a dangerous man, and the people have already lost so much throughout this trying year. Especially in Benwick. The people seek to quench their thirst for justice, and I aim to give them a taste, even at such a slight dosage. For this alone will not heal and rebuild, but it will act to satiate their souls."

Fervently, Credence dabbed at the sweat congregating on her pronounced forehead. Amyr appeared unimpressed, and he shifted his weight, renewing his trek.

"But, wait!" Credence sped to Amyr's side. "Can we not hold out for at least one more day?" she pleaded.

The blissful thought of Ancel spending successive days and nights in the dungeons briefly tempted the Arbiter toward relenting. "Denied," stated Amyr, engraving the word with finality.

When Amyr began to walk again, the cleric lingered behind, wanting to say more, but in the end, she did not follow.

44

Linette woke with Amyr's words still dripping in her mind. The night before, he had cordially knocked upon the door almost immediately after the lampyr had left her. Believing it was a servant come to tend the hearth or perform some other perfunctory duty, Linette had released the bolt and bid the outsider come.

Regret and anguish sluiced her memory, recalling how the laif entered her chambers, acting as if he would be welcomed by her. Expecting to be welcomed.

"This will all be clear soon," he had said, opening his arms widely. After taking an uninvited seat, he had spoken again. "I care for you deeply, and if you wish me gone, then simply say—" Covering his lips with an index finger, the laif suppressed a playful laugh. "Forgive me, please *indicate* as much."

Linette had vehemently pointed to the exit, indicating exactly as much.

Naturally, Amyr ignored her. "You do know that Lord Ancel has proven himself false on more than one occasion. The fact that he concealed his identity from you is a mere symptom belying a grander ailment."

Striding into his view, Linette continued to point toward the door.

"You don't mean that." Amyr placed his chin onto interlocked hands. "Oh, if only you would have seen the plans I had for us. The estate! The gilly fields! The look on your dear father's face at the reveal!

How your sister wept with pure joy!" His claims filled Linette's face with turmoil. "Can you not see?" The laif sat up as he watched his words beginning to take root. "Everything that I do, I do for you."

Turning away, Linette scrubbed her hand across her face in frustration, from forehead to cheek. After a moment, she spun back around, and once again bid the laif to leave.

"Why do you mar yourself like that?" Amyr rose and Linette shrunk back. "The lampyr only just healed you." He motioned toward the dressing still pressed to the side of her neck, two distinct crimson specks bleeding through. "Ah. You still believe Ancel to be true, I see," said Amyr, not twitching one muscle toward departure. "What if I told you that I have proof to solidify my claims? Will that sway you to verity's corner?"

Keeping her eyes firmly fixed on Amyr, Linette sidled behind an armchair, staring at the laif as if a dagger loomed behind his cloak.

"Are you still cross about the wagon ride?"

Linette's fingers strangled the brassy palmette engraved atop the chairback.

"There are a great many things that I wish you to see! I need you to see!"

The girl was not swayed; her eyes gleamed as defiantly as a cornered fennec.

"I needed you to see my sentinels' ire! An ire that only a traitor can conjure from fair minds! If it weren't so, I would have spirited you on the most regal palfrey in the kingdom! You must believe me!"

In response, Linette heatedly tapped her neck where the bandage was secured, and then swirled a finger over her face. Her scowl deepened, riveting pocks on her chin.

Amyr winced. "The injuries you sustained were mere theatrics. You are no worse for the wear." The laif attempted a step closer, but Linette shifted away. He growled in frustration. "I am sorry for that. If you wish it, I can see the sentinel punished?"

Linette's only response was to employ both hands to strangle the palmette.

Turning back to his chair, Amyr dropped his weight onto the cushion. He stared into the flames, his fist thoughtfully keeping his head aloft. "You know," he began at length, flicking his eyes toward Linette, "that we have over a dozen witnesses who confirm Ancel's treachery. Think hard, Linette, and perhaps if you look deep within yourself, you'll realize that you should join them on the stand." He shifted his weight abruptly, planting both feet on the floor. "At any point, after he stole you away from your kin, how many warning banners waved? Surely, there had to be more than one occasion of doubt that had risen about your captor. Something must have simmered to the surface."

If her skeleton could have leapt from her flesh to ensure an escape, Linette very well might have seized that option. She did not wish to abide this laif even a minute longer.

"Linette!" Amyr suddenly appeared in front of her. "You are rendering your hands raw!" The laif had crossed the room, grabbing her hands that she had unconsciously wrung raw. "Please, sit," Amyr said gently. "Please, allow me to say my piece, and then I will depart."

Linette felt almost sick as she relented. She sat bolt upright on the furthest fringe of the seat, her rigid posture drawing the cushion over the edge. She was ready to get up and walk away the moment his speech concluded.

After taking the seat directly before her, Amyr offered her a wan smile. "Once I spoke with Bilka, of Benwick's council—" A rap upon the door cut the laif off. "Enter," he commanded, not bothering to turn around.

Two servants strode into the room. The one balancing a tray deviated tentatively when he saw Amyr. The other stood by the door in strict observance. It was clear to Linette that the young man carrying the drinks was new to service and must be in training.

"Ah, yes," Amyr drawled. "This must be the mulled wine that I requested..." he trailed off, swiveling his shoulders to look at the supervisor, "An hour ago."

A grim darkness swirled about the woman by the door with her hood drawn. Linette did not care for her in the least, and would be glad to see her gone. Taking the wooden cup into her hands, Linette nodded a *thank you* to the beaming servant. His pristine teeth were confined inside a broad grin, and he seemed as one about to relinquish a long-kept secret. Linette began to stir uncomfortably as he grinned at her overly long.

"Thank you, lad," said Amyr dismissively, selecting his cup and chasing away the radiating heat with a gentle blow.

The servant flinched, closing his mouth, and refraining from uttering whatever he had been mustering. "My Lord," he said, awkwardly bowing to Linette first, then to Amyr. "Nighty-night." The servant bustled from the room, receiving a slight buffet to the back of his head as he passed the supervisor, though it appeared as more of an endearing tussle of hair than a corrective slap.

"Nighty-night," Amyr mumbled into his wine, taking a drink. "Go on," he urged. "It's not poisoned, I assure you." He took another sip and smiled at her. "Delicious."

Linette glanced at her cup on the table and pensively mouthed the word *hot*.

"Well, give it a few minutes then," advised Amyr, "it's very good."

Unnervingly, the supervisor had yet to leave. She glowered as she stood beside the closed door, clinging to the wall like a stain.

"Now, where was I?" Amyr's shoulders rose and fell. "Yes, yes, I had spoken with the Benwick council to verify the rumblings. Rumblings of what, you ask? Why, the rumblings that indicated our Lord Ancel was in league with those covetous, vile archenlaives."

Whether the supervisor had bristled at Linette's bristling, she could not tell. But both women seemed to take offense at the statement.

"I know, I know," said Amyr, gulping more wine. "This is quite good. You really should try it. Anyhow, to make a long tale slim, there had been an interaction on the battlefield, betwixt Ancel and the archenlaif karbaled that raised more than one eyebrow."

The silence weighed thick as Linette waited for Amyr to press on with his supposed condensed story. The laif slurped and swiped his bottom lip with a finger. "And once this suspicion was shared between the witnesses, each at first tightly holding onto such a dreadful accusation, the truth eventually unraveled into the light."

Linette needed proof. She knew when speaking falsehood that the Arbiter was free from his own magics. It was a failsafe that prevented absentminded and unintentional suicide.

"I can see by your countenance that you do not believe me," stated Amyr, setting his cup aside. "Recall, if you will, when I told you that I had proof?"

Linette responded with a dull nod.

"Jukaliska." Amyr pointed behind his shoulder without shifting his forward gaze. The hooded supervisor peeled away from the wall and walked into the light. "Yes, Amyr," she grated. Linette could not recall hearing a voice so dreadful. With one hand, Jukaliska cleared the cowl from her head, revealing laif ears.

Laives don't serve like this! Linette rocked back in her seat, the cushion nearly spilling out from underneath. *And she does not look a regular laif!*

"You seem troubled," Amyr said fondly. "Have you never been in the presence of a real live *archenlaif?*" He turned to the archenlaif. "Tell me truthfully, is Ancel in alliance with the archenlaives?"

Jukaliska craned an affirmative nod. "Yes."

* * *

Ancel felt the cold steel glance his fingertips before gliding over the heel of his palm.

"Our little secret," the servant whispered into Ancel's ear. "You'll know when the time is right." Before stepping backward, he spoke once more. "We believe in you."

A sudden scrape of metal jolted the servant back another healthy step. The noise signaled the entry of a handful of Amyr's sentinels, each one resplendent for battle.

"Is the prisoner secured?" a quavering voice called from beyond the dungeon cell.

The foremost sentinel nodded his close-visored helm toward the servant lingering in the shadows beneath the sliver of a window.

"He is," the servant passed along, nodding briskly. His eyes darkened as they shifted toward the shackles secured to Ancel's wrists.

"Arms behind his back, I hope?" the voice queried.

Dutifully, the servant resumed nodding. "Yes, yes, they are."

Ancel quietly began working the bulky key the servant had slipped into his hands, trying to find the best way to hold it without giving away its presence. Finding the shackles' eye would be tricky and the sudden appearance of this Church vicar aggravatingly prevented ample time for practice.

The sentinels parted and a goaler entered with truncheon in hand. "On your feet!" she commanded. "Turn around!" was her second order, made while twirling the truncheon at his face.

Turning to face the servant, who appeared petrified at this event, Ancel offered an encouraging smile. The shackles rattled as the goaler gave them a firm tug, and sniffed with approval.

"He is secured!" the goaler announced to the vicar waiting outside, turning a heel to stand by the wall. A gratuitously tall middle-aged man stooped beneath the cell opening, lifting his robes from the filthy floor beneath.

"Very well," the vicar sneered, discarding the wobble in his voice. "Launcelot, son of Ban, the Lord of Benwick, allow me to introduce myself. I am Vicar Rowan. Where I hail from is not important anymore, and like you, I once held a title and land."

Shifting his weight onto one foot, Ancel moved to turn around and face the vicar.

"Hold fast now!" Rowan nearly squealed. His fear had clearly returned, restricting his vocal chords. "Please stay where you are, if you will," the vicar said, gaining control of himself. "Today I have been given the privilege of presenting you with a choice, Ancel, if I may call you that?" He did not wait for a response and continued, "It appears that you are at a crossroads, Ancel, and it has fallen upon me to present you with your options. All of Camelot is watching, Ancel, awaiting your decision, on bated breath. Understand that the charges being brought come with an insurmountable load of firsthand testimony."

"But not one shred of evidence," Ancel replied calmly.

"I have been advised of your cleverness, Ancel." Rowan plucked at his cuff and rubbed his fingers together. "I am not here to hold a conversation, as much as it would please me under alternate circumstances. Unfortunately for you, the answers that I require are distilled to a simple yes or no. Help me to help you, Ancel." The Churchman spoke almost pleadingly, taking a tiny step toward the shackled captive. "You must simply admit to your treachery, Ancel. There is no need for explanation. Just confess your crimes and seek absolution. If you do so, I assure you that your death will be administered painlessly in private, free from the public eye."

Ancel's right shoulder twitched. "And the other road I may take?" he asked.

"Why judgment, of course."

"Of course."

"What shall it be, Ancel? All of Camelot is watching."

45

Amyr had voiced his wish for the trial to be held on the newly furnished tourney grounds, but those persistently contrarian Benwick advisers had been staunchly opposed. "Think about those who are hard of hearing," the female human, Bilka, had said with condescension.

The other minister, Byron, had stepped forward to add his piece. "And think of the children!" It was as if it had all been rehearsed. Before Amyr had the chance to inquire further regarding exactly how "the children" pertained to the discussion, Bilka had signaled to the nearby servants by clapping her hands briskly. Mere moments after, the Arbiter had been led to a large pair of arched doors, their size being the only thing remarkable about them.

"We believe that this will be to your liking, Lord Amyr," Bilka had said through thin lips that barely moved.

In truth, her use of the speculative word "believe" had been her saving grace. For had the insipid harpy spoken with certainty, she would have dropped right then and there. It would have been quite satisfying to see in the moment, but ultimately would have proved a disappointment, seeing as she was one of the witnesses meant to testify against Ancel. Each and every arrow, no matter how dull, was necessary when pursuing such prey.

Now seated high above the chamber floor, Amyr gazed down at the proceedings, a sour expression sculpting his face. Positioned in a luxurious compartment tucked up into the framework of the cathedral hall, he felt like a ridiculous bird perched inside a rocky crag. He greatly preferred to be at eye-level, or even just slightly above eye-level, but the overseers had insisted he take the seat of prominence. Being this far removed was entirely foreign to him, but he would make do. After all, he was not in his basilica. This was Benwick, and when his ends came to fruition, none of this would matter in the least.

The Benwick council had appointed that unnerving vicar, Rowan, to manage the prosecution on behalf of the realm. Certainly not Amyr's first choice for the position, but no one had asked for his counsel on the matter, and, truly, they could have done far worse.

Gangly and awkward, Rowan lurched about at the base of the stand that had been erected for testimonies. The attendees had filtered into the theatre, filling every seat. At first, excited apprehension had been apparent in their gesticulations and speech, but now that they had been waiting for an uncomfortable amount of time, they were growing restless. And Rowan's incessant pacing at the front of the room was not helping.

Amyr's eyes swept over the witnesses hemmed into their partitioned seats, and noticed, to his dismay, that the space beside the sallow-faced Kenna was vacant. The seat reserved for his Linette. Slamming his hands down upon the plushy manchettes of his throne's armrests, Amyr vaulted to his feet. Along his sudden rise, a pretty figment snagged his eye among the roiling throng near the entryway, locking him in place.

"She came..." he breathed, easing back into his seat. To Amyr, the girl moved through the room as a fragile silken scarf, skimming between mortals. Of all that he had seen and known, experienced and built, the sight of this girl navigating a crowd somehow surpassed it all.

"...and she's mine."

* * *

The cemetery had been a poor choice. Stacey had been unaware that Benwick had accumulated quite a ghoul infestation over the years. Being awakened by the sound of your name being hissed in an unnatural whisper over and over tended to prevent one from attaining proper sleep. She had culled the ghouls that had dared nose too close, but it still left all the others to disrupt her rest.

As Stacey made her way toward the castle proper, she spied a throng of sentinels ushering a shackled prisoner toward the front gates. The dungeons had only one opening, and the path to the front gate skirted the curtain walls. Wisely, the architects had not connected the dungeon to anywhere within the keep, but it meant that bringing a prisoner inside for sentencing proved an aggravating duty. Especially if the prisoner was less than tolerant of a leash, or, Creator forbid, wounded to the point of needing a litter.

"I must move," Stacey muttered to herself.

This event was something that she could not miss. The trial of Lord Ancel trailing so close at the heels of war smelled of intrigue. And it also smelled of a farce. The entire kingdom seemed to be set against this man whom Carlysle had sworn to be upright and just. Say what you wished about Sir Carlysle, but Stacey knew no matter how intoxicated she became, she could always sense a grift. Somehow through the fog, Carlysle could peg a person as good or ill almost instantly.

"*That whelp,*" Stacey whispered to herself, echoing a fragment of Carlysle's final words to her. Carlysle had known from the start that Ector was not to be trusted.

Upping her pace to a run, Stacey managed to join the sentinel's march and slide in with the last batch of folk allowed entry through the gates. Behind her she could hear the unmistakable din of outraged men and women.

"Should have woken earlier," one of the guards said, crossing spears to bar further access. "The hall is full." The clinking chains of the portcullis drawing to a close further punctuated his statement.

The walk from the gates to the hall hardly registered to Stacey. Willfully she dismissed any memories of her last visit to this place when she had been in love with a son of Benwick, and Jekar had been alive. Before she knew it, she was seated in an amphitheatre with raised rows that descended in a gentle gradient funneling toward a stage. The opening announcements had already been made, but Stacey did not feel that she had missed anything. Everyone knew what they were here for.

A lanky man in formal church garb paced back and forth on the floor beneath the stage. "The first witness," the man hurriedly announced. Above him the sentinels had only just begun seating the prisoner. Clearly, the sound of the chains scraping upon the dais rankled the churchman. He curled his shoulders to his ears and shook his head. "That I would like to call forward," he continued, "is the accused's former betrothed, The Honourable Kurrva Pentracil, daughter of the esteemed Barrett Pentracil, Duke of Rhionydd."

The pale woman beside Stacey heaved a wilting sigh as the graceful witness invaded the kiosk and maneuvered the chair to her liking before taking a seat. Placing both hands in her lap, Kurrva fidgeted with the rings adorning her fingers.

"It bears repeating," the tall vicar finally stood still, "though it should go without saying, that it would be most prudential for you if you choose your words carefully..." he dramatically trailed off and lifted a finger above him.

Stacey looked up sharply. A compartment she had overlooked seemed to suddenly appear above the stage. Within its shallow recess was the Arbiter. *Of course he would be here,* she thought. *Why wouldn't he be?* Such powerful magic was usually detected by her feral senses, but Amyr had somehow slipped completely underneath.

"If a question feels a bit too perilous," the vicar continued, "I suggest you remain silent, and I will gladly move along."

Kurrva nodded her head with eyes downcast. "Yes, Rowan," she said meekly.

"Now," said Rowan, teetering toward Kurrva, his heels clipping his robes. "Please state your name."

"Kurrva Pentracil." The woman had not stopped fiddling with her rings. "Of Rhionydd."

"Thank you," stated Rowan, swerving his head, engaging the audience that cupped the chamber, from shoulder to shoulder. "Now that we have established that you are not an imposter, you may say your piece."

"What would you like to reveal to Benwick—" Rowan stopped himself short. "Nay! For Camelot!" His flourish of phrase coaxed a smattering of applause from a few pockets in the chamber but it bit off almost immediately.

"He forgets himself," Stacey said quietly.

The woman beside her overheard and smiled in silent agreement.

"Explain your relationship with the accused," Rowan prompted.

Straightening up, Kurrva ceased her twiddling. "We were to be wed." She spoke with her eyes plastered above as if an axe head dangled there. "Our fathers sought to bolster the alliance betwixt our realms."

"Ah," Rowan licked his lips. "I'll make this brief. Was the accused a *loving* paramour?"

"No."

"Was he attentive to you?"

"No."

"If not you, then what were the accused's energies focused toward?"

As her head turned, her chest heaved. She finally looked at Ancel, bloody and marked with the cuts of a captive. "I cannot say for certain," she said at length. "He was always at study. Learning languages, tongues, customs. Foreign interests, I gathered." Her lip curled. "Unseemly, I believed, for someone who was in line to inherit Lord Ban's mantle."

Casting a glance to the Arbiter, Rowan settled his chin and strode through the center of the chamber. "Your betrothed, the accused, meddled in *otherworldly* affairs?" He arched an eyebrow and crossed his arms, concealing his hands into loose sleeves. "I will not beg you for further testimony."

Dismissed, Kurrva gathered herself and strode from the stage. Not another moment would be spent in consideration of Ancel's fate. The grace he had bestowed seemed long forgotten. *Life can be funny like that,* Stacey thought.

The next witnesses were servants who squirmed in their seat, attesting to Kurrva's claim, that yes, indeed, Ancel was a man who spent great stretches of time in his study. This did not sway Stacey's opinion in the least, but she did not hold a bias against the man on trial. Many heads bobbed around her, accompanied by thoughtful expressions that bloomed into scowls. Moustaches hid lips that muttered and kerchiefs veiled mouths that whispered words such as *false* and *traitor*. Others mopped their brows in disbelief, easily coerced by the words of a jilted lover. Though not all were convinced. Not yet at least.

The servants, Stacey noted, spoke apologetically. She did not find a measure of enmity in their voices. This may have been induced by the lingering threat of instant death, but all the same, Stacey found it remarkable. She wagered, surveying the hive around, that this detail would go unnoticed by most.

"The next witness I would like to request," Rowan paused, scratching at his sideburns. "Kenna Turinleure of Benwick."

A stocky boulder of a man gradually rose to his feet from the witness section, gripping his cap as if it would fly off on its own. By his gait, the man seemed to have lived a life of labor, and he eased past the others in their seats with the care of an ox. In hindsight, this Kenna Turinleure certainly should have been positioned closer to the aisle. Eventually the man wriggled free and plodded toward the stage. Somehow this length of his journey, even free from complacent knees barring passage, seemed to take the man much longer than expected.

"Kenna Turinleure," Rowan addressed the man. "Please state your name."

The color, if the man had any to begin with, drained from his face. "Kenna Turinleure," he stammered, "but you can call me Ken." This elicited a few cheerful laughs.

Rowan was not amused. "Please," the vicar rolled his wrist dramatically, "reveal, if you will, how you came to know the accused."

Wriggling in his seat, Kenna removed his cap and balanced it upon a shaky knee. "Well," he began, sounding parched. He cleared his throat and resumed. "Well, the accused first introduced himself to me as a Benwick messenger."

"A humble Benwick messenger?" Rowan inquired.

"I suppose so," replied Kenna. "He was bringing a message."

"As messengers so often do," said Rowan. To his chagrin, titters of laughter ensued. He continued, cutting through the mirth. "And you did not recognize this courier as your new Lord?"

Kenna lowered his head. "No, I did not."

The woman seated beside Stacey abruptly bowed her head and began mouthing words into her hands, though not one syllable registered above a whisper.

"And just when did you come to the realization that you were being fooled, Kenna?"

Shoulders quaking, Kenna looked up. "I had no idea! I swear!"

"It's alright, it's alright," Rowan said placatingly, turning toward the audience. "Mistakes do happen."

Kenna smoothed his moustache and leaned back, rocking the chair. "The last few days blur together for me, you understand?" he stated. "And I don't wish to die if I were to—"

"We understand," Rowan interrupted, raising a finger. "So it's safe to say that you only came upon the truth within the last few days, as you stated?"

"Yes."

"Magnificent."

Rowan cut toward Kenna swiftly utilizing his full gait. "There was an incident regarding *ogres?*" He suggested quietly, so quietly that none could hear the phrase outside the kiosk.

Brightening just a shade, Kenna nodded. "There was this one afternoon—we were seated at the table eating, enjoying an afternoon stew—"

"Who are 'we'?" Rowan interjected.

"Oh." Kenna adjusted in his seat. "It was me, uh, myself, my daughters—Linette and Perla, and the uh, the accused over there." He pointed toward Ancel, then peered into the crowd as if he were looking for someone.

Stacey suddenly noticed that the woman beside her had tears spilling down her cheeks, her shoulders shaking with silent cries.

Clearing his throat, Rowan urged the witness to press on.

"We were enjoying an afternoon stew," recited Kenna distractedly, squinting into the crowd. "This was before I knew that we were dining with our Lord, of course, or else I would have served something a bit classier. But, well, I'm a simple farmer, and my one daughter seemed to be smitten by this 'messenger,' and well, a father should know when to keep his distance when it comes to such things—"

The heel of Rowan's boot scuffed sharp against the floor, gaining Kenna's attention. The vicar eyed the balcony overhead. Rambling in the Arbiter's presence was exceedingly dangerous.

Abashed for a moment, Kenna released a pent-up breath and frowned. "The ogres came from the forest," he spoke rigidly. At the mention of ogres, a series of gasps and mutters permeated all over. "I was frightened. The accused was not. He got up and strode out to the ogres. He spoke to them. Then they went away."

"They went away?"

"Never saw 'em again."

"Without bloodshed?"

Kenna gave a crooked nod as if he swallowed bitter tea. "Without bloodshed," he repeated with finality.

Producing an awkward whirl, Rowan addressed the hall. "There you have it!" he declared. "The accused studies other worldly wonders and confers with monsters!"

To Stacey, the correlation that the vicar drew did not hold water. How did it matter that the man held uncommon interests and peaceably resolved a conflict with ogres?

"You are dismissed," Rowan waved his hand with a flourish. "Thank you, Kenna."

For a single beat, the old farmer's eyes sunk to the floor. "I'm so sorry, Netty," he groaned just above a whisper, securing his cap.

"Netty?" Stacey repeated, following Kenna's laborious return.

Beside her, the woman's tear-streaked face abruptly turned toward Stacey. A question formed on her lips but she was disrupted by Rowan's next announcement.

"I would like to call a daughter of Kenna Turinleure forward," the vicar scanned with a hand to his brow. The woman shrunk. "Perla Talbot, if you would be so kind. I merely have a single question to ask."

A woman, clearly with child, took the witness stand and corroborated everything her father had said with a simple yes. Having survived the assertion, Perla Talbot was escorted from the stage.

What was the point of that? Stacey wondered. *If the man had been lying, he would have simply keeled over.* A brush against her elbow drew Stacey from her thoughts. The woman next to her had returned to an upright position. The tears had been swept away, but her eyelids held back a resurgence. Her lips trembled as she mouthed another muted phrase.

"Sir Tamarah Gant of Benwick," beckoned Rowan. "Please come forward."

Dressed in a crisp green and black tunic, a knight Stacey recognized entered the box. Her hair was bundled taut to the back of her skull, restricting the path of her eyebrows.

"Please state your name."

The knight folded her arms. "Sir Tamarah Gant," she said, looking toward Ancel, revealing two distinct dots on the right side of her neck.

"I hope that I do not sound overly brazen," Rowan began peering between Tamarah and Ancel. "But may I ask, how did you die?"

Tamarah's eyes did not leave the prisoner. "Save for Sir Ector," she said, "all of the knights in my company died."

"And yet you live?"

"Luckily, I was felled by ice spears early on," Tamarah adjusted her seat so that she squarely faced Ancel. "The rest were unfortunately finished by werewolves." She paused, staring at Ancel. "I cannot attest to what happened thereafter on that battlefield. I can, however, discuss what I saw at Fort Navarene."

"Fort Navarene, you say?" Rowan's frown rumpled his knob of a chin. "Please go on," he encouraged.

"I was there," stated Tamarah. "I was at *the* battle at the foot of the fort, fighting for our lives, fighting alongside *Sir Sandrin*." She practically spat the knight's name, and Stacey caught the prisoner flinch. "You remember him, don't you? How about Belfast? Does that name ring any bells? Or Deverin, our revered battle lampyr, do you recall him?" She breathed hard, directing the questions at Ancel. "Anyhow, as you can tell," she tempered her breathing and flicked her eyes to the side, "I am still breathing, so I am clearly not lying." Returning her gaze to the accused, she continued her speech. "At the time, it seemed like an exchange between foes..." she trailed off, fearing that speculating any further would mean her end.

"You watched the accused converse with the archenlaives?" Rowan scooped Tamarah's words into a discernible bowl. "Is that what you are saying?"

"Not just any archenlaif." Tamarah leaned forward, her eyes narrowed, "the karbaled."

Intermixed with incredulity and anger, a wave of voices swirled throughout the great hall. As Stacey thought back on the ice that had sprung forth during that horrid battle, men and women alike sprang to their feet in contempt. Believing themselves righteous, the insults they hurled were beyond apology.

Sedately, Rowan attempted to calm the flood. "My good people, if you please," he scowled, though his eyes betrayed his delight. "Please. This is a trial. There must be order."

In resignation, Rowan simply placed his hands behind his back, waiting out the storm. Tamarah leaned heavy, her hatred silently fixed. And yet, Ancel bore it all without a sound.

Once a modicum of calm descended upon the room, Rowan spoke again. "Please, my good people, refrain from such outbursts in the future." By the time he had finished his statement, silence had finally been attained.

Rowan's eyes scanned the box seats allocated for the royals of the realm. His gaze stopped at the box with the green and black pennant dangling beneath, the seats within empty. Swinging his attention back down, Rowan smoothed the coarse hairs on his chin. "Thank you, Sir Tamarah," he said without looking her way. "Now, I would like to call the other remaining son of Benwick to the chair."

46

Tamarah was still in the witness chair when Ector approached, arms folded, staring daggers at Ancel.

"Tamarah," Ector began, before remembering that every word inside the box was amplified. His voice reverberated among the joists high, high above.

"Sir Tamarah." Rowan crouched as he approached the kiosk, looking much like one who had just spotted a curio on a low shelf. "You are dismissed," he said, his voice rising as his spine straightened. "Please vacate the seat."

"One more thing," said Tamarah, releasing a clenched hand to scratch one ear. "Ancel, before Creator and Arbiter, I want to ask you something."

The sentinels shifted their stance when the prisoner looked up.

Stepping between, Rowan offered an objection; "The accused will have his chance to speak after —"

"Shut it!" Tamarah shouted, rising. "The accused does not need to answer if he does not wish to." The knight stepped forward and leaned heavily against the inner trusses of the kiosk. "He can hide as a coward behind courtroom rules..." She focused on Rowan and offered a challenging sneer. The vicar said nothing and patiently tucked his hands into the folds of his robes.

"Just *how much* do the people of Benwick mean to you?" seethed Tamarah. The column she gripped began to creak under the immense pressure. "Your brothers, your liegemen... after Navarene, after all we lost and sacrificed..." she broke off, turning to Ector for a fleeting moment, before rounding back. "When your King called for you, when the people cried out for their Lord, while the world blistered with ice and wind — Where were you? What was so important, Ancel? Does your father's legacy mean so little that you would even turn your face while pissing on it?"

Her outburst was met with only silence. The disgraced Lord of Benwick's face was a bloodied, bruised mask that did not crack.

"Will that be all?" Rowan gently asked. "If you would be so kind," he waved his hand in the air, indicating anywhere off stage, "return to your seat."

"Yes," Tamarah sighed, swiping her nose, "that's all."

In Tamarah's wake, Ector felt closer to victory than ever. Finally, the entire realm was seeing what he had suspected for so long. Beneath Ancel's chivalrous and intelligent exterior, there lurked an insidious, vile daemon. And for the first time, Ancel had been seized midway through a scheme.

We have you now, Ector thought, lowering down onto the seat. *Nowhere to run.*

After stating his name, Ector began to divulge his suspicions concerning his older brother from youth until the present. He recounted the times Ancel had been absent or had hidden something from the family. Ector delicately painted the canvas with as much speculation as he could manage without speaking false.

"You must understand," said Ector, selecting his words carefully, "it was never so much the *what* he did, but it was more the *how*. If you catch my meaning? Sneaky is not the right term for it..."

"Sly?" offered Rowan. "Disingenuous? Devious? Shifty?"

"Yes." Ector batted the air. "The first one, *sly*. Like there was always something below the surface. There was always something more."

"And right now?"

"And right now, I want to know the *why*," Ector regarded Ancel. "Why would you abandon your post at our hour of greatest need? You should have been there to protect Nolan and Gabriel! Your own brothers, your own flesh and blood! Their shredded bodies are hardly recognizable anymore after what those werewolves did —" He pried a moment open to calm himself. "And when the king was nearly felled, had it not been for that archer... Where were you? Where were you when the evil fae descended? When the gargoyles took to the skies in reply? When Arthur's horse released a tremendous roar and transformed into an avenging monster, and drove the remaining archenlaives west, where he is still pressing?"

Ector gasped in a shuddering breath before he continued. "And where were you when your brothers led the final Benwick charge against the Karbaled and Vetarled, sustaining the brunt of the werewolf force. If we had not done so at that precise moment, Arbiter strike me down if this be a lie, then the whole of the war would have been lost!" He lifted his eyes to the heavens, awaiting his doom. But death did not come knocking, and Ector heaved a sigh. "Why weren't you there? What was so damn important?" Bitterly, he swiped his brow with the heel of his palm. "If my visor had not been closed when I pierced that young spellcaster's back —" Grief, not death, arrested the knight.

Beyond the stage, Ector could hear the murmuring of the crowd above his own cries. He cursed himself for being so frail. But judging by the smile on Rowan's face, this disclosure of raw emotion registered as a solid blow against Ancel.

"And what of that force that flanked the field?" Rowan prodded the sullen knight, his words acting as a stick. "Moments before you vanquished the evil casters."

Ector swiped the tears from his cheeks. "Yes, yes," he said with a throaty sniff. "Well, I wasn't alone when the karbaled was dealt her defeat, but yes, there was another force that unexpectedly joined the field." The knight paused, lifting his chin. "A force from the forest."

"Was this another contingent of archenlaives?"

"No."

"Perhaps the werewolves had a few late arrivals?"

"No, not werewolves."

"Well, then," Rowan feigned a perplexed expression, forking his chin with thumb and forefinger. "What manner of force did you espy?"

Ector turned to face Ancel. "Ogres," he revealed.

Satisfied with the orchestration thus far, Rowan watched in amusement as a hush fell while the realm connected the dots. Another rising of outrage began to fester and build.

"Have you no class?!" The Duke of Garlot unexpectedly barked from the balcony. He was on his feet, baring his teeth at the crowd. "This is a trial for a man's life, not a tournament for fools! You have forgotten yourselves!" The din resolved itself into a hush. Huffing as a bear before it returns to its cave, the duke nodded at the vicar. "Proceed," he stated, and glowered for a few more moments before taking his seat.

A few people had filed out of the chamber, whether in revulsion or protest, it was difficult to tell. Or perhaps, for some, such proceedings were too intense, and their delicate sensibilities had been pushed up to their summit.

Rowan's eyelashes fluttered in disbelief. Ector could tell that the vicar had been planning to use the outburst to gather strength for his next proclamation, and now the duke had stripped him of those valuable seconds.

"Will that be all?" Ector asked Rowan, trying to move things along. "May I return to my seat?"

Rowan regained his footing. "Indeed," he said graciously. "Thank you for your time, Sir Ector." With his awkward grace, Rowan paced a few steps in Ancel's direction.

"Regrettable, we have merely two more witnesses," Rowan said to Ancel with false apology in his voice. "Then you will be given your chance to speak. But I fear that once the final witness rests her elbows upon that chair, what we shall hear will render any defense moot."

Ancel flexed his left shoulder as if it were assailed by pins and needles. "Get on with it then," he returned through clenched teeth.

What are you trying at, brother? Ector thought, peering curiously at Ancel.

"The next witness I would like to request," the gangly vicar called. "Is Byron Cleven of Benwick, a member of the Benwick council. In the consideration of time, he has been appointed to speak on the council's behalf."

Ector stepped back to allow the man clearance to hurry past. Upon his ascent to the stage, the spear that Byron clung to issued dull thuds that vaulted from wall to distant wall, resonating in every ear above and below.

Ector recognized the weapon immediately. *That dragoon... what was his name? Bactern? No. Bactaal? Yes! Bactaal gifted that spear to Ancel after the karbaled's defeat...*

Taking the witness chair, Byron held the spear as a king would a scepter. Not a shred of shame glossed his demeanor, though he appeared as a puffy housecat wearing an ill-fitting sweater. Ector had to applaud the way the man championed his amateur display of stoicism. After all, fooling oneself is the inception afore fooling others.

"Byron Cleven is my name given at birth," replied Byron to the vicar's prompt. "I am a member of the Benwick council, as was stated, appointed by Lord Ban."

"Wonderful," said Rowan approvingly. "And I see that you have brought something..." The vicar bowed, relinquishing the lead.

Byron lifted his eyebrows. "You must mean this fearful-looking bringer of doom?" He playfully bounced the base of the spear, snagging it further up the haft. "This weapon was found inside Ancel's quarters within the keep. A chambermaid, who fluffs pillows and does whatever it is that chambermaids do, complained of hearing a voice each time she set about her work beyond Ancel's antechamber. Once she passed the threshold, she complained that it was only a matter of time before a voice would begin to utter phrases to her."

"Oh, how dreadfully surprising," commented Rowan.

"Most," Byron agreed. "Upon the first instance, the poor thing fled for a guard. And when the guard strode into the room to investigate, he heard *nothing*. It was the strangest thing! From behind the guard's back, the maid heard the voice plain as day. It was inquiring about the guard's identity. Afterward, when the maid pressed the guard, he revealed that he had heard nothing of the sort. Only a quiet room with a remarkable spear leaning nonchalantly against a wall." Byron leaned forward, a smile forming on his face. "Those were his words, not mine — *leaning nonchalantly* — I have admitted on a number of occasions how underappreciated our guards are..." he smugly strung a series of chuckles together, "but I digress."

Peering from above steepled fingers, Rowan encouraged the man to go on. "Please continue," he said. "What a most peculiar happenstance, I must say."

"To be sure," admitted Byron, placing the length of the spear onto his lap, parallel to the floor. "Begrudgingly, the senior maid eventually acquiesced to the frightened chambermaid's incessant pleas for a reassignment."

"How generous of her."

"Most certainly," Byron nodded. "But wouldn't you know? The next chambermaid was afflicted the same as the first! And the next, and the next, and so on until the senior maid, at her wit's end, decided to take it upon herself to investigate."

"Don't tell me!" Rowan interjected, placing one hand on his clavicle. "She heard the voice as well!"

"Well, I never!"

Byron listlessly skimmed his thumb along the onyx blade. "And that seasoned maid," he went on, "staunchly determined to uncover the cause, remained in the room as the voice tickled her ear spaces something awful. In the past, she had seen the extrication of goblins from wardrobes, wraiths banished from belfries, and ghasts knocked from chandeliers, so this sort of occurrence was not pushing the boundary of reason."

Ector was taken aback by the brazen manner in which the man spoke; slinging phrases about beneath the Arbiter's watchful eye. On the battlefield, where hierarchy meant nothing, he had seen such heedless displays by self-important knights, and more often than not, such pompousness was soundly rewarded with a cloven helm.

"Well, wouldn't you know," continued Byron, "the maid, using her ears and a system of deduction, determined the source of the mysterious speech!" The man ineptly twirled the spear into one hand, nearly catching the tip on his leggings. Once the weapon was vertical, he drove its heel against the floor, fortifying his claim. "This spear!" he announced with an enthusiasm that forced a wince onto many faces in the crows.

Despite the ridiculousness of Byron's performance, the truth in his claims could not be denied. "Its origins are a mystery to me," he said, leaning the spear into a forward corner. "And I will not make any guesses beneath the Arbiter." Meekly feigning confusion, the man shrugged toward Ancel. "All I can do is encourage you to draw your own conclusions."

Well played! Ector sat amused by Byron's deft play as the world around him exploded. *He appears quite the fool, but Creator's crupper, that man is anything but.*

When the room was once again filled with turmoil upon the councilman's conclusion, Stacey turned to the woman beside her. "Want to move up?" she shouted, gesturing toward a vacant space nearer to the stage. The woman sucked a breath and nodded.

"Good people!" The Duke of Garlot bellowed overhead as Stacey, hand in hand with the quiet lady, made for the front. "Good people! Plea —!" The man was cut short. In fact, the entire room was cut short. Even Stacey's footfalls along the cushioned aisle were rendered mute. People all around were moving their mouths, testing their voices, but nothing came forth. An unyielding silence penetrated the air.

"That is enough." Amyr was standing, glaring down from his alcove. His voice echoed in the perfect quiet. "Not another outburst." Flicking a wrist, Amyr returned the volume to its natural level.

"Apologies, Arbiter," said Rowan peering upward with his hands folded as if in prayer. "Let us take this moment to reflect in silence on what we have seen thus far, good people." The vicar turned and dismissed the councilman with a cordial nod.

The new seats afforded differing angles, giving Stacey a new perspective. She swung her head all around taking it all in.

In contrast to Stacey's non-stop scouring, the quiet woman's head had not moved since taking her seat. The prisoner was some fifteen paces away, and Stacey wagered it was the reason for the vacancy of these rows. It appeared no one wanted to be so close to the villain of this story.

Continuing to look around, Stacey's eyes fell upon the talking spear that Byron had brought to the stage. Curiously, the man had left it behind in the kiosk.

Stacey recognized the weapon, recalling when Ector had withdrawn it from his tent... *Ector!* She spun her head to the left. Her new location had unwittingly brought her closer to the witness section. To her great dismay, the knight was directly on the other side of the aisle, leaning forward with his chin sunken, contemplatively rubbing the bridge of his nose. *He has yet to notice me!* she thought with a dose of relief, sinking lower and shielding the side of her face with a hand.

Rowan broke the silence. "Foreign weapons, unseemly research," he began to recount Ancel's supposed transgression, "consorting with ogres, discussions with an archenlaif karbaled..." he trailed off. "If only we could speak directly with the enemy, with an archenlaif in the flesh." Locking his hands behind his back, Rowan strolled into the light at the forefront of the stage. Until now, he had been avoiding the bright curtain. Shadows underlined every pock upon the vicar's face. "Oh, wait a moment," he paused dramatically, his upper lip curling. "We can."

Only moments earlier, the proclamation would have been met with a torrent of cries. But the Arbiter's prior spell had left a rather sedating effect on the onlookers. Stacey could see fingers clenching armrests, veins popping from foreheads and necks and temples, teeth grating, and heels rolling toward arrested toes; a restrained display of scorn ready to burst.

"Sentinels." Rowan turned to the prisoner's escort. "If you will." Acknowledging the command with shifted weight, four sentinels from Ancel's guard detail crossed the stage behind the vicar, disappearing from sight. Moments later five figures approached the stage, the central being a most austere figure held within the midst of the sentinels.

To Stacey, the archenlaif looked to be no more than an angry laif who had missed a few meals. Removed from their threatening plate armour, Stacey found the enemy no more special than any average laif warrior. Perhaps gifted scholars wielded better visual acuity than her and were able to discern the scant musculature differences that drew a line between laives and archenlaives.

Stacey shrugged, watching the witness take the stage. *They all probably taste the same.*

Each sentinel detached from the escort and assumed a post at the four corners of the witness box. Leaning a few feet from the shackled archenlaif, was the spear that had yet to be removed, which Stacey found to be rather troubling. Surely she was not alone in observing this. Despite the shackles and calm disposition, archenlaives were notoriously dangerous, especially around humans.

"My name is Jukaliska," the archenlaif replied to Rowan's initial question. "And yes, I am an archenlaif." A smile upwardly heaved her prominent cheekbones.

"How did you come to be here?" Rowan asked, tilting his head to the side.

The smile fled the archenlaif's face. "I was captured."

"How unfortunate for you," Rowan sucked at his teeth, "but fortunate for us. Now, if you would be so kind..." The vicar extended a hand.

"Please, identify, if you will, the weapon that reclines unassumingly be-fore you. Is it archenlaif?"

"It is of archenlaif make," replied Jukaliska without hesitation.

The tension in the hall tightened along with each jawline within Stacey's line of sight.

"And do you know how the accused may have come upon such a weapon?"

Jukaliska shook her head. "I do not."

"Could it have been a gift?"

With her eyes toward Amyr, Jukaliska sighed. "I will not speculate."

"I will reword my question," Rowan backed a pace. "Do archenlaives give gifts?"

The archenlaif narrowed her vision. "Yes..."

"Alright, alright," Rowan said calmly. "And can archenlaives speak with, oh, I don't know, monsters within the forests?"

"As all laives can, yes," returned Jukaliska sharply.

"Hm," Rowan dabbed a finger to his bottom lip. "So, I would not be off-base if I were to assume that *ogres* are a monster that you may con-verse with?"

After the briefest glance at Ancel, Jukaliska nodded. "We may."

Rowan took advantage of the short exchange between the prisoners. He bent down at the waist, locking his arms behind his back. "And is the *accused* familiar to you?" he inquired darkly.

Amyr shot to his feet, daring another commotion.

The crowds roiled but did not break, awaiting the affirmation that they all sensed was forthcoming.

Ancel seemed to be staring fondly at Stacey. No, she was mistaken. His eyes were fixed on the woman beside her. Following the quiet woman's gaze, Stacey discovered that she was looking back toward Ancel, silently mouthing words to him. No, not words. Just one word, over and over.

Stay.

47

It happened all at once.

The archenlaif nodded affirmation, but her pronouncement was drowned out. Where Rowan was standing within the crescent of light from the ceiling, shadows violently flickered, darkening the vicar. Stacey shielded the woman next to her, fearing the descending creatures to be dark fae. An inhuman shriek pitched from the entryway, then a sound like thunder commenced. The sentinels guarding Jukaliska squared their halberds and hurried toward Rowan.

Ancel fought at his bindings, the sentinels behind him were stirring, distracted, unsure of where to pledge their weapons.

Jukaliska somehow had the spear now held within her shackled wrists, and rushed toward center stage. The sentinels, focused on protecting Rowan, did not see her.

Inside his perched box above it all, Amyr was grappling three heavily armoured men. One assailant was atop him and seemed to be easing a dagger toward his throat.

Debris tumbled from the royal boxes overhead. The ground level onlookers were held suspended in shock. Unconsciously, Stacey tugged at the invisible cord inside of her and changed in an instant.

Stacey's heightened senses took over. Avian and equine scents filled her nostrils. She looked above her, it was a dense flock of birds, not dark fae, that swirled all around, spewing feathers and plucking at

Rowan's robes. The archenlaif was among them, immersed in melee with the sentinels.

Fabrics fluttered as the thundering made its way past. A stable of riderless battle chargers led by a glorious laifhorse, gradually slowed to a canter before the elevated stage.

Simultaneously, the sentinels behind Ancel rushed toward the archenlaif, aiming to join the others. Taking advantage of the commotion, Ancel leaned back, easing his rear upward, and brought his shackles to his front.

Having dispatched the first three sentinels rather quickly, Jukaliska engaged the fourth, deftly piercing the sentinel's trailing leg at the onset. In desperation, the wounded sentinel released his halberd and lunged for the archenlaif, attempting to grapple her. If he could stop her for just a few moments, it would allow time for the rest of the sentinels to overtake her.

A scream came from above, then a body tumbled toward the rushing sentinels. Amyr had discarded one of his attackers, pitching him over the balcony. The man continued to scream along his course toward the ground. Striking a point in the archenlaif's favor, the scream ended in a barrage of clattering steel and fallen sentinels.

Ancel leapt over the contingent that had been his guard. A few had been rendered unconscious from the unexpected assault from above, and the others were still unsteadily trying to climb to their feet.

Jukaliska, having dispatched the fourth sentinel, spun around in time to meet Ancel. Her spear missed its target, though only by a vapor's width. Raising his arms over his head, the Lord of Benwick brought his fists down hard onto the stunned archenlaif's face. The archenlaif, who was not yet quite aware of how dead she was, swatted at a jagged rod protruding from her left eye. In an instant, Ancel was before her yet again. Having retrieved the spear, Ancel pivoted hard on his left boot, and drove the heel of the weapon into the archenlaif's abdomen.

Spewing and choking, Jukaliska cursed Ancel as he angled his shackles over her face. When he slammed his wrists down onto the device protruding from her eye, the archenlaif fell silent. Wrenching his shoulders and gritting his teeth, the man worked and twisted the device deeper into the archenlaif's cavity.

Grim realization dawned on Stacey as she determined just what it was that Ancel had lodged in the archenlaif's eye. She couldn't help but laugh to herself. *A skeleton key.*

After a faint click, Ancel was finally free from his bondage. The shackles released, falling away and battering the dead archenlaif about the ears.

The turmoil within the hall had not abated in the least. The balconies were filled with havoc. Amyr was still embroiled in conflict; sparks flew as he deflected sword blows with his vambraces. The commoners were being assaulted by fowl, but fearing that they would be trampled by the enraged destriers, they cowered and hid where they were. Rowan, receiving the worst from the skies, had fled screaming deeper into the theatre, out of sight. Several war birds could be seen fervently attempting to carry the vicar off, and a few of his final cries emanated from several degrees above the ground.

At some point, unnoticed by Stacey, the quiet woman had wriggled free. Fearing the worst, she frantically scoured the area. From the feathered host above, an emboldened magpie careened toward her, disrupting her search. After a quick riposte, the shuttle of black and white plumage disappeared somewhere into the rows behind.

A few of the sentinels had risen and shambled toward Ancel, though it seemed their senses had yet to fully congregate. Heedless of their approach, knees bent, Ancel waited for the laifhorse to swing near. It was then that Stacey's eyes found the quiet woman. She was running with absolute disregard toward the tarnished Lord of Benwick.

Miraculously, the laifhorse slowed to a canter, allowing Ancel time to bound onto its back. Free from the excess weight of armour that it was accustomed to, his jump was a tad early and overeager. He clung to the ridges along the flanks of the laifhorse, struggling to assume control while his chin jolted the beast just behind its left ear.

"Bring him down!" Ector roared from the witness section, his forehead and cheeks emblazoned with lacerations. He was swatting at a raven that seemed determined to take more than just a pound of flesh. The sentinels that he shrieked at suddenly froze. And as if in reply to his call, a concussive detonation emitted a surge that swept the rafters. Every soul above the ground level was knocked flat. The humans around Stacey appeared disoriented, but for her, the pain lancing through her brain was excruciating. She dropped to her knees, smashing an elbow on her way down, and pressed her snout to the cold stone.

Amyr had held the heavily armoured foe at arm's length for long enough. With one palm pressed flat to the woman's breastplate, the Arbiter decided that the time was nigh.

Never before had Ector been so furious.

When the balcony that the Arbiter had been tucked into exploded, the fragmented shards pierced a great number of the birds that had been violently battering at his head. He was quite grateful for that. But the engulfed girders that swung loose, pouring flames onto the stage, not so much. For the flames created an impassable barrier for the sentinels attempting to give chase. Instead, the sentinels turned to aid their screaming comrades flee the pressing inferno. Thusly allowing Ancel the scant moments he required to escape.

Upon his departure he managed to sweep a young maiden up while she endeavored to escape. The poor dame must have been blinded from the cinders, for she was running toward the traitor with her arms wide. The smoke must have entered her lungs as well, for Ector did not hear a single note of panic as Ancel drove the beast through the great opened doorway.

With her chest pressed to the jagged bones of the charger's neck, every fiber of Linette wished Ancel to take her back to Joyous Garde, despite Amyr having caught them there previously. But if she knew it to be a foolhardy idea, then certainly Ancel was well aware of it. The laifhorse's mane whipped against her face as the beast hurtled through the village, and soon, the scenery gave way to familiar meadows.

Within a blink, she saw a tawdry cottage with toys scattered all about. The laifhorse was running so fast. If her eyes were not playing games, she recognized that exact home from the piteous wagon ride to the Keep. Briefly Linette felt sheer weightlessness as the laifhorse leapt a wide chasm in the road. Then another. This was the same road. The course Ancel chose was a retracement of that horrid journey.

"He will not stop." Ancel spoke into Linette's ear. The knight's forward lean had formed a welcome shield around her. "He will not stop until he claims possession over you."

Of all the things he could say to her, a plea for her to believe his innocence, apologies and promises for reparations, excuses of a convincing nature—instead, Ancel chose to speak of her peril.

"If you wish to be let free," said Ancel. "Nod your head."

Linette tensed rigid, refusing to allow a solitary muscle to waver.

After a moment's passing, Ancel spoke again. "I will not hide, for he knows where to find me."

The forest appeared out of sorts. Both young saplings and centuries old trees had been uprooted and toppled, breaking the line of distinction between forest and garden. Joyous Garde had clearly been hit with a storm.

"A tornado touched us," Ancel said, releasing a pent-up breath. He dismounted before assisting Linette. Appraising the forest with a wary eye, he continued, "We must be cautious of the forest. I fear the drevnigosts are no longer loyal."

Arching backward, Linette tried to rake out the soreness that had developed during their hard ride. Miraculously, Ancel hardly seemed flagged at all. As he steered the laifhorse in the direction of the castle, making sure to maintain a healthy distance from the fallen trees, a lone figure streaked toward them from beneath a mossy causeway. Breaking from Ancel's side, Linette forgot all her aches and slid onto her knees to greet the creature. She ruffled Gomer's fur and hugged him tight about the neck, causing him to yelp with joy. His tongue lapped the air around her face, but when he spied the spear in Ancel's hand, his muzzle dipped almost sullenly.

The cheer within Ancel receded as well. "What is it?" he inquired, following the dog's gaze beyond the desolation.

Peering into the darkness, Linette felt an indescribable presence looming somewhere between the shattered bracken and the roots forlornly grasping for the skies. She turned to Ancel and signaled the word *time*.

"I cannot say," Ancel replied, fixated on the forest. "But I think it best that we move into the keep." A sudden stirring in the trees caused the knight's shoulders to tense. "Now," he said. "Now!" he repeated with a shout.

Gomer snarled, stepping toward the thicket. Resolutely, the laifhorse took up beside him, and both beasts strode toward the huddling gloom. All at once along the forest boundary, spectres began to rise from the soil. A chorus of tongues filled the air. Steadily growing in volume and numbering in the hundreds, voices in varying pitches began to speak of violence. They spoke of blood and ruin, dismemberment and wailing all focused on humans. It seemed that the drevnigosts had claimed ownership of Joyous Garde, and Ancel and Linette were interloping beyond a ward of some hurried, shallow making.

After rounding a bend beneath a silverite archway, Ancel shot a forearm across Linette's chest, stopping her. "Without sacrificing haste," he said. "I think it best that we traverse with caution."

Keeping a gentle hand on her back, Ancel stayed a step behind Linette. When weaving between the first columns, she thought she saw a laif standing between two monuments on the left. At first it seemed to be a trick of the eye for when passing another column, the laif would no longer be where she had seen him. But then he would appear again at a further distance, standing and seeming to watch her. She passed a circular pillar, briefly barring him from sight, yet he somehow disappeared within that narrow margin. Over and over, the laif flickered in and out as she moved. Gratefully the garden's exit had finally come within stumbling distance.

Once she passed beneath the archway and out onto the central promenade, she could no longer feel Ancel's hand pressed against her. The weight had been brushed from her back, leaving her with a sudden feeling of isolation. She slowed and rounded on the flagstone. Behind a filmy translucence, Ancel raged silently against the apparition that barred his passage through the archway. His face a mask of wrath, screaming and hammering upon the magical barrier.

Calmly, Linette walked toward Ancel.

The fury he had been suppressing for some time was visible. He feverishly rained blows down upon a structure not made to be broken. When she placed her palm flat against the obstacle, Ancel eased back to breathe. She shook her head, wishing she could soothe him again just as she had done when the rains had fallen. With her other hand, she formed the sign for *home* and nodded at him. Ancel smiled and wiped the spittle from his chin. He understood that when this was over, she wanted to stay here with him until time drained itself elsewhere.

As Ancel placed his palm to Linette's, she felt a presence emerge behind her back. The scuffing of sabatons and the distinct rattle of maille to plate drew the presence into clarity.

When he looked beyond the woman, Ancel's wrath clearly was renewed and somehow doubled. He battered the impregnable glass with the base of the spear, driving his shoulder into it when that proved fruitless. In a last desperate effort, the enraged knight reversed the spear and brought the blade head down upon the working, striking a wound that rippled outward. For a split second, Linette could hear Ancel's voice from the other side. She signaled for him to do it again. Setting his jaw and bending at the knees, he launched himself forward. The spear penetrated the barrier, but did not shatter it, as Linette had hoped.

"Take hold!" Ancel urged.

She nodded, grasping the spear several inches beneath the blade.

Grinding on a heel, Ancel hauled the spear back through.

Linette's knuckles were the first to go into the barrier, then without any resistance, the rest of her followed. An itchy tingle briefly overtook her flesh, and if she had voice, she would have laughed at the curiosity of the feeling. Upon returning to Ancel's side, the sensation went away.

Locking eyes with who lay beyond, Ancel snarled as Linette embraced him about the waist. His anger was brought to a simmer as he returned the gesture, securing an arm across her back. Linette wished to remain safe in his embrace forever.

Ancel brushed away the hair lingering upon her forehead, and gently kissed her above the brow. "With me!" he said urgently.

As they worked their way back through the arrangement of shrines and pillars, the spectral laif was completely absent from the periphery. Absent, for now he trailed them.

Racing back toward the forest, Ancel noticed an opening created by a fracture in the wall. Abruptly he pivoted, scoring earth beneath his heel, and caught Linette around the waist. The jarring shift caught Linette off guard and she choked on her breath, causing Ancel to slow a step. At that same moment, an arrow shattered upon a column to their right. Instinctively, Ancel brought Linette to his chest, carrying her, and spun another way. Every time he set a new path, arrows would burst at the juncture, forcing him to select a different direction.

Linette caught sight of an archway ahead of them, but after rerouting so many times, she could not determine which it was. If it was the ensorcelled one, it would mark the end of the chase. But if it was the initial entryway...

Ancel charged headlong, and Linette feared that they would break against the working. She braced herself and tucked her face against Ancel's chest. She unexpectedly heard Gomer's bark nearby, lifting her spirits and betraying the archway's identity. Nevertheless, Ancel lowered the spear and drove himself harder. They made it through without being separated. Slowly, Ancel lowered her to the earth. When she turned, the breath of relief she had been about to take hitched in her throat.

Thousands of treeborne faces swung, snapped, and focused directly on her. Ancient guests hemmed the forest, forming a wall that stretched infinitely.

The voiceless child. The threatening voices resumed, flooding the air. *Traitor. Chattel, come nigh. What was once, will be again.*

Ancel's head never stopped moving, scouring the area for any way out.

There is no escape. The drevnigosts hissed as one.

Unlike Priraeda, these creatures were anchored to the soil and had no discernible legs. Though it prevented an advance, it did not make them any less terrifying. Defiantly, Gomer barked and bluffed charges, causing only a few ancient guests to balk. The laifhorse, in contrast, merely showed his teeth.

"Let me ask the questions this time."

That voice. Linette turned to her right, knowing the voice was to the left. She wanted to delay this moment as long as possible, delay the ending of this dream.

"Do you think me a common spellweaver?" The runes etched upon Amyr's exposed leg armour flickered molten. He stood a mere fifteen paces to their left while a contingent of holy sentinels filled their right. Once again, they were trapped in Joyous Garde.

"No," Ancel replied. "I do not think much of you at all."

The truth struck, and Amyr's countenance waned. "Clever. As always. Anyway, I was not speaking to you." He directed his eyes to Linette. "I want you to think for a moment." The laif had yet to make a move toward them. "If you had my powers the man shielding you right now would be dead. Would he not?"

Linette shrugged.

"Oh, come now!" Amyr said angrily. "I saw the doubt shroud your face back in Benwick! Even forgetting the fact that he betrayed an entire kingdom, drawing innumerable widows and widowers into new depths of despair!" Finally, the laif took a step forward. "Ah, but if only you would have seen the estate that I built for you! A broad field yearning for shadesgill! You should have been there to see the joy in your father's face..." He winced, retracting his step. "But you weren't there, were you?"

It was true that on the eve of Ancel's judgment, Linette had been kept awake by the archenlaif's statement. The next day she had sat and watched as the witnesses for the tribunal managed to sway many hearts and minds. But her mind, though hampered and a bit frantic with suspicion, had been anchored by her heart. She knew Ancel to be a true knight, and a true knight would not betray his realm. All she saw from the witnesses was envy, speculation, and half-truths balanced upon a very thin blade. After all that, the Church's lynch pin—the witness that their spectacle hinged upon—weighed upon the testimony of Camelot's archest of enemies.

Though quite honestly, she had reconciled her decision to stay with Ancel long ago. The expression on her face must have been enough for Amyr to grasp her feelings. His eyes twitched toward the sentinels, silently urging them forward.

Before the sentinels took their first step, Gomer and the laifhorse were upon them. Blood sprayed in a mist from differing directions within the mass of bodies. Linette watched, horrified, as one sentinel clutched his throat, failing to suppress the crimson leaking in torrents. Then Ancel took her up once again, sprinting at full pelt toward the guarded forest. Within the span of a hurried breath, a tight volley of arrows brought the knight down.

Skidding to a halt before the grasping ancient guests, just shy of their reach, Linette scrambled toward Ancel, fearing the worst. Three fletchings protruded from his right shoulder, but the snarling coming from him proved he was still very much alive.

Using the spear as leverage, Ancel returned to his feet.

The archers, though not for lack of trying, did not achieve another hail. As they drew, the laifhorse bore down upon them, and they wasted their final arrows on the beast. *Final arrows* for their quivers were spent. *Wasted* for the laifhorse, driven to blind fury by his death throes, rent the archers into grume.

"Not while I live," Ancel promised Linette, turning to face what remained of Amyr's soldiers, "will they take you."

Beyond the approaching sentinels, Gomer, a bloody mess, crawled pitifully toward the dying laifhorse. Three sentinels lay in his wake, unmoving.

Dusk was deepening. The shadows reached Ancel and Linette before the armoured bodies spreading them.

With interest and growing amusement, Amyr watched silently from the distance.

48

Swords sing on the battlefield and daggers hiss in the dark. Arrows blend with the wind and warble along their avenues. Push blades sneak and skulk, releasing gurgles when they murmur. When beaten, shields laugh as bells announcing holiday. Halberds, poleaxes, and dagda hammers do not barter or haggle, they bellow demands, no penitence is offered in their wake.

Stumbling backward, clutching his gut and dropping his halberd, the first sentinel died screaming.

That was what Ancel found remarkable about this spear. Every weapon he had ever wielded had had its own voice. But this spear spoke in cold silence—more so than a final breath's escape.

The way their companion wailed on the ground in such a piteous manner gave the sentinels pause. Death was taking his time to arrive.

Ancel would have used their fear to his advantage, piercing lungs and sundering tissue from bone before they took another step forward. Instead of pressing forward, he took a few measured steps backward, mindful to keep a safe distance from the lashing and jeering trees behind. Oh, if only this contest was hosted in phases, one clutch of foes at a time...

Somehow Linette lost her footing, perhaps catching her heel upon a root, and fell. The sound of the air escaping from her stomach caused Ancel to whirl around. Several ancient guests were desperately groping for her as starved blind men after bread. One managed to hook a talon to her collar and began to reel her toward the forest. The anguish on her face almost drove Ancel from sanity. His first step toward the trees seemed to be imbued with an incantation. The ancient guests recoiled in terror, twisting their trunks away from him as far as their roots would permit. In his panic, the creature dragging Linette flung her sideways. Weightlessly, the woman skimmed above the grass for a few moments before her shoulder snagged on a knoll. Her body crumpled, and she rolled to a stop as one no longer drawing breath. Ancel recognized that withered posture immediately.

Inside heartbeats, his tide of rage dipped into howling grief. Resurfacing on the other side of his mind's desolation, he could not recall what had just happened. His prisoner tunic was drenched, clinging tight to his skin. A metallic coppery flavor pervaded his tongue, and the air smelled of boggy earth. The mockery that had filled the air had ceased, ending abruptly the moment he opened his eyes.

Heaving air into his chest, he stood inside the forest. It appeared like another tornado had plunged down, uprooting the ancient guests. But a tornado would not exact such precise waste. Every leaf blade, every strip of bark, every stalk of grass, each piece of flora glistened with ichor as if it all had been submerged. Thick roots supported the dead whose husks were still attached. Branchlets dangled from upper boughs. Shards of bark were lodged into forking trunks. Moss was spattered in places where moss could never creep.

Imperceptible at first, shrill screeches gradually bled into clarity. Ancel blinked and turned toward the outskirts of the devastation. Ancient guests were flailing in horror. The derision previously held within their countenances was now only a frail memory. The soil from which they grew was torn and mangled by their fevered attempts to flee. An ill venture, for none could hope to succeed.

As Ancel picked careful steps toward Joyous Garde, the ancient guests' pleas suddenly renewed into a frenzy. The din swelled despite the knight's waning interest. His jaw ached and he found it painful to move. In the gloom beyond the lawn, unmoving holy sentinels stood beneath the crest of a hillock. Torchlight blazed across armour and cloth. The slightest figure among them was merely visible from the neck up.

"If you would be so inclined," Amyr's voice broke through the gloom, "discard that spear before taking another step. I would like to end this quickly."

Ancel's eyes focused, letting him see what he had not noticed, the slits of glimmering steel held beneath Linette's throat.

He had been mistaken. She was still alive.

The five remaining sentinels had regrouped, converging around the Arbiter. Their halberds were focused in Ancel's direction. Fearing another step, the knight capsized the spear and plunged the blade into the soil. Voices pealed the air again. The ancient guests were enlivened by what they saw as the knight's impending ruin.

Curiosity twisted Amyr's lips as he watched the spear haft lurch and totter to a halt. "Perhaps you can explain to me," he said leisurely, "for it escapes my comprehension, why the Lords of Benwick, both past and present, never bothered to harvest the hide from their drevnigosts?"

Ancel was not looking at the Arbiter. "I'm sure it crossed their minds from time to time," he murmured.

"Did it ever cross your mind?" Amyr asked, leaning to his left, coaxing Ancel's attention from Linette. "Certainly it cannot have gone above your notice as to how powerful such weapons can become when forged from..." he trailed off, eyes lifting somewhere else. "Priraeda. Not a moment too soon. Welcome."

Ancel had not heard the creature's approach.

"Lord Amyr," the voice creaked as the closing of a thousand gateways. "You have roused me from my slumber as a free drevnigost." He eased his great trunk down toward Ancel. "It was blissful."

Since childhood, Ancel had known the curator of Joyous Garde to be a kind and peaceful sort of creature. He had tended the gardens and orchards, keeping watch over the land and forest without once displaying any hint of discontent. On many occasions as a child, the drevnigost had placed the young Lord up into his highest branches to take him on excursions deep into the forest. And to his parents' chagrin, often passed deep into the evening.

Ancel looked at Priraeda with contrition. "I had no idea that you were—"

"Unhappy?" Priraeda hastily finished the statement. Moving faster than Ancel had ever witnessed, the drevnigost snapped to his full height. "Why would centuries of forced servitude make one miserable?" He sniffed. "You smell of slain kin."

Speaking to his sentinels, Amyr angled his chin to the side. "Bring her forward." The sentinels immediately ushered Linette toward Amyr. Her face was contorted in agony. The delicate fabric of her gown had accumulated crimson along its collar trim.

Looking upon her, the Arbiter's expression softened. "Be with me," he said. "I am giving you this—"

With tremendous speed, Linette lashed out. The base of her fist carved a deep trench that spewed blood in its wake; sable fluid cascaded in torrents. The Arbiter reeled back, clasping the side of his neck in utter confusion. He staggered and fell, contorting sideways, but swiftly bounded back to his feet. The sentinels lunged and held Linette in place.

Sound fled. Nothing dared to stir.

Amyr glowered ruinously at Linette.

In steady increments, blood dripped from the hooked implement locked in her trembling fist where a shard of an ancient guest's claw had snapped loose inside her wound.

"Extend your arm!" Amyr was crazed in fury. Between his fingers the blood continued to course. Linette did not react, and Ancel could not tell who Amyr was addressing, then Priraeda spread an obedient limb that loomed directly overhead. "For all that I have done!" screamed Amyr, convulsing with pure rage. "You die this day!"

Amyr flicked a hand at Ancel, and the knight felt his body transform. Instantly, he diminished, thin as a chord and felt his raiment release, fluttering free. He tried to move his limbs but found he had none. Rushing upward, the ground receded beneath him. No longer human, he felt agile and stretched. All at once, his perception settled and he felt himself dangling right before Linette's face. Panic overtook her countenance. Never before had she looked at him in that manner.

Then Ancel was yanked higher. But he felt much heavier now. Something weighed heavy within him. It felt like warm flesh pressed stiff. He felt constricted, tightening more and more as he was heaved higher and higher. He had no control. Suddenly realization flooded into him. He tried to scream, tried to shred himself into pieces. He struggled and seethed, but he was powerless against what he had become. And he could feel the life draining from his beloved within his grasp. Helplessly, he could feel himself strangling her as he rose toward the skies. He could feel her feet kicking, finding nothing but open air. Air that would never again enter her lungs.

Ancel's climbing ceased and he was now face to face with Priraeda. Nothing but hatred brimmed from the ancient drevnigost's gnarled carapace as his eyes followed Linette's dangling corpse. "Die, little one." Looking toward the noose that had killed her, he spoke again, "and you,

Lord of Benwick: may Avalon shutter and bar her gates before your entry."

Ancel, the rope who had hanged his beloved, was lowered and Linette's body was untethered and wrenched from his grip. The sentinel tasked with extricating Ancel from the drevnigost had the visor on his helm lifted. Pity was inscribed upon his sodden face. His lips were yet concealed, but their tremors were evident, rippling on the hollows of his taut cheeks.

"My Lord," the sentinel called out cautiously. "What shall I do with..." he was at a loss for what to call the bundle of braided humanity.

Amyr shifted his weight. "I see nothing," he spat, turning away. The scarlet wound upon his neck glistened damp.

Another sentinel spoke up. "My Lord, if we kill him, and word reaches the kingdom of what transpired..." she too trailed off momentarily before finding the words. "Will he not be deemed a martyr of sorts?"

The conversation grew faint as the distance lengthened, and Ancel wished he was not privy to it. He wished only for death. If only the sentinel with the tormented eyes would throw him into a pyre and not turn back.

"A martyr for whom?" Amyr demanded, rounding on the sentinel.

A thundering pause passed between them. The sentinel wisely chose not to reply. When Amyr spoke next, there was no waver in his voice. "For cowards? For whom we have no fear? Or perhaps for the downtrodden who yet curse his name? Nay, he will only be remembered as a turncoat and murderer. I will make certain of it."

49

⌘

"Them birdos must have stripped the lass naked!"

Stacey swiped away the drool that had accumulated on her cheek. Her head felt as if it had caved in upon itself. The horrid sound from the Arbiter's balcony had knocked her completely senseless. *How long have I been on this floor?*

"Father, give her your tunic."

"But what about Linette?"

"We can't do anything for Linette," the female voice oscillated like she was shaking her head. "But we *can* do something for this poor woman."

"My belly is gonna show..."

"Creator's marble steps!—Oh! She's awake!"

Easing up onto one elbow, the pain that had accumulated in Stacey's head began to funnel sideways, scraping against the back of her eye sockets. With a groan she fell back down, but not before seeing who was speaking over her and about her.

Kenna Turinleure was leaned forward clasping the bottom hem of his tunic. "Alright, alright," he said through the fabric overtaking his head. "Glad I wore these fancy braes today."

"You and me both," his daughter Perla said with hollow enthusiasm. "Let's just spread this atop her..." At first the fabric felt chilly. "Like so."

"What happened?" Stacey asked. As she sat up, she could taste the dust that had climbed her nostrils and was now in the back of her throat. "How long was I out? Did I miss anything?" She quickly forced the tunic over her head so it fell enough to give her a semblance of modesty. It smelled of grain and sod.

Kenna bit down on the side of his mouth and squinted an eye. "Not sure what the last thing you saw was," he said, rubbing the back of his head while admiring the recently vacated hall. "But, well, I'd say a whole lot."

"Who would have thought that the servants were sympathetic toward the archenlaives?" Stacey said to Kenna as they approached the Benwick keep's stables. "Huh."

Kenna nodded his head in agreement. The topless man's jovial tummy would normally have turned more than a few heads as they strode through the various lounges on their way out, but no such moments happened. The castle was nearly empty leaving only a strange abandoned feeling.

"Right after the explosion and Ancel and Linette's flight, a little lout climbed the stage and announced, 'Nothing changes for me, but for all those above us—everything will change!'" Perla lowered her finger self-consciously after the imitation. "Er, or something along those lines."

They passed into the stables and Kenna dabbed a finger to his top lip, trying to recall which stall they had secured their horses inside. "Even some of the guard joined with the servants," he said distractedly. Suddenly his eyebrows jutted up. "Oi! There be our ladies!"

Stacey peered at the man, sensing great unease beneath his perky moustache. He was exceptional at hiding his feelings. She wanted to inquire more about his daughter Linette, who turned out to be the quiet woman she had sat beside during the trial.

Kenna placed a hand to his mare's saddle. "Like I said, you're more than welcome to spend the night with us."

Perla seemed to sense Stacey's refusal, and spoke up just as she was about to decline. "It would be a most welcome distraction for us." Stacey was taken aback when the woman scooped her hands up. "Please?" she asked.

"I wouldn't want to take up any space—"

Kenna made a funny noise. "Pshaw!" It sounded as if he were trying to articulate something but had been interrupted by his own outburst. He looked a little embarrassed and heaved his shoulders, turning to Perla. "Recently we have been gifted quite a large estate..."

"Father!"

"What?"

"I told you I won't lay my head there until..." Perla teared up and began rubbing the bump on her stomach.

Stacey often felt out of place being a werewolf amongst humans, but somehow, in that moment, she felt their difference even more keenly.

"It's just that," said Kenna with a sigh. "As of late, we have been through a lot, and some new company would be so very welcome."

"Father."

"Alright, Perla," he huffed, his shoulders sagging. "We'll join you at the old place tonight."

"I still feel like I am intruding," admitted Stacey.

Kenna's moustache rippled as a heavy sigh escaped from his nostrils. "We own two farms now. I have been staying at the new *bigger* one. And Perla has been staying at the old *smaller* one."

Stacey was growing more and more uncomfortable. "It's fine, really."

"And well, you see," Kenna continued, staring at the hay strewn across the floor planks. "Perla's husband went missing during the battle at Fort Navarene, and well..."

"I get it, alright, I'll stay with you."

"She's been sleeping at the old home in the hopes that if he should return—"

"I'll come with you."

How Perla managed to have both of Stacey's hands wrapped in hers again, she did not know. "Oh, that would be so nice!"

The sun seemed weary upon its set.

Stacey leaned against a post, staring out at the fields beyond the Turinleure's porch. Her stomach was happy and full. She laughed as she picked her teeth, remembering the last meal she had eaten. Perhaps in some other stretch of this world ghoul meat was considered a delicacy. Wherever that may be, she did not wish to ever sojourn.

"How'd ya like the stew, lass?" Kenna had carefully eased out of the front door with full cups in each hand. She had smelled him before she saw him. *Grain and sod.* A comforting scent.

Stacey accepted the offered cup. "It was very good," she replied. "Thank you again."

"There was coney in it," Kenna said brightly, lifting his cup and pulling a long sip. "Could ya taste it?"

"Whoa, really? I wondered what that was." Stacey had obviously tasted the coney. She could taste everything. "Your daughter cooks well."

"Aye," Kenna nodded. "So are you a knight from some other realm who has lost her way?"

Stacey was taken aback. "Uh..." She tipped the cup and took her time swallowing. Though she could hide the fact that she was a were-wolf, the warrior insignia on her neck was a different story. "I am currently without a liege or lord, or anything really. I have only just received my belt."

"Ah." The farmer rubbed his chin. "Where's the knight who knighted you from? Garlot?"

That was a good question. Stacey wracked her brain. "Sure," she replied at length. "Garlot, yeah." She lied.

"Sturdy knights come from Garlot," Kenna said with a hearty swig. He brushed his moustache with the back of his wrist. "Or so I hear."

They nodded at one another as quiet fell between them. The ale Kenna had poured was fairly decent. The hops and malt intermixed on her tongue in a way that she did not find offensive. In addition, after swallowing, she could taste a lingering hint of brambleberry. *Not bad,* she thought. It was nothing like the gutter swill Carlysle used to drink every night. *Whatever got her there quickest.*

"Your knight," Kenna broke the silence. "Where is your knight now?"

"Eh," Stacey grunted, suddenly finding a lump in her throat. "Don't know."

Kenna felt that he had tread upon touchy grounds. "Ah, I see," he said.

An unforeseen *something* struck Stacey in her sinuses. A pinprick that caused her to reel and snort.

"Whoa! Careful!" Kenna said, batting a cautionary hand. "This is more of a sippin' ale, to be honest."

Stacey pounded the handrail. "I'm alright." She scoured her nostrils with her index finger. "I'm fine." She looked for advancing shadows in the dimming landscape. Her senses had activated while everything around her remained placid, untouched.

"Welp..." Kenna turned for the door, sounding distant, his empty cup in hand.

Stacey looked at her own cup. She had barely touched it. Night had fallen. *How much time just passed?*

"I'm heading in for my pipe," said Kenna, peering back from the doorway. "But there's something that I want to show you."

After giving the twilight a final distrustful sniff, Stacey turned toward Kenna. "Lead the way, sir," she said with forced cheer. That *something* was still out there.

She followed the man through the house, concluding in a small study. The room was boldly fragrant with pipeleaf, and an unfamiliar floral scent hung back somewhere behind.

Kenna had strode to a bureau. With his back to her, he spoke. "Do you know what this is?" he turned around slowly, holding a glass dome with a solitary silver flower huddled inside. The flower exuded a magical aura, brightening the glass and illuminating Kenna's soft chin.

"Is that...?"

"It is," Kenna replied. "It's silver shadesgill."

"It's magnificent."

Kenna nodded, extending the dome over to her.

"Why are you showing me this?" She peered curiously at the man while setting her ale on an end table.

Folding his hands behind his back, Kenna rose slightly onto his toes. "My daughter—" he cleared his throat. "Linette," he said forcefully, trying to quell the emotions brimming up from his throat. "She grew these on a small plot of ground out on our lawn. A very small plot. She loved those damnable things. Sometimes, I thought she loved them even more than her old Pa." The man attempted a chuckle, tears glistening on his lower lids. "Didn't think I'd get this choked up talking about it! But here I am, eh? Well, before I become a blubbering mess, I felt like I should remind you that time is fleeting. And, well, I don't really know the bad blood between you and your knight, not really my business, but

I wanted to tell you that you never know how much time you'll get with those you love."

As he returned the shadesgill to its place on the bureau, Stacey could hear the man beginning to break down. Then that *something* smacked her in the nose again. This time, she knew what it was. And it was close. It was another werewolf.

Beyond the room, Stacey heard a faint knock at the door. She rushed out of the study, startling Kenna and sending papers fluttering in torrents.

"Coming, coming," Perla said, wiping her hands upon a towel. "Who could be calling at this hour?"

"Don't answer that!" Stacey barked.

She was too late.

At first, the hinges creaked open, then suddenly the door surged open with a shuddering crash. Perla's scream rivaled the blast from the hall that had rendered Stacey unconscious.

The claws were the first to spring from Stacey's hands, then within the next step her fangs were at full tang. When she cleared the threshold, knowing the other werewolf would be there, she faltered to a knee. She had expected to find torn limbs and furniture soaked with Perla's blood, but instead found nothing of the sort.

She saw a man on his knees, embracing Perla around her waist. He was weeping with his head pressed against the child growing inside her womb. Fervently, she was running her fingers through his silver hair.

With tears pouring from her eyes, Perla looked up to grin at Stacey. "He's home!" she laughed. "Don't you see! My husband has finally come home!"

50

The cord of rope lay sprawled upon the face of the hillside, untouched. The ghost of Ancel confined within its fibers strove for nothing more. An existence, a sentence, one and the same.

Perhaps this is what I deserve after all, he thought. *A man guilty of slaying mountains in order to save the hills...* his thoughts drifted away. A basket perched on a nearby table, positioned near the ledge for easy collection, drew his attention. Behind, the fruit orchard provided an appropriate skeletal backdrop. The vast tunnel of branches was now completely empty, barren of leaf and fruit. A spectral winter seemed to have strangled all its vibrancy, crippling a resurgence of life. He hardly recognized it anymore.

But that basket. He knew that basket and what resided within.

An eternity staring at a bushel of faewort. Creator, what did I do to deserve this? You know their allegations to be false! I can still feel her flesh grinding and tearing against my knots. Her residue is branded to me. Must I also stare at something that reminds me of her? Oh, Creator why? Bring sleet of salt to crumble me to dust and a hard rain to sweep me away!

In his sorrow, vengeance was far from his thoughts. And in his lament, he did not hear the approaching footsteps.

"Ah, there you are," said Amyr. "Right where Tocine left you. I feared a raven would have bundled you into her nest while I was away."

Ancel felt hands lifting him.

"Up you go," said Amyr. Then, slowly, methodically, he wrapped the rope around his wrist. "Your final destination awaits."

Within a blink, Ancel's fingertips felt cold again. His ears popped. The transformation back to human was dizzying. His optics were no longer roaming untethered within a long malleable object. Now locked in place on his skull, his eyes took in his surroundings. The room was cramped and comprised entirely of stone. It was circular with a radius of no more than five paces. From the uppermost slant of a window, clouds wafted nearby. There were no tapestries, no furnishings, and no imagination in the structural design. It was a prison cell.

He sat propped against the wall where Amyr had left him. Though he had regained control of his limbs, he had no interest in moving. He was beaten, finished.

If he had any care left, he may have been startled when a chalice appeared between his outstretched legs. Instead, he rolled his head back against the stone.

"This is where your story ends, Lord Ancel," Amyr said, materializing before him. The First Laif was the epitome of splendor. Light emanated from his armour, splashing the chiseled walls with a glossy silver sheen. At his neck, the gorget was missing, revealing the wound that Linette had exacted. It had since been cleaned. The Arbiter lifted a finger to the laceration. "A lesson learned," he said bitterly, then shook his head, dispelling the malice. "Let us drink." In his hand was a chalice not unlike the one teetering before Ancel.

Ancel remained as if he were still braided twine, unmoving. The spirit required to even raise his chin was absent.

"Come now," Amyr purred, drawing eye-level. "Why must everyone always be so suspicious of the drinks I offer?" He stood, moving back a step. "I assure you, it is not poisoned, though it does differ greatly from what swirls in my cup."

Leave me, Ancel wished to say, but found himself unable.

"Oh, yes," Amyr's smile spread as a slowly drawn dagger. "I have revoked your speech. Can't have you telling a lie and dying, now can I?" Amyr strode to the window. His chalice clinked on the stone. "That would defeat the purpose."

Ancel's head returned to his chest.

"First, we drink," Amyr raised a toast. "To the future!"

The chalice before Ancel remained on the stone floor.

"You will not be stripped of your senses, I assure you."

The prisoner ignored the laif.

"The sooner you drink, the sooner I leave."

That statement earned Ancel's attention. Adjusting his pose, Ancel leaned forward and retrieved the offering. His back returned to the wall. The fluid descended his throat, coursing a hot pathway.

"That was delicious," Ancel lied, his voice no longer missing. Believing his death to be forthcoming, he welcomed it, releasing all the tension in his body as the discarded chalice rolled a circular pattern on the stone beside him. A few moments passed and the chalice came to a halt against his thigh, and yet he still drew breath.

"Welcome to Avalon!" Amyr spread his arms, sounding almost gleeful. "I jest, I jest," he said as Ancel continued to wilt. "That concoction or decoction, I can never keep them straight—is a decoction the one that is boiled down?—Ah! No matter! The *potion* you consumed will not only prevent you from dying when you speak false to me, but it will also prevent you from dying... ever."

"I... I am immortal?" Ancel stuttered in dismay.

"In a sense, yes," Amyr traced a finger along the rim of his cup. "Your soul will remain on this plain. Avalon is closed to you. Hekk does not want you. There will be no passing on. Your flesh will rot on your bones, and yet you will continue to be. Eventually a skeleton, a husk, for all time."

"For falling in love."

Amyr's finger ceased its spin. "For taking that which did not belong to you," he snarled. "I have been alive for so long. I have witnessed many downfalls stemming from lust and swore to avoid such ruin. Not once have I entertained a partner in my bedchambers. Not once have I committed any manner of carnal act with another laif, or human, nor any other creature." He turned for the window and took another pull from his cup. "I am the last of the first laives. How do you think I have survived for so long?"

"Then Linette..."

"Why did you get in the way?" Amyr flung his empty cup out the window. "I never believed a human could possibly encapsulate so much beauty. So much indescribable perfection. For the first time since after the Creator sharpened my ears centuries ago, did I ever feel such a stirring. I had finally found someone to love. Through no ensorcellment or trickery—Linette could not speak, could not vocalize falsehood. That trait coupled with the symmetry of her features and the demeanor that carried her aloft. She had been made by the Creator just for me!" The Arbiter's mouth clamped down. "Then you appeared."

Ancel shrugged.

"Why couldn't you allow me to have her?"

"That is not how love works," Ancel stated. The laif's armour seemed to grow tawdry under his gaze. "One's perception does not dictate another's affection."

Resting an elbow on the sill, Amyr propped his head on his hand. "How poetic," he scoffed, turning his head to the clouds. "Tell me true; if you had heard the call to war, would you have left her?"

"Who says I did not hear the call?"

Amyr cocked his head at the knight. "I do," he said with doubt. The laif was unaccustomed to distinguishing lies from truth. "That proved to be your downfall."

"Did it?"

"Look around you!" declared Amyr. "The realm believes you false! A paragon of liars! In the dankest of taverns, the filth and traitors spit at the very mention of your name!" His tone suddenly dimmed to a near whisper. "The annals will write you as such: Lord Ancel, the villainous traitor, using treacherous means, stole through the dark of night to Linette's doorstep and tricked her and murdered her." Amyr laughed into his collar and waved a dismissive hand. "Eh, it requires work, but you surmise my meaning."

"Do what you will," said Ancel. "I care not."

Amyr rolled his head back to stare at the rafters. "I see," he said at length. "I think it best that I take my leave." Disappointed, the laif folded his arms across his chest. "Do you have any words afore I leave you in this cradle of endless solitude?"

An echo of Ancel's former self rattled beneath his flesh. "Would that they serve nectarines in Avalon?"

The arch of the laif's eyebrow was the last that Sir Launcelot of Benwick would see of another creature.

Snowflakes invaded the silent room, spinning and weaving from the window.

He should feel the cold. But instead, he felt nothing.

51

❧

The Cloth had yet to retrieve their dead. Fallen sentinels created irksome barriers for Famyl as he crawled into the slowly dying laifhorse's view. Lucidity streamed from the beast's eyes, insinuating that life still resided within, however fleeting. When the laifhorse finally noticed the dog, he heaved a sigh and tried to rise. Only his head managed to leave the sod, and even then, it was only for the flicker of a moment.

Faithful to the very end, Famyl thought. And while the First Laif wondered the origins of this laifhorse, the beast shuddered its final breath. *Farewell, my friend.* Famyl wished to move closer, but he was already stretched beyond his mortal threads. A tunnel had been closing ever since one of his lungs deflated, and he knew that he would be returning to the Hold within a few meager breaths.

Watching Linette die was more than he could bear. As an immortal, watching mortals perish was not something new. But Linette, he felt for certain, should have passed peacefully many years from now in a soft bed surrounded by family. Not in that way. Not in that manner.

Oh, Creator, how weary am I of corruption. From the beginning, elves were given such a gift, and yet see how we squander it. Such a waste! I thought to escape it all by living peacefully with a magnificent example of your creation. Now look what has become of her, what has become of your creation! So many lives torn asunder, so much greed, so much discontent! Oh how they waste the

537

gifts meant for good at every turn, at every opportunity! Send me into a body far from all this! Far from the treachery of laives and the greed of men!

"Is your grief becoming hatred?" An all-too familiar voice entered his ears. A laif in plain garb stood over him holding Ancel's drevnigost spear. With a downward shrug, he planted the haft inches from Famyl's tear streaked muzzle. "I know of the place you seek," the Creator said softly, easing down onto his knees. "An island reached by fowl but not by vessel—a land governed by a curse. Do you really wish to reside there until the very end?"

Famyl felt as if a warm blanket had been placed upon his brow. "I do wish that," he said with eyes locked on the laifhorse. "I wish that with all that remains of my being. And that this glorious beast might accompany me there."

"That can be arranged," the Creator obliged, rising to stand. "I will make you into a creature of myth. A beast that brave souls will yearn for the chance to discover. Many, seeking your gift, will try to find you. For merely finding you will prove most arduous. And even those who sacrifice all to arrive, will, in the end, perish." The Creator turned his face to the spear. "That is, until..."

"Until?"

"You will know when that day arrives." The laif's thumb played at the blade of the spear.

"How will I know?"

The Creator's eyes moved to rest upon the hillock where Linette had died. "His blood," he said gravely, "will smell of her."

Epilogue

"**C**are to offer a few words, Fig?" the knight asked the dapper wisp upon his shoulder.

After a series of whimpers and throaty sniffles, the fae wiped the tears from his pillowy cheeks and straightened up. His wings gradually spread with confidence as his chin surveyed the gravestones populating the abandoned laif cemetery.

"Error was..." Figharth cleared his throat. His eyes slid down to the rectangular plot of freshly turned soil, and the fae tried to dampen another shudder. "Error was a true horse, in the truest sense of the word. And he was a true lion in the most brutally honest sort of way." That was all Figharth could manage before concealing his face with a forearm.

"Well said." Sir Gwayne crossed an arm beneath his chin to pat his index finger against the small fellow's back. "Well said."

It seemed that the rain fell exclusively in the clearing where they stood. The surrounding trees of Fenrirfang appeared almost untouched, their leaves barely registering nods. The knight didn't mind it at all. Others found the dark clouds of the summer rains to be bleak, but he welcomed the shade.

"He was a good friend and companion," offered Gwayne. He could not help but think wistfully of his own horse. Like Error, Delilah had been culled long before her time.

"They will pay," Figharth had regained composure and spoke forcefully. "They will pay for what they have done!" Despite the gloomy skies overhead, a shadow seemed to pass over his face.

"Whoa, Fig," Gwayne was caught off guard by the wisp's sudden shift to fury. "I thought you wanted to return to Leandra—"

"I changed my mind!"

Angry spittle droplets pelted sharp to the corner of Gwayne's left eye.

"Those kapreta were only the beginning! I will unite the banners! All those responsible for Error's death will come to ruin! Mark my words!"

Gwayne rubbed a knuckle into his eye. "Maybe we should—"

"Mark my words!" Figharth's feathers trembled with rage. Raindrops continued to strike, streaming under his fine garb and soaking his downy feathers. A sneeze interrupted his tirade, and with it, a shiver followed. "Error's death shan't be in vain!" he announced, shuffling closer to Gwayne. The knight obliged by lifting his chin, supplying shelter for his friend. The sudden fervor had taken its toll, and soon Gwayne could hear the sounds of mourning coming from the wisp once again.

Blinking against the downpour, Gwayne eventually gave up and closed his eyes. He had not yet planned his next move. For all he knew, Galahalt and Elkara would not return for another century or more. Perhaps Figharth's idea of revenge was as good a place to start as any. And if that be their chosen path, then they had quite a road ahead of them.

Gwayne waited for Figharth's sobs to subside. "What does *Jatel* mean?" he asked, not bothering to open his eyes. Many of the markers were graven with the title. At first he had believed it to be a house or family name, as the word was fairly prevalent. But one well-worn inscription had read: *A Jatel long before dubbing, until the end.* "Were they some order of laif knight or something?"

"Not sure," Figharth sniffed. "Why don't you ask him?"

Gwayne's eyes shot open.

"It means friend."

ACKNOWLEDGMENTS

Thank you for reading this book.

Tom Kent, Ryan Krebs, Hiram Ring, and Scott Telle:
For your advice, criticisms, and keen sense of what
should never, ever be included in a fantasy novel.

Tremendous gratitude goes out to the
legendary fantasy artist, Jonathan Myers, for his
brilliant representation of Lord Amyr for this book's cover.

Gina: For being the most brilliant of
proofreaders, editors, humans, and wives.
I thank God every day that our paths crossed.

Dad: Though you'll never read a lick of anything that I will ever
publish, I think you would have liked this one the best.
I can't express just how much I wish we could discuss (over cigars)
your favorite plot twists, and where I succeeded at character development.

But we never will.
All along, I thought we'd have more time.

ABOUT THE AUTHOR

M. Warren Askins lives in the Northeastern
United States with his family.

There's no such thing as happy endings...

Scan the following code to check out his current list of works.